The Call of The Aïdin Planet

A TALES OF THE HORIZON™ BOOK

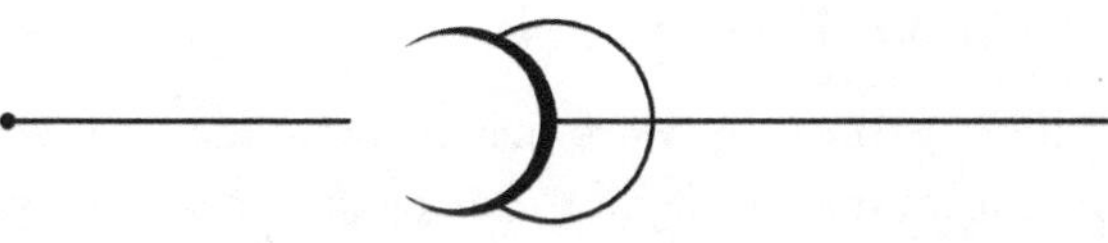

The Call of The Aïdin Planet

L.Z. Dáin

THE CALL OF THE AÏDIN PLANET ~ Book One of THE LEGACY SAGA
Second Edition

For information about the copyright holder and other inquires, please contact the publisher.

Tales of the Horizon
Seattle, WA 98110
United States

inquiry@talesofthehorizon.com
www.talesofthehorizon.com

Book design by TALES OF THE HORIZON LLC
Cover art by Alex Storer — www.thelightdream.net

L. Z. DÁIN, TALES OF THE HORIZON, and colophon are trademarks of TALES OF THE HORIZON LLC, a media producing and publishing company.

ISBN 978-1-950978-22-9

Also available in hardcover and in ebook formats:
ISBN 978-1-950978-23-6 (hardcover edition)
ISBN 978-1-950978-02-1 (epub edition)

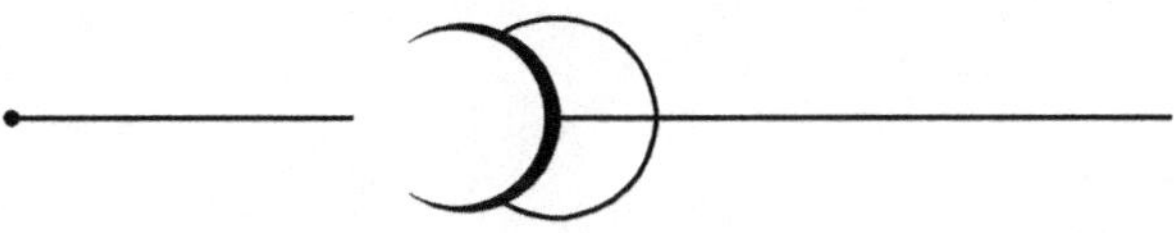

Ever there is a broader horizon awaiting you!

— An~Ríordáin

Contents

⚡ ⚡ ⚡

⚡ ⚡ ⚡

The Call of the Aïdin Planet

Book One of The Legacy Saga

Main Characters

Althesal: Human female from the planet Thel of the Eir System (*Eta Cassiopeia*). Main protagonist and one of the seven main characters in the story. Dean of the Guilds of the Path of Exploring of the Thelian civilization. Issën and Science Director of the multi-galaxy union of civilizations — *the Union or Laendänl*.

Daothel: Human male from the planet Thel of the Eir System. One of the seven main characters in the story. Apprentice in the Bio-Soul Sciences Guild under the mentorship of Nesdil.

Ethën: Human male from the planet Thel of the Eir System. One of the seven main characters in the story. Specializes in Light-Sound Sciences and Light Harmonics.

Laidé: Human male from the planet Lyaty of the Nauth System (*El Nath*). One of the seven main characters in the story. Special Advisor in inter-galactic relations and diplomacy to the Chancellor of the Union.

Mhali: Human male from the planet Seelë of the Merope System in the Pleiades Cluster. One of the seven main characters in the story. Marshal of the Ranger Corps, Islnom-1 of the Laïs Galaxy (*Milky Way*).

Nesdil: Human female from the planet Thel of the Eir System. One of the seven main characters in the story. Specializes in Life Harmonics Sciences. Teacher and mentor of Daothel.

Soen: Human female from the planet Esdänl of the Alcyone System in the Pleiades Cluster. One of the seven main characters in the story. Member of the Order of the Wanderers.

Thaël: Human male from the planet Thel of the Eir System. Ambassador to the Union and member of the High Council. Dean of the Guilds of the Path of Providing of the Thelian civilization.

Ulhloom: Humanoid from the Realm of Lhool (*the People of Lhool*) in the Alaïs Galaxy (*Andromeda Galaxy*). Ambassador to the Union and member of the High Council.

Vuensé: Human female from the seventh planet of the Alcyone System in the Pleiades Cluster. Chancellor of the multi-galaxy union of civilizations — *the Union or Laendänl*.

The Story Teller

Planet Earth, Sol System ~ Year 2022 CE

"I study Humans", he said while gazing at the sky. "They are intriguing."

"You said *they* as if you weren't Human!"

Resting the book on his lap, he smiled and asked, "Don't Humans intrigue you?"

I refused to answer. He was sitting on my bench, and I was the one asking the questions!

In the weeks since I had come here for a quiet time, no one had visited this secluded spot of the park overlooking the lake. And today of all days when work at the Foundation was testing my resolve and when my frustration with the injustices of the world was at its highest, this stranger had chosen to invade my privacy. To protest his intrusion I had sat next to him to eat my lunch with as much display and noise as I could muster.

But as I ate, the book he was reading had attracted my attention — *Utopia*, by Sir Thomas More. I had then blurted, "That's an interesting book! Not many know of it today." What was I thinking? I had invited him to remain in my spot and start a conversation. Now he was asking me a question!

Unfazed by my refusal to answer and looking intensely into my eyes, he said with a twinkle, "Yes, Humans do puzzle you."

I felt my irritation melt away. Everything in him was disarming: his smile, the look in his eyes, the tone of his voice… He was my age, in his mid-twenties, and dressed with elegance in fine, though somewhat exotic clothes whose origin I couldn't guess — as I really looked at him, I noticed his whole bearing was regal.

"Mmm… I guess they do…" I replied glancing at the ground to break the intensity of his gaze. "Although I'm beginning to think I care too much about them."

"Interesting…" he said with a slight nod of his head and a bemused frown. "In all my travels I've never heard such a statement. But then, what can one expect? Humans are a surprise at every turn!"

There it was again! Who was this man who spoke of Humans as if he didn't belong with us?

"Who are you?" I couldn't refrain from asking.

"I am known as *An~Ríordáin*; though my friends just call me *Ríordáin*. You too can call me by this name if you want. It has been a while since a Human from this planet called me so."

Oh God, I am dealing with a lunatic! What have I done to deserve this day? — I must confess, however, I felt both attracted by his presence and afraid of his peculiarity.

My face must have betrayed my reaction because he used his disarming smile on me once more. "I can assure you, I haven't lost my reason." After a short pause during which he kept bombarding me with his smile, he added, "Now that you have a name for me, shouldn't I have a name for you?"

"Claire…"

"Clai-re", he echoed with his musical voice. "Good name! It speaks of the light you are."

Thus began the most marvelous adventure of my life! That day we conversed for a few more minutes. So enthralled was I by the mystery emanating from him that with reluctance I went back to my work. During that afternoon and evening my mind drifted, again and again, to him.

⚡

The next day I ran to the park when my lunch break finally arrived. Afraid he wasn't going to be there, I slowed to a crawl at the bend of the path leading to the bench. My heart was pounding and skipped a beat when I saw him.

"The air smells of spring", he said with his eyes closed as I approached. The breeze played with his silky and wavy brown hair, and the sunlight filtering through the trees made him appear otherworldly.

The previous evening I had researched his unusual name — *An~Ríordáin* — and found it was a title in the old Gaelic kingdoms. It meant, *The Royal Bard*. Thus, I sat next to him and asked, "Ríordáin, who are you?"

Turning towards me with a puzzled face, he said, "I am your friend! I gave you my name."

"Yes… but I want to know more about you — where you are from, where you live, what you do for a living… those sorts of things."

"Ah, that!" He rose his face to the sky as he said this before adding, "Humans are mysterious, aren't they? They are curious about the things with a beginning and an end, yet overlook that which is timeless in them and all around them."

"B-but that's who we are. Don't we all have a beginning and an end?"

"Let's not take that path right now, Claire. You aren't ready to understand."

I didn't know what to say to that. The thought that he was not in his right mind came to me again. It didn't last. In my job at the Foundation as the Director of Grants, I dealt with all types of people from many countries and cultures, and with different levels of education. Some are a challenge to understand, but in the end we always find a meeting ground to make things happen. Ríordáin was no different, although more exotic and intriguing.

"See, Claire, your life-path isn't much different from mine!"

His words startled me. Did he know of my job? That wasn't difficult for anyone to find out… Then, it struck me — he had read my mind!

"No, I don't read minds", he said as soon as the thought came to me and shifted his body to look at me directly. "You broadcast your thoughts without control and in all directions, and they impact the minds of those around you."

"Y-y-you concede that you read thoughts. Isn't that the same as reading minds?"

"No, it isn't. No one in the Universe can intrude into the mind-soul of another. Ever! The seat of the self is the strongest locus in Time and in Space. But anyone can pick up on the thoughts a mind broadcasts. You do so everyday in your job, though unaware of it, with all those with whom you relate and seek to understand." He paused studying my reaction, then added, "I do something rather similar to what you do at work — There it is. You wanted to know what I do, now you know."

The inflections of his speech were musical, and to my surprise I had seen in my mind's eye and had felt in my heart what he had said. It was then for the first time I grasped that the thought and feeling behind his speech reached my mind and heart before his words reached my ears. That was the reason I didn't question the strangeness of his statements. Deep within I knew he spoke in truth.

"One day you will remember how to do that, too", he said as a matter-of-fact, not bothering to add he had heard my thought. "Before you can remember, however, you need to find peace in your heart. Your job doesn't frustrate you. You are quite good at it. Your restlessness comes from seeking answers to the deepest questions of life in a world that, as yet, offers not much meaning."

"Since you appear to know the questions I have," I replied, "why don't you just give me the answers?"

"Oh Claire, it doesn't work that way! Remember, I am a student of Humans. Similar to you, I am on a quest for answers to certain questions."

"Then, perhaps we are looking for the same answers!" — I didn't know where that came from! Conversing with him was a dance in which at every step one followed the other's lead.

His eyes brightened and with a wink he said, "Perhaps we are, Claire… Perhaps we are…"

I had to leave for work with those last words. We never agreed to meet 'a next time'. But I knew he was going to be there the next day, sitting on *our* bench, waiting for me.

That evening, in the quietness of my home, I reviewed our two conversations. It was then when I decided to write down my encounters with him. I didn't want to forget a word he said, or any detail of the times we were together. Something was happening to me. It wasn't anything romantic. Instead, I felt a grounding and a familiar force coming from him, and I kept thinking: *Ríordáin, in truth, who are you? Why have you appeared in my life at the time when I feel so lonely, ready to give up on everything I've achieved, and turn my back on the problems of this world?*

⚡

A thrill of excitement ran through me when I saw him the next day but halted when I was about to greet him. He knelt on the ground, speaking soft words to one of the many squirrels of the park while caressing its back. The animal was relaxed and looked at him as if it understood his words. He then rose and walked to the bench. The squirrel followed him, but he said something to it in words that sounded as a chant, and the animal scurried away to resume its hide-and-seek nut games among the trees.

Ríordáin wasn't a person for formalities or small talk, and our conversations were driven by the flow of the moment. I knew he liked my direct approach. "You talk to animals", I said as a greeting.

"All beings in Space and Time respond to the vibrations of the voice", he replied.

"That sounds New Agey, or mystical."

"It's science, Claire. Simply, you haven't arrived at that point on the journey of life where you remember the power of the voice."

"Ríordáin!" I blurted. "You make statements that lead me to think you're some sort of sage or mystic!"

"I am neither."

"Then, are you a scientist from another world?"

"No, although I understand why you see that in me too", he replied and became absorbed in thought, something he did frequently, as if looking for the right words to say.

"Humans do love to place themselves in boxes!" he whispered after a time and turned to study me with his deep, honey-colored eyes. Slowly he next added, "Know, dear one, that science and religion are the pursuits of young Humanities. One day you will discard them both. Then you will discover a boundless freedom to truly live and create with the exactness your scientists search for and with the limitlessness your religionists hope for."

It took me a long moment to absorb what he had said. His words had said one thing, but this time they had been carried on a silent feeling whispering to me: *Don't wait until that time, Claire. Be free. Now!*

That did it! The bitterness and frustration I had carried in my heart for months regarding the selfishness of our current economic and social systems came out unrestrained. I then flooded him with the tale of the hell we and our planet were living, and he let me talk on and on with an understanding face.

I ended saying, "You speak of us as if we were perfect beings, and trust us as if we had a secure future — I want to feel that way too. But, we aren't going to make it. We are destroying ourselves, and Nature with us, one step at a time. The worst is, we are splitting up into a multitude of separate camps. Those of us who endeavor to make this world a better place for all are losing the battle. I see it everyday in my work. We tell ourselves we are moving forward, but the reality is other. In the mad pursuit for material wealth and comfort, we are moving away from the very foundations of what it means to be Human."

"But moving away from established foundations is what makes you Human!" he said when I paused to catch my breath. "Your blind spot is that you act oblivious of causes and effects, and when you run into trouble, you wonder why."

He knew I wasn't buying that argument because he changed his tone and added softly with the musical cadence he used on occasion, "The Humanity of this world will make it — I don't doubt it. You have been gathering momentum for a long time to fulfill your destiny, and that momentum is unstoppable."

Upon hearing the music of his words, an unexpected calm washed over me and a ray of hope shone in my heart. It had been such a long time since I had felt a moment of peace, all I did was stare at him, not wanting the moment to end. When I could again speak, with a whisper I asked, "You speak of a destiny for us. What destiny?"

He didn't answer right away and gazed to the sky for a time. Then, when he lowered his eyes, he spoke with an uncharacteristic intensity: "Yes! This is the right moment in this locus of Time!" Taking my hand in his and with fire in his eyes, he added, "Dear Claire, I am going to tell you the Story of your planet — you are ready to hear it. Many others in this Universe know of it, but not the people of Earth."

Again, he became silent for a time and when he resumed, said, "The Story of Earth, and of Sol, your star system, is entwined with the story of *La'Aït* — which is the region of Space your scientists call 'the Local Group' of galaxies. It's a story which goes far back in time. But that would be too long of a tale. Let's begin, instead, nine hundred thousand years before this present time, with events centered on a world located twenty light years away from Sol, in the Eir System — which you know by the name of 'Eta Cassiopeia'. The name of that world is *Thel*."

"At that time", he continued, "Thel was a paradise planet… still is. Its Humanity was the most advanced and influential among Galactic Humans… still is. But something was discovered on Earth, and an unstoppable chain of events began which you, and we all, are still living."

I was dumbfounded by this turn in our conversation.

"Let me show you", he said still holding my hand. "Don't be afraid and close your eyes."

With a muted nod I did as instructed. Next, I heard him intone a soft musical chord and felt a tingling spread throughout my body, which didn't last. I felt sinking… rapidly… in something akin to water… for a fraction of a second. The sensation was so unexpected that I instinctively reopened my eyes.

"What—?" My protest was cut short by wonder. We were in a park, yet not the same one. The wrought-iron bench had changed to one made of a soft, warm and cushioned material. Trees, flowers and grasses unknown to me surrounded us. Pavilions and sculptures of a strange but beautiful design stood nearby. And the sky… it was lavender and with a blue-white sun! Groups of the most attractive Humans I've ever seen walked together, engaged in conversation among themselves. A few were sitting alone, studying some sort of holograms. Others appeared to be enjoying a quiet time. There were also with them non-Human beings of various other races, also beautiful and graceful in their alienness.

"W-where are we?" I managed to whisper.

"We are in a locus of Time that for you is nine hundred thousand Earth-years ago. We aren't on the planet Thel of the Eir System, not yet. Instead, we are in the city of Llën, on Esdänl, a planet of the Alcyone System in the Pleiades Cluster. This is where and when you and I will begin witnessing together the Story of Earth as it unfolds."

I was having a hard time processing his words. He noticed this because he paused and, placing both his hands on my temples, said, "Your body cannot yet withstand the pure 'light' of Time for extended periods, so at the beginning we will keep these visits short."

After this first visit we returned, in the same way we had departed, to our bench at the park of my city on Earth. We still sat on the bench… and he still held my hand… and my lunch time wasn't yet over.

He then explained to me that we hadn't abandoned Earth's current *locus of Time* while visiting there. That he had gathered from that other locus some of its 'light' around us to allow us to witness the thread of events he wanted to show me.

"Claire, don't seek to understand right now the ways I talk about Time. As the Story of Earth progresses you will learn that Time is much more, and of a different nature, than your present understanding of it." Then with a wink he added, "Mastering Time is part of your destiny, and soon it will become the new horizon of exploration for the people of your planet. You will then marvel at what awaits you!"

At first, we kept our encounters at noon. As the Story progressed, I suggested we meet more times and in other places. For months I have taken notes of this amazing journey through Time — although he insists there isn't such a thing as 'traveling through Time', that this idea sprouts from misunderstanding the real nature of Time and of the Human Self.

I started writing down the experiences with him because I didn't want to forget any detail. Lately, though, I have wanted to share them with others. Ríordáin has assured me that he is helping me remember every detail of it. That my exposure to the 'light' of Time, together with him, synchronizes our minds. In retrospect I realize he knew that one day I was going to make the Story available to others because he said early: "Write the Story as if you are telling it to friends, and in a style and with descriptions appropriate for the understanding of Humans on this planet."

We still meet. He hasn't finished. Although our friendship has deepened with time, he remains surrounded by an aura of mystery. Seldom he speaks of himself, but I noticed early that storytelling is his passion.

The Beginning of the Story

Planet Esdänl, Alcyone System ~ 900,000 years ago

"Humans aren't exclusive to Earth, nor is your planet the first to house Humans."

Ríordáin thus began the Story when we arrived that first time to the city of Llën of the planet Esdänl, and after I recovered from my initial shock. With my hand in his, he led me through that park along a broad walkway made of a white, crystalline material.

"A large number of Human civilizations", he continued, "have existed for a long time in this and in other galaxies. Most of them participate in a community of worlds for mutual support and friendship. This community is known as *Laendänl*, which in your language would mean something close to *Enlightening Union*. We are now at the headquarters of the Union — this whole planet is.

"Humans first appeared in numerous star systems of seven of the galaxies in the Local Group, nearly all of them at the same time. Many theories of their mysterious origin have been woven. It is accepted, however, that Humans appeared rather suddenly six hundred million of your years ago, and that they established themselves on uninhabited worlds, on which they rapidly developed advanced civilizations.

"Early in their history, in the group of star systems where we are now, the Pleiades, the Union was established to forge bonds of kinship and support among the worlds housing Humans. Since then, this Union has expanded to include thousands of worlds from those seven galaxies."

As Ríordáin spoke, I felt a strange familiarity with that place and with his account. For all my life I have loved science-fiction stories, most so those that present a positive and uplifting view of other civilizations and that go beyond the cliché, 'Earth Humans are the good guys, Extraterrestrials are the baddies'. But what I was experiencing at that moment wasn't fiction — I was witnessing pages of history which on Earth we are yet to discover but that, nonetheless, we sense in the deepest recesses of our being.

At that moment the walkway came to a fork, we took the left one and entered a pergola covered with a vine loaded with pink blossoms. Ríordáin brought me to a halt and gestured to me to breathe in, deeply. The flowers were minute but their perfume was beyond description! My body immediately felt invigorated and, mentally, I felt more lucid.

"There", he said with a wink. "These plants come from the planet Thel. I knew you and your body were going to love them. Can we now continue?"

Without waiting for my answer, we returned to the main path and he resumed:

"Many other sentient, non-Human races also call these seven galaxies 'home' — they are known collectively as *Amethen,* a term which means 'friends'. A great many of these other races also participate in the Union on equal footing with Humans, as you can see around us. Those who choose not to join the Union are either friendly or indifferent to Humans. Contrary to what Earth Humans imagine, most beings in the known Universe aren't aggressive, or conquerors, since the Universe has a way to weed out those who show those tendencies before they reach the capacity to propel themselves towards the stars."

"The Amethen races are much older than Humans, and no records exist of their origins and earlier histories. It is known, however, that for hundreds of millions of your years they evolved slowly and lived in harmony with each other. That all changed seven hundred million years ago when other players came uninvited to the seven galaxies, and the lives of the Amethen were seriously disturbed. Legends tell that the intrusion sparked a great turmoil, and that it was marked by two major events: a 'malady of the mind' and a war. This malady is described in the legends as *The Blight of the Ancients*, and the war as *The War of the Kskiln.* Even though these two events happened before Humans, they are relevant to the Story of Earth, as the two of us will witness later.

"In the aftermath of that time of turmoil, some rogue groups from Amethen races joined the intruders and formed an alliance — with the peculiar name of *The Others* — to seize star systems and to profit from the chaos of the time. Later, when Humans appeared, The Others saw in us a menace and vowed to eliminate us. To this day, they are still attempting to do that."

Ríordáin halted his telling and our walk when a graceful, beautiful and elegant young woman, about my age, strode towards us in the company of an also-handsome young man. I thought the woman and the man were coming to meet us, yet to my astonishment they walked *through* us!

I shuddered, even though I hadn't felt anything, and looked aghast at Ríordáin.

He then rushed to say with concern in his voice, "I should have told you this. No one here can see us. Our mind-souls are clothed with only a small amount of the 'light' of this locus of Time, enough to allow us to experience the events as they happen to the actors I have chosen to assemble the Story of Earth. Let's journey with her. Her name is *Althesal* — she is from the planet Thel that I mentioned to you before. Her companion's name is *Laidé* — he is from the planet Lyaty of the Nauth System, known by your people as the star *El Nath*. Both are key characters in the Story."

Ríordáin then sounded a word and what happened next, I still can't fully grasp how it is possible: somehow he and I became the woman Althesal and began to witness that present moment of her life as she lived it — this "witnessing from within" happens in every instance when we experience an event in the Story. "We aren't inside her mind, or her self", Ríordáin whispered to me. "We are simply witnessing her contribution to the creation of this locus of Time as she lives her life and as it's recorded in the 'light' of Time."

And here is, dear reader, the first part of the Story of Earth as I witnessed and understood it.

— Claire De'Lys

An Unheard of Tragedy

"How is it possible a Humanity destroyed itself?" Althesal asked her companion the question that hadn't left her mind the entire trip from her planet. The two of them strode along the broad path. She was on her way to the High Council Chamber, summoned by the Chancellor of the Union. The Councilors were going to ask her the same question, and she had no answer for it.

"The information we have is sketchy, Issën Althesal", Laidé said while striving to keep pace with her. "A party of independent traders from the Nostelat System sent news of the tragedy. All we know is these traders had already made contact with a group of Humans on that planet and had established a regular business relation with them. They—"

"You mean, they were smuggling technology restricted to the Union!"

"We don't know that, Issën… Well… yes, they probably were… The point is one of them was unable to remain silent and sent to the Chancellor copies of the ship's logs from their last five trips to that planet, accompanied by a short note. Of course, these are logs from a Nostelat ship, and their quality is… poor. Nonetheless, the first four logs reveal the traders were dealing with a peculiar group of Humans, belonging to a Humanity half way through a first-level civilization, and who were secretive, aggressive and demanding. Through some of the visuals, telemetry and conversations recorded on the logs, we concluded that a rapid deterioration of that planet's bio-sphere was occurring. But the surprise is in the log from their last trip there. When the Nostelat craft arrived, eighty-five standard galactic days after their fourth trip, no one was waiting for them and the planet had become a desert, with not a trace of living beings."

"And the contents of the note?"

"It says: *'The fools destroyed themselves. We saw it coming. Yet, we gave them the goods they requested. It was just business!'* — That was all."

They continued their march in silence. To Althesal the entire affair sounded surreal. It didn't help that she felt spacey at that moment. Every time she used an ös-craft to travel between star systems, it took her some time to feel grounded again. She inhaled deeply a few times to clear her head.

She hadn't visited a Nostelat world, nor met any of their inhabitants. All she knew was they were among the least developed Humans in the Union, liked to ignore the rules, and had no attraction for the sciences and the arts. Yet, those traders 'saw it coming', while she, who had dedicated most of her life to study bio-souls, couldn't imagine the psychological changes a Humanity would have to experience to destroy itself and its planet's biosphere!

"Is this party of traders available for me to talk to them?"

"Unfortunately no, Issën. We have been unable to locate them. We suspect they have gone underground... They are good at that."

Althesal halted to look at him. "Tell me, friend — and stop addressing me as Issën! — can we trust those logs? And what about the note? This is your area of expertise."

She liked him because he was bright, pragmatic, and thought outside the box; although, as a good Nauthian Human, he was too formal at times. They had become friends since the time he had lived on her planet while studying her people's culture. He now worked for the Chancellor as her personal advisor on planetary cultures and diplomacy. It was him who had contacted her the previous evening to let her known the Chancellor requested her presence for an emergency meeting of the High Council.

"Yes, Iss— Yes, Althesal. The logs are authentic. The Rangers themselves concluded they do belong to a typical Nostelat craft and are recordings of five trips to the fourth planet of the Sol System — which, according to the logs, its inhabitants called by the name *Yfel*. Some segments are missing, but these probably contained information that would have led to identifying the traders. Also the visuals of the Humans are blurred, probably to avoid the use of those logs against them in the Courts, if it comes to that. As for the note, it uses the language and voice-code of Nostelat traders. It is recorded in an æl-crystal, which only those in a high position in their Syndicates are allowed to use."

With a sigh Althesal regarded him, then turning they continued on their way.

The summons had come at the worst possible time in her life. A month earlier, her peers on Thel had, in a surprise move, elected her to the office of Dean of the Exploring Guilds. Although an honor, she had been chosen to stop the intrusion of the Providing Guilds into the affairs of the other Thelian Guilds. As if that wasn't enough, other responsibilities beyond those on her planet came with the job — she became the Issën or Director of Sciences of the entire Union. Since then, her quiet life of teaching and research had become one of ceaseless meetings and administrative duties. She wasn't used to that. Next, twelve days after her election, her closest friend and life-long companion, Ethën, had told her he was leaving their planet, tired of "the non-sense" happening on Thel. He had asked her to go with him.

This was Althesal's first visit to Llën, the aerial city where the High Council had its offices. It was also her first time on the planet Esdänl, where more than 1,250 federations and leagues of star systems, comprising over 18,000 civilizations, were represented. Laidé escorted her along a broad path surrounded by gardens. Groups of delegates met under the shade of trees of as many origins as the delegates themselves. They were surrounded by a profusion of blooming plants also gifted by many worlds. The feeling and look of the city were similar to the aerial cities of her home planet, and for a reason. Many years before she had been born, her people had built that aerial city, and three others on Esdänl, as a gift to the Union. She knew well it had also been a statement of her people's scientific and technological prowess and superiority, so that no one would forget it.

The path took them to a spindle-shaped building towering over the city. At its base, all around, the arched entrances leading to the various floors and sections of the building rose tall. Laidé directed her to one of the arches. There, as soon as they both stepped through the opening, in the time it took her to blink, they were transported to a vestibule on the apex of the building, 120 floors from the ground. A silent nod from him told her they had arrived to the High Council Chamber — a circular dome made of a crystalline light-field with changing hues on its exterior surface, to reflect the diversity of peoples of the Union.

When she entered the Chamber, the Councilors were already waiting for her, in silence and without their aides. Laidé led her to a podium facing the almost-circular row of seats where the Councilors sat. Next he left the Chamber with soundless steps.

For a long moment no one broke the silence, and she felt twenty-five pairs of eyes studying her. But she held them in her gaze too. She had met before the Chancellor and a few of the Councilors. Most of the others, she recognized their faces. Some smiled at her. A few were stone-faced. She sensed a tension in these but couldn't identify if it was eagerness or anxiety — *This isn't going to be easy!*

"Issën Althesal!" The Chancellor's orotund voice startled her. "Thank you for coming to this Chamber on such a short notice, and welcome. We look forward to having a long and fruitful relation with such a distinguished person as you are. We wished your first time with us would have been under other circumstances."

Althesal was going to return the greeting when Chancellor Vuensé continued:

"On your way here, you were informed of the recent developments in the Sol System. Undoubtedly, you have many questions. Know that so have we. Thus, to obtain more information on this tragedy, the High Council has an urgent mission for you: we want you to organize and lead a research expedition of bio-soul scientists to that system to discover the actual cause of the destruction."

Her legs suddenly felt weak. Clasping the podium with both hands, she asked, "To Sol?… A research expedition?… Isn't that system in a region of Space controlled by The Others?"

"Not all the star systems in that area are under their control," the Chancellor replied, "and Sol is unclaimed. Besides, you aren't going to go there alone. The Ranger Corps will assist you. Assemble your team and figure out what you need. When you exit this chamber, you will find Mhali, Marshal of the Rangers, Islnom-1. He is waiting for you. His orders are to assist you in this operation."

Althesal's mind raced — *The Rangers? My teams are scientists, not infiltration forces. No one will want to go.* "Chancellor, may I ask, what is the High Council expecting to find there? I need to know it before I ask anyone to risk their lives."

For a moment the Chancellor studied her before turning briefly to regard the other Councilors. Most of them nodded back to her. Althesal observed with curiosity that the Councilor from her planet, Ambassador Thaël, had not. Without counting the enormous political power of the Chancellor herself, the power of the Thelian Ambassador to the Union weighed more than any other.

"Everything I am about to tell you, Issën, must remain within this Chamber until we have answers." The Chancellor's eyes bored into hers as she added, "The gravity of the situation confronting us requires wise handling. Do you agree to this request?"

Althesal admired Chancellor Vuensé's wisdom, nobility and utmost respect for the guiding principles of the Union. The matter was indeed of deep consequences if she and the Councilors had thought wise to act without the normal transparency of the High Council.

"Yes, Chancellor. I will abide by your request."

"Good! — You know the Sol System is one of many in our Seven Galaxies to which the Union hasn't paid much attention. Our efforts to deter The Others are spread throughout too many worlds, and not enough resources are left to explore systems where other Humanities or Amethen races may be developing. Yet, we shouldn't have ignored Sol since it's located close to a few member worlds, including yours. Now circumstances are forcing us to correct this oversight. Let's hope it isn't too late."

A few of the Councilors shifted in their chairs and regarded each other, evidently uncomfortable with those words — *She is good at Her job!* Althesal thought, *rubbing their noses and showing me the ones who could make my job difficult.*

"However," the Chancellor continued, "the reason we have decided to send now a group of Rangers with a group of bio-soul scientists to Sol is because the recent news from that system, together with a fresh analysis of the records of the movements of The Others around Sol in the past five hundred years, hint at the possibility they may have infiltrated that system in spite that a Humanity lived there. Then, the question we in this Chamber have is: Did The Others play a role in the demise of that Humanity? If that was the case, it would be the first time they have dared to destroy a Human world. From the logs of the Nostelat craft the Rangers surmised The Others didn't have dealings with the Humanity of that planet. Could they have used a long-range psy-weapon? Again, if this was the case, it would be a first time, and we need to determine the nature and effects of such a weapon."

Althesal took a deep breath. She had thought of that possibility when Laidé had let her know of the reason for the summons, but she had quickly dismissed the idea. The Others never exterminated peoples, or made worlds uninhabitable. They incorporated them into their dominions and profited from their civilization and resources. They were empire builders. But if the High Council suspected their involvement, only one thing could have happened.

Years back rumors had surfaced in the Bio-Soul Sciences community of the existence of some fringe scientists experimenting with energies to control the psycho-mental development of entire civilizations. A debate had then ensued regarding the theoretical and ethical bases for that type of experimentation. At the time she had thought it was impossible — perhaps with sentient beings of a primitive psycho-mental nature; but not with Humans, whose mind-soul component was one of the strongest among the known sentient races. Efforts to locate those scientists had yielded nothing, and the whole affair had then been dismissed as a baseless rumor.

"Are you suggesting, Chancellor, The Others found a way to affect and derail the psychological and mental development of Humans on a planetary scale? Is proof of this what the High Council is expecting to find there?"

Several voices answered at the same time. Some Councilors nodded, others shook their heads.

Althesal rose her eyebrows — in spite of the differences of view among the Councilors, the High Council always presented a unified stance in any affair concerning the Union.

"Yes, Issën," the Chancellor replied to her after imposing silence, "your words describe what some of us fear. The Nostelat logs reveal a progressive deterioration of the psychological state of those Humans, and a marked aggression towards each other — something which we have never seen... or imagined. With the knowledge and experience you have, can you confirm if it is even possible for someone to have altered their psyches and minds?"

As a reply, Althesal proceeded to give an account of those old rumors, of the ensuing debate among bio-soul scientists, and of the actions taken by the Trans-Galactic Association of Bio-Soul Sciences. She answered the Councilors' questions to the best of her knowledge. But after a time it was clear to her they wanted a 'Yes' or 'No' answer, and some felt frustrated because she couldn't provide it. She understood their pressing need for answers. The consequences of such a power in the hands of The Others would be far reaching. They had never held a superior position over the Union in force or in technology.

"We thank you for enlightening us, Issën", the Chancellor said when the discussion was exhausted. "Now you understand the reason we must send a research expedition to the Sol System, and the need for silence until we have answers."

"I do—" her words came in a whisper.

Light! What was she going to do? She couldn't deceive her teams to volunteer for such a mission. The Others could be anywhere in the Sol System. If they were in truth responsible for the destruction on the planet Yfel, the terms of non-aggression towards inhabited Human worlds, set forth by the Armistice of Adhara, would have been violated — and this meant open hostilities against the Union, again. There was also the problem of those dissenting groups among Humans who were tired of the long conflict and wanted to sign a final peace deal by partitioning the galaxies, even if it entailed massive relocations. If word spread revealing the Union had lost its advantage to contain The Others, it would empower those dissenting voices. These factions were naive, of course. The Others never wanted peace. They were conquerors. They had left a long trail of broken treaties and armistices, and they loathed Humans with viciousness. Thus, finding out what had happened on that planet wasn't a simple scientific inquiry, and she had to find a way to make it happen!

She glanced at Ambassador Thaël, who now stared at her with an inquisitive face. It puzzled her that his whole demeanor had been neutral during the entire discussion. She couldn't believe he didn't have any concerns — *Is that what we have become? Impassive and disconnected from the plight of others since nothing can touch us Thelians, not even The Others.* This wasn't the first time she felt saddened by some of her people's sense of superiority. Yet, as in those other times, in her heart she knew she didn't have to act in like manner. Thus, an idea began to form in her mind.

Straightening her body, she looked once more at Ambassador Thaël directly in the eyes, seeking to prepare him for what she was going to say — his face didn't show any change. Next, she turned towards the Chancellor and with a set determination said, "I do understand the gravity of the situation and the task the High Council requests of me. Regardless, Chancellor, I can not organize that type of expedition. I can't ask any of my teams to go there and risk their lives knowing The Others may have already infiltrated the Sol System."

The Chancellor didn't react, but a murmur rose in the Chamber. Althesal ignored it and continued:

"I offer, instead, another course of action for your consideration. We have developed on Thel a new class of survey probes designed to catalog and study the populations of bio-souls on planets. The probes can likewise analyze a broad spectrum of energy factors to assess their biological, psychological and mental environment. It is a new technology, but the tests we have done tell us it works, and well. These—"

Ambassador Thaël had cleared his throat and with a deep frown regarded her. The existence of that technology hadn't been disclosed to anyone outside certain circles on their planet. It was the norm on Thel that every new discovery or invention had to pass through a special office of the Thelian Council to assess its potential impact on the well-being of other civilizations. But, in recent years this mandate had been tainted with political ambitions, and new technology was now seen as political tool in dealing with the Union. This distortion of the original mandate filled Althesal, and most of her peers, with disgust. It was the reason her friend Ethën wanted to leave their planet. It all had begun with Ethën's formulation, 620 years back, of the principles for 'standing sound waves' in the ös harmonic fields of Space to create "live crystals". Inter-stellar travel and communications had been revolutionized since then, and it had provided the Union with a decisive advantage over The Others. But because of this, Thel had then been catapulted to the highest seats of power in the Union, something that most Thelians felt no attraction for.

She resumed knowing well that later she was going to face the consequences of her decision: "These probes, Chancellor and Councilors, can likewise read the echoes left in the ös-sphere of a planet by any known form of energy. We can thus assess the types of influences bio-souls have experienced as far back as ten thousand standard galactic years. Since we are looking for anything that may have recently affected the Humanity of Yfel, I propose to the High Council we send probes of this type, from one of the stealth transports of the Ranger Corps, to that planet, to every other planet in the Sol System, and to its interplanetary spaces."

A Glimpse into a World Beyond

Planet Thel, Eir System

Gentle musical tones awoke Althesal. It couldn't be morning, she still felt tired. With effort she opened her eyes and saw the stars through the domed ceiling of her bedroom. It was midnight. The pale light of the small companion planet of Thel — Othy — and of Thel's only moon shone low on the horizon. The standing light-field that made the dome sensed her waking brain pattern, and the communication frequency became active. Almost-invisible ripples formed on the field, and she heard the voice of Ethën:

"Althesal! You have to see this!"

"Oooh, it's you…" She slowly rose and donned a robe. Then she intoned a short, soft word, and the whole bedroom became lighted with a projected replica of the lab where the data transmitted by the probes was received.

"You won't believe what one of the probes discovered!"

She flinched at the volume of his voice.

"They awoke me first", Ethën continued. "The probe malfunctioned, but I came here and fixed it, then it happened. They couldn't believe it either. I—"

"Ethën! You aren't making any sense."

The other two researches in the lab laughed, and Ethën grinned at her. Althesal had entrusted him with the leadership and organization of the survey operation of the Sol System, free from the prying eyes of the Thelian Council and under the umbrella of the Chancellor of the Union. Her hope was he would change his mind of moving to another world.

"Well…" He ran a hand over his unruly wavy hair. "The probe sent to the third planet entered its atmosphere late last evening—"

"*Third?*" She still felt sleepy.

"Correct. When the probe became active, the data transmission it sent was scrambled and fragmented. The team here tried several fixes, but nothing worked, and decided to call me. Something around that planet is different. We had to recalibrate the probe several times before the transmission became readable a short time ago. The data stream still has gaps, and some readings are missing, but you aren't going to believe what we are seeing!"

Ethën nodded to one of the researchers, and Althesal became immersed in the multi-sensory stream of the data transmission. As if she were the probe, she glided through the air above a beautiful meadow in bloom. Dazzled by the profusion of colors, she blinked. A gentle breeze caressed her face, and the aromas it carried made her breathe deeply. No longer she felt sleepy, and the freedom of the gliding probe became hers. She even ducked when a vibrantly plumed bird flew close to her — she laughed at her foolishness. When her laugh subsided, the lavish sounds of that remote world enfolded her body. To her delight, the sensory experience kept going. Majestic trees, she had never imagined, rose in the distance, appearing to touch the few clouds in an azure sky.

Everyone in the lab was silent, observing her. Two minutes into the transmission she sat at the edge of her bed and with a quaking voice said, "I must be dreaming."

"No, you aren't dreaming, Dean Althesal", the younger of the two researchers said.

"But, it is an…" She felt a knot on her throat, and the next word came as a whisper, "*Aïdin…*"

"Yes! An Aïdin Planet!" The same researcher trumpeted, and gave a triumphant look to Ethën.

Ethën shifted on his feet, his initial enthusiasm now gone. "Hey, let's not confuse a magnificent bio-sphere made by Nature with a legend. Yes, this planet appears to be an outlier in that star system, but there are better explanations than to say we have found a mythical world."

Althesal said nothing to this. It was an old argument between the two of them.

During her studies she had encountered a significant number of records that appeared to confirm the existence of some of the stories described in the legends of old told by the Amethen. She wasn't alone. Many researchers from other worlds and races had also found evidence suggesting that in the earliest times life in the known galaxies included elements and experiences appearing to defy natural law. A number of Galactic Human and Amethen cultures accepted without question the legends of the earliest times as true events, even though much of what the legends described didn't fit in the current observations of science.

Ethën, by contrast and similar to most Thelians, held firmly to an empirical perspective to understand the Universe, and one's path through it. For him the legends didn't pass the test of science.

Althesal argued that one shouldn't reject, up front, the records. For his part Ethën insisted he wasn't doing that. He saw the legends as untenable and unreliable since they came from many cultures and had many differences among them, even when referring to the same subject. The subject of the Aïdin Planets was the most commonly debated legend between the two of them.

"Do we have other readings from the probe?" Althesal asked, still unable to contain the feelings that had taken hold of her heart.

The two other researchers rose from their seats and started talking to her, simultaneously, stopping once they realized what they were doing. They laughed, then took turns to point out data from the probe other than the sensory stream:

"That planet has so many groups of bio-souls, the probe is struggling to classify them all." — "Thousands of the bio-forms are new, and the count is still rising." — "There are no records of such a balanced and harmonious world." — "The flow of the life processes through that planet's ös-sphere and into the bio-sphere and the planet's core is perfect and musical." — "Yes, that planet is a symphony."

At first Althesal listened to them with full attention, but after a while her mind drifted off. Since she had been a child she had felt a strong fascination for the Aïdin Planets of old. No one truly knew how they looked, yet everyone imagined them. According to a few legends, these were rare, garden-like planets from the age before Humans appeared in Space. Those legends told these planets had been created by an enigmatic race of luminous beings who commanded with songs the forces of Space and Time. But the planets and their creators had disappeared at some point in that distant past. What intrigued her most was that a few of those legends linked these planets with the origin of Humans. They told that Humans had been seeded by the same beings who had created the Aïdin Planets.

"Althesal! Are you okay?" Ethën's voice brought her back to the present.

"Are there Humans on that planet?" she asked him with a trembling voice.

"Probably no. We looked into that right at the beginning. The sensors to detect the Human presence are among those refusing to work. However, the analysis of the data sent so far shows no indications of Humans living there."

"No Humans… Are you sure?" She couldn't hide her disappointment.

"What should we do with these data, Dean Althesal?" one of the researchers asked.

It took her a moment to realize she needed to make a decision about those findings. Both Humans and Amethen in the many worlds of the Union were going to want to see them — most children had heard of the legends, and the longing to rediscover an Aïdin Planet was found in countless hearts.

The probe sent to the fourth planet had already revealed a complete destruction of its bio-sphere and its Humanity, confirming the Nostelat traders' logs. The readings had shown the echoes of a sudden and violent dissipation of the molecular structure of the forms of the bio-souls which once had made their home on that world. But the data hadn't confirmed, nor ruled out, if The Others were responsible for the catastrophe. The findings, however, on the third planet could change everything regarding the Sol System. Many member worlds of the Union would want that system to be protected. At the same time a few members would shy away from doing anything to reignite a direct conflict with The Others. Althesal didn't want to be caught in the middle of such a dispute.

"Before we rush to any conclusion," she replied to the researcher, "let's have someone with expertise in the songs of bio-spheres, and their effects upon other worlds, review these findings — Nesdil, at the Life Harmonics Institute, is the right person for this. I want all the data we have to be ready for her by tomorrow morning."

Ethën and the other researcher were adjusting settings in the four-dimensional live replica of the probe at the lab when Ethën next spoke: "Now that we are talking about engaging Nesdil, I would like to involve also an acquaintance from Planetary Harmonics Science. There is something around that third planet still affecting the probe, at this very moment. He would be of help in identifying it."

"Very well", she replied after thinking about it. "You can engage him in the project if he is willing to abide by the secrecy required. But I don't want news of these findings to be shared with anyone else until we are sure of what the probe is showing us, and have the High Council's approval. I will inform Chancellor Vuensé of this discovery after we have Nesdil's analysis of the data. The Councilors will have to agree with us that the nature of the operation has changed and we can't keep this to ourselves. Also, we need to be ready for—"

"Not again!"

The cry of the researcher working with Ethën startled her. The live, 4-D replica of the probe had vanished.

Ethën turned and asked the second researcher, who was monitoring the actual probe, "What happened?"

The woman continued scrambling with the controls before turning to answer him, "The probe… The probe is gone… for good."

"That's not possible!" Althesal said before Ethën reacted. "Direct the cameras of the deployment module towards the probe."

"I just did it, Dean. Besides, we had one of its sensors continuously sending to us visuals and telemetry of the probe itself. The probe is gone. Not even the echo of its communication beacon shows anymore. It is as if the probe never reached that planet!"

"Contact the Rangers on the transport. Tell them about the probe and ask if they are detecting any unusual activity in the area. Perhaps someone or something destroyed the probe."

"No, Dean, it wasn't destroyed", the researcher insisted. "It vanished — one moment visible, gone the next one!"

Althesal rushed from her house to the lab. They played the multi-sensor stream several times and analyzed the twenty-two minutes of data available. Nothing explained the disappearance. The Rangers also informed them that, since they had arrived to the system, nothing unusual had been detected in the system or nearby. They too confirmed the probe had vanished from the transport sensors for no apparent reason, leaving no debris.

While Althesal reviewed the data, Ethën conducted all the procedures to detect any malfunction in the deployment module and reviewed the records of the diagnostics of the probe. Something had affected the probe as soon as it had penetrated the planet's ös-boundary, and the instruments had detected nothing of it. He then began to pace, stopping to look at something in the transmission, or in the instruments, and to ask the same questions he had already asked to the two other researchers. At some point he sat in front of Althesal and said, "That was the last probe left in the deployment module for that sector of the system, and the transport has no more modules. The Rangers already released those for the rest of the planets. Let's send another craft with probes to that planet!"

"That won't be easy", Althesal said, pressing her lips. "I've been shielding you from this, but right now we aren't in favor with the Council of the Paths for having used these new probes without the permission of the Trans-Civilization Relations Office. In addition, many in the Providing Guilds think we have gone too far by ignoring the proper procedures, and they will do all they can to stop or delay the making of new probes."

"No, they won't", the younger of two researchers said. "They will change their minds once we tell them of our discovery of an Aïdin Planet."

"I doubt it", Althesal replied to the young woman. "After all, we are talking about legends that our people dismissed a long time ago as the product of unsophisticated minds."

"Some of us think", the young woman added, this time regarding Ethën, "the legends are based on real historical happenings — muddled by the passage of Time, but pointing to past events, nonetheless."

"It doesn't matter what we in this room think!" Althesal didn't want to enter into a debate of the legends. "The point is a good number of our people in the Providing Guilds are no longer familiar to us. Pride and a sense of exceptionalism dwell in their hearts and blind them to anything else. They will refuse to build more probes for this project because they can't control it."

"Who cares about the Providers!" Ethën said while rising from the chair. "I'm sick of their intrusion into all research. Let's go there… ourselves… to that planet and settle this enigma."

The two researchers nodded.

Althesal didn't reply right away, her eyes staring at the starry horizon through the transparent light-field that was the lab's building. Othy and Thel's moon had already set, and the central star in the Constellation of the Heart, Sol, winked at her in the distance.

"Yes… that may be the only way…" Her soft voice trailed away. The possible discovery of an Aïdin Planet had awakened in her an old feeling — the feeling that binding one's identity to a culture, to a world, and even to being Human, was ultimately a limitation… that 'home' was somewhere else, beyond the cosmic horizon… that it was time for her to move on from being a Thelian.

Corridors of Power

"Destroyed? All life?"

Ambassador Thaël looked at his friend, Councilor Ulhloom, as he echoed Chancellor Vuensé's words. Was there a tone of fear in Ulhloom's normally soft spoken voice?

"My people haven't heard of such an event since... since before the founding of the Union", his friend added. "The Nostelat people are deceivers, and I had hopes they weren't acting any different this time. A hoax — that is what I expected of those logs."

Ulhloom's golden, semi-transparent, humanoid form made him resemble a living work of art. As he paced quietly across the room, the light in his body sparkled with a rhythm of hues revealing his feelings. His race, the People of Lhool, was one of the oldest among the Amethen, and it was considered by most as the wisest — Thaël agreed.

"That's what the probe confirmed", the Chancellor replied. She was summarizing to Thaël and Ulhloom the preliminary report on the planet Yfel that Marshal Mhali and Althesal had sent her that morning. "What happened on that planet", she continued, "was a sudden event — not in the nature of an explosion but of a destructive and fast chain reaction that engulfed the entire atmosphere and bio-sphere and broke down the molecular bonds of everything it touched. The energy released by the conflagration must have produced a powerful outward-bound shock wave. Thus, whoever or whatever initiated the chain reaction was also probably destroyed in the event."

Thaël shook his head, "That's not the way of The Others!"

Both the Chancellor and Ulhloom nodded in silence, their faces reflecting the uneasiness he also felt.

"There is more", the Chancellor continued. "After Marshal Mhali received the findings of the probe, he ordered the deployment of an autonomous, stealth drone to explore the interplanetary space around that fourth planet. The drone collected metallic debris outside the planet's ös-sphere. The lab analysis showed they are made of a crude alloy of mostly iron, a metal which, according to the Marshal, neither The Others nor any known civilization uses for their craft or space technology." After a sigh she added, "Definitely, The Others weren't responsible for the events on that planet."

"Back to where we started." Ulhloom halted his quiet and slow pacing to regard the two of them. "Other possible explanations are even darker."

"What's in your mind, Ulhloom?" Thaël asked. He couldn't understand his friend's uneasiness. "You implied at the beginning of this conversation that a planet-wide destruction of this type has happened before."

Ulhloom didn't answer right away and just stared at him.

The three of them followed the same routine every time they convened to talk about problems confronting the High Council. They met at the private conference room of the Chancellor's offices. She usually sat by the broad panoramic window with her back to the breathtaking vista of the city of Llën; Ulhloom, like all his people, didn't like to sit much and paced around; and Thaël sat facing the Chancellor across the large table. Those quiet, informal meetings had started spontaneously eleven years back, when dealing with one of the not-so-rare crises between new and old members of the Union. During the meetings they exchanged information, intelligence reports and ideas, and coordinated strategies, which they then brought to the entire High Council for consideration.

"We remember…" Ulhloom closed his eyes and started to answer with his usual staccato speech, without finishing the sentence. Thaël was, by now, used to that. It was the manner of speech of the People of Lhool when they were recalling past memories from their subconscious. Each individual of the Lhool was a collection of former selves under one present-self, and each individual was still aware of those former selves and life experiences.

"The Blight of the Ancients — you heard of that legend." Ulhloom opened his eyes. "Many call it so these days. The Blight is no legend. We remember… We lived through those times… Friendship and harmony, before then, we had among all races. Aggression and war were unknown. One day it started with entire peoples destroying themselves and their planets for no apparent reason… A blight of the mind and soul it was! It lasted long enough to make us realize we share the Universe with Powers of dark and unwholesome intentions to whom all of us are mere playthings."

Thaël and the Chancellor looked at each other, their eyes wide. That was the first instance the two of them had heard their friend speak of the history of his people before Humans appeared. With their reserved, forbearing and pacifist attitude, the People of Lhool seldom called attention upon themselves. To hear Ulhloom speak of the Blight of the Ancients was even more revealing, since neither Thaël nor the Chancellor knew how the People of Lhool regarded the legends of old.

"Do you think we are now confronted with something similar?" the Chancellor asked Ulhloom with her tactful tone. "Something which would explain the behavior of the inhabitants of the planet Yfel?"

"We cannot know with certainty, Chancellor. The thought of the Blight did come to me when this affair intruded into my peace. After this report, I cannot ignore the Blight, or something as dark, is a possibility."

Thaël shifted in his chair. How could an old legend, even if it touched on a real event in the far past, explain a present-day event? — "There must be another explanation", he muttered.

"And what would that be, friend?" Ulhloom halted his pacing to face him, pleading with his face that he would offer a better explanation.

When Thaël didn't answer, Ulhloom continued, "Let me answer for you: *The Humanity of the planet Yfel was born with a twisted heart. With self-destructive traits. Without connection to the Universal Stream of Mind-Soul —* No Thaël, that would be a first! — Needless to say, it contradicts the intrinsic goodness of our Universe which you, Thelians, promote."

What could Thaël say to that? Ulhloom was right. It had to have been something external to that Humanity. Moreover, his friend hadn't concealed this time the dread he felt at the possibility the Blight of the Ancients had returned. But still Thaël couldn't accept that an event so far in the past could explain the catastrophe on Yfel. Why hadn't such a phenomenon, or malady, resurfaced in the intervening time?

The Chancellor noticed his distress and came to his aid. "Let's postpone this conversation until Issën Althesal's team finish the survey of the entire system. If I recall well, the Blight of the Ancients affected, not isolated planets, but entire star systems and regions of Space. Is this true, Ulhloom?"

"Yes, Chancellor. Once it appeared in a system, it spread like a vicious plague from star to star."

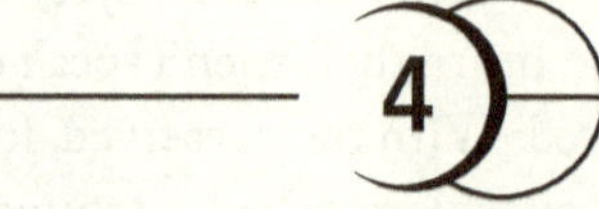

Time Shepherds

Nesdil felt apprehensive that someone would discover her whereabouts. Even Althesal and Ethën, her closest friends, would give her a lot of grief for what she was about to do. To her knowledge, no one of her fellow Thelians had ever defied the decision made by their ancestors to not set foot on their planet's surface. But there she was, about to land on a large island of the Meridional Ocean.

It all had started one month before with a recurrent dream, short and unclear. In it, a group of beings clouded by a sparkling mist called to her. Every morning after the dream, the feeling she needed to visit the planet's surface to look for them didn't give her rest. For days she had hesitated, but the dream kept returning. Then two mornings back, she had made up her mind to heed their call.

On the previous day she had visited the large continent where her ancestors' cities once stood tall and majestic. For hours she had surveyed the land from the air. Yet nothing was left of their former civilization, and nothing either in the landscape stood out as the place she had to go. That night, back at home, however, she dreamed once more — this time hearing the call much clearer. Thus, that morning she had returned to the surface with a prompting in her heart to explore the Meridional Ocean. Her prompting had been right. Soon she found that large island.

Gathering all her resolve, she landed on a clearing at the edge of a forest. An invigorating air rushed inside the cabin when she opened the hatch, erasing her last doubts. To her surprise, groups of animals came to greet her as soon as she exited the solo-craft. She didn't recognize their species. The first to approach were small canidae, with a sleek fur, tan in color, and with tall, graceful ears. They waged their tails and licked her hands. A few others were cervidae, walking with a noble bearing and bowing to her as they came. There were also large and colorful ground birds, talking among themselves, with an approving look, about her presence.

But her astonishment increased when she went to explore the forest — the greeting party decided to accompany her! Similar to children on their way to an outing, some rushed ahead with joyful strides, stopped and turned around to see if she was still coming before resuming their march. The young of the canidae — which she ended calling *doïel* for their ceaseless playfulness — were… well… they were puppies. They begged for her attention with short musical barks, rubbed themselves against her legs, and lay on the ground in ecstasy when she scratched their heads behind their tall ears. Flying birds also joined the procession. They chirped or sang to her while gliding from tree to tree, some ahead, others behind. It all gave her the impression she was being shepherded.

When she entered the forest, she felt at home! It felt alive in a way she hadn't experienced. Yet, she also sensed she was being observed, and the feeling became stronger the further in she went — a presence, an intelligence, studied her. It was elusive and undefined, all around. She had sensed none of it during her trip to the large continent.

What can it be? — she asked herself while meandering with her companions under the canopy of mighty trees. *Was it wise for our people to have abandoned the surface of our world? I ought to know what is observing me. It feels natural, belonging to the planet. Yet, it also feels otherworldly.*

Distracted with these thoughts, she didn't see it until it was too late. Thus, when her foot found no solid ground, she tumbled down through a deep hole, landing on her back and hitting her head against something hard. Then, right before she lost consciousness, she saw them!

She awoke at the touch of something cold and wet on her left cheek — it was the nose of one of her doïel companions. She also felt a weight on her abdomen — one of the puppies lay there, asleep. Several of them also napped against her body, keeping her warm, and two stood like sentinels guarding her. She lay on a soft patch of grasses shadowed by a large tree, and her head hurt. The pain made her remember having fallen into the hole.

Did I crawl out of it by myself?

The memory of having seen them came next, and the hairs on her nape rose. The promptings from her heart had been right: the beings on her dream were on that island!

She rose and felt dizzy, not for long. Next, she searched for the hole but couldn't find it, nor could she find any footprints different from those of the creatures of the land and her own. The daylight was by then fading, and she decided to continue her search another day.

"You look dirty, Teacher", Daothel, her young apprentice, said to her when she arrived at the Institute to return the recorder she had taken with her. He was the one who had encouraged her to visit the surface when she had told him about the dream. He too had requisitioned for her the solo-craft she had used. "If someone sees you now," he added barely holding his mirth, "they will think you fell all the way down from the city to the planet's surface!"

She hushed him with a frown. Then, as she turned around to leave for her house, he spoke again, this time with concern, "Wait! You have blood on your hair!"

"It's just a scratch."

"Not so, it's a lot of blood. Let me see… You also have some sort of paste mixed with the blood… Wait…" He called for a flask from a dispenser nearby and scooped a sample of it.

She turned around, and he held the flask in front of her face. With a chuckle he asked, "Did you do this to yourself, Teacher?"

"Of course not!" she replied and next told him her whole adventure while he examined her to rule out a concussion and then cleaned the wound.

"Strange," he said after removing the paste, "there isn't a cut or a scratch at all in your scalp, only a slight linear discoloration. Whoever applied this paste knew what they were doing."

That night Nesdil dreamed once more of those strange beings. This time she saw them much clearer and heard them urging her to go to them. Soon!

The next day, after a restless night, when she arrived at the Institute, Daothel was waiting for her.

"You have to see this", he said and led her to one of the photo-sonic re-search chambers designed to analyze complex bio-forms. He activated it, and a large representation of a live bio-cell sprang all around them, filling the entire chamber. The music sounded by the bio-chemical and bio-physical processes in the cell reached their ears, confirming that the sample cell was still alive.

He let her listen in silence for a long while before he spoke: "I isolated this bio-cell, and other similar ones, from the paste on your scalp. The first impression is that its song is normal for the bio-sphere of our planet. Yet, listen to this sub-harmonic…" He touched a point in the nucleus of the cell, and a sole sub-harmonic became audible. "This chord doesn't belong to our planet. I mean, it doesn't match anything we know."

She nodded in silence.

"But that's not all, Teacher." He zoomed into the nucleus of the cell to the level of the strands of DNA swimming in it.

"What's that?" She had to blink a few times. Portions of the DNA emitted a bright, iridescent, pulsating light while phasing in and out of sight.

"Those are extra sequences in each of the chromosomes. I checked in the database of the Bio-Soul Sciences Guild and in the Libraries of Esdänl. No one has ever encountered them, not on any world of the Union or on any other world we know of. The strange sub-harmonic chord is sounded by that extra DNA." He pause for a moment to look at her, then added, "If it weren't for these anomalies, I'd say this cell is from a hominid."

"There aren't hominids on our planet!"

"Yep! That's what intrigues me", he said with pursed lips.

⚡

Two days later Nesdil went back to the island — this time Daothel insisted in accompanying her. The doïel came to them when they were unloading a gravity-modulated sled carrying equipment. From their barking sounds she knew these doïel were from a different group, yet they greeted the two of them as if they were old friends. She had the feeling then that the doïel were going to escort them to the location where the mysterious beings on her dreams were waiting. She was right. As soon as the two of them were ready, without hesitation the creatures began moving in a straight line towards the forest and urging them to follow.

Daothel had wanted to accompany her in her two previous trips, but she hadn't allowed it to protect him from those among their people who would object to those visits to the surface. As she had suspected, everything on the surface captivated him, and he behaved as a child without parental oversight. He touched and smelled every plant and rock, and played with the doïel puppies, rolling on the ground with them. His joy was so contagious that some of the adults joined in the fun. Nesdil had never seen among their people such a free and joyful spirit, reminding her why she had chosen him as her only apprentice.

When the fun between Daothel and the pack subsided, the doïel led them along an invisible trail, at a steady but unhurried pace. At some point, they climbed a knoll where short bushes loaded with yellow berries grew in profusion. Both young and old doïel rushed to them, and Nesdil could smell the sweetness as their teeth crushed the juicy fruits. Daothel, of course, wanted to join them in the feast, but she held him back.

"Our bodies may have forgotten how to process that", she warned him.

After the repast, the puppies wanted to nap, but the adults shepherded everyone on their way.

Towards the end of the morning they arrived at their destination. This time it wasn't a hole in the ground but an entrance, on the side of a hill, to an underground passage — tall and wide enough for eight to ten Humans to walk abreast.

"Before we enter, let's set recorders to capture the music of this place," she told Daothel, "including any sounds at the feeling and mental levels that may be present. We will retrieve them when we return."

Once the equipment was set, they entered the opening on the side of the hill. The doïel were by then all asleep and didn't stir.

A broad passage, of the same dimensions of the entrance, stretched in front of them. It had a gentle downward incline. Its floor and arched walls were regular and smooth, covered by a crystallized material.

A fluttery feeling of anticipation lurched up in Nesdil as they commenced their descent. Daothel for his part was taking the adventure as if 'this is how everything in life should always be'.

After fifty paces or so he halted and said to her, "Let's get some light. We don't want to fall into a hole."

When he was about to turn around to activate the lights of the sled, a soft, white light burst forth, illuminating the entire passage. It was all about them without a visible source. Speechless, they regarded each other. Next, both, at the same time, rushed to touch the wall of the passage. It had a soft vibration.

"Can you hear it humming?"

He nodded. "It comes from this material."

They continued descending along the gentle slope while a feeling of welcoming swelled in Nesdil's heart. A warm breeze touched their faces, and the air smelled fresh with a hint of orange blossoms. From time to time they saw openings to unlit passages but kept going in silence, guided by the light. Then, fifteen minutes or so after they had entered the passage, they arrived.

"Hold it there, Teacher!" Daothel grabbed her arm and forced her to stop.

So enthralled was she with the spectacle that she hadn't seen the drop. The two of them stood on a circular ledge at the equator of a large spherical space, about twenty-five lont across [54 meters]. It was perfectly round and with smooth walls, like the passage they came through. It too was illuminated by the same type of soft light. But what had captivated her attention was the group of sixty or so beings who stood in mid air regarding them.

They were the beings on her dream — slender, about four quont in height [1.44 meters], with a remote resemblance to lemur species she knew existed on other planets. They had soft, beautiful features, and a short golden fur covered their entire bodies and their long tail, which ended in darker stripes. They stood upright with a smile in almost-Human faces. But the most striking feature was their appearance. It fluctuated between solid and translucent while emitting soft iridescent flashes.

"Greetings, friends. Once more your *now* and our *now* are one."

The greeting sounded in her head; they hadn't spoken. Instead, a gentle music had touched her, eliciting tingles throughout her body and forming those words in her brain. She was entranced, seeking to explain all she was experiencing, while a feeling of otherworldliness and familiarity, at the same time, sought to overwhelm her.

Daothel spoke at that point. "I hear their greeting, Teacher... *'Once more'* they said! — Who are they?"

She found her voice and, without thinking, replied, "*Asli...*"

It surprised her to call them so, but it made sense — *Shepherds*, in the language of the Old Races.

A surge of well-being rose in her body as soon as she called them so, and an image of them guiding the doïel came to her mind as a confirmation.

"They are using a form of telepathy", she whispered. "I can't identify it."

"It isn't telepathy", Daothel replied and closed his eyes for a moment. Then, opening them he added, "They aren't communicating directly to our brain — that's for sure. I sense them reaching to our entire bodies... from inside out... somehow."

As he finished speaking, a live image of the nucleus of a bio-cell flashed in Nesdil's mind.

"I see it too", Daothel rushed to say. "Now I understand. They are touching the cells of our bodies with... it isn't thought... it's their flashes... it's the music of their flashing bodies..." After a moment he added with triumph, "They are playing with our DNA as it were a musical instrument to communicate with us!"

The Asli, all at once, bowed to them to confirm his conclusion, and Nesdil felt another surge of well-being. A realization then dawned on her — her dreams hadn't been dreams at all. The Asli had used her sleep time to learn to communicate with her, from the cellular level up to the brain and mind — which also told her their powers reached all the way from the island to her people's aerial cities, and perhaps beyond.

She wanted to ask so many questions to them, yet before she could, their soft music coming through her bio-cells started again, eliciting in her not only understanding but a visual sensory experience.

"You *two, five* others, and *we* are together in other *nows*." She heard them say with emphasis. "In one of them you ask us to tell you our tale in this *now*, so that you remember your tale. Here is our tale: In the beginning, in our first *now*, we and your people are one. Then, our oneness ends, and we become other than you… Other, because the *nows* move around us, avoiding us. Not so for you."

Their tale wasn't easy to follow. Yet with it, images of a remote past came to her mind. From these she understood that the ancestors of the Asli had been the only hominid species on her planet. Then, at some point, an extraneous Power had split the species in two groups, one larger and one smaller, and that same Power had transformed their group, the smaller one, into their present state. Both groups had continued living along different evolutionary paths — the Asli on that island, the others on the main continent. Apparently her people were the descendants of the larger group. Yet, the intriguing thing was her people had never noticed the Asli's existence.

"In *That* which sources *Time* we live", they continued. "And from there we enter any *now* we choose be in."

At this point they paused and bowed again to the two of them, as if seeking confirmation they understood their tale. She was feeling wave after wave of gentle musical touches. Their language was complex, with multiple levels of meaning, resembling an entire symphony carried on the waves of a simpler song — that of their DNA.

"Events are precipitating!" they added with a rapid flashing of their bodies. "You must see and understand so that your *locus of Time* continues its intended weaving — Observe!"

She turned to Daothel and asked him, "*Locus of Time*? — What are they saying?"

However, before he could reply, she felt as if she was about to faint. It took her a moment to recover, though she felt lighter and giddy. Daothel was still standing next to her, but his appearance had changed. He was taller and robed in a bluish light, and he studied her with such a face of wonder that it prompted her to look at her own body — she was also clad in light! From her hands and feet issued rays of a lavender hue.

The Asli had vanished. So had the cavern. But the two of them weren't alone. The most beautiful beings she had ever beheld were with them — Human in appearance, and more. Like daystars they shone with noble and serene countenances. And similar to the two of them, their bodies and garments were light itself.

They all stood in circle on a barren mountaintop — three dozen of them. Above them, dark and menacing clouds rolled through the sky. Lightening, rain and ashes fell, making the twilight even gloomier, but the radiance from their bodies formed an impenetrable shield around them. In spite of the darkness, Nesdil could see far into the distance where valleys and mountain ranges lay broken and scorched. Further away, oceans roared in turmoil as quakes shook beneath them. No life was left. They were witnessing a dying world, torn apart and robbed of its essence by warring, unseen Forces.

"Now is the moment!"

The magnificent musical harmony of these words startled her — such was the contrast of that beautiful voice against the cacophony of death all around. Nesdil looked at the one who had so spoken. She knew him! At the same time she knew it wasn't she who knew him. She was looking through someone else's eyes and self.

At his exhortation all those in the circle closed their eyes. It was then that somehow she also knew what needed to be done. She thus closed her eyes, rose her awareness, and focused it at the point where Time springs forth into existence. A few moments after, the intensity of a light forced her to reopen her eyes. The light, cold and white, emerged from a small vortical opening in the fabric of Space, in the midst of their circle. It was about two handspans in width, with a mighty sparking point at its center, and spinning at a great speed with a four-fold motion.

She knew then it was time for all of them to sing, and for that dreary world to hear the song of life anew. And singing they did. And louder and louder their song rose with indescribable majesty and beauty. And at the rhythm of its notes, the vortex at the center of the circle gave off wave after wave of fiery sparks which spread throughout the desolation unto the horizon.

To Nesdil's wonder, everything the song and the sparks touched was then infused with new life and made whole again.

Soon the quakes ceased and the clouds parted, and the rays of a bright blue-white sun spread along mountains, valleys, rivers and oceans. Order came to a world that had lost it.

Then, when a ray of that bright sun touched the mountaintop where they stood, their singing took a new cadence, and the sparks coming from the vortex this time rushed to penetrate the ground everywhere — yet not to remain there. Each one next burst forth and up again into the light of day in a spiral dance of joy. And with their dancing, greenery covered the lands and insects appeared to begin their labors as the caretakers of all plant life.

At this point, once again their singing changed rhythm, commanding the sparks with a new task. This time, pair after pair dispersed together in a slow-moving dance, and as leaves fall to the ground in the autumn, the pairs fell upon the lands and into the waters. And at the tune of this new rhythm, each pair of sparks gathered upon themselves air and moisture while revolving around one another, and from their dancing complex molecules were given form. Without rest the sparks danced until the waters, the lands and the winds became peopled with beautiful and joyful animals of countless species.

It was thus that their singing gave life anew to that which had been dead, and Nesdil felt a joy that made her also whole and new with every harmony.

Then, when all was restored, with a grand finale the song reached out to the stars. In no time others like them joined in the chorus. Singing, these other Humans thus approached the newly-restored world, and on their wake carried, asleep, in envelopes of light, thousands of sentient, non-Human beings of a race unknown to Nesdil.

With care the arriving ones settled the sleeping ones on valleys and meadows of the now-a-garden world to begin anew the life the warring Powers had from them stolen. And when the sleeping ones awoke, the song came to its end.

All done, the mysterious vortical phenomenon at the center of their circle collapsed upon itself.

Once more Nesdil felt dizzy, and in the blink of an eye she was back in the large underground space with the Asli. They were enveloped in a swirling mass of sparkling particles which bounced back and forth between them and the spherical walls. Yet, the sparking particles didn't last for long before they were gone.

"What did just happen?" She heard Daothel ask. He was still standing next to her.

"I-I am not sure."

Twin Songs

Althesal watched in silence as Nesdil moved in rhythm with the light and harmonies on the lab's central platform. Her friend's eyes were closed, listening to the music, and joy was on her face. Abruptly the music ceased, and her body came to halt with an awkward step.

"What happened?" her friend asked her new apprentice, Daothel.

"That's all the data Dean Althesal brought", Daothel said, quickly lowering his eyes when he saw Althesal studying him.

"For heavens sake, Althesal, why do you this to me?"

Althesal grinned back to her. "I told you, we don't have much."

"Play it again, Daothel… and don't let her Dean-ness intimidate you." Her pleasant laugh filled the lab.

The central building of the Life Harmonics Institute resembled a vast performance hall designed to reproduce the most delicate sounds naturally emitted by bio-souls. Its interior, a circular wall, was made of hundreds of hexagonal niches — each no wider than two handspans and covered by a dampening acoustic field to neutralize external sounds. These niches also served to house and protect the largest collection of records in the Union of the fundamental chords, and their harmonics, of the bio-spheres of a multitude of planets in the Seven Galaxies.

Half way through the second time they played the data, Althesal noticed that Nesdil's apprentice rushed to retrieve a recording sphere from one of the niches. He then placed it inside the photo-sonic field where a similar sphere, with the probe's data she had brought, was playing. The photo-sonic field translated the data into the music that sounded throughout the Lab.

When the data finished playing for a third time, as the platform descended to the floor level, Daothel strode towards Nesdil and whispered to her, "Teacher, they match!"

She nodded. "I too suspected it when we played the data the second time."

"But, what does it mean? Do they know that we—?"

Althesal couldn't figure out what was happening, and to add to her confusion Nesdil hushed him. Next the two walked together in silence to the console where the small, crystalline, recording spheres hovered. Her friend touched the input field and entered the fundamental cord and harmonics she had identified in the data transmitted by the probe. Once done, the two of them came to her.

Nesdil sat on a chair and gestured to Althesal and Daothel to also sit. With her eyes closed her friend took a few deep breaths to clear the remains of the probe's sounds from her body.

Their people had the most sophisticated hearing sense and organs of speech among Humans and the other known sentient races of the Seven Galaxies. They were capable of listening and of voicing sound frequencies in a broad range of ultra and infra-sounds no other race could match. But on their planet they weren't the only ones with that ability. More advanced than its Humans were the *eos*, a unique natural kingdom found nowhere in the known worlds but on Thel — the eos could also hear, and sound, a broad spectrum of light frequencies.

When Nesdil opened her eyes, she asked Althesal, "Where did you obtain this data?"

"I can't tell you", she replied, still puzzled by the interchange between her friend and her apprentice. "What do you think of it?"

"So-o-o… this data must be from that secret project of yours that everyone is talking about." Feigning a disapproving look, her friend then asked, "Are we now keeping secrets from each other?" It was a game they played since the two of them were young. It worked every time, in both directions, and they ended sharing what the other wanted to know.

Althesal sighed and said, "You are going to be the first one to know when Chancellor Vuensé grants me permission to tell others. I promise it, dear. Now, tell me what you think."

"You aren't going to like my answer — I warn you! The data is limited, but it reveals a bio-sphere with an unusual complexity and richness. However, if this data is from a planet, which I think it is, by all known standards that planet shouldn't exist."

Althesal, now more curious, leaned forward, "What do you mean? Why shouldn't it exist?"

At that moment with a swift movement Daothel rolled his chair closer to the two of them, and Nesdil gave a glance to him before replying to Althesal:

"Because the fundamental chord of that bio-sphere is *not* in harmony with the standard pattern of the Music of the Spheres characterizing known Space. In itself, it isn't a dissonance. On the contrary, the music of that bio-sphere is of a rare majesty and beauty. Yet it's playing a tune of its own, under a master musician, but independent from the universal symphony in our multi-galaxy environment."

Althesal tried to contain her excitement. She took a look at Daothel, measuring him up — she had heard of him several times but had only met him that morning — then, slowly, she let the question drop: "Could that world be an Aïdin Planet?"

The young apprentice gasped while Nesdil frowned and locked her eyes with Althesal's for a moment before rising her gaze towards the domed roof.

No one spoke for a time. The only sounds came from Daothel as he fidgeted with his hands.

"You know I've wondered for long about Aïdin Planets…" Nesdil whispered. "Yet, it eludes me how we will know if we are seeing one."

"We won't know by seeing it with our eyes", Althesal replied smiling while resting her back on the chair. "A certainty will arise in our hearts."

"Hmm… You speak as a Wanderer… of intuitions and certainties… the substance of dreams and hopes. Can we still dream and hope at a time when we demand tangible proof for the certainties in our hearts?"

Althesal nodded. For a reason she could not grasp, talking to Nesdil about it made her more certain of what they had found in Sol.

"And your heart tells you, that world is an Aïdin Planet?"

"Yes." Her answer, though barely a whisper, echoed throughout the large chamber. "Although Ethën thinks otherwise. But you know how pragmatic he is!"

"Yes…" Nesdil nodded. Too many times the two of them had had debates with Ethën regarding the power of one's feelings and intuitions, besides the mind, to help one understand life and the Universe. "Well…" her friend continued louder, "for sure that planet of yours is an enigma. However, I don't want to dampen your hopes because here we are confronted with a much deeper mystery than the one you have in mind."

Althesal remembered Nesdil's interchange with her apprentice, and her certainty was replaced by doubts. Clasping her hands, she asked, "Deeper mystery?… What are you talking about?"

Nesdil signaled to Daothel, who went back to the photo-sonic console where the two recording spheres were still immersed. "Listen to this", she said to Althesal while gesturing to him.

Daothel announced and played the isolated chord and its harmonics recorded by Nesdil from the data Althesal had brought, followed by the chord and harmonics recorded in the second sphere. Next, he played the two of them together. Two more times he repeated the same sequence.

Althesal stiffened as the sounds reached her. When the silence returned, she asked, "What's the meaning of this?"

"Tell me what you hear", Nesdil asked.

"Of course they are the same chord! Any child can tell you that!"

"Yes, they are the same chord and the same harmonics, but… one is from the bio-sphere data you brought to us; the other… well… the other is from a recording Daothel and I made recently on an island in the Meridional Ocean of our planet."

Althesal felt the blood drain from her face, opened her mouth to say something, then closed it again.

"I told you that you weren't going to like my answer", Nesdil said softly to her. "Now, if we are going to clarify this mystery, you need to share with us the source of your data. We will also tell you the circumstances in which we recorded the matching sounds."

⚡

Althesal returned to her offices at the Exploring Guilds Administration early in the afternoon. She canceled all appointments and told her assistant not to disturb her for the rest of the day. She needed time to think about her next move. The story Nesdil and Daothel had told her hadn't left her mind. Her entire world had been turned upside down. Several times she listened to the two recording spheres Nesdil had given her as if they could tell her more of the mystery surrounding those sounds.

From her desk she could see far in the distance another of the aerial cities of Thel. It shone as a jewel of great intricacy and beauty. Twenty-four of them housed the entire population of her planet — 240,000 Thelians. Her people had built them fifteen generations before her. Made entirely with materials condensed from light-fields, they tapped into the ös-fields of the planet to supply their energy needs and to remain in place in the air at an altitude of 834 lont [1,800 meters]. Moving from the planet's surface to live on them had been a turning point in the history of her people.

But something had happened back then. As the cities had reached the right altitude, a slight shift in the ös-sphere of the planet, in its electromagnetic component, had been recorded. For a time after, people had complained of minor neurological symptoms and sleep problems. Tests had then shown minute alterations in their brain-wave patterns, which had become permanent since then in all those who lived on Thel. The changes had been explained through the science that had made possible the creation of the ös-field modulators keeping the cities in the air. Now, if those mysterious beings Nesdil called 'the Asli' were to be believed, that explanation wasn't the right one. According to them, another event had happened to the planet at the same time, but the Asli had been silent about its nature.

"What's the matter?" Ethën's head peeked through the door opening. "You are ignoring my calls."

She stared at him as he came in, walked to the food dispenser and grabbed an eesple [a kiwi-like fruit], then sat across from her to eat it.

"By the way," he spoke before she could say anything, "Marshal Mhali and I talked earlier today. The module with the probes sent to the fifth planet is almost there — that's the last planet to study. Unless we have another surprise there, the survey of the entire system should be finished in two days."

She gave him a dismissive nod, covered the two spheres with her hands, and asked him, "Do you remember when we were kids and I made plans to travel in Time so that we could journey to our future and see if we were still together?"

"How can I forget that! You've always been a dreamer… a dreamer of big dreams — I love that in you."

"Yes… and you have never discouraged me… Well, now I wish we could travel to our past."

He regarded her with his broad smile, swallowed a bite of the eesple, and asked, "What for? To visit that planet of Sol?"

"No! To see how our people evolved here."

"I don't follow you. Is that from your visit to Nesdil? What does she think of our enigmatic planet? Is she coming with us to investigate it?"

"Oh, yes, she is coming… if ever we go there. But not for the reason you and I want to go. The enigma is… more convoluted."

He finished his fruit, then asked slowly, as if he were treading on shaky ground. He always did that in everything involving Nesdil. "Convoluted?

Does she then agree with you that we found an Aïdin Planet?"

"She can't tell. The problem is… something else has come up." She paused to regard him before showing him the spheres. "Listen to these two recordings. The sphere on my right contains the fundamental chord and harmonics Nesdil isolated from the song of the bio-sphere recorded by our probe, while the one on my left is the dominant chord and harmonics of the song of a bio-system Nesdil recorded recently."

Althesal next played the two chords and harmonics for him in the same order Daothel had done it at the Lab.

Ethën frowned as he listened. When the sounds die out, he asked, "How did she obtain that second recording?"

"She traveled with her apprentice to the surface of our planet, to a—"

"What! — That's not the Nesdil I know!"

"I had the same reaction. Though I think it's her new apprentice — his name is Daothel — who challenges her to go beyond her boundaries. You will like him when you two meet."

He nodded. "So, what's the story with the second recording?"

"It's a long one, and she can tell it to you better than I can."

"Go ahead, nonetheless."

She then proceeded to tell him the story while he listened with a growing skeptical face. When she arrived to the description of the Asli, he shook his head:

"Is Nesdil kidding? There have never been hominids on our planet! No fossils. No other records."

"That was my reaction too. Yet, the fact is, they are down there and appear to have evolved there, on that island. Why our people never knew of them, I can't fathom."

She let Ethën digest the revelation. It arose so many questions that it was hard to know where to start.

"Hmm…" Ethën said after a while. "This is going to be big news — the missing link between us and the animal kingdom!"

"I thought of that too. Though I think it's more complex than a direct connection. That's the reason I wish we could travel back in Time… But let's not go into that right now… Listen to this: those beings summoned Nesdil because they had something of great importance to show her, something which concerns her, Daothel and five others — that's what the Asli told them. It turned out they wanted to show Nesdil a vision of events that took place in the past on another planet. In the vision…"

When Althesal ended the account of the vision as she remembered, she paused. By telling this part of the story to Ethën, she re-experienced the same strong feeling that arose in her when Nesdil told her of it: an unexplainable feeling of sadness for those luminous Humans in the vision, mixed with a pressing urgency to fulfill a task for which she had been born but couldn't define.

Ethën too was visibly shaken by the story — his skepticism now gone.

Taking his hand in hers across the desk, she whispered to him the end of the story: "Nesdil and Daothel spent a whole day with the Asli asking them questions. They also found that the Asli's bio-forms, as well as the bio-system of their island, have the same fundamental cord and harmonics the third planet of Sol has — that's what is recorded in this second sphere."

She let go of his hand, and Ethën rested his back heavily on the chair. He sighed, then shaking his head slowly he said, "Evolution doesn't work like that! It doesn't create duplicates. No way! Someone or something has to be responsible for that similarity." After a short pause, he added, "Those beings in the vision and the singularity they used?"

"That's also what I think", she whispered. "Nesdil too. Though her apprentice isn't sure that it explains all."

Althesal took a deep breath. The unknowns were piling up. A simple survey of a star system had become an entangled mass of findings without a discernible pattern, connecting their planet, and perhaps their people, with a planet in a neighboring star system. More perplexing to her was that, because of their strong reactions to the Asli's revelations, the mystery appeared to want to draw Nesdil, Daothel, Ethën and her into it too.

Feeling again the sudden urge to do something, she rose from her chair while saying to him, "As soon as this work of mine here allows it, I'm going to visit the Asli and see what more we can learn from them. We too need to figure out how to obtain more information about that third planet. If its bio-sphere was affected by the same Power that made the Asli, that singularity in the vision could still be there... At the least, it may have left more clues."

"Don't expect me to sit here and wait for you to tell me how your trip went", he said pretending to be annoyed. "I've always wanted to visit our planet's surface, who hasn't? As for obtaining more information on that other planet, our only option now is to travel there."

"I thought of that too." She looked at him directly in the eyes knowing what he was going to say next.

"Easy thing to do", he began slowly. "You and I could use one of our trans-planetary craft — I guess Nesdil and her apprentice would want to come too — and do a preliminary stealth survey. One day is all we need. No one will ever know, not even The Others if they are there. Let's do it!"

She didn't answer right away. In her heart she wanted to do so. She knew that involving the High Council, and Marshal Mhali and his Rangers, to find answers to those mysteries would only complicate things. Yet, she also knew the entire affair wasn't just a personal quest. Thus, she replied to Ethën:

"No, this isn't our way. Our people pledged to abide by the Protocol of Union when we joined the Laendänl, so that with our example other worlds may rise above their present selves towards greater horizons."

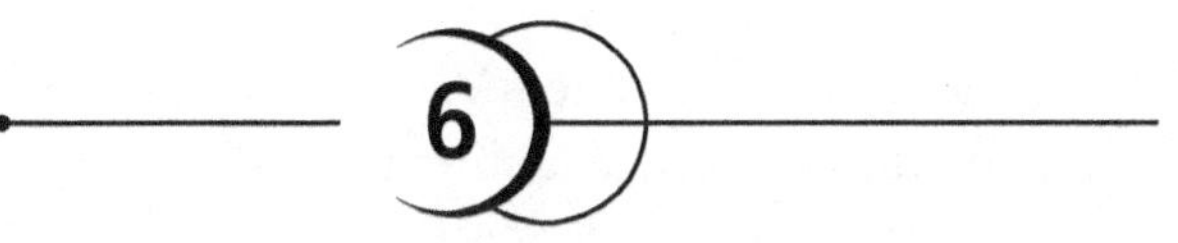

Lifeless Dust

The Ranger on watch on the bridge had detected them heading towards the system, and Marshal Mhali had ordered to move the transport to the other side of the ös-sphere of Sol to observe their intentions. Three craft, one carrier and two escorts, followed a direct path towards the planet on the fifth orbital harmonic. The deployment module with the probes to study that planet was going to arrive there at the same time as them, and the module's stealth technology wasn't designed to conceal it from The Others. He had then made a decision.

"Is this wise, Marshal?" the Captain asked him. "We could destroy the module from here."

"It may alert The Others of our presence", Mhali replied. The live-crystal he held on his hands felt cold, and its bluish glow reflected on the Captain's eyes.

"Let me do it. I can retrieve the module. You shouldn't risk it, Marshal."

"I need you here, Captain. The probes surveying the last two planets are still out there, and no other person on this transport knows of their technology as you do, if something goes wrong. That leaves me as the only one available to densify a solo-craft and pilot it." He placed the live-crystal at his feet, on the floor of the launch bay. The Captain moved away from him, and Mhali added, "I will return in no time… and Captain, inform Issën Althesal's team on Thel of this situation so that Ethën isn't surprised when in their monitors the module doesn't arrive to its destination — I talked to him this morning and told him that everything was going according to plan."

Mhali focused his mind on the live-crystal, and with his will power gave energy to the pattern programed in it — the light in the crystal flared. He then held in his mind the image of a complete solo-craft. The crystal hummed the familiar melodious tones. Within seconds, inter-stellar ös light densified around the crystal, and around him, in the shape of the craft he had visualized — a spheroid, four lont across [8.6 meters], flattened at the poles. He then sat on the only chair in the craft. A panoramic window at its mid section gave him a 360-degree view. The chair was his personal touch since the craft usually came with a full-body-support stand, but he always liked to include a pilot chair. His parents had taught him to be a pilot on an older craft with chairs from the time before the live-crystal technology had been developed.

He next sent the telepathic message to the First Officer on the bridge: "I am ready."

A large opening in the hull of the launch bay appeared. With his mind Mhali instructed the PI [Programed Intelligence] of the solo-craft to exit through it. Once outside, he visualized his intention to be beside the probe-carrying module. The live-crystal hummed again, and the craft rose above the dense physical levels to the ös light fields that made up the ös-sphere of the system. He watched in silence at the spectacle. The mighty ös light-fields coming from Sol, visible only at the first ös harmonic, surrounded his craft while it slid along the pathway to its destination. He was going to be there any moment — for the Captain and crew on the transport, his craft had suddenly vanished from view, only to reappear almost immediately at the target location near the fifth planet.

Mhali loved traveling through space, and nothing surpassed the joy and freedom of piloting a solo-craft. He just wished it could be under different circumstances.

Soon the craft matched the speed and trajectory of the module, which traveled along the physical level of the dense ös-fields [solid, liquid, gaseous]. His craft, still at the higher, first ös light-field, enclosed the module fully. He next sent a mental command to the live-crystal, and the craft and his body returned back down to the dense physical ös-fields. He stood up, took two steps to reach the module and powered it down.

"I have the module", he communicated to the Captain.

"Excellent! Marshal. The three spacecraft of The Others continue on their original course. They are heading towards the other side of the planet from where you are. So that you know, those craft have no insignia to iden-tify them."

"Understood. I am—"The glow of the live-crystal flickered, and he felt a downward pull. He lost no time and refocused his thought power on the crystal, but the downward pull accelerated. He was falling towards the planet!

"Marshal, what's happening?"

"I lost control of the crystal. Something isn't right with it."

"We are moving to intercept you."

"No! Stay where you are. The Others mustn't know of our presence. Those are the Chancellor's orders."

He continued his efforts to regain control of the live-crystal with his well-trained mind. Yet, tendrils of a strange reddish light came through the floor of the craft and penetrated the crystal. He fought with all his will power to reach its PI of no avail — a small area of the hull at his left became translucent; other translucent patches started to appear. Once a live-crystal was deactivated, a craft could retain its form for hours or days, or even indefinitely, if it was at rest and exposed to balanced forces. Exposed to the attracting power of a planet while inside the various flows and normal turbulences of the electromagnetic components of the ös-field, was a different matter. He was going to have a rough landing.

There was nothing else for him to do but relax and let his Ranger training take control of the situation. He had learned and practiced the maneuver he was about to do during his days at the Academy, though that had been years back.

Time slowed down as he began to breathe in and out. With every exhalation his mind and feeling energies cascaded down and magnetized the ös light-field around him. Next, focusing his mind, he modulated that ös light, and it began precipitating into a semisolid, jellylike light-substance, surrounding his anatomy tightly and swelling to fill the entire craft. He kept focused on his breathing. It was a matter of minutes before he hit the ground. Using his expanded proprioceptive sense, he then assessed the distance left and readied himself for his last step in the maneuver. Using the energy of Sol's ös-sphere, he shifted the polarity of the jellylike light-substance to match that of Sol. As he expected, the force of gravity from the planet lost most of its control on him and the craft decelerated. Only some momentum remained.

Well… Here it goes!

The first bounce was the hardest. His body took it well. After several more bounces the craft came to a complete rest.

At once he released his control of the jelly-like substance and, almost instantaneously, it returned to its normal state as light. With this, to his surprise, the craft dissipated into its component light-fields. The live-crystal then fractured and dematerialized too. The module was intact, though a reddish light flashed a few times inside it, making him suspect the probes had suffered the same fate.

From the long-range-sensor survey made by his crew when they had first arrived to the Sol System, he knew this fifth planet would support Human life. He thus took a deep breath, and the air felt charged with vitality. It was a relief since he didn't want to submit his body to additional stress. His main concern now was that he was stranded on a planet controlled by The Others.

He lost no time and focused his attention on his surroundings, alert to any eventuality. The afterglow of the sunset told him he had landed near the equator of the planet, though it was windy and cold. He next adjusted his eyes to the twilight and his body to the cold. A vast plateau, covered with short grasses, extended in all directions. In the distance, to the north, the lights of a tall complex of buildings shone. He felt a chill down his spine, their outline reminded him of the bases The Others had on some planets. He hoped no one had noticed his descent. Regardless, it was time to break his silence.

Mhali then gazed towards the sky, and with his mind projected the thought-words: "Captain, I am on the surface of the planet. Condition optimal. The craft is gone, but the module is with me. The live-crystal dissipated during the descent after an unknown force took hold of it. It could be a new defense system The Others have developed and which has escaped our attention."

All Humans are capable of mind-to-mind communication, but not many choose to develop this faculty to its fulness since it takes a great discipline. It was a standard training for the Rangers, and they achieve great mastership of it. They can share thoughts across vast distances, through the fifth trans-galactic harmonic light-field of Space — the realm of Mind of sentient beings.

"I receive you, Marshal", the Captain replied. "The three spacecraft are about to land on the opposite side of the planet. I wait for your orders."

"Do not attempt to rescue me. Move the transport outside the system. Until we know more, we must treat this operation as an infiltration to a star system controlled by The Others. From my position, I can see a complex of buildings that could be one of their bases. I will explore the area to assess the situation and keep you informed."

"Understood."

Those who didn't know well thought that the Rangers were a military force. They weren't. The Ranger Corps of the Union was a close knitted, hierarchical institution of self-reliant individuals, Humans and Amethen, under the command of the Chancellor. They were trained in the art and science of first contact with other cultures and races. They too established and strengthened relationships wherever they went — although they joked among themselves that they were a type of sophisticated diplomat who also needed to know how to survive in the wilderness with their bare hands. They never used weapons, nor were Ranger craft equipped with any. The Others, nonetheless, feared them — it was because of this fear that most considered the Ranger Corps as a deterrent force. In truth Rangers were those Galactic Humans and Amethen who chose to develop the faculties of Mind-Soul faster than others, and place themselves to the service of the common good.

Mhali hid the module in a large crevasse of a nearby outcrop. Next, he began moving towards the buildings in the distance. Questions crowded his mind — What The Others were doing on that planet was the most pressing one; they had breached the Armistice by entering a star system where Humans dwelt.

In spite of his dire situation, he felt relaxed and confident. The smells and sounds, and the feel of the grasses under his boots, reminded him of his native planet, Seelë of the Merope System. Soon he was moving fast. He hadn't been on a field mission for some time and had missed it. His feet touched the ground lightly, and his Ranger suit shifted hues with the surroundings, making him almost invisible. Several times small animals crossed his path, stopping to look with curious eyes at the unexpected, sudden encounter. Besides them, the land showed no signs of being inhabited. Even the vegetation became sparser the closer he approached to his destination.

Before midnight he arrived. A tall fence waited for him. It rusted away and was covered with short, sharp spikes on both sides, making climbing it a perilous act. A fog had risen, and lampposts with a cheerless light stood as sentinels at regular intervals. Inside, five narrow towers rose in defiance to the sky; a soft reddish light surrounded them. The place was deserted. All he could hear was a deep rumble under his feet. At that moment a slight tremor shook the ground. It was the second he had felt since his descent.

What's this place? This isn't a base of The Others!

A dark night had replaced the twilight, and the towers had a ghostly appearance. He next began to move with caution along the fence, looking for an entrance. He found one on the north side of the complex. It was un-barred and he went in. An increasing tingling spread throughout his skin the closer he came to the towers, but his inner senses told him his body wasn't in any danger. The towers, solid and conical in shape, had different heights and were made of a dark material. Reddish threads of an almost-invisible energy issued from the ground around each one, spiraled along the polished surface, and joined the others high above their apexes in a focused beam shooting upwards towards the upper atmosphere.

A harvester of energy from the core of the planet? Hmm… The Others aren't that foolish! — He walked around the towers and noticed the ground was covered with a lifeless, dry powder — *What's happening in this star system? The Humanity next door destroys the bio-sphere and itself, this planet is heading towards an even-more catastrophic fate, and the third planet is surrounded by a force we can't explain. What are we missing?*

He needed to gather more information before finding a way to return to his transport, but it would have to wait. The descent and the run had taken a toll of his energy. His body asked for rest, and he didn't know when he was going to be able to sleep again, undisturbed. Thus, he exited the place and walked to an outcrop he had seen close by. He contacted the Captain once more and gave her a detailed account of his findings, with the order to send the information to the Chancellor and to Issën Althesal. After this, he found a depression among the boulders and lay down. His Ranger suit kept him warm, and the ground was a soft sand. A family of small rodents scur-ried around, unafraid of his presence — they were going to keep guard for him. The fog had, by then, moved with the wind, and the starry sky brought him memories of his childhood. His parents had likewise been Rangers, and many times he had camped out with them in remote locations of their planet in a night not unlike that one.

He awoke before dawn. He wanted to use the cover of darkness as much as he could. His body felt rested and full of energy. It wasn't going to need water or food for two more days. He had already decided to continue walk-ing north, beyond the energy collectors. His intuition told him he was go-ing to find answers there.

When Sol rose in the eastern horizon, he found himself at the edge of the plateau. A lush and well-cultivated valley extended below him. A few dark pillars of a shape similar to the towers, smaller, stood scattered throughout the fields forming a regular pattern. He noticed the absence of towns or villages and decided to explore the valley.

Small trees and shrubs soon gave him cover. The descent became easier when he found an old road showing no signs of recent use. By mid-morning he was close to the valley floor and decided to abandon the road.

The first sign he wasn't alone were footprints, old and new. Soon after, he heard movements… and a grating voice.

"Lazy! Worthless creature! Get up!" The sound of the words were in an unknown language, but his mind had so translated the harsh and violent thought of the one who had spoken.

He moved closer, hidden by a patch of shrubs, and peeked through their branches — *Humans! How can this be?* — He had expected to see a party of The Others.

A man, dressed in a sort of uniform, used a cane to punish a young woman. She lay on the ground next to a makeshift tent. Her face and body told Mhali she wasn't yet an adult. Another youngster, a male, with a discomposed face stood silent looking at them. The two youths were dirty and dressed in tattered clothes. The man hit the girl again. Mhali felt disgusted. He had never witnessed anything resembling that type of violence, not even in planets controlled by The Others. As if that wasn't enough, stagnant pools of filth and two dozen other shabby tents surrounded the trio.

"She is sick. Please don't punish her", the young man pleaded.

The man in uniform turned and hit him on his shoulder with the cane as the youth dodged the blow directed to his face. "Shut up! Speak when you are asked."

The youth flinched, suppressed a cry, and took a step back. The man then turned and hit the young woman again while shouting at her. She tried to rise. She was pale and weak.

Mhali's body was tense. His heart pounded. He had never seen a Human doing violence to another Human, nor even imagined it. He couldn't withstand the horror of it. His Ranger training, however, told him to be cautious of any intervention — he was going to compromise his presence, intervene on the affairs of a people who hadn't requested it, and place his mission at risk. Ignoring his better judgment he stood up, nonetheless, sounded a word, and the substances of his physical body rose in vibration to match the lower ös light-fields. Everything around him became still. Next, he walked through the shrubs as if these weren't in his way. The man and the two youngsters couldn't see him approaching — he now moved above their physical bodies' level of dense ös-fields and range of perception. In eight strides he reached their position, touched the man's forehead with two fingers and sent a powerful pulse of his energy to the man's brain. The man collapsed unconscious. He next sounded another word and returned down to the dense physical level.

The young woman was too weak to show any reaction, but the young man, though shocked by what had happened, rushed to stand between her and Mhali.

"I come in friendship!" Mhali sent the thought to the two of them and rose his right hand in greeting.

The young man's eyes widened. Mhali knew then he had heard his thought. Mhali smiled at him and, pointing to the young woman, added, "Let me help her." Most Galactic Humans are a beauty to behold and have a disarming presence. Mhali was no exception. And, as it is natural to all the people from his star system, when he smiled to the youth, a stream of his heart energy went to him, to elicit a state of easiness.

This time the young man shifted on his feet and inspected Mhali from head to toe. His expression remained defiant, and Mhali began to suspect the youth had seen Galactic Humans before. It was possible. A few Galactic Humans, unable to find their place among their people, sometimes joined the ranks of The Others. They were then treated as precious tools to foster The Others' scheming plans against the Union.

"Who are you?" the young man asked with a stern face. "You speak to my mind." He straightened up in a vain attempt to reach and look at Mhali directly in the eyes.

"I came from the stars to learn about your planet. Let me help her."

The youth thought for a moment, looked at the unconscious man, then moved aside.

Mhali knelt next to the young woman and took her hands. She was feverish, dehydrated and almost unconscious. Bruises covered her bare shoulders, arms and legs. Placing his right hand on the girl's forehead and the other on her solar plexus area, Mhali assessed the imbalance of her energies. It wasn't as much as he had feared. Then, with a deep inhalation he established a connection with the universal Life-Energy suffusing all Space. He became a bridge for it and passed the energy to the girl, alternating the flow through both hands. The bruises began to fade, and color returned to her face. It all took less than fifteen seconds before the girl took a deep breath and opened her eyes.

The young man gasped and knelt facing Mhali. "W-who are you?" His body shook, and tears flooded his eyes.

Mhali's answer was a smile. Then the two of them helped the young woman sit with her back against a dirty pillow. "Bring her water."

The youngster hesitated and looked at the man on the floor.

"He isn't going to awaken for a good while", Mhali told him.

"She is my younger sister, Eeëna", the youth said while helping her drink the water. When she finished, he rose and with a bow of his head added, "Thank you, visitor from the stars. I am Keeël."

Mhali still held the hand of Eeëna, who regarded him with thankful eyes while with her mind asked him, "Do you have a name?"

"Mhali is my name", he replied. Then, digging in a pocket on the left side of his Ranger suit, he produced a small nut and offered it to the girl. "Eat this. It will help you regain your strength."

"She hasn't spoken since The Entitlement", Keeël rushed to say.

"I can hear her," Mhali replied with a wink, "and she is hungry."

The girl smiled. Next, with an awkward movement she took the nut, placed it in her mouth and chewed it in slow motion. Right away her face brightened. After she swallowed it, she asked for more with an extended hand.

Mhali laughed. "One will give you energy for several days. More will make you sick." He then produced another one and gave it to Keeël.

"Thank you, Mhali from the stars", Keeël said, again with a bow of his head. "We are indebted to you."

His manners are noble and his heart is good. What are these kids doing in this situation? — But before he was going to have a conversation with them, he needed to deal with the unconscious man.

"Will someone miss him?" Mhali asked Keeël.

"He is the Controller of this valley and works alone. In three days he has to send his next report. If he doesn't, someone will come to investigate."

Mhali lifted the man with ease and carried him outside the camp to a spot Keeël led him to. With care he set the man down under a tree, on a patch of soft grasses, and made sure he could breathe without restrain. Close to the tree, a tubular vehicle rested on the ground. It had room for five passengers. An antenna protruded on its rear; tendrils of a reddish light hissed as they were captured by it. This confirmed his suspicions. Their civilization was powered by the energy of the core of the planet.

"When is he going to awake?" The anxiety in Keeël's voice returned as they walked back to the tent where Eeëna rested. "Will he remember what happened?"

"You don't need to worry. He will sleep for a day or two, then he will feel tired and unable to move much for days. His memories of the events will begin returning in sixty to eighty days, but he will not know why he collapsed. He isn't a problem now. It's the two of you and what happens next."

"Eeëna and I can't stay here!" the youth hastened to say. "The other laborers saw me this morning leave the field with the Controller and knew we were coming to see my sister. They will talk."

"Whe-re c-can y-you g-go, Kee-ël?" Mhali was beginning to use their vocal language together with thought transmission. Their language wasn't as complex as others he had learned.

Keeël regarded him with wonder before answering, "When our parents were alive, my father wanted to escape to a place in the north where a small group of our people are gathering a resistance group. We could travel there, but we need to leave before the other laborers return this afternoon."

Groups resisting established forms of government were common on planets under The Others' occupation, but Mhali knew that any information they could provide would be incomplete. He still needed to see for himself what The Others were doing on that planet — although that wasn't part of the survey operation, it had become his primary mission, specially now that he knew the planet was a Human world. He hesitated, however. He had set loose a chain of events around the two youths, and he couldn't leave them alone to face them.

They left the camp at midday in the vehicle of the Controller, which the youths called a "slet". Mhali had advised against that course of action but consented to it when he saw Eeëna wasn't yet fit to make the trip on foot. The slet used a primitive propulsion system of magnetic fields to counteract the force of gravity. It traveled fast, and in silence, but couldn't rise more than eighty lont [173 meters] above the ground. The youths were in good spirits and saw in Mhali a liberator and a protector. Their plan was to travel east, along the base of the plateau. Keeël knew well the land. His family and other families had stewarded it for generations until six years before. Then, an Elite group had declared itself the sole owner of the resources of the planet, had dissolved all levels of government, and had appointed themselves as absolute rulers — 'The Entitlement', that's how the Elite had called their decision. Those who had resisted had been either killed or made slave workers.

Keeël proved to be a good and fast pilot, and they left the valley well before the night arrived. Following the course of a river, they entered a land of canyons and broken hills. In a system of caves somewhere beyond these, the Resistance hid.

They rested for the night in a meadow. Eeëna was recovering her strength fast. Before going to sleep Keeël assailed Mhali with questions. He told them about Galactic Humans and the Amethen, and their Union of civilizations. And from him he learned that three years after 'The Entitlement' the Elite had introduced a group of beings from the stars as their friends. They had come to help the Elite end disease and bring prosperity for all. But it had been a deception so that those who were still resisting the Elite would surrender without a fight. With those other beings on their side, the Elite fully extended their rule by force and fear. It was then when the Elite's Controllers came to take over the land their family had stewarded. During the event one of the Controllers had killed their parents in cold blood when their father had objected to the making of his employees migrant slaves. As an additional punishment, Eeëna and Keeël were also made into slaves.

That night Mhali contacted the Captain and told her of his experiences since they had last communicated. He emphasized to her the importance of passing the information to the Chancellor and Issën Althesal, and of keeping hidden to The Others the presence of the Ranger transport. He had no doubt now that the fifth planet was under the control of The Others.

Keeël insisted on keeping guard the first half of the night. Mhali rested but watched in case the young man would fall asleep. The youth, though, kept his word, and the night was warm and quiet when Mhali relieved him from the watch. A few nocturnal animals came to inspect their camp, even large ones described by Keeël as dangerous to Humans. But these sensed in Mhali a friend and approached with curiosity, even allowing him to pat them.

What am I doing here? Mhali pondered as he watched the stars on their path along the vault of the heavens, his home. *I am becoming attached to these two youths. My path is somewhere else… But what future do they have? The Resistance isn't going to offer them anything lasting. Moreover, I need to find a way out of this planet, and I doubt the Resistance will help me with this.*

Early the next day another tremor, stronger, struck the land. Keeël dismissed it, telling Mhali the shaking had begun 110 years before, and by now people took tremors as a normal occurrence since they seldom produced any damage. "No, our previous governments showed us proof the tremors aren't related to the energy towers", he said in reply to his question. "The quakes began seventy years after we started using them." Mhali shook his head at this. However, he didn't bring up the subject again, even though one or two light tremors a day rocked their feet.

They traveled that second day without hindrance. Keeël had studied the map of the region with his father and had a good idea of the direction in which they would find the Resistance. More than once, however, they entered canyons with no way out and lost precious time. Eeëna felt better but still didn't speak. Mhali had no experience with her malady and didn't know how to help her.

On the third day they left the canyons behind and entered a narrow valley covered with forests and flanked by tall mountains. Large boulders rose among the trees, here and there. "Phew… I was wondering when we were going to see them!" Keeël said. "We should arrive before this evening."

It was early in the afternoon of that third day when they saw the first signs of trouble. First, they noticed the absence of birds and other animals, and a deep silence enveloped everything. Mhali's inner sense also told him something was wrong. They thus continued with caution. Then, further up the valley, the trees changed. Although still covered with green leaves, they looked lifeless. At that point Mhali asked Keeël to land in a small clearing. His suspicious were confirmed when, with the palm of his right hand, he assessed the energy of a tree trunk without touching it — it was dead. Burn marks, not larger than a handspan, were seen here and there, and a foul odor rose from them.

"Alas, the Resistance is already dead", he told the two youngsters. "We need to change our plans."

"How do you know they are dead?" Keeël asked while seizing the branch of a bush. The branch immediately crumbled to the ground and, in the process, released a dusty gas. The youth stepped backwards with a jump. "What's this?" he cried.

"I'm almost sure your people don't have the weapon to produce this type of damage. Only a perverse mind would design such a weapon! The Others are most probably responsible. It appears the weapon breaks down the structure of water into its atomic components… a weapon designed to kill living beings with a minimum damage to buildings and objects. They must have used it to eliminate the Resistance."

Keeël and Eeëna insisted, however, that they continue towards the hideout. They couldn't believe the Resistance was dead. "The caves protect them", Keeël argued with Mhali.

Before proceeding, Mhali contacted the Captain to tell her of the new finding. She, in turn, informed him that the three ships of The Others had left the planet that morning and were heading out beyond the system. Next, the two of them discussed, and agreed, the weapon used to destroy the forest was new, and that it was possible The Others were using that planet as a testing ground. "The Others must know, for sure, the energy collectors are changing the energy polarity between the core of the planet and its ionosphere, and that the planet is heading for a catastrophic fracture of its crust", Mhali said to her. "We must conclude they don't care if their tests add to the damage."

Mhali would have preferred to continue on foot by himself, but the two youths had their minds set on reaching the caves. As a compromise, Keeël flew the slet under the cover of the lifeless forest. However, the slow pace navigating the obstacles tested the youth's patience, and it took all of Mhali's power of persuasion to make him understand the danger they were in.

As Keeël had estimated, at the end of that afternoon they arrived to the caves. Mhali had been right too. An air of dead was everywhere. Nothing moved, and the silence was ghostly.

Mhali forced the youth to land the slet away from the entrances, hidden behind a large outcrop. He next told the two youths to wait for him there. All the vegetation around them was lifeless. Mhali's senses detected no living beings, but footprints on the ground told him a small group wearing boots similar to those of the Controller had been there… recently — *Agents of the Elite,* he concluded. A few of the footprints mixed with the others weren't Human, but he couldn't determine to which race of beings they belonged. There were also two large imprints on the ground as if two craft had landed there. One appeared to have been left by a small shuttle craft, while the other left a large, irregular indentation and had burned the soil — *What type of craft left this?*

Next, he approached the main cave. As he walked with caution towards its entrance, a cold, prickly and unwholesome rustle of air hit him on the face. He shuddered but went inside.

A few bodies covered the floor of the tunnel near the entrance. They had cold burns all over, and for their positions he suspected they had died not knowing what had hit them. The cave wasn't deep, and soon he found himself in a main hall where large tables and benches stood arranged in rows. Bodies lay everywhere. All had burn marks on their skins and clothing, and some had body parts that had crumbled into dry chunks and dust, mostly from their upper torso, arms and heads — *Why? What could have done this?* — All that horror was new to him, and after assessing the situation he knew he wasn't going to find the answers there. Thus, he turned to retrace his steps. It was then when his mind saw the pattern: every one of the bodies with crumbed parts had died face down, and all of them were adults. There was only one explanation — *The bodies were inspected because those who brought this destruction needed to confirm they had eliminated the leaders of the Resistance. Did they?* — At that thought a foreboding hit him, and he darted for the entrance.

He should have known better! Keeël stood there, and to Mhali's horror, the youth held in his hand a small silvery ovoid, inspecting it with his face close to it.

He was too late, and there was only one thing he could do.

Mhali sounded a word, rising his body to a higher ös level, and rushed towards Keeël. All the youth saw was the small ovoid yanked away from him by an invisible hand, crushed, and thrown through the air in an arc above the trees. Mhali next sounded another word and startled the youth with his sudden appearance.

"Quick! We must leave now!" he commanded the youth. "They came looking for the leaders of the Resistance. That was a spy probe. They didn't find all of them, and you just showed yourself to them. They will think you are one of them. We must assume they aren't far away and will be here soon. Let's move."

Before the two of them reached the slet, however, they heard the scuffle and a cry from Eeëna. Two men dressed as Controllers had seized her. Another stood next to the slet with a snarl on his face, not a Human but a Dreki. The girl was still resisting her captors, and none had seen Mhali yet.

With an effortless jump Mhali rose high through the air above the canopy and, placing his hands together, sounded a word of power. A thunderclap was heard. The lifeless trees all around crumbled into piles of dust, and the three assailants, together with the two youths, collapsed unconscious. Mhali landed on his feet in the midst of them.

He checked the youths before the others, making sure that everyone was breathing and had not injured themselves when they fell. Next he studied the Dreki. It was a male and had no insignia on his uniform, although its design appeared to indicate he was of a high rank — *To which of the dominions of the Overlords do you belong?* he wondered.

He had been right in another observation. One of the imprints he had seen on the ground was that of a small shuttle craft of a common design used by The Others, and it now rested on the ground nearby — he had found his way back to the Ranger transport!

⚡

Keeël awoke with a start. He lay on a soft bed covered with clean, silky linens. Mhali sat on a chair across from the bed, and regarded him with his deep green eyes and an inquiring smile. Eeëna stood next to the bed with a big grin on her face.

"Everything is fine, brother."

With effort he sat on the bed and reached out to grab her hand. "Eeëna… your voice… Ouch, my head and my eyes hurt!"

"You'll be well in no time, brother. I'm well. These people — they are wonderful!"

A soft white light suffused the room. Its walls were smooth except for large oval areas of textured interlaced spiral patterns. "Where are we?" he asked.

Eeëna took three steps to one of the textured areas and rested a hand on it. In a split second it became transparent, and stars, hundreds of them, peppered the darkness of Space. "We travel on Mhali's spacecraft."

"How?… Mhali, what happened? The last thing I remember is the two of us running towards the slet."

"I rendered you unconscious. I couldn't let them see me, nor harm either of you. I brought you here on the craft they traveled. After that, my people returned their craft to the same spot and erased all traces of our presence. The two Controllers and the Dreki are probably awake by now, but they will never know for sure what happened to them. They may think that someone from the Resistance stunned them unconscious while rescuing the two of you."

"What's going to happen to us?" Keeël said after a moment of silence and staring at his hands. Day after day for three years he had wanted to be free from their oppressors. Now that he was free, he felt empty, confused, directionless.

"You can go wherever your heart desires", Mhali replied. "If it is your choice, we can return you to your planet. You are also welcomed to live on any of our worlds. Everywhere our peoples will receive you with open arms, and you can start a new life. I know that my sister and husband would be delighted to include you in their family — I already talked to her. They have two kids close to your ages."

"Let's go with Mhali's people, brother. For what I've been told, the people of the Merope System are all like Mhali." Eeëna grabbed both his hands and looked into his face. "There isn't any future for us on *Mal'ek*."

All he could reply to her was a silent nod.

⚡

Mhali sat cross-legged on the padded floor of the small observatory, on the highest deck of the transport. Eeëna and Keeël were asleep in their cabins; their biological clocks still running in sync with their planet. Operation Sol had come to an end, and the crew were busy on the decks below retrieving the last probes and readying the transport for the return home. Some of the Councilors of the High Council were already unhappy with the lack of answers and the new questions the operation had produced.

That's how life flows, isn't it? — He was also leaving the Sol System with questions. His intervention to protect the two youths had taken him on a path he had never expected to travel. Similar to most Galactic Humans, he had forgotten how to take risks and go into the unknown — *It was worthy, though,* he concluded.

Sol shone in the distance with its grand and beautiful display of ös swirls and orbital harmonics. But in his heart Mhali felt uneasy looking at it — it beckoned to him to unveil the mystery it harbored.

7

Revelations from the Age of Legends

Althesal was eager to visit the Asli, but her load of work had conspired against it. Besides, it hadn't been easy to coordinate a time for Ethën, Nesdil and Daothel to accompany her to the island without raising suspicions. Thus, meanwhile, in the evenings she had researched all available information on the Aïdin Planets. To her surprise, besides what she already knew from the legends and from academic works on them, not much was found. She had likewise uncovered little information regarding the Sol System. It appeared to be so unimportant that its only mention was in maps and navigational charts.

Frustrated with the lack of findings, by chance she had met Daothel one day while walking back to her house and had mentioned to him the lack of sources of information on those two subjects. He had then suggested the unorthodox idea of going to *the Mæl* for help. She had considered it but was skeptical of the information they could provide. She had heard the Mæl had a changeable understanding of the Universe, spoke in paradoxes, and had no particular view on anything — although many did agree, they were knowledgeable on the subject of the history of the Seven Galaxies.

Eventually, the unexplainable attraction she felt for the third planet of Sol won out, and she decided to act on Daothel's suggestion. Visiting the Mæl would take no more than a few hours of her time, and she could do it in an evening. Thus, quietly and without letting anyone know, she traveled to the closest star where a group of them lived — *'Eneb* was its name, in the constellation of the Swan. She used one of the small star-to-star shuttle craft available at the transportation center on Ïthel, her home city. It was her first time piloting that class of craft, and she found its PI much more capable than that of an intra-planetary solo-craft.

Thus, with the free time available during the trip there, she searched for the information her people had on the Mæl. There was only one entry on them in the library system, a video record. She called for it and had to suppress a cry when the hologram sprang into life in front of her — the narrator was her father and his voice sounded as if he was speaking to her, right there on the craft! He said:

Dear one,

I have been asked by the librarians to record my experience with the Mæl during my travels. To start, I must say they are remarkable beings. You won't be disappointed!

The Mæl, or *Master Chroniclers* as most call them, are 'star beings' — belonging neither to the Young Races [Humans and Amethen] nor to the Old Ones [races which, according to the legends, vanished before Humans appeared]. They dwell on stars, not planets. Their homes are the Portal Stars — those few in the vastness of the known galaxies characterized by a natural spatial phenomenon connecting their core with the galactic core of their respective galaxy, and through it with the cores of other galaxies and the Portals Stars in them.

Throughout all the known history, those who travel from one galaxy to another have had to use Portal Stars to arrive to their destinations. In the process, as one journeys through the pathway that connects each of these stars to the galactic core, one's mind-soul enters into a synchronous vibration with the first harmonic light-field of the Ös of the star, leaving a record on it of the contents of one's mind. This is the reason these Portal Stars have become vast repositories of knowledge, information and memories, which the Mæl process and classify with their astounding minds.

But know that the Mæl don't keep the knowledge so obtained for themselves. They know it belongs to all. Thus, they love to share it with others, and for this they have built visitor stations orbiting each of their Portal Stars. Everyone is welcomed to learn from them, with one condition: no one can go to them for knowledge with intentions contrary to the well-being and harmony of the galaxies — which they zealously guard.

Her father went on with a few other notes on them. When he finished, her mind drifted to him and to her mother. Unlike most Thelians, the two loved to travel to other worlds, doing research on their cultures. It was them who had instilled in her the joy of exploration since an early age. Although she hadn't seen them in over a year, they did make the point to communicate with her regularly. She missed them, but they enjoyed their lives and that's what mattered to her.

"Althesal…" Her thoughts were interrupted by the soft voice of the PI. "We have arrived to the visitor array orbiting 'Eneb and will be entering the landing bay promptly."

Good! Only twenty minutes travel! At this pace I'll be back home before midnight.

Through the front window of the craft she could see that one of the Mæl waited for her in the center of a large chamber next to the landing bay — *So, their capacity to sense the mind presence of others reaches well beyond the ös-boundary of their home-star,* she concluded since she had come unannounced.

She descended from her craft to a controlled atmosphere that matched that of her planet, and with some caution she walked towards him — for some reason, she thought of *it* as *he*; although she knew his kind were beyond gender classification. He stood unmoving, regarding her with piercing deep-brown eyes. He was much taller than she was, and his body was made of a slender and cold violet flame in which his face, not unlike that of a Human, appeared close to the level of her face.

Her father had mentioned that his kind had no speech but were masters of many forms of telepathy. Thus, she used thought-words to reach his mind, "Greetings, Master Chronicler."

He made no sign, mental or otherwise, that he had received her greeting. Instead, she felt his presence connect with her mind in what appeared to be multiple channels. Almost immediately she felt that everything she was, had been, or aspired to be, was exposed to him. She flinched at the strangeness of the contact, yet there was no way to hide from the power of his mind. Doubts then assailed her that coming to that place may not have been a good idea.

Overcoming an urge to turn around and leave that place, she willed her body to relax and faced him with as much poise as she could summon. She next looked at him directly into those deep wells that were his eyes and said:

"Now I know the reason few dare to come to you for knowledge, Master Chronicler. I feel naked and vulnerable!"

"Yes, it feels so, Althesal of Thel. Not for the reason you think, though", the Master Chronicler replied to her mind. His flaming face had changed to a gentle and paternal expression, which softened his imposing towering form and his intrusion into her mind. "That which is of light cannot be concealed in any manner. Isn't the mind-soul of Humans made of the purest light of all, young one? Aren't your thoughts extensions of that pure light?"

She knew he didn't expect answers to those questions and said nothing in reply, uncertain as to how to proceed.

In silence he continued for a time studying her with keen interest.

"Of your people, few have ever used the Portals," he reached her mind when he broke his silence, "and my kind wonders why Thelian Humans don't venture beyond their star. Countless races are known to us, while yours remains a mystery."

She didn't know what to say to that and turned the conversation to the reason for her visit. "Thank you for coming to meet me, Master Chronicler. I assume you are already aware of the knowledge I need."

"A peculiar and most interesting being, Althesal of Thel, you are", he replied while circling her. "To us you come, though in you — deep in you — the knowledge you seek of Sol and of Aïdin Planets already resides."

She suppressed a gasp. That wasn't what she had expected to hear! When she had been young, she had felt she knew much more than what she was aware of in her conscious mind, and that this blind was in her so that she could fulfill a destiny. She had buried those feelings and no longer thought of them. Had the Master Chronicler read them, or was he implying that her destiny was connected to the Sol System and to Aïdin Planets, and that was the reason that knowledge was veiled?

His face changed to something akin to a smile. She then realized he had read her thoughts and wasn't going to tell her the answer to that question.

"Could you, at least, tell me the reason why that knowledge is inaccessible to me?"

"To unveil that which you veiled before donning a form, young one, I cannot. Yet, for knowledge you came, and without it you will not leave. Listen… Real were the Aïdin Planets of old — at least in the minds of those to whom we gave passage to other galaxies during the Age before Humans. From those travelers we learned of a time when a blessing these Planets were. That time, however, lasted not. At the end of what you call 'the Age of Legends', as a curse on all beings, and on Space itself, that's what they were considered."

A curse! — she had never heard of such an expression to describe them. All the stories spoke of them as idyllic places many longed to visit.

"Puzzled by my words you are, young one. That was, though, the thought of those who lived during those times. It was from many of them that we learned the following story. In the details it varies, yet a thread connects it all. Listen to it…"

The Master Chronicler's tone and form of telepathy changed as he began to tell the story, and Althesal had the impression that he was reading from a record left by someone else. The story went:

Long before Humans, and after the earliest of the Young Races developed interstellar traveling, the Aïdin Planets were discovered. By then, after a lengthy eon of turmoil between the two primordial forces of the Universe, Space had settled into a steady rhythm, and for all beings in the known galaxies harmony was the norm. The Young Races, on their numerous worlds, were steadily developing as self-conscious and creative beings, and *the Åh* — those beings who nowadays people call *the Old Races* — took care of guiding them and of teaching them the ways of Nature and Space.

The reason those planets were called 'Aïdin' no one remembered. It was recalled, though, that the sounding of the word *Aïdin* carried a power — "a sacred utterance", some called it — but its specific use was lost in time. It too was remembered that they were unlike normal planets, since they moved on unnatural orbits, independent from the stars which housed them, and were surrounded by mysterious, multicolored, flowing light-fields that beckoned to outsiders.

All the locations of these planets had been charted and many visited them. For this purpose expeditions and pilgrimages were regularly organized.

In spite of these planets' popularity, the Beings who dwelt on them were an enigma to all, even to the Åh. Their origin no one knew, nor the reason for Their presence since Their appearance and behavior suggested that They, similar to their planets, were outsiders to Space. Regardless, Those Beings were benevolent and welcomed visitors. Their bodies were made of a rare and beautiful light that was felt as the rays of a morning sun after a cold night and that gave off a perfume not unlike the perfume of flowers. But the most striking and enduring memory travelers had of Them was that those Beings *sang* — and entranced were those who visited Their worlds with otherworldly and uplifting songs.

"Why was it so striking that They sang?" Althesal interrupted him.

"Because, young one, in those ancient times no one could sing — not even those to whom you now call 'birds' existed then. And because They sang, They were given the name *Manaï* — that is, 'Masters of the Voice'."

That was new to her, and it didn't escape her the phonetic similarity between the end and the beginning of the two words, *Manaï* and *Aïdin*.

The Master Chronicler was waiting for her with a broad smile on his face, and she rushed to say, "Please continue."

Of all those who went to visit the Manaï, the Young Races were the ones who felt most the effects of their visits. The Åh too visited them, as did the Tharan and others of the Hyperboreans. But to these mighty and formless beings the attraction was more for the Manaï's unsurpassable beauty and inscrutable mystery than for the Aïdin Planets themselves.

The curious thing was, besides Their singing and Their shimmering light-form, no one could remember other details of the Manaï, nor what visitors experienced while on their planets. Perhaps so it was because Time wasn't the same there as it was everywhere else — it seemed not to exist! Nonetheless, after a sojourn on those mysterious worlds, visitors invariably felt renewed in body, mind and soul. They overflowed with such an inspiration and such a deep joy that living and creating became an easy and fulfilling path. So much it was that it led to a period of rapid development in the Seven Galaxies, during which many new civilizations were born, and those already established advanced at a pace that astonished the Åh.

'The Golden Age of Aïdin' — thus would that time be known in the memories of many, and all were so joyful and fulfilled that no one could conceive it could ever end.

But one day the unexpected happened. It started as rumors brought to spaceports by explorers, travelers and traders. They all told the same stories:

"Entire races are behaving strangely…"

"Peoples are going mad…"

"An unknown sickness of the soul has appeared…"

"The inhabitants of that planet are killing each other…"

"These others on that other world are destroying their own creations and themselves…"

"Those over there have lost their desire to live and are letting themselves die…"

"Peoples are doing violence to their own and to other races…"

"It is mayhem…"

No one had ever heard of, nor imagined, such happenings before. Wanton destruction and war were unknown to all. Until then, the heart and minds of all those of the Young Races were good and kind, and all felt they were an integral part of the harmonious flows of the Universe — they knew the Universe loved them and provided for them, and they reciprocated this love by treating all beings and things with respect.

Of course, something had to be done, and leaders, guides and overseers rushed to find the truth of the rumors — the stories told were too horrible to be believed! Thus, they sent reconnaissance missions to the troubled worlds.

Alas, the rumors were soon confirmed.

"A scourge, a blight, clouding the mind and the heart has appeared!" The emissaries reported. "It is a blight of the soul afflicting only those like us! Entire worlds are affected!"

But that wasn't the extent of the findings. Before long something more was discovered that stunned everyone: "The Blight affects only worlds in the vicinity of Aïdin Planets!"

"How is that possible? Have the Manaï caused this to occur?" Everyone asked in dismay. The fact was those worlds had flourished faster, and their peoples were the happiest and kindest since the Aïdin Planets had appeared.

Overnight all expeditions and pilgrimages to the Aïdin Planets came to a halt. No one knew what to do, and fear took hold of many hearts. Trade and commerce between worlds also suffered, and inter-stellar traveling was reduced to a minimum. Even the word 'blight' was feared, and every unconventional behavior gave reasons for suspicion and dread.

The Åh knew otherwise, however. They knew the Manaï weren't responsible for the scourge. As a dark, yet invisible intruder, the Blight had come from beyond the Seven Galaxies. Thus, because the Åh loved the Young Races, they did all they could to heal the malady. But their efforts did nothing since they weren't healers and had no knowledge of the intricacies of the hearts and minds of the Young Races. It was then when they did the only thing they could think of: They went to the Aïdin Planets to consult with the Manaï and request their help.

The stories tell that the Manaï listened with great attention to the Åh, but that, in their child-like innocence, They failed to understand what the Åh told Them. Several times, with the patience of a parent, the Åh conveyed to Them the situation, each time with the same result. In the end, the only recourse the Åh had was to invite the Manaï to see the situation for Themselves. It wasn't easy either to convey to Them the invitation, but eventually the Manaï understood and accepted it.

That was the first time, and perhaps the last, the mysterious Manaï traveled outside their planets. And it too became the first time They experienced the cacophony of sickness, disharmony and ugliness. To the surprise of the Åh, in great pain They recoiled from the scourge, wanting to flee from the cacophony. Yet, as They were about to flee, something halted Them... something in Them... something They didn't know They carried in Their hearts... Thus, it came to pass that as the Manaï witnessed the suffering of peoples and the devastation of those worlds, *Love* awoke in Them!

Steeped in Love and wasting no time They then reacted to the need, and with Their songs began to heal all those affected by the Blight.

From world to world, on a ray of mighty light, the Manaï traveled, and in the span of one of Their songs each planet and its peoples They restored. The stories tell that not two of Their songs were the same, as not two peoples and not two worlds are ever the same. And such was Their love that never before did our Universe hear songs so wondrous and majestic — songs which no one now alive imagine are possible...

The Master Chronicler's account faltered at that point. He appeared to be lost for words. After a pause he whispered to Althesal in a melancholic tone, "My kind still hears the echoes of Their songs... We wish others could... Perhaps your people, young one, hear those echoes too. After all, you were made for that."

Her people? Made for that? — Althesal was stunned. However, before she could ask the Master Chronicler to clarify that extraordinary comment, he continued with the story.

Eventually, all those who could be healed were made well, and for those races who were already gone the Manaï made of their worlds gardens of hope so that their mind-souls could have a place to return and continue their path when the Universe so would tell them.

Once Their work was finished, alone, in silence and quietly the Manaï retreated to the sanctuary of their Aïdin Planets.

From the Åh themselves, and from daring explorers, the news of the healing of the Blight by the Manaï, and of Their innocence, spread.

The news should have restored life to normal for everyone — Alas! it didn't. Although the Blight was gone and worlds had been healed, the Young Races had lost their former innocence. For the first time in the history of the Seven Galaxies, they conceived of such a thing as *Evil* since nothing else could explain the Blight's origin. Thus, that uninvited guest which came with the Blight — *Fear!* — didn't go away. Mistrust of others replaced the easiness of friendship that had before existed, and many looked for and imagined unknown enemies lurking everywhere. Even the enthusiasm for visiting the Aïdin Planets again couldn't be summoned, and from then on only a few adventurers sought to do so.

In time it became evident to the Åh that although the Blight had been healed, a malady was still affecting most of the Young Races... that the scourge had left a damage in their hearts. And because of it, creativity and progress became rare; culture and commerce were no longer shared between worlds; traveling was infrequent, even travel between lands on the same world; and only a few were interested in what they, the Åh, had to offer.

After a time, no one spoke anymore of the Aïdin Planets. Even the few adventurers who wanted to visit them could not find them. *Perhaps the Manaï took them away to other galaxies, or perhaps they are now invisible to all* — so they thought, but no one knew. The fact was, those wonderful places and Beings were gone forever, and only a few among the Young Races mourned the loss.

As he finished his tale, the Master Chronicler, regarding Althesal with his paternal eyes, added, "Know, young one, that the story of the Aïdin Planets ended with a sad note: though the Manaï hadn't been responsible for the Blight, forever that scourge became associated with their Planets. A doubt remained anchored in the hearts of many, who asked — *Did those Planets attract Evil to the galaxies we call home?*"

In the silence that followed, Althesal attempted to digest the unusual story. Some would probably question its veracity. Yet, in her heart she felt it spoke of a real event in those earliest times. More so, it suggested an explanation for the current events in the Sol System — the catastrophe on the planet Yfel and the unusual behavior of the Humanity on the planet Mal'ek found by Marshal Mhali, both could well be attributed to the Blight of the Ancients.

The Master Chronicler must have read in her a deeper thought because at that moment his expression changed to one of concern. "Sol!… You want to go to Sol!… I advise you, young one, be careful in your quest to decipher Sol's mystery — that system was sealed off to all in times of old, and for a good reason… Be also careful too with the desire you harbor of the Aïdin Planets — know that wise laws rule the appearance and the disappearance of all things and all beings in Time and in Space; to bring back that which should remain gone, or to bring forth that whose time hasn't yet come, seldom ends in good."

As he spoke to her these thought-words, Althesal acknowledged that in her innermost being she, indeed, wished for the return of the Aïdin Planets. For her entire life she had thought that Humans had more in them than they recognized; yet they had, instead, become content with settling in and mastering Space. She harbored the hope the Aïdin Planets were real so that they could show Humans a greater horizon of what they could be. This innermost wish had been re-awakened in her by the third planet of Sol, and by Nesdil and Daothel's experience with the Asli. But as she thought of this, it sank in her what the Master Chronicler had said of the Sol System — *"Sealed off to all!" — For what reason? By who? Who has that kind of power? Could the Manaï be still with us and no one knows?*

"Ah! Young one!" the Master Chronicler interrupted her pondering once more, this time with a pensive face. "Others before you have had similar thoughts to yours… long, long ago… yet the consequences of their attempts to restore the Aïdin Planets are still with us — Yes! I speak of those Humans in the vision your friends were shown. They believed they were doing good by seeking to make Aïdin Planets of worlds damaged by war. And, yes! they had with them a spark of the Primordial Fire which emboldened them, a Fire that wasn't theirs to use. Know that attempt after attempt they made, but in vain… Although mighty those Humans were, Aïdin Planets were beyond their efforts, and for their zeal a heavy price they paid. Less they became… so too did Space… like them, it became less."

Stunned by these statements, she stuttered, "W-what do you mean, Master Chronicler? Your words are riddles."

"Are they, Althesal of the metamorphosed planet?" he replied with emphasis. "Change you are. It travels with you… even at this very moment…" Then, abruptly, on waves of sadness he added, "My kind was torn asunder because of those attempts to bring back the Aïdin Planets… We tried in vain… We tried to reunite all of us again… but desist we were forced by the futility of our efforts to heal Space and relink the Portal Stars beyond the rim…" Next, as if realizing he had spoken too much, he said, "Long it has been since any of my kind has dwelt on these matters…"

He was going to say one more thing but stopped and became absorbed in contemplation.

Althesal didn't know what to think of his astounding revelations. That wasn't what she had expected of her visit, and the Master Chronicler appeared to be deeply disturbed by the entire subject.

When his silence extended for a long while, she thought he had finished with her. Yet, when she was about to thank him and depart, he asked:

"Do you know, young one, why those mighty beings who called themselves 'the Åh' are no longer with us? Do you know why no one can travel beyond the boundary of our group of galaxies? Why the Portals have no access to galaxies beyond our group?… More so, young one: Are you aware that your creators gave up on Thel when they witnessed its failure?… It is all connected, young one — even Sol… It is all connected…"

Holding her in his gaze and not hiding the sorrow those questions carried, he bowed to her with his flaming form. Next, without taking his eyes from her, he glided backwards, away from the visitor array and towards the corona of the star, while projecting to her mind a last thought: "Change, indeed, you are. It travels with you! Althesal of Thel."

Dumbfounded, she stood there letting the meaning of his last statements sink into her mind — *It is all connected…*

She had come for answers regarding the Aïdin Planets, and all she had found was more questions. Once more she felt an angst over the entire mystery of these Planets, and over the possibility that they had found one. In her heart she felt her entire existence was entwined with them, and she couldn't understand the reason. All she knew was that, similar to most Humans, she harbored a deep longing to return 'home'… to a state in which one is free from the limitations imposed by Space and Time… and those Planets were somehow connected with 'home'.

It took her a long while to realize she was alone in the landing bay and staring into the radiant orb of 'Eneb.

8

The Metamorphosed Planet

It was morning in the aerial city of Ïnthil, on Thel, and the Hall of Records was deserted when Althesal and Ethën arrived. Not that many visited it at other times anyway, since History was a subject Thelian Humans felt no attraction for. The Hall had been built mostly for visitors and scholars from other worlds, and to comply with a membership requirement of the Union. It was grand, nonetheless. It couldn't be otherwise for a people who were masters of harmony and proportion, of science and art.

Althesal had suggested to visit it when Ethën took with his usual pragmatism her account of the extraordinary revelations the Master Chronicler had made. She was confused. Too many views taken as established facts by their people were now challenged. She didn't know anymore what the truth was. The Hall of Records was her only hope to clarify the statements made by the Master Chronicler about their planet and their people.

The Hall was a large hexagonal open space, without walls or roof, enclosed by an imperceptible light-field to protect its interior from the elements. A twelve-strand helix rose at its center, about ten lont tall [22 meters]. It was a resonator, not unlike a giant tuning fork, made of a crystal tuned to the second harmonic ös light-field of their planet. It vibrated in sync with the natural properties of this harmonic of the Ös, which recorded every change in consciousness experienced by mental beings on the planet, not at the individual level but at the collective one. This natural record-keeper was accessed through six photo-sonic display stations placed around the base of the helix.

They had been unsure on which historical period to start their search.

Their only lead was a vague memory Ethën had. Someone had told him —
he thought it had been their friend Laidé, when he had studied their culture
— that the earliest Thelian Humans called their planet *Theleth* instead of
Thel, and that it was an ancient word from the language of the Åh which
meant 'metamorphosis' or 'transformation'. So far their search had confirmed that.

"It could be a simple phonetic coincidence since our ancestors didn't have
a written language", Althesal said when they found that reference.

"When did we start writing?" Ethën asked while doing something to the
display station they were using.

Althesal was standing next to him and took her time to answer him.
When she had been an apprentice on the Path of Life Weaving, she had
surprised her teachers by deciding to study their people's history. It fascinated her how her people had been a harmonious and unified society since
its beginning, and how they had used the power of their voices since earliest
times to affect all types of light-fields and forces, and to make wonderful
creations in tune with Nature — that wasn't the case with Humans elsewhere.

That way of life had been, however, deeply shaken when their planet was
discovered by off-worlders. Her people had been shocked by their techno-
mechanistic ways and by their materialistic thinking. However, after their
initial reaction, Thelians had adapted to having relations with other worlds
while preserving uncontaminated their way of living in tune with Nature.

"We started writing", she answered Ethën, "when we were discovered by
Galactic Humans. The communication gap between them and our people
lasted for a long while since those particular Humans didn't use mind to
mind intercourse. It was the off-worlders who started writing down what
they were grasping from our vocal sounds. When our people noticed their
attempts, we relieved them from this effort by designing our current syl-
labary. Although, because our people were quickly learning Galactic Standard language, soon after the Standard became our preferred language in all
communications with off-worlders."

Ethën kept silent. He loved to play with light-fields and sounds, and
Althesal seldom gave attention to his usual distractions when they talked.

"I keep reviewing my conversation with the Master Chronicler." She
changed the subject back to their search. "It's clear to me he wanted me to
know that our planet was in a process of transformation to become an Aïdin
Planet, and that it was part of a larger effort to bring these planets back."
She next asked him the question that bothered her most, "Do you think we

are a 'designed' Humanity, as the Master Chronicler implied?"

He halted what he was doing to look at her. "I don't see how we could confirm that, unless we find concrete proofs that tell us so. But then, it wouldn't be just us. It would have to be the entire evolution of our planet's bio-sphere that was engineered."

She nodded slowly to him, "Yes, that would be a way to see it."

The interconnection of all the species and Humans on their planet was a subject she had also studied thoroughly. All species were remarkably beautiful and friendly, and showed unequivocally their direct evolutionary relation. Now that she thought of it, some off-worlders could think their planet wasn't natural. Just a look at the kingdom of the eos would make them think so — it was a kingdom extremely unusual in form and behavior, and the fact that they, the Humans, shared with its eight species most of the sensitivity to the same spectra of light and sounds was even more strange. And to all that was now added the mystery of the Asli.

The photo-sonic display blinked at that moment, and Ethën frowned at her while it re-started. "I doubt we were designed", he said. "We have sufficient data to confirm our planet went through a natural evolutionary process — admittedly, at a faster pace than most known bio-spheres. Besides, there aren't records of unnatural events affecting our evolution. Thus, an outside intervention, if in fact it happened, had to be applied over a long time and mimicking natural factors. Finding it today would be almost impossible without knowing the nature of that intervention."

"What bothers me", she said, "is that, when the Master Chronicler spoke of this, he wasn't telling me the conclusions of travelers who had used their Portal Star. No, he spoke from his own direct experience. Let's assume that he is right, that we didn't meet certain expectations and that the intervention in our planet was halted — and that means, something happened to us, or to our planet. But then, looking at what we are today, by which measure could we as a people, or our world, be labeled 'a failure'?"

"Agree", Ethën replied. "By all accepted standards of development we aren't that."

Althesal moved closer to him, attempting to figure out what he was doing to the console. His hands, however, moved so fast inside the photo-sonic field that she soon gave up.

"On the other hand," she continued, "the Master Chronicler didn't say anything regarding the fate of the other attempts made somewhere else. He only mentioned the Sol System, that it had been isolated for a reason, and that the pieces of this puzzle are all connected."

When Ethën didn't say anything to that, she began wandering away from the console thinking on the question that had just popped into her mind — *Could it be that the third planet of Sol was also intervened and needed to be protected to avoid another failure? That would make sense* — she answered to herself. *It would explain the reason the probe vanished… Who is behind all this? The Manaï?*

As she turned around the base of the helicoidal resonator, she saw Ethën waving at her with a face of excitement, signaling to come to sit next to him. She rushed to him and sat down looking at the display. The images in the four-dimensional field were now larger and much clearer than right before.

"Look at this", he said pointing to a small symbol. "This marker indicates the time when our people stopped calling our planet by the name of Theleth."

Althesal observed that the marker was exactly in the middle of the historical time previous to their people being discovered by off-worlders. Timelines in the displays were represented by spiraling threads of light of various colors, corresponding to the flows and movements of the collective awareness of their people. At the particular moment Ethën indicated, the spiral was made of three major threads — *The three Life-Paths of our people,* she knew right away — the Paths of Life-Weaving, Exploring and Providing that defined their entire civilization. Secondary threads were seen born from and entwined with these, revealing the diversification and richness of their people's understanding of themselves and life. It was a dance of light threads, intermixing and mingling to form new ones, yet all harmonics of those three main ones.

Ethën next zoomed-in on that same historical moment to reveal more details. It was then when Althesal saw the reason for his excitement — another main thread, finer, subtle and silver in color, spiraled with the three main ones, although independently and free from harmonics!

"Another Path!" she cried. It had to be. It was the only possible interpretation.

Ethën stared at her in silence, then looked back at the display and kept zooming in and out.

Althesal's heart pounded. She knew the natural records of a planet couldn't be altered. It was impossible. What they were seeing in the display was exactly what the second ös light-field of their planet had recorded of the movements of the mental life of their people. "Why has no one seen this thread before?" she asked him. "Historians come here frequently from other words to study us. They should have discovered the existence of that other

Path."

"No, they couldn't", Ethën answered with a grin. "These photo-sonic displays haven't been updated in a long time. I enhanced their sensitivity just now. That's the reason we are seeing it." Then, lightheartedly he added, "We should treat visitors to our planet better!"

She gave him a quick node. "Too much attention to other matters."

"There is more", he added. "This thread appeared at the very beginning of our civilization — here — and for a long time it was the only Life-Path our people followed. Then later — here — our current three Life-Paths were born from it."

"What? A source Path! — Are you sure?"

"That's what it shows here! And there is even more. That Path kept going for thousands of years after the other three were born, and it only disappeared when our people left the planet's surface to live in the aerial cities."

"That's impossible! We have other types of records from the times we lived on the surface, and there is nothing in them about a group of our people living a separate Path."

"Sorry… Our planet doesn't lie. It recorded the event. Yet, for some reason, the majority of our people didn't notice it happening — I agree, that's not possible, unless… unless the group following that source Path went to live in isolation, in a retreat somewhere, when the rest chose to follow the three other Paths."

As he said this, an idea came to Althesal: "That silver thread can't be a record left by the Asli. Nesdil and Daothel think their sentientness isn't founded on mind but on feeling — besides, they are still with us and these planetary records don't have anything of them. Regardless, can you isolate the energy signature of that silver thread and correlate it with the energy signature of the bio-system of the island of the Asli?"

"I see where you are going." He frowned. "I'll need to access the data Nesdil collected. Let me see if I can do it from here…" He then, with a quick turn of his head to look at her, rushed to add, "You will tell Nesdil not to give me grief for accessing her records! Will you?"

Althesal waved a hand in assent and let him work. Her mind raced — *A source Path and it disappeared! This is going to shake our people deeply. Most will take it as having lost our way.*

"Oh light!" Ethën cried with excitement.

A shiver went through Althesal's body. His excitement told her the answer.

"It has the same energy signature!"

She just gaped at him. Next, with hesitation she said slowly, "T-That only means that whatever power made the Asli and influenced the bio-system of their island, it also influenced our people… at least some of them."

"Or", he said, "it affected *all* our people, and probably our natural world, but something happened at some point in our history that changed the majority — who then began traveling the current three Paths — and only a minority remained pure to the original life-path. That could be the failure the Master Chronicler told you about."

"Yes… But, what was that original life-path? What could have happened to create a split? And, what happened to those others? Where are they now?"

He shrugged, but his face betrayed he had a hypothesis.

"You are thinking of Sol, aren't you?"

He assented with a grin. Then a change happened in him and with a troubled face kept looking straight into her eyes.

She knew his heart. Like her, he didn't want to put in words the most shocking conclusion from their findings — Their planet and their people had indeed been designed to bring back the Aïdin Planets!

9

Live Writing from the Past

The trail zigzagged up the steep slope of the mountain range. Laidé panted. Drops of sweat ran down his face. His guide, old in years, had offered to carry his rucksack during their last rest and had suppressed a smile when Laidé had declined. But with every step he took, his pride eroded, not unlike the small rocks under his boots rolling downhill and making his ascent harder. For the one-hundredth time he asked himself that morning how he had become involved in such a situation. He could have said 'No', but he wanted to become a diplomat and a career diplomat never says 'No' to anyone.

It all had begun when, against all forms of protocol, Chancellor Vuensé had come to his apartments to entrust him with a mission. She had suggested to him to travel under a false name and to dress as a trader, which made him feel as an outlaw. But that wasn't all. She had never mentioned he had to climb a mountain! He disliked informality… and the outdoors… and rucksacks. Give him reception halls, conference rooms and libraries — there he thrived.

After a journey along seldom-used trade routes, he had landed before dawn on the only spaceport of the planet Orphes, in the outskirts of the Laïs Galaxy [Milky Way Galaxy]. No one else had disembarked, and the craft had left as soon as his feet had touched the ground. The solitude of the place had made him shudder. His instructions were to travel to a certain village, but in the data records of the Union he hadn't found much about that world, not even a map. Thus, he had been forced to wait for daylight and for someone to appear. In a turn of good luck, when the daylight was breaking, the old man had come to him to offer his services as a guide. Although, after they left the port, the man seldom spoke a word.

By mid morning when his pride was all but gone and he was about to accept the offer of the old man, the path took an abrupt turn and leveled off. They had entered a pass between two mountain peaks. A cold wind greeted them, and it felt good on his face and bare arms. His guide said nothing to him but, cupping his hands around his mouth, sounded a short tune resembling the call of a bird. A group of twenty or so children of various ages appeared from behind some trees, singing in a language he couldn't recognize. He guessed it was a welcome song because they approached him with merry faces and carrying refreshments.

"How did they know we were coming?" he asked his guide.

"Son, you think of us a backward planet, with no technology or concert halls. Yet, as soon as a visitor arrives, everyone of our people knows it. It's simple. Every living being creates an eddy in the Web of Life, and we sense its movements. We also know you came to see the Wanderer."

"Humph! So much for my disguise!" he snorted, and let his rucksack slide to the ground, then looked for a place to sit. With hesitation he ended plunking his body down on a mossy rock.

"Those are your games, son, not ours", his guide replied while sitting on the ground with the agility of the youth.

Laidé hadn't eaten anything since the morning of his departure, afraid the strange-looking edibles at the four spaceports where he had changed crafts would make him ill. But the refreshments the children brought were simple nuts, fruits, pastries filled with honey, and cold scented water. He devoured them all with an almost improper speed while the children observed him in silence. They had beautiful, chiseled features and were dressed in handsome, colorful clothing, free-flowing and comfortable. Some sat next to him, others next to his guide. One of them said something to his guide, and the two began to talk in sonorous cadences. Laidé had never heard a language so musical — *It would be the envy of the Thelians*, he thought. He finished swallowing and listened with intent — *These people for sure speak with their hearts. They would make wonderful diplomats!*

He thanked the children in Galactic Standard when he finished eating. They nodded to him with a grin.

His guide then rose and this time told him, "We are almost there."

One of the older girls took his rucksack. On impulse, he placed his hand on a concealed pocket in his shirt where he carried a letter the Chancellor had entrusted him to deliver in person to a Wanderer named Soen. The girl smiled at him and strapped the sack on her back. He hadn't brought much with him. One extra set of clothing and some toiletries. He was going to deliver the letter and return to the spaceport right away. The Chancellor wasn't expecting him to carry back a reply from the Wanderer, and he didn't want to remain a moment longer on that world.

Soon after, the mountain pass widened and gave entrance to a narrow valley. Laidé halted. Where the valley began to spread out, a strange formation rose. At first he didn't know what he was looking at. It appeared to be a large garden-forest located on the banks of a small river fed by mountain streams and waterfalls. Then he realized it was a village with curved streets forming a large six-petaled flower. At its center, a building dominated a hexagonal plaza. The large building and all the houses were each a living tree whose branches drooped to the ground and had been woven together. Ogee arches made with the branches formed windows and doors. The trees were in bloom, and the scent of their white flowers reached him. Well-tended gardens, surrounding each and all, complemented the picture.

Far in the distance, the valley opened to a wide plain. As pearls strung upon a silver ribbon, a number of similar villages nestled along the river.

He was so mesmerized by the beauty of it, he didn't realize his guide had gone ahead. Although the girl with his rucksack and all the other children were still with him.

"Do you like it?" the girl asked him in Galactic Standard while pointing to the valley.

"Yes! I've never seen such a marvel. Why is it kept as a guarded secret?"

"The Wanderers know of us, and they love to visit", an older boy with intense eyes replied.

"Do you live in the sky?" a small girl asked next.

"Y-yes." He wasn't good with children, but these ones defied the image he had of them. On his planet, children were considered unformed Humans, unruly and unpredictable, and only through training and education they finished becoming one. These ones exuded happiness and ease. At the same time, they had the poise of mature souls.

The trail led them to the center of the village. It was high noon, and the few people he saw greeted him with a smile and a musical 'Welcome'. The children dispersed but not before going to him and wishing him a good stay. Some asked if they could come later to visit. Only the girl with his rucksack continued walking with him. His guide stood on the other side of the large plaza, talking to another man.

"What is your name?" Laidé asked his young companion.

"Meera", the girl replied.

"Thank you, Meera, for your company and for carrying my rucksack. I am Laidé."

The girl nodded, "I know."

The wind buffeted his body as they crossed the plaza. It forced him to roll down his sleeves. But his admiration of the place grew with every step he took. The floor of the plaza was made of planks of wood of different colors and sizes, polished and fitted tight together. Most had intricate, etched designs. The entire floor was a perfect, seamless work of art.

"Each youngster designs and etches one when they become a grown-up", Meera said when he stopped to admire a design representing a group of Humans and Amethen walking together along a spiral structure rising towards the stars — that was something he hadn't expected the people of that planet would think of!

He smiled at her and realized he felt relaxed for the first time since he had left his home on Esdänl.

When they reached his guide, the old man said to him, "Wanderer Soen is not in the village. She will return this afternoon. I will take you to her house. She is expecting you will lodge with her."

"How does she know—" He didn't finish. The look of the old man was telling him: 'What a foolish question!' — He felt annoyed with himself.

His guide left him and Meera by the front door of one of the houses, on a street not far from the plaza. Before leaving the old man offered to accompany him back to the spaceport when he would be ready to depart.

The door to the house was an ogival plank with an etched design. Meera opened it and entered first. Laidé was expecting to see a rustic setting, yet when he crossed the threshold, he froze on the spot. The interior of the house was an open space, about ten lont across [22 meters] and seven lont tall [15 meters]. The boughs were woven loose, and a pleasant light filtered from the outside. At the center rose the trunk of the tree, straight, broad and smooth. A stairway wound around it to reach three large platforms, each at a different height and arc placement. Elegant furniture of various woods, fabrics and colors, and a double-spiral crystal sculpture near the stairway complemented the space. But the most striking feature was the tree — the same myriad of minute flowers covering its exterior also covered its interior, giving the space an exquisite touch.

"This place outshines the most majestic halls of government I've visited", he whispered to Meera.

In reply, with a smug voice, the girl said, "Wanderer Soen is my friend.

I live next door. She's teaching me to become a Wanderer." Then she dashed upstairs to the first platform, came back without his rucksack, and rushed towards the door while shouting, "My mother is waiting for me. I'll come back later."

Laidé waved his hand to her, then walked around the stairway, still dazzled by the place. In spite of the cold wind outside, the house was warm and cozy. The large room was tastefully divided in spaces for sitting, eating and working. The floor was also made of etched planks, much smaller than those on the plaza. At the rear, partitions made with the boughs created privacy for a toilette room and a room with a deep tub in which warm water, probably from a natural hot spring, poured in continuously and silently from a broad spout, to exit through an overflow drain. There was no kitchen or a place to cook that he could see. Instead, a well-stocked cupboard offered fresh fruits, nuts and an array of pastries that made his mouth water. With hesitation he took the smallest pastry of all. It was filled with a sweet, nutty paste. He tried others, each more delicious than the previous one.

"I am glad a person of your standing finds pleasure in those simple pastries."

He turned around praying that the source of those words wouldn't notice the flush on his cheeks. He swallowed with a gulp and blinked. No words came out of his mouth when he tried to speak. On the other side of the room, by the front door, stood a young woman, about his age, gorgeous and graceful. With a twinkling smile, she regarded him. It had to be Meera's mother.

"I-I am waiting for Wanderer Soen", he said, then added in a hurry, "Meera let me in."

"I know. You look tired and need some rest. Go upstairs and sleep some. I'll make sure no one disturbs you." With these words the woman turned and left the house.

It took him a moment to grasp what she had said with her winsome voice, so mesmerized was he with her beauty. She reminded him of someone but couldn't figure out of whom. He shook his head, the exhaustion of the past few days was settling in. However, before sleeping he needed a bath.

⚡

He opened his eyes with difficulty. He wanted to sleep more. The daylight was waning. When he remembered where he was, he jumped from the bed and dressed in clean clothes. The warm water of the bath had relaxed his muscles and his mind, and he had fallen asleep as soon as his head had touched the soft pillow. He felt rested and ready to finish his mission so that he could return to his normal life on Esdänl. Along the entire journey he had been clumsy, and he now realized his vast knowledge of cultures and races hadn't prepared him to move with ease among the peoples living on the fringes of Galactic Humanity. He needed to do better… He was going to do better!

"The children like you", the young woman who had come earlier said to him when he descended the stairway. "I had to tell them to come back another time. They wanted to hear stories from you."

He couldn't come up with anything to say. The young woman was even more beautiful than he remembered. She sat on a chair, looking at him with the same twinkling smile than before. Several round sheets of a sort of textile with some writing lay on the table in front of her.

"You don't talk much, do you?"

He became aware he was staring at her and with an awkward bow of his head hastened to say, "I am Laidé of Nauth, and you are?"

Grinning, she stood up and walked to him, then placed a hand on his chest and said, "Let's do it your way." She next bowed her head. "Welcome, Laidé of Nauth. I am Soen."

"Y-y-you?… I-I thought you would be an old—" How stupid of him! He had just insulted a Wanderer. He bowed his head again. "My apologies, Wanderer. This whole mission has confused me, and I am not myself."

"You too are surprisingly young for such an old mindset and manners!" she replied and began to laugh with mirth.

Everything about her was disarming, and he couldn't contain himself, joining her in the laugh.

The life of Wanderers fascinated him, perhaps because it was so different from his. They were free-spirited Galactic Humans who thought the essence of being 'Human' is to be free of attachments to place, culture or protocols — *Humans are visitors in the Universe. They came to transform it with their presence and creative power – not to take possession of it!* — thus said the only tenet to which Wanderers adhered. They were highly respected for their wisdom and the knowledge of peoples. Similar to Rangers, they also cultivated their higher Mind-Soul faculties. They did so, not in schools or academies as the Rangers did, but as they wandered from world to world, sharing of their skills and knowledge with others and learning from them too.

At the same time Wanderers reminded him of his people in their quest to unearth the true origin of Humans. Although, unlike his people, which loved books, maps, manuscripts, and all arcane sources of knowledge, Wanderers studied the oral traditions of cultures. It helped them to integrate themselves with the peoples they wanted to live with along their wanderings. They weren't historians in an academic sense, but it was accepted they were more knowledgeable than most scholars who dedicated their lives to History. Among Wanderers, there were those who followed the various threads of the ancient legends. He had heard of Wanderer Soen only recently and knew she was renown for her wisdom and had dedicated much of her wandering to study the legends of the Aïdin Planets.

After their laugh their eyes met, and she continued with her beautiful musical voice, "The truth be said, you have more in you than you acknowledge to yourself. Visitors to this planet are rare, and those who come seldom venture on foot along the mountain trails." Then, with a gentle movement of her hand, she touched the left side of his face. "You are cold", she said and turned. In three strides she was by the double-spiral sculpture, at the base of the stairway. With a quick movement she next rotated one of the spirals to change their angle of intersection while speaking, "Your people are from warm climates, and the evening is chilly."

A soft light and a warm radiation filled the house immediately, though Laidé barely noticed the change. He couldn't keep his eyes away from her. The movements of her body and her colorful dress made her appear floating. She was the most intriguing and attractive Human he had ever encountered. He had met Wanderers before, but Soen had an enigmatic presence reminding him of those beings of whom the legends spoke.

She next went to the cupboard, took two rounded cups, poured in them a liquid from a pitcher, and came back to the sitting area, suggesting they sit down. He sat first, and she gave him one of the cups before taking a chair across from him, by the table. The cup was more a bowl than a cup, and he had to hold it with both hands. It was made of a light-weight crystal, unpolished, yet without rough edges. The liquid in it had the appearance of water. At first, the cup felt cold; yet, within seconds, it warmed up and the liquid in it changed its color to a pale blue. He almost dropped the cup and, in question, rose his eyes towards Soen.

"Try it", she said. "It's now attuned to your body and mind." The liquid in her cup had a pale green color.

"What is it?" he asked.

"Pure water from a mountain spring. The cup is made of a crystal which, when in contact with your hands, becomes a transformer for the energy of your heart. The result is water that balances you at every level. This isn't technology but Humans working together with the natural world — 'natural technology' you could call it. The people of this planet collect the rough crystals that Nature provides in abundance at various locations. Next, they use a simple technique, submitting the raw crystal to a sound made by their voices. Invariably, each crystal cleaves and the result is two cups or bowls."

He sighed. "Nothing here is what I expected." Then he drank the water. It had a light sweet flavor and felt invigorating.

"The people here tell a story", she continued, "describing how this planet was made by Powers no longer with us, and that they were entrusted to keep it pure. They have done a good job at it and, in the process, have kept themselves true to their essential Human nature... for the most part."

"Is that the reason you are here?"

"Many Wanderers see this planet as an oasis and come here for a rest. This is my second visit. The first time I came out of curiosity. This time, however, the people here requested my presence to help them solve a schism."

Laidé raised his eyebrows. "A schism? These people?"

"No-o, it doesn't involve them." She regarded him for a moment, then slid towards him the round sheets of textile she had been studying when he came down the stairs. "Read these."

Laidé was proficient in hundreds of languages — all Nauthians were, because of their brain structure and the conditions in which their minds had evolved. He took one sheet and immediately gasped. The glyphs on it had begun to move as soon as he had touched it. They emerged from a point at the center, forming a spiral pattern, marched along it, and disappeared at the edge of the sheet. "Live writing!" he whispered in awe. "This is the stuff of legends!" He took other sheets, one at a time. They were made of woven, flexible fibers of a silver-white metal, which he couldn't identify. All the sheets behaved in the same way. For several minutes he studied them while Soen observed him in silence with her deep gray eyes.

He eventually gave up and said, "I can't believe I have these in my hands! Where did you find this treasure? Scholars and librarians in all the galaxies will want to study these. Although it will take years to discover the key for this language."

"They were found on the planet Lughai of a star system next-door, sealed in containers made from the same metal. The sheets and the containers appear to be indestructible. Few people outside Lughai know of their existence. It is what these sheets represent that has created the impasse between the two cultures inhabiting that planet. Because they couldn't arrive to an agreement, they sought the help of the council of leaders of this planet, since both planets have become close friends. Then, those here asked for my help when their efforts to solve the impasse didn't produce any result."

"Can you read them?"

She shook her head. "I haven't been able to make any sense of them. The curious thing is the writing becomes alive only when Humans hold the sheets in their hands. This tells me the sheets and the language were made by Humans or for Humans. I presume the language requires a mind and a brain structure uncommon to us and, perhaps, no longer with us."

"Are you saying these artifacts are from the Age of Legends?"

"How else can you explain this?" She took one of the sheets and held it against the light for him to see. The glyphs became invisible and the image of a beautiful Human with a luminous body appeared on the thin material. The figure moved against a starry background, and with a hand touched different points on it, causing the background image to zoom from constellations to star systems to planets.

Laidé rushed to take one and hold it in the light. More Human figures, but this time the constellations, stars and planets they touched were different. He did the same with the others. Each was different. "Maps!" he said.

"They do resemble maps, but of what? Human worlds? Aïdin Planets? Something else? The challenge is those constellations are almost impossible to identify with a two-dimensional chart, and the relative position of those stars will be different now. Where and when were the creators of these charts positioned when they drew them? How can we know? Our only hope is to translate their writing. But then, that too will have to wait until those who discovered these sheets allow them to be studied. I have them today with me only because the delegates of the two cultures of Lughai trust that, as a Wanderer, I am not going to take sides or betray their desire that these sheets remain a secret." She paused to study him, then added, "And I know, you too will abide by their desire."

"Of course!" He looked at the maps again, one by one. One caught his attention. The Human figure pointed to a binary star system and to its fourth planet. It reminded him of the Thelian world and of its Eir System and neighboring stars. Dismissing the idea, he placed the sheet back on the table and asked Soen:

"How does an archeological finding threaten a civilization with a schism? Are both cultures Human?" He was in his element and felt intrigued by the nature of the affair.

"Both are Human and both are refugees who felt the need to relocate when The Others took over nearby star systems, encroaching their native ones. That's the extent of their similarities. One group of people landed on one side of the planet and the other on the other side, not realizing the existence of the other. It took each many years to rebuild their livelihood on the new planet. Only eighty standard galactic years ago they became aware of the existence of the other. At first they were joyful to discover they weren't alone, even though their cultures were different, and bonds of cooperation brought them closer. Then, when they had enough number of people, they all voted to comply with the 'Protocol of Union' so that the Union would accept them and protect them from The Others. It was when they were deciding the contribution their planet was going to offer to other Union planets, that the discovery of these sheets was made. It was on a third continent, by an expedition of explorers from both peoples. The discovery changed everything."

"It isn't uncommon for refugees", Laidé said, "to have different views on how to organize the main thrust of their new civilization." He took one of the sheets and held it against the light, the thrill of touching such an artifact still in him. "I don't understand how this discovery separates them instead of uniting them. This is going to be one of the most important archeological discoveries in the history of Galactic Humans. Their planet will receive a lot of attention when this news is made known."

"That's the source of their conflict — one culture wants that exposure, the other doesn't."

⚡

Laidé awoke the next morning with a start. He had forgotten to give the Chancellor's letter to Wanderer Soen! That was unlike him. He dressed in a hurry, took the letter, and rushed downstairs. The house was silent and empty. It was mid morning. He called her name, but no one replied. He then placed the letter in his pocket, ate a light breakfast, and strode outside looking for her. He didn't know where the negotiations between the peoples of Lughai took place, but of all places it had to be in the building at the center of the town.

When he arrived there, the building was empty, and nothing indicated it had been used recently. Puzzled, he turned around to exit and the old man, his guide, was standing at the threshold of the door, looking at him with the same kind but unreadable face of the previous day.

"The Wanderer would like you to join her." He said no more and proceeded away.

Laidé sighed and followed the man. They exited the village in the opposite side to the mountain pass and took a well-kept trail among tall trees. Birds and scurrying creatures moved around, unconcerned with their presence. Soon the two of them arrived to a meadow where Soen sat on the grass surrounded by children. Most of them were the same ones who had welcomed him the previous day, including Meera. They all rose and came to him, joyful to see him, and invited him to sit with them. He looked at Soen and in reply she nodded.

The old man then turned around and left them.

The grass felt soft when Laidé sat down, next to Meera and across from Soen. The experience was new to him, but the light and warm of the yellow daystar felt comfortable and inviting.

All the children observed him with intent and expectation. Then, the small girl who had asked him if he lived in the sky said to him, "Please, tell us about your people."

His heart jumped into a race. He had never addressed a group of children! He looked at Soen for help. She just regarded him with that twinkling smile of hers. When he realized she wasn't going to rescue him, he turned towards Meera. The girl grinned with a face of conspiracy and nudged him on his side. He felt trapped and breathed deeply a few times to calm himself while pondering on what to tell them. Then, slowly at first, he began:

"The home of my people, the planet Lyaty of the Nauth System, is a world different from this one. It doesn't have forests or rivers… or mountains… It's beautiful too, in its own way. All my planet is covered with waters, and our towns and cities are floating islands, drifting freely along the ocean currents. We aren't a numerous people — about one hundred and eighty thousand of us on that large world. Yet, we haven't always lived there.

"A long time ago, when we were a small fraction of that many, we lived among the stars, traveling from planet to planet, never staying in one place for more than one or two standard galactic years. The thing is, my people always felt this attraction for legends, specially those regarding the origin of Humans and the mythical planets called 'Aïdin' — You have heard of them, yes?"

"They are in the stories our parents tell us", answered an older boy with a melodious musical voice, about Meera's age.

Laidé smiled to him and noticed the light-blue gemstone of a medallion on the boy's chest when it reflected the sunlight to his eyes. He then continued:

"We were well received in all the worlds we visited and had many friends,

Humans and Amethen alike. The elders of our people today tell us we were happy with that life. The only thing we didn't enjoy — and you will agree — was to acquire new friends only to leave them after a short time. But we thirsted for the tales, the legends and the history of others. We loved to hear them, with the hope they would lead us one day to find the whereabouts of the Aïdin Planets. From these tales we made songs and plays, which we later performed for others on many worlds.

"Then, one day everything changed. A delegation from the Union of worlds… the Laendänl — you know of it, don't you?"

The children nodded.

"Well, a delegation came to us and asked for our help with the language of an Amethen people who wished to join the Union. My people had lived with them several times. We enjoyed each other's company because they too loved stories and plays… they still do. Eventually, the help my people gave made possible the understanding between them and the Union. It was at that point when we realized we had something of value to offer others, besides stories, songs and plays.

"Soon after, more and more requests similar to that one came to us, and our voyaging became diplomatic missions instead of a quest. That brought its own challenges. At first, all my people traveled together to the planets where we were needed. Then, it was decided that smaller groups could accomplish the missions more speedily. We had always voyaged together and lived simple, and with this new way we experienced separation and entered the life of large cities, palaces and plenty. Alas! That changed us, and after a time my people made the decision to settle on the planet where we live today. It was a momentous and life-altering decision. But we were going to have a place where we could be together after diplomatic missions, and the drifting islands would remind us of our voyaging past. Thus, about twelve thousand standard galactic years ago, we replaced our thirst for stories and tales with the study of cultures and peoples in libraries, always seeking to learn more about others."

"You sound sad", a boy said to him when he stopped to catch his breath. "Don't you love yourselves right now?"

Laidé regarded the boy for a long moment before answering such an unexpected question. "We do find joy in what we have become, because we help others. However, of lately some among my people, especially the young, feel restless. They advocate that we should start again our voyaging through the stars. They think our destiny lies there. Some of them have started to travel in small groups, although not yet far from our home world.

They want to feel, by themselves and not through stories, the joy of the quest for the sources of the legends of old."

The entire morning he continued with his telling. At some of his stories, they all laughed, specially those concerning his youth when he had disagreements with his parents and mentors, which had been frequent. He had never shared those stories with anyone and now realized that, by the standards of his people, he had been a rebel. A part of him felt proud of that.

Lunch time came, and they all walked together back to the village. The children dispersed as soon as they arrived to the plaza, and Laidé made his way back to Soen's house in her company and that of Meera and the boy with the blue-gemstone medallion — Cael was his name. The four of them shared a simple lunch, during which Meera and Cael asked him questions about the Union, questions which Laidé would have expected but from adults. It was then when, with a start, he remembered the letter and, taking it from his pocket, gave it to Soen.

She thanked him, read the Chancellor's handwriting on the envelope, and let it fall to the table.

For a moment Laidé felt confused. Then, unable to contain himself, he blurted, "Aren't you going to open it?"

"Later." She sighed.

He felt embarrassed for his outburst. "My apologies, Wanderer. I understood it to be an urgent missive." At that moment a realization came to him, and a heaviness took hold of his heart.

The youngsters had observed with curiosity their interchange, and Cael voiced the thought in Laidé's mind with a question to him: "Are you going to leave us now, to return to Esdänl?"

"No!" Soen piped up, startling Laidé and the children. Everyone gaped at her. She smiled back and continued addressing Cael with her usual voice, "He just arrived from that long trip and may want to stay with us for a time, to rest before returning."

Laidé didn't know what to say to that. Meera regarded him with a pleading face. Cael, with his intense eyes, waited for his reply.

"Well… the Chancellor didn't say when I should return to Esdänl… I could take some days off."

Mira and Cael relaxed at these words.

Yes, he did want to stay. He had realized that while sharing the stories of his people with the children. But he didn't know if he would be intruding on Soen's space and her present mission. Thus, using the same maneuver Soen had used, he addressed Cael instead of her, "If Wanderer Soen think it appropriate, I would like to meet the delegates from Lughai. I don't know what I can offer them… Perhaps I could answer questions they may have about the Union."

Cael glanced at Soen, who answered to Laidé, "They know you are here and who you are. If they want to talk to you, they will certainly let you know."

Laidé noticed Meera winking at Cael, and the boy rushed to say to him, "We are helping this afternoon to harvest the flowers that sweeten our foods. Come with us. It isn't far away. There will be music and dance when all is finished."

Once more Soen left him to decide for himself. Music and dance? It had been a long time since he had been so informal. "Yes," he replied softly to the children, "I would enjoy it, very much."

⚡

That evening at the house, after an enjoyable afternoon with the people of the village and, of course, with Soen, Laidé asked her the question puzzling him the entire day: "Where are the delegates of the planet Lughai?"

"The situation has changed, and we need to talk", she said in reply while sitting down and inviting him to sit across from her.

His heart sank. She had the letter in her hand, and he sat down in slow motion. Soen had been withdrawn all the way back to the house — she was going to ask him to return immediately to Esdänl, with a reply to the letter, and he'd rather not leave so soon.

"My mother's letter—"

He swallowed, widening his eyes. "Y-y-your mother? What do you mean? Chancellor Vuensé?"

With a candid smile she regarded him.

Of course! he thought. *She resembles the Chancellor! The similarities have been there all the time staring at me — their eyes, their smile, their use of certain expressions, the tone of their voices.*

She handed him the letter. "The letter is addressed to the two of us. You can read it."

He took it as if handling a dangerous thing, not knowing what to expect, and began to read it holding his breath — a letter wasn't the way the Chancellor would address him! The letter started with some words, directed to Soen, regarding him. It introduced him as the most trusted advisor her mother had and that he was in possession of sensitive information regarding a secret operation in the Sol System. Afterwards, the letter asked him to tell Soen everything, including the unusual findings on the third planet.

When he finished reading, he rested the letter on his lap and looked into the distance. None of the Councilors of the High Council knew about the findings on the third planet of Sol; not yet. Besides Althesal and her team, only the Chancellor, Marshal Mhali and he himself knew of them. He was having a hard time dealing with the secrecy surrounding the entire affair — his people considered secrecy as the worst transgression to the common good, and as something only those with twisted hearts would use to achieve selfish ends — and now he was asked to include in this circle of secrecy an outsider to the High Council!

"Laidé," Soen whispered, "you don't have to tell me anything if it goes against your principles. I can see how uncomfortable you feel. Mother astutely plays the game of politics. I never felt attraction for it. But in this case, she isn't playing her game. She's asking for our help. When I was growing up, she taught me a concealed written language she devised to communicate with my father, and in this letter she says between the lines that the operation to the Sol System has divided the High Council into several factions, and she doesn't know what to do about it. That the findings on the third planet are going to test the integrity of the Union."

"But, what can I do?" He spoke louder than what he had intended. "I don't have any power in the Union… What's she expecting of me?"

"I don't know her plans, but I can see she is expecting this situation will require unusual decisions and, perhaps, stepping outside all protocols. The manner she sent you here, hiding your true identity, tells me she wants to know if you are ready for the unexpected and for being her eyes and ears in situations that may challenge your principles. As for me, she wants to know my thoughts regarding the findings on that planet."

Laidé listened with intent. It all made sense. He had already thought the High Council wasn't prepared to deal with the situation in Sol, least of all with a radical change in the tactics of The Others. What Soen hadn't said was that her mother had sent him there so that Soen could assess if he was worthy of the trust her mother expected from him. Four days before, he would have doubted his strength of heart to step outside the principles of his people and of the Union. But this mission to deliver the letter had taught him he had lived with a limited perception of real life, and that the heart couldn't be encased in formalities and protocols — it had to be free to live life. The people of Orphes, especially the children, had shown him that.

⚡

Early the next day Soen waited for him downstairs. A light breakfast laid for him on the table where she sat. Her greeting was what he now expected of her — unpretentious and direct to the point:

"I am going with you back to Esdänl. But before we do that, we need to finish the negotiations with the delegates of Lughai. They want to meet with you."

The previous evening, Soen had been silent the entire time when he told her about the operation in the Sol System. She hadn't even reacted to the possibility of it harboring an Aïdin Planet — *Wanderers! Nothing impresses them!* had been his thought.

After his breakfast they left the house and walked to the large building at the center of the village. As they approached it, Soen told him that the delegates had met the evening before and had come to a final decision about their impasse.

The building was empty when they entered, but chairs were arranged in a circle. The two of them sat in silence, next to each other, facing the main entrance. Soen was quiet and pensive.

Not a minute had passed when he heard voices. Thinking it was the delegates, in respect he rose from his chair, but soon his mouth dropped at the sight. The children, his new friends, came into the hall, entering in pairs, one clad in a golden colored dress, the other in an ocean-blue. Meera and Cael were at the head of the procession. Each carried a slender, sealed vase of a metallic silver-white. They came to the circle of chairs and took position in front of them, twenty-eighty in number, with Meera and Cael taking the chairs opposite to him and Soen. Laidé was still standing, unable to comprehend what was happening, when Cael signaled to him to sit. When he sat, all the children except Meera and Cael also sat. Next, Cael addressed him:

"Laidé from the People of Nauth, forgive us the pretense of the past two days — We are the delegates from Lughai!"

Laidé grabbed the arms of his chair, dumbfounded, but Cael didn't give him time to recover.

"We needed to know you first, and your people through you, before we could tell if our decision had been right. During the last thirty days, with the help of Wanderer Soen, we visualized different avenues of the possible future of our people. During this journey we realized that our parents, when they stood aside and left to us the decision on the future of our planet, our future, they showed us the way to deal with the archeological discovery — they showed us the discovery doesn't belong to us but to all Humans. However, along this journey, we also discovered the lack of a true unity among Galactic Humans. Were we to give the discovery to the Union, it would be wrapped in the politics of the present, and its true meaning lost. Were we to keep it for ourselves, it would consume our people at a time when we have yet to find the new path of our lives. Thus, we came to the conclusion that a steward of the discovery, one who would understand its true value, was needed until the time when all Galactic Humans will be ready for it.

"Wanderer Soen", Cael continued, "suggested various civilizations — yours included. While studying them we found out that your people are already stewards of the seed of unity among Galactic Humans and of the longings found in all Human hearts.

"Now that we know you and can call you 'our friend', we arrived to a final decision."

Cael turned to Meera, who then said:

"Laidé of the Nauth, our friend, we place in trust in the hands of your people the sheets of live writing and everything associated with the discovery, including access to the archeological site and other potential sites. Your people will study them as they see fit, and will keep them until the time when all Galactic Humans will be ready — and this too they will decide."

All the children next rose at once and Soen with them. They all beamed with smiles. Laidé rose as an automaton, stunned by the revelations and the trust the children had in him and his people. Meera and Cael proceeded to walk ceremoniously towards him. The two bowed to him, then one by one handed him the vases.

A knot had formed in his throat, and tears rolled down his cheeks. All he could say to them was, "You remind me and my people of who we truly are. Thank you. Your wisdom has no match."

10

Corridors of Power

"Doubts I have…" Councilor Ulhloom said to Thaël and Chancellor Vuensé as they began their meeting, "doubts The Others are responsible for the destruction of the Resistance camp on the fifth planet of Sol. Their Overlords dislike changing tactics. Why now? Since the Armistice they are rebuilding their dominions… have freedom to express themselves. Doubts I have they would dare intervene on a Human world — and killing Humans! much less so. They remember when the Union had them neutralized and contained — their peoples withered."

Ulhloom had left Esdänl as soon as the three of them had received Marshal Mhali's report of his unplanned visit to the planet Mal'ek. Upon his return four days later, Ulhloom had requested they meet. When Thaël had first entered the conference room, it hadn't escaped him that his friend, normally easy-going, now appeared to carry a burden on his soul.

Thaël too had doubts. The same thoughts had passed through his mind. He too remembered well those times previous to the Armistice of Adhara when rare was the day without news of skirmishes between The Others and the Union, and of reports of peoples, from both sides, displaced from their planets by the conflict. Those days had also tested the commitment of his people to be part of the Union — war and conflict Thelians couldn't understand. It was at that time when he had been appointed as the Thelian Ambassador to pressure the High Council into starting negotiations with The Others. That hadn't been an easy task either, but it had come to a conclusion when Thaël himself, with Ulhloom and Vuensé, had sat with the Overlords to negotiate the terms of the Armistice.

"You aren't the only one to disagree with the Marshal's conclusions, Ulhloom", the Chancellor said. "Things aren't clear to me, either. Regardless, this report has stirred a hornet's nest among some of the other Councilors. I am seeing a split in any decision ahead of us. What worries me is that, for the first time in the history of our Union, some of our fellow Councilors are speaking of launching an all-out offensive against The Others to eliminate their threat once and for all."

Ulhloom's semi-transparent body changed hues quickly, revealing his worries. "That reaction was expected, Chancellor. Yet, a reaction is all it is. No one is ready at this point to make a decision on this affair. The presence of a Dreki at the Resistance camp could be explained in other ways. These days the Overlords have no need for stealth — bluster and overwhelming threat, those are now their ways. No, this Dreki the Marshal saw, and the three craft without insignia the Ranger transport detected, suggest to me rogue elements among one of the Overlords' ranks."

"That could be the case", Thaël said. "However, the nature of the destruction is horrific. The weapon used, if it was a weapon, is an explicit violation of the Armistice of Adhara — and that's the argument some Councilors have, that the Union is in its right to counteract."

Ulhloom looked at him. "That too is a way to see the destruction. Yet, clarity in this affair none of us has. We are not at the point of action. All we now know is the destruction was not caused by weapons or any form of technology we are aware of. The Rangers know the entire arsenal that each of the Overlords possesses. They would have noticed the development of a new weapon."

"But then, Ulhloom," he asked, "how can we explain the devastation Marshal Mhali witnessed? Does it match anything in your memories? After all, you suggested in our previous meeting that the Blight of the Ancients, as you remember it, could explain the catastrophe on the planet Yfel. Can this destruction be explained by that?"

The Chancellor observed their interchange in silence. Thaël had noticed she had been withdrawn since they had received the Marshal's latest report. "We have entered an unknown and dark path, and we can't rule anything out", she had confided to him the day before.

"We remembered not such a destruction in the times of the Blight", Ulhloom replied to Thaël's question with a muted tone. Next, pausing to recover his normal steady tone, he added, "However, the visuals of that forest, the Marshal's suit recorded, sounded an alarm in me… a hint of a memory deeply buried to my present self. It prompted me to travel home to enter *the Stream* and witness that which is our people's past, to remember."

Thaël had once visited Ulhloom's home — the Realm of Lhool, a trinary star system of the Alaïs Galaxy [Andromeda Galaxy]. He had been surprised that the nine home planets of the People of Lhool were similar in their bio-sphere, appearance and feel. His friend had then explained that, throughout their long history, the People of Lhool had recreated their bio-spheres multiple times to match the natural cycle of renewal through which they, as a people, experienced every 8,000 standard galactic years. In that visit Ulhloom had taken him to observe the Stream — a system of light-made 'rivers' in the first-harmonic frequency of the Ös, one on each planet, serving as repositories of the collective knowledge and memories of the People of Lhool. Right before the Lhool start their joint, 5,000-year-long hibernation-renewal period, they all enter the Stream to imprint on it their recently acquired knowledge and memories. Later, after the renewal process is over and they all re-awaken, those who want to learn something from their past do so by entering one of those 'rivers'.

"When I entered the Stream," Ulhloom continued, "I had expected to behold memories of my people's far, far past… after the Blight was healed and when dark Powers brought war upon us. What I beheld, however, wasn't from that time. It was from our recent past — a mere nine thousand years ago. My people were then called to assist three worlds that had experienced a localized destruction resembling the one Marshal Mhali witnessed in that forest."

"Where?" The Chancellor hastened to ask. "And why wasn't the Union informed of this?"

"They were isolated incidents, Chancellor, on remote planets of the Alaïs Galaxy whose inhabitants aren't members of the Union. The incidents were too far apart from each other to see a pattern in them. Besides, those of our people who were called to help never reported those incidents to our government."

"I understand", the Chancellor said. "Did you find in the Stream the cause of the destruction on those three worlds?"

"I asked the Stream the same question, but none of those of our people who witnessed the devastation arrived to a clear answer. One of them, nonetheless, left on the Stream his personal view on the matter after having done extensive research in the chronicles of races as old as ours. His conclusion was the destruction had been caused by an *'Ancient Darkness'* — *'by incursions of agents of the Ancient Darkness'* to be precise — and that those three incidents *'may signal the Darkness is returning!'*"

An eerie quietness descended on the conference room, as if the sole mention of those words could create a link with that 'Darkness'. Thaël felt uncomfortable with that thought and shook his head. This made the Chancellor look at him. Her eyes appeared distant, but after a moment she also shook her head. She then asked Ulhloom:

"And what is your thought on that conclusion?"

Ulhloom's body changed the hues of its light radiance a few times while considering the answer. Thaël then knew what was coming. He could anticipate the answer by reading the change of colors of his friend's body and listening to the music they made. Ulhloom was going to allude to an undercurrent in the life of the Union, which didn't threaten the cohesiveness of the Union but that resurfaced from time to time.

"Unlike Humans, who knew Them not," Ulhloom began, "we of the Amethen races still feel the loss of the Old Races. They taught us and guided us when we were young, and for a longer age than the one we now live with you Humans. The end of that age started when life took a sharp turn and we were exposed to the Blight, and later to the war inflicted upon us by those malevolent Kskiln. At the time we believed an ancient Power from beyond our galaxies — an 'Ancient Darkness' some called it — was behind both events… It was during that war that the Old Races' attempts to protect us took them to their doom… Such was the might of that Darkness!

"Humans", Ulhloom continued, "have been spared of such experiences. Thus, they doubt the existence of unseen Powers in this Universe, both good and evil, who may affect them… us all. Humans are still young and daring. These differences between both our peoples' histories will now arise. When word of the happenings in the Sol System will spread, most of the Councilors and Ambassadors from Amethen worlds will stand together in their view that the Ancient Darkness is returning, that it must be contained." Ulhloom turned at this point to face Thaël directly. "They will look for those who can save them — and they will look at you, Thelians, for that. In contrast, the Councilors and Ambassadors from Human worlds will take the stance that the Union can deal with any menace."

The Chancellor nodded slowly, "Yes, that's what is going to happen, unless something else throws a new light on this strange affair… However, my question was more personal. I would like to know your thoughts on the conclusion reached by the one of the Lhool who said the Ancient Darkness was returning."

Ulhloom looked at her with his shrewd eyes and took time to answer.

"Dark days are upon us", he eventually said softly. "Happenings none of us living today has seen, or imagined, are coming… The one of the Lhool you ask about, the one who did that extensive research, is one of my former selves. He felt so distressed by the certainty of the return of the Darkness, and by our powerlessness to defeat it, that the memory of it he no longer wanted to carry and buried it as deep as he could!"

11

The Forgotten Quest

Daothel hesitated at the entrance to her home. What would happen if Dean Althesal didn't believe him? Brushing off his concerns and gathering his resolve, he announced his presence by singing a short greeting. The house's exterior standing light-field translated his tune into ripples of a soft light, matching the harmonies of his voice. There was no turning back.

"Ah! It's you, Daothel." He heard her pleasant voice come through the tall, open oval that served as the entrance. "Please, come in."

He entered with measured steps and suppressed an exclamation — the house was more beautiful than he had imagined! The vestibule led him to a broad circular atrium whose height spanned the three levels of the building. He was on the middle level. Looking down, he could see a comfortable living-dining space in the midst of a beautiful interior garden. On the third level, he surmised, were bedroom suites.

"Find me in the studio."

He followed the sound of her voice. The studio was on the same level he had come in, and before reaching it, he passed by two open rooms, which he guessed were one for music and the other for craft-making. Exquisite and rare works of art, of various types and origins, adorned the spaces with great taste. He slowed down to take everything in. The house was indeed the expression of a song of great beauty — it lived up to its reputation; the Dean had designed it herself.

"Welcome to my dwelling", she said with her melodious voice when he reached the spacious studio. "You are a good surprise. Please, take a chair."

She sat at her desk and with a wave of a hand dismissed the display she was working on. Besides her desk and four chairs around a work table, shelves lined most of the walls. On them rested hundreds of books, maps and manuscripts, in many languages, shapes and materials. These were the type of things his people hadn't ever created, or had any need for. Although he knew Dean Althesal was knowledgeable about many other civilizations, races and bio-souls, he hadn't expected her to use such things.

Realizing the Dean waited for him, he crossed the room in three strides and sat on a chair in front of her desk, then took a deep breath before speaking. "Excuse me, Dean, for coming unannounced. I went to your offices, and your assistant told me you were working here today. However, matters beyond my control bring me to you."

The Dean leaned back in her chair and regarded him. Her friendly smile eased some of his disquiet.

"I have come to extend to you an invitation to meet with Ciän the Wise. He knows your duties are many these days; nonetheless, he asks of you to honor his request at the briefest possible time."

Dean Althesal's smile froze on her face. Then, leaning forward and placing both hands on the desktop, with emotion on her voice she said:

"You've been chosen by Ciän the Wise to be his successor!"

That was an answer he wasn't expecting! For a moment he couldn't come up with anything to say. Then with a muted voice he replied, aware he was going to excuse himself, "The Wise One contacted me three years ago and began to initiate me into the Way of the Synod of the Wise. Yet, long is the path ahead of me before I can even sound a harmonic note of his life-song."

She shook her head in dismissal. "You honor all of us, Daothel. It isn't difficult to see who you are."

He bowed to her slightly and waited for her reply to the invitation.

"Does Nesdil know of this?"

He shifted his body in the chair. He had never talked to others about his initiation — it was something which grew in the silence of the heart. "Y-Yes, Dean. The Wise One spoke to her. Then, together they came up with a list of skills and areas of knowledge for me to master."

"This is a wonderful happening!" Her words were spoken softly, as if to herself, and he didn't understand what she meant by them. Next, with a big smile she added, "Well, let's not keep the Wise One waiting. Are we meeting in Eiral?"

"Yes, Dean. The Wise One would have liked to come to you. However, the matter he wishes to discuss is most delicate. He deems the silence of the Halls of Eiral are more suitable for the need."

"And this matter, you know of it?"

"Although the Wise One has discussed it with me on various occasions, new developments have him both intrigued and concerned. Of these new developments I am not aware, yet they prompted the invitation to you."

The Dean rose from her chair, and he rushed to do the same. Soon they were on their way to the nearest transport pad, not far from her house.

Eiral was the aerial city on Thel where the Synod of the Wise had its Halls, and where the twenty-four Wise Ones also lived a life of silence and quietness. The Synod was the highest decision-making body in the Thelian society. Their dicta weren't concerned with the organization or with the administration of the civilization, but with guiding the evolutionary development of the many groups of bio-souls of the planet and its companion world, Othy. In principle, a Synod's decision could override a decision made by one of the three Parliaments of Mentors or by the Council of the Paths itself. However, the Wise Ones focused more on the steps into the future, than on the present, for their world and people. Thus, it was expected by all that they would remain neutral in the daily affairs of the Parliaments and the Council.

As the two of them approached the transport pad, the Dean broke her silence: "You are still young, Daothel. How does it feel to be chosen by one of the Wise Ones?"

He realized she had noticed his uneasiness on the subject and wanted to let him know he could trust her. Thus, he replied, "Ciän is unlike 'the Wise One' I had imagined him to be. He is friendly and fun to be with… his wisdom flows from the peaceful and uncomplicated way with which he sees everything. Most times he acts towards me as an older brother, as one who has experienced life a little longer than myself. I like that he shows me how youth and Wisdom don't exclude each other — 'It is a matter of expressing your timeless identity', he says."

He gave a side glance to the Dean to gauge her reaction. A broad grin adorned her face.

"This isn't the first time, Daothel, an apprentice is chosen to succeed one of the Wise Ones. This should also ease your concerns."

"Yes, Dean, I know it happened before… Iolthel the Wise comes to my mind."

"Oh! I was thinking of others. I didn't know Iolthel had heard her calling when she was an apprentice. Do you know of her life?"

"Ciän the Wise has told me of her. Not much is known, but the Synod has kept some oral stories and anecdotes of her life, work and mission.

Likewise, a few of her musical compositions have survived — you should hear them; they are delightful and mysterious at the same time. The Wise Ones think these songs were composed when she was 'seeing' into the patterns of Time."

"I would like to", she replied.

"They are kept in the Library of the Synod… It's regrettable our people aren't attracted to know of our past. They would discover Iolthel's wisdom and dicta still guide our hearts and minds. Many don't know the founding of the Synod was her most outstanding contribution to our way of life."

The Dean sighed, slowed her pace, and said, "I wish we would have someone like her today with us."

What was she implying? That he could be like Iolthel? She had looked at him with fire in her eyes when she had said that. He halted, forcing her to also stop, next asked without being rude, "Why do you say that, Dean?"

"As a people we lack something. I haven't been able to identify it, but it's clear to me we are fettered by our Paths. Iolthel lived during a time of great changes in our civilization, and many saw in her a source of inspiration and strength. But she was likewise of strong will and had to contend with opposition — something which the members of the Synod today don't experience. Do you know she opposed the Council of the Paths' decision regarding the aerial cities, which were built during her time?"

"Yes, Dean. I know of it."

"She spoke strongly against abandoning the natural world of our planet, leaving it without the Human touch. Yet most couldn't understand the reason for her opposition to this when the move was intended to protect that natural world. And, as you may know, soon after she disappeared, still in the prime of her life, leaving a vacuum in our civilization that hasn't been filled since then."

The Dean sounded nostalgic, and Daothel looked at her with renewed admiration. She knew of Iolthel the Wise, and apparently well. Not many Thelians, not even in positions of influence, had Dean Althesal's breadth of knowledge and experience. To him, she was more of a mystery than Iolthel herself. For a start, she had traveled to many worlds with her parents when she was young, and even in the present she still had many off-world friends — no other Thelian he knew of had done that. His Teacher, Nesdil, spoke of the Dean frequently, as if wanting him to look up to someone whose life had so much to teach him.

After this interchange they entered in silence the transport pad. Daothel felt by then relaxed and concluded that his anxiety had been unfounded.

People of such standing as the Dean would accept and understand that, although he was young, he was on the Way of the Synod.

⚡

"Have you seen one of these before?" Ciän the Wise asked Althesal.

He was old in years, approaching 3,200. Yet, only the light of his eyes revealed the wisdom of old age. His body was still young and supple, and Althesal could see the light inside it glowing strong. He had come to meet her and Daothel to the only transport pad in the city of Eiral. He next had led them to a quarter of the city, away from its public Halls, where clusters of small buildings sparsely located sprouted from the garden forest surrounding them. She hadn't visited that area before, and the harmony of its song struck her with its peacefulness. When they had entered a building in one of the clusters, Althesal had realized with surprise that it was the private studio of Ciän the Wise.

"No, Wise One", she answered him while he placed the object on the palm of her hand. It was a crystalline ring, with the appearance and weight of an emerald gemstone. It was cold to the touch, and she didn't feel or hear any sound coming from it. "What is it?"

"That's an old recording device used by some of our people when we lived on the planet's surface. It's crude but has the advantage its contents will withstand the passage of Time, unaffected by the surrounding light and sounds frequencies of Space. This one was found among the few possessions left by Iolthel the Wise after her disappearance."

Althesal couldn't suppress a quick glance to Daothel, and the youth's eyes sparkled back to her with a twinkle. He had known Ciän the Wise wanted to talk to her about Iolthel and had skillfully prepared her for the matter the Wise One wanted to address.

"Only recently and after many millennia", the Wise One continued, "it was Daothel who found the way to know of its contents. Let him show you."

Daothel received the ring and placed it, standing up, on a tabletop. Next, with a swift motion of his hand, he started to spin it and then released it. Soon the ring gained momentum on its own and became a blurred sphere. At this point Daothel sounded upon it the fundamental chord of the song of their people's soul. With this, an opening appeared on the north pole of the rotating sphere and a fanning ray of emerald light rose from it. Slowly, at the eye level, the ray resolved into the face of a young woman, who thus began to speak:

"Greetings, dear ones. You have found this message for a reason. My name is Iolthel, the last one of our people standing on the surface of our planet. I leave this message to you because I am about to embark on a quest from which I may not return. This quest is the only recourse left to me.

"Seven millennia ago the Time Seers of our people heard a change in the song of our planet, a change I still hear — *Is it coming from our people, or is it from the bio-sphere of our world?* they so asked themselves. They then searched tirelessly for the cause, yet finding it they did not. They knew, though, the change bespoke of a loss since during their time they also observed that fewer and fewer Time Seers were being born among us.

"I too followed on their steps and have searched for the nature of this change and loss without finding its cause. Now I am the only Time Seer left on our world.

"Because our people will miss the guidance of the Time Seers when I am gone, I sponsored the creation of the Synod of the Wise — a group of those among us whose wisdom, love and insight could guide our people with their example, and shine a light onto the way forward for the three Paths, until Time Seers may again be born among us.

"Looking at the sameness that has befallen the life of our people, I have no doubt something has gone missing from our collective soul. As our skill and mastery of the Power of the Voice has grown in us, the Power of the Eye has faded — that power to conceive greater horizons and aim our steps towards them. Yet, as Sound and Light are the two halves of Space, so are the Voice and the Eye the two halves of the wholeness of Human — lacking one of them, a people are doomed to fade.

"Now you understand my quest — to find the cause of our loss and to attempt to restore the wholeness of our people. The only compass I have is my heart. If I fail, all hope rests in the Synod to continue this search for that wholeness with which we were born at the dawn of our existence. If the Synod fails, the sole hope left is *you!*

"Farewell, dear ones. I have no advice for you where to start. All I know is this message will reach you at the right moment in time."

After those last words the face vanished, the recording ring slowed its rotation, and Daothel grabbed it before it fell over. No one of them spoke for a long while, during which Althesal felt Ciän studying her. The implications of Iolthel's message were staggering.

When Ciän broke the silence, he said to her:

"You may have well concluded from this message, as we did, that the Synod hasn't followed the mission Iolthel intended. Did she speak of it to the first members of the Synod? We must assume she did. However, the many changes and reorganizations that took place when our people moved to the aerial cities probably obscured her instructions to them. Also, the fact that we were discovered by Galactic Humans soon after, that must have altered the mission of the Synod as an institution. It became respected, yet removed from the daily life of our people and of the three Paths.

"This recording ring survived all these thousands of years because someone who knew of its content placed it in the Library of the Synod. Otherwise it wouldn't be here today — it could have been Iolthel herself, since she also started the Library of the Synod. I discovered it under other artifacts by a series of synchronous happenings, unrelated to what I was actually looking for. Thus, I am inclined to think that Iolthel the Time Seer *saw* the journey of her recording along the passage of time, and she intended for us to be its recipients."

Was Ciän also including her?

Noticing her reaction, with a smile he added, "Yes, you too, Althesal — more so, I'm inclined to think it was to you that she left the message. Iolthel's quest was born from the same questioning you have had since early age. For some time I've noticed your voice in the Song of our people. Your singing is strong and clear, more than most others, and it introduces improvisations impossible to miss. And these improvisations reveal your dissatisfaction with the sameness our lives have become. Thus, when five days ago you found in the Hall of Records evidence of a Source Path for our three Paths, besides the surprise it gave us, I then knew you were ready to know of her message… I knew you had found what the Time Seers had looked for — the cause of the change in the song our planet… I knew also that you are the right one to find out the fate of those who traveled that Path, and to find the way to restore our wholeness."

Althesal was speechless. As if Ciän's idea that the message was intended for her wasn't enough to shock her, his other conclusions added more to the confusion she felt. Taking a deep breath, she whispered, "How do you know of the Source Path, Wise One? Ethën and I haven't spoken of it to anyone."

"The Time Seers haven't returned, Althesal, and the Power to See into the patterns of unfolding Time is not with us. Yet, the power of remote-seeing across Space is still with us and can be developed." He ended smiling with a touch of mischief impossible to miss.

"Am I to assume, Wise One, that you also know about my work for the High Council of the Union and of my research on the Aïdin Planets?"

"Yes, Althesal — but how I know isn't important. In addition to handing you over Iolthel's message, I have invited you here to let you know that all of us in the Synod are ready to help you and your friends with your quest, or 'research' if that's how you want to call it. We aren't going to dictate to you where or how to seek, nor do we ask you to report to us. Support in all you may need is what we offer — that's all. Would you accept this help?"

Ciän and Daothel regarded her in silence, waiting for an answer.

"I-I don't know what to say, Wise One... Of course, I accept your support. It isn't difficult to see that our people have lost something from their identity — although I haven't connected this loss with the disappearance of the Power to See the unfolding patterns of Time... until this moment. However, so that you know, for all my life I have felt it isn't just our people who are missing something — all Humans are, everywhere. We have forgotten who we truly are. We conquer Space with little effort. Otherwise, we are prisoners of Time, even though the longing to be free from its shackles is in all of us."

She paused and lowered her eyes. She hadn't intended to say that last part. Yet, as she had spoken, her mind had made a connection: both, restoring the Aïdin Planets and Iolthel's quest had one and the same purpose. To be whole and free from Space and Time was what the legends told people experienced on the Aïdin Planets, and that was also what the Time Seers used to speak of — for Humans to move towards horizons with an ever-expanding identity until the ultimate freedom was reached. Could that have also been the purpose intended by those who had metamorphosed Thel? To create a Humanity that would advance faster than others to a fuller freedom and be way-showers to all Humans? But her people had failed and a split had occurred, and the whole plan had come to nothing — Was her mission truly to revive the path of the Time Seers? No, it couldn't be. She was just a simple researcher, and she hadn't the power to 'see' the patterns of Time.

Then it dawned on her: Had the mysterious singularity the Asli had shown Nesdil and Daothel also been used on Thel to alter its bio-sphere and their people? The Master Chronicler had called it 'a Spark of Primordial Fire'— Was it truly that or something else? But where was it now? Had those who traveled the Source Path taken it with them when they left? That was the most logical explanation to the changes her planet experienced at the time the aerial cities rose from the ground. Had they taken it to Sol?

She looked up, aware of the silence in the room. Ciän regarded her with a kind face and a wealth of patience. "This quest may not be what the Synod expects", she said softly to him. "Are you aware, Wise One, this isn't just a mystery concerning our people but involving at least one other world, and perhaps more?"

"That, Althesal, is the reason we are certain you are on the trail of the Time Seers. The first members of the Synod traveled to our planet's surface looking for Iolthel a few years after she went missing. Only her belongings in the dwelling where she had lived they found, and not a trace or a clue of her whereabouts. They searched for her across the lands and oceans, and even on Othy, until they had to accept she was gone. The mystery of her disappearance has perplexed the Synod since then... until now, when recent events and discoveries have begun to throw some light on her quest. That island in the Meridional Ocean—"

"Excuse me, Dean! And excuse me Wise One!" Daothel rushed to say with concern in his face. Next, regarding her, he said, "Ciän knows of the island of the Asli. Our people aren't aware that the Wise Ones do visit the surface of our planet on occasion to assess the evolution of the many bio-souls there. It was during one of these visits, a year ago, when Ciän and four others of the Synod discovered the existence of the island after noticing a slight change in the song of the Meridional Ocean. But all they found was an uncharted island. Thus, when recently Ciän told me of that island, my reaction betrayed to him that I also knew of it. Then, I thought it wise to disclose to him the existence of the Asli and their underground complex."

She regarded him, containing her discomposure. None of this she had expected, though she should have when Daothel had told her about his initiation under the sponsorship of Ciän — the relationship between the Wise Ones and their chosen successors was one of complete openness and trust. "I understand, Daothel", she said to him. "I would have done the same. It is, however, unsettling that all these apparently disconnected events and findings are carrying us in the same direction and that I have no choice but to go along."

"Yes, Althesal", Ciän said to her while gesturing for them to sit. "That's what life, lived in its fulness, is about — a song and a dance carrying us forward. We want, and try, to be in control of every step we take, yet we forget that the ground where we are going to step also has a say in our dance and song. We are never alone... Now, I want to know your intuitions regarding that third planet of the Sol System."

A Song of Desolation

Ethën was spellbound. He could well have been standing on a remote alien world as he beheld the magnificence of the Asli and the polished, spherical underground chamber that was their home. That the Asli — a hominid species — moved through the air with ease challenged his view of the order of the Universe. He also felt apprehensive at the possibility he wasn't going to understand them. Daothel had explained earlier to him that they used the song of the DNA in the bio-physical cells to communicate, and he wasn't good at focusing on the physical sensations of his body.

But his apprehension dissolved the moment he, Althesal, Nesdil and Daothel were welcomed by the Asli. Their magnetism and friendliness touched his whole being with something akin to bliss. The four of them had finally found a time together to visit them, and not a moment too soon. He was full of questions.

Dispensing with introductions, and before Ethën or the others could say anything, with their musical language the group of sixty or so Asli communicated to their brains: "Observe!"

The Asli next proceeded to disperse, in no apparent order, towards the periphery of the enormous chamber, while a fountain of sparkling light-particles erupted from a point at its center. These soon became a rotating spiral that resolved into a four-dimensional horn torus, filling about one-half of the space.

"*Loci of Time* — the sparks are." The Asli's song reached him and the others in their wordless language.

Nesdil had explained to him before their visit:

"Time for the Asli, as far as I understand them, is a symphony of *now-moments*, each sounding its own note and harmonics — the Asli call those moments *loci*. But these loci aren't equal to the divisions we give to Time, nor to what we perceive as past, present and future. To start, they said loci have no equal duration because they are created by the events in consciousness of the collective of self-conscious beings on each planet. Then to add complexity to their view of Time, they said that each now-moment, or locus, doesn't move linearly but in four dimensions of Time, and in the process it interacts with other loci to form patterns of an ever growing complexity, creating a fifth dimension — this means, they said, that all our yesterday, todays and tomorrows interact with one another to form patterns of Time and that, because of this, the tomorrows influence the present as much as the yesterdays do."

What all that meant, he could only guess. Of one thing he was sure: to his keen eyesight those so-called loci were something not made of a normal light, nor was their luminosity intrinsic to them. It appeared they were outsiders to Space and elicited from it a luminous reaction as they "touched" it.

As he pondered on that, one of the loci expanded, and the entire mass of them resolved into a pastoral scene of undulating hills on an island.

"Wow!" he heard Daothel, at his left, exclaim. "I can sense the breeze on my face and smell the fragrances of the land!"

Ethën felt he was there too. But there was more. His eyesight appeared to have become more acute, and he could see each detail of that island.

The hills were covered with grasses and short plants in bloom. Woods and orchards grew in the small valleys between them. The only feature that wasn't natural was in one of the valleys in the distance — a mysterious cylindrical, glowing structure of great size, rose from the ground. Everything else he could see had its perfect place, even the position of each hill with respect to the others, as if someone had sought to make of that island a well-designed landscape.

But what drew his attention wasn't the scenery. It was a group of the most noble-looking and handsome Humans Ethën had ever beheld. They ascended along the slopes of the tallest hill, climbing in perfect order and effortlessly, and forming seven streams along the grass-covered slopes — about three hundred individuals in each stream. They all had the appearance of young, genderless adults, dressed with a similar clothing, if clothing it could be called, as it was a rainbow-colored light undulating and shifting in hues as their bodies moved. Yet, contrasting with the magnificence of their looks were their demeanor and the song they crooned — a deep sadness appeared to burden them!

"Who could they be?" Nesdil whispered at his right. "Their loss must be so intimate to be so desolate."

Ethën couldn't make sense of the words those Humans sang. Yet, their voices were more magnificent than those of his people.

The seven streams of Humans eventually reached the plateau crowning the hill and proceeded to mix with each other to form one group, arranged as a perfect circle. It all happened without affectation, or because of a studied choreography. No, everything in them had the precision of harmony, proportion and beauty — even their sadness.

In the silence that ensued after their march and when their singing ceased, a realization came to Ethën: *Could they be those who followed the Source Path?* Before he could look for any sign that would help answer the question, seven flaming figures, bluish and bright, and as tall as him, appeared above the Humans. The flames descended and circled them three times, in the process creating a shimmering luminous field that enveloped them all. As soon as this field was formed, all the Humans on the plateau, together with the flames, became airborne, slowly and straight up. Then, when they reached about 120 lont [260 meters] above the hilltop, they all vanished.

Ethën felt a deep sadness as all this happened. But it hadn't been because of the sadness of the Humans. It was those seven flaming figures. In his heart he knew they were more than flames — *Who were they? Could they be the Manaï?*

But things hadn't finished. After a silence and a slight shift in the light, a short and loud sound difficult to describe — perhaps a single note — reverberated throughout the hills. It had sounded remote and ethereal, as if coming from a higher dimension. Looking for the source of the sound, the only thing Ethën saw was that the hilltop now appeared hazy.

"Do you see that?" Daothel asked to no one in particular.

"Where?" he rushed to ask.

"There, at the summit of the hill… Unfocus your sight."

Following Daothel suggestion, he saw it.

A spherical field of some type of force exited the hill through the plateau. Then, when more than half of it became visible, Ethën saw that 'flames' similar to the others — yet this time nine of them — circled the sphere. There was more, though. At the center of that spherical field, a spark of an intense brilliance throbbed, its gentle pulsation impressing iridescent changes throughout the sphere. But none of this lasted. Once the entire sphere left the ground, it contracted at a great speed until only the spark and the nine flaming figures were left. They next hovered for a short while before ascending through the air, where they were lost above the clouds.

With the Humans and the spark gone, the island changed — not in topography and contents but in its liveliness. It became ordinary, lacking in something, and Ethën felt that a coldness now blew across the hills. Almost immediately the entire scene dissolved back into the many sparkling particles inside the Asli's chamber, leaving Ethën with an emptiness in his heart and feeling the cold of that ordinariness.

Involuntarily he shook to free himself from that coldness. Next he turned to ask Althesal about those Humans, but his words died before he spoke them — a concentrated mass of loci hovered three handspans above Althesal's head, swirling and rotating as if these were a miniature spiral galaxy crowning her. Her eyes were closed, and she appeared to be in a deep state of concentration.

"Touch her not!" He felt the music of the Asli reach his body and brain with these words. When he lifted his head to look at them, two Asli were gliding towards Althesal. The concern on their almost-Human faces was unmistakable — *They hadn't expected this!* Ethën realized.

Nesdil moved quickly to stand next to Althesal.

"Touch her not!" The two Asli repeated while studying the mass of loci.

"A bridge across nows." The music-words of one of the two Asli came to him; although these weren't to addressed them but to the other Asli.

"The essence of *Aïdin* is in all nows; so is her essence", the second one said. "She summons It."

"Yes, she remembers", the first one added. Then pointing to Daothel, Nesdil and him, this Asli said to the other, "They all remember."

"Some of it", the second one replied shaking its head. "When the three others come, together they remember the other nows."

Nesdil, Daothel and Ethën glanced at each other, puzzled by this interchange.

To Ethën nothing made sense — *The essence of Aïdin? ... Remember what? ... Three others?*

Then, without warning, the mass of sparkling loci above Althesal's head vanished, and he had to step forward to hold her as she lost her balance while coming back unto herself. The iridescent light emitted by the bodies of the Asli was all that remained of the former display of loci of Time.

"Time is friend and harms not", the two Asli said to the four of them.

They had regained their normal joyful and child-like countenances. "Remember *you* in those other nows — you each must — so that this present locus continues its intended weaving."

Ethën still couldn't comprehend much of what they communicated. Althesal stirred, and he held her closer to him. Daothel then rushed to retrieve the sled they had brought with equipment, and with Nesdil's assistance he carefully led her on it. She was pale and weak.

"She needs some rest", Nesdil said after touching Althesal's forehead. "Something isn't right with her. She is cold. Let's return to the open air."

Ethën hesitated, he wanted answers. He hadn't yet talked to the Asli, and he needed to. Althesal's hand was in his, and he felt her attempts to squeeze his. She gave him a weak smile, and he knew then that she also wanted answers but that it had to be another time. He bent over to help her lie back on the sled. "It's going to be fine", he said to her as she closed her eyes.

As the four of them exited the chamber and entered the gallery connecting with the outside, he gave the Asli one last glance. In a strange Human fashion they waved their hands to them in farewell and held a broad smile!

⚡

Upon returning from the island, the four of them had retreated to Nesdil's private studio in the Life Harmonics Institute. Althesal had felt better as soon as they had exited the underground gallery. They were at a loss to interpret the connection between those loci of Time and her. Why had she been the only one so affected? It disturbed Ethën, and her, that she didn't remember anything from the moments she had been under the influence of the mass of sparkling particles.

Once they had dined together, after a lengthy discussion about their experience, they simply sought to spend some quiet time to mull over all they had been through.

The scene the Asli had shown them appeared to have taken place on the Asli's own island. They had surveyed the entire island from the air, and the hills matched the ones they had seen in that scene. The main difference was that mature forests now covered most of them.

As for those Humans, the four of them thought they had to be those of their people who had lived by the Source Path. But questions was all they have — What had been the true reason for them to split from the rest of the Thelians and for leaving their planet? Who were those flaming beings which had taken them? And where had they all gone?

Regarding the spherical energy field with a spark-looking phenomenon a its center, it had to be a new type of Space singularity. According to Nesdil and Daothel, it did resemble the source of power in the vision the Asli had shown them in their first visit to them. Still, the four of them had also many questions about it — Had it been the power used to produce the metamorphosis of the bio-sphere of Thel over time? If so, who had been responsible for its use? And where was it now?

More pressing, and above all those unknowns, were the more personal questions: Why the four of them? And, as the Asli had told them, what was that they had 'to remember'?

Similar to most other instances, Ethën couldn't be at peace with the enigma until he understood it in its entirety. However, at that point in the evening only Nesdil and him were still engaged in conversation. Althesal and Daothel were absorbed in their own thoughts.

Ethën sipped the traditional Thelian evening tea made from the nectar of several flowers combined to form a song of flavors. But at that moment the harmonies of the infusion in his body didn't help to unwind his mind.

"Why can't the Asli be straightforward and tell us what it is we are supposed to remember?" Ethën asked Nesdil as he paced, still disappointed that he hadn't talked to them.

"They are of their own nature and need not live up to our expectations!" Nesdil answered sternly, forcing him to stop his pacing.

"Sorry. You are right. My frustration isn't with them. I'm tired of this mystery! A simple scientific survey of a neighboring star system has become a bundle of disconnected data in which our planet, the third planet in Sol, our lives, and the lives of beings of whom we know nothing, appear to be intermixed. And now the Asli bring in the Time factor to make matters worse… *Remember!* they said. Remember what?"

Nesdil waved her hand to him. "Relax! The best we can do is to let things be, for now. And stop pacing! — you're making me dizzy."

"Nothing makes sense!" Ethën grumbled and plunked himself down on a chair away from the others.

Determining, exactly, when the Humans and when the Spark had left their planet was, to him, a starting point to make sense of the mystery. Althesal and Daothel had argued that these had been two separate events, that a length of time had spanned between the two of them. Nesdil and him hadn't noticed anything to make them think so.

"The Humans' departure", Althesal had said, "was the probable cause for the change in the song of our planet that the Time Seers noticed millennia before Iolthel's time, while the removal of the Spark explains the change the planet's electromagnetic field underwent when our cities went up in the air."

Oh, she's probably right! Ethën thought. *What doesn't make sense is that our people noticed nothing of this.*

"It does."

Ethën jumped in the chair, startled. Was Daothel reading his mind? The youngster had spoken little since their return to the city. The experience had affected him deeply.

He rose and asked the youth, "What are you talking about? *What* does?"

Nesdil and Althesal also regarded the young apprentice with inquiring faces.

Daothel stood by one of the windows. Turning to face them he replied, "This whole affair… You said to Teacher Nesdil, 'Nothing makes sense'. I say, 'it does'. The Asli have engaged us with a purpose. We weren't randomly selected. They contacted Teacher Nesdil first, and they must have known that the three of us were going to come along at some point. In fact, they were expecting us. That's clear. And they are conveying one simple message — to us — that will make us remember something of vital importance. Though I think they haven't finished."

"And what would that message be?" Althesal spoke in a way that told Ethën she was thinking along the same lines Daothel was.

"I can't grasp it yet, Dean. The only thing clear to me is that a connecting thread exists between the loci of Time they are exposing us to and our present life."

That was too much for Ethën. "Are you talking about our past lives?" he asked him. "Are you saying we were there, during the time when those Humans left?"

Daothel turned towards him and shrugged in reply.

"For what purpose?" Ethën insisted. "For what purpose would the Asli want to remind us of our lives in other *nows*? And for—" He cut short what he was going to say next. It surprised him that he had used the same expression the Asli had used, and this made him think that Daothel could be right.

The youth didn't answer his question. No one did. Could a thread of Time truly connect the departing scene with the vision Nesdil and Daothel had first experienced, and with the current events in their lives?

The notion that the essential Self of every Human was non-spatial, and unfettered by Space, had been proven beyond doubt through multiple scientific approaches, well before Ethën had been born. So was the idea of reincarnation of the Self across Time. But the repeated scientific attempts made by many to retrieve memories from that path across Time had come to nothing. The obstacle was accessing Time itself — it refused to be isolated from Space. Althesal had discussed this enigma with him in many instances, and she was of the idea that something key in understanding Time was still missing; that the studies weren't approaching it in the right way. That's why the Asli's reference to "loci of Time" and to the symphony of patterns they formed intrigued Ethën. It provided the first new approach to this subject, that he knew of, in a long time.

Althesal rose abruptly from her chair, interrupting his thoughts.

"I'm tired," she said, "and we aren't going anywhere with this conversation. All we have are conjectures." Then, she turned to leave but hesitated. Facing again the three of them she added, "Let's agree on something. Let's keep to ourselves, for now, the similarity of the fundamental chord of that island with that of the bio-sphere of the third planet of Sol, as well as the existence of the Asli and the experiences we had with them. Too much is at stake for the Union to add these mysteries to our official report of the survey of Sol. Besides, we don't know enough about these experiences to even explain them to ourselves... And, one more thing", she added. "We shouldn't mention a word to anyone about the discoveries we made regarding the past of our planet and our people. The impact of such a revelation on them we can't predict. It is best for the Synod to take care of it when they so choose. Do we agree to all this?"

Ethën wasn't going to lose any sleep because of that and replied, "Fine with me."

Nesdil, however, shaking her head said, "I don't like it. Once we take the road of secrecy, where do we stop?"

"You're the one who started with the secrecy!" Ethën retorted. "Besides, it isn't an unethical decision, as you imply. It's refraining from divulging an incomplete scientific observation until we have sufficient facts to complete the picture."

Nesdil turned unfazed to look at him. "My first trips to the surface of the planet were a personal affair... or that's what I thought at the time. But the whole thing now is about something concerning our people."

"I see it differently", Daothel interrupted. "This isn't about ethics or science. The four of us, and apparently three others we are yet to meet, have started a journey no one else is traveling — a journey which appears to be written in the patterns of Time."

13

A Star of Many Shades

"No, mother…" Soen replied.

Laidé and she were at her mother's house and had just finished reviewing the full report of the operation in the Sol System. In the report, three planets appeared to hold the key to decipher the happenings there — the third, the fourth and the fifth. She needed to be cautious. A complete picture of the situation still eluded her.

"No," she repeated, "that third planet isn't an Aïdin Planet. I disagree with Issën Althesal's conjecture. If we were to apply her argument to that planet, we may as well say Thel is an Aïdin Planet. We all know it isn't. Even the Thelians in all their primacy, and with all they could gain from it, discourage this idea."

Laidé, widening his eyes upon hearing her words, amused her once again. He still wasn't used to her plain speaking. The two of them had arrived to Esdänl the evening before, and she regretted not having spent more time on his native world, Lyaty. Presenting the archeological artifacts of Lughai to the leaders of his people gave her a unique insight into the Nauthians. But her mother's letter had been on her mind the entire trip.

They sat on a terrace overlooking the woods Soen used to explore when she had been younger. The air in Llën was crisp as she remembered it, and the morning fog hadn't yet risen above the horizon in that colossal aerial city. She felt invigorated, and happy to be back. She had hoped to see her father, but he was working on a remote world of the Cealaïs Galaxy [Triangulum Galaxy], designing the trans-planetary relations building complex for a new member of the Union. Her mother had canceled all appointments that day to meet with the two of them.

"Then, daughter, tell me what you expect an Aïdin Planet to look like", the Chancellor replied while pouring fruit juice into Laidé's glass and waving her other hand to tell him not to feel embarrassed. "I have asked this same question to Issën Althesal."

"And what did she say?" Soen asked.

Her mother stopped and regarded her with a subtle frown, letting her know that she was avoiding to answer, then replied, "That those were just comments and not conclusions, which she had included in case the High Council decides to send the findings to other scientists for further analysis. However, she and her team don't really know. She told me it was something they felt in their hearts."

"That's a Wanderer's answer!" Laidé blurted. His mouth twitched, and Soen felt certain he fought a laugh at her expense.

"Yes, it is." She grinned back at him. What she didn't say was that there was another answer which could, perhaps, provide an empirical approach to identify those planets.

In her 'Wandering' and study of legends, oral traditions and ancient records, the Aïdin Planets were often described as "outsiders" to normal Space. Following this thread of research, in a remote star system believed to have harbored one of these planets, she had found a background light-signature in interplanetary space different from the natural background spectrum of light frequencies. She had thought it was worthy of investigation and was going to test her theory in other systems after helping the people from Lughai. But her mother's letter had thrown her plans into disarray — by an uncanny synchronicity, it was in the Sol System where she had planned to test her theory next. Now she was unsure of her following move.

"Could we review now the sensory stream transmitted by the probe sent to that planet?" she asked.

Her mother walked to her desk, under a canopy in a corner of the spacious terrace, and came back with a recording sphere. Laidé was already standing, waiting to assist her.

"I'll do it, Chancellor."

With the small crystal sphere in the palm of his hand, he whispered the key word upon it and let it float in the midst of them. A spherical light-field sprang up, showing the Sol System in detail. He then said the words, "Planet Three", and the three of them became immersed in the multi-sensory transmission of the probe sent to that world.

Soen felt the joy of gliding with the probe along a landscape that was beauty itself, but she didn't allow the feeling to distract her. She observed with intent every shadow and movement in the visuals, and listened for certain sounds. As a trained Wanderer, she could sense and see minute signs and indications of processes which only Rangers could also detect — the legends told that Nature on Aïdin Planets was unlike those found in any other world, and she looked for evidence of that. When the recording finished playing, she didn't know if to feel relieved or disappointed — the planet refused to unveil its secret! Perhaps the malfunctioning of the probe explained the absence of any unusual signs. Or, perhaps it was one of those elements of the legends product of the imagination of bards and storytellers.

She next asked her mother about the difficulties the probe had encountered, and how the Thelian science team had interpreted them. They talked about this, including the conclusions of the Rangers on this matter. Ultimately, no one could say what had caused the probe to malfunction and to disappear.

"Mother, what are you going to do with this information? Are you going to share it with the other Councilors?"

"Eventually… but, first, I want to have a clear idea of what is happening on that planet. There is enough posturing now among some of them, and I don't want this finding to be mixed with the investigation of the catastrophe on the fourth planet."

"Chancellor," Laidé interjected, "with all due respect, it may be wise to consider everything happening in the Sol System as only one issue. We haven't confirmed The Others have a presence on that third planet but must assume they do. It would be atypical if they haven't already explored and mapped the entire system to assess their claim."

"That's what puzzles me." The Chancellor frowned. "They haven't claimed the system. The Armistice Inspectorate hasn't received any official notice. Moreover, Marshal Mhali, upon his return from Sol, ordered a review of the communications of The Others intercepted by us in the past one thousand years, and no mention is made of the Sol System, or of its planets, in any of them. His Rangers reviewed the communications even further back in time; they obtained the same result. Why would they announce with fanfare their claim on other star systems, and not do so with this one?"

"All appearances tell us they already have a claim on the fifth planet," Laidé replied, "and perhaps they will file the claim soon." Then, pursing his lips he added, "Although, it would be the first time they incorporate a planet into one of their dominions and not the entire system."

Soen nodded slowly. On their way back from Lyaty, she and Laidé had studied and discussed Marshal Mhali's report of his experience on the fifth planet. One thing the two of them couldn't understand was The Others having an alliance with that planet's leadership. Something didn't fit. The Others' tactics were never to establish alliances but to subjugate. Why to start now? What was different? The Overlords knew for sure they were risking being irreversibly crippled by the Union if they were found violating the Armistice by interfering in any way on a Human world.

"It could be that they don't want to claim that fifth planet either…" Soen caught herself voicing an idea that had just come to her mind. She hadn't seen the situation in that light before, but it now made sense. In a fraction of a moment all the data of the survey of the Sol System, and all she knew of it, fell into place. There were some missing pieces in the picture, but her inner sense told her it had to be the only explanation.

Her mother and Laidé gaped at her. With her eyes, her mother demanded a thorough explanation for her statement. With his face, Laidé was telling her, 'That's the most outlandish idea I ever heard. The Others never simply visit planets; they take possession of them!'

Ignoring their reactions, she continued, "Could it be that Marshal Mhali misread his experience on that planet? After all, the information given by two isolated youngsters can't reveal everything about the presence of The Others there… Could it be that something else is happening there that has drawn the attention of one of the Overlords and made them behave uncharacteristically? All we know is the government of that planet and The Others have an arrangement of some sort, and that Mal'ek's civilization has an unusual social order and a suicidal science. Yet, anomalies abound in the Sol System."

She realized she was giving reasons to her mother to send the Rangers back to the Sol System, which was something she wanted to avoid. However, the detailed reports of the Rangers and of Issën Althesal had given her a more complete picture of the system: its mystery appeared to be darker than what she had thought at first.

Her mother regarded her with her penetrating eyes for a long moment, and Soen knew her questions had given her mother the answers she was looking for. Next, without saying a word, her mother rose and strode towards the interior of the house.

"Soen, you know something you don't wish us to know", Laidé hastened to say to her. "Even I can sense it. I respect your silence. You must have a reason. I hope, however, you realize this affair is so unusual that we cannot entirely rely on established procedures and protocols. One false move could mean the end the Armistice and a new cycle of conflict with The Others; and that's just for a start."

Soen remained silent but couldn't suppress a shudder. Laidé had just articulated what she had been trying to ignore. Had she become attached to the knowledge she possessed and to her discoveries, even though 'detachment' was the Wanderers' only philosophy? When she became a Wanderer, she had rejected the secretive behavior some of the Wanderers had embraced. Now she had become like them! Yet, why did she feel such a strong urge to protect the third planet of Sol from any intrusion? Was it because she sensed the power of Aïdin might be found there, and she doubted Galactic Humans were ready for it? — But now The Others were there. What was she going to do?

Her mother returned to the terrace a few moments later with a bearing that left no doubt she was the Chancellor of the Union. The only words she said to the two of them were: "I have invited Marshal Mhali to meet with us here, this afternoon. Lunch will be ready shortly." She then turned and entered the house again.

⚡

Soen hadn't met Marshal Mhali before. He wasn't what she had expected of one of the highest ranking officers in the Ranger Corps. He was about her age and with a presence that spoke of nobility and wisdom. At the same time he was friendly, relaxed and uncomplicated — she liked that. He had developed and mastered the higher faculties of Mind-Soul faster than anyone in the history of the Corps, and had ascended through their ranks with a speed that had astonished everyone. In spite of his young age, her mother had appointed him Marshal of the Islnom-1 of the Laïs Galaxy, where the heart of the Union, the Alcyone System, and its most important planet, Esdänl, was located.

Besides her father, Mhali and Laidé were her mother's most trusted advisors. And since his appointment as Marshal, Laidé and he had become good friends.

Soen connected with Mhali at first sight, as if they had already shared many experiences together. Her mother noticed this because Soen caught her a few times observing the three of them with the smugness of a proud mother.

Mhali listened to Soen's questions and analysis of the situation of the Sol System with great attention and without any attempt to defend his official report of his experience on the fifth planet. After she finished repeating what she had said in the morning to her mother and Laidé, Mhali addressed her with his rich voice:

"Your analysis reveals a knowledge of the Sol System, none of us who are seeking to decipher this affair possesses. I wonder the source of it! Wanderers love to be mysterious and are attracted to investigate the unusual, but in remote places. I never thought they could move so close to Alcyone without being detected by my Rangers!" He ended with the disarming expression of those from the Merope System.

Soen had known he was going to be more perceptive than her mother and Laidé. It didn't matter now. During lunch she had decided to share with them all she knew. She still wanted to protect that third planet, but she had come to realize that an unstoppable chain of events had been unleashed and the best chances to do so was to trust the three of them. She thus replied to him:

"Rangers and Wanderers are the two halves of the same whole, and we tend to think and act similarly. As you, we move frictionless through both the common and the uncommon pathways others use. It is the frictionless interaction with everyone and everything that unveils knowledge to us."

Mhali nodded with a pleased face and waited for her to continue. No thought communication passed between them, but Soen knew he understood her well. He expected that, next, she was going to tell them how she knew more of the Sol System.

Her mother and Laidé watched with interest the match between the two of them. Soen had already told them she had visited that system; although they didn't know yet what she had found there.

She began her story:

It was two years ago, after an arduous search and a lot of persuasion, that I met the boss of the Nostelat syndicate who had dealings with the Humans of the planet Yfel of Sol. Econost is his name—

"That scoundrel!" Mhali couldn't hide his disgust. "You visited his lair! I should have guessed he was behind all this! He is the most elusive and foxy of the Nostelat bosses. Few claim to have seen his face. I don't know how you did it, but your powers of persuasion must be extraordinary!"

Her mother shook her head in reproach but in a way that Soen knew she was in fact saying to her, "I would have done the same, daughter." Laidé's reaction was different. He looked genuinely scandalized at her.

She gave them all an innocent smile and continued:

Rumors had reached the Order of the Wanderers telling of mysterious happenings in the interplanetary spaces of the Sol System, and also warning sane explorers and travelers of going near that system. They too spoke of beings resembling Humans on some of its planets, yet so strange in their behavior and social order that those few who had interacted with them thought they weren't Humans at all but some aberrant, lesser race.

I was intrigued by the rumors and decided to find out more. Those Humans could provide new insights on the origin of Humans and, perhaps, throw a light on the paradox confronting all of us who study this subject — the fact that we have in our galaxies Humans who descend from higher beings, and Humans who evolve from the natural world.

Mhali nodded in silence.

The first step I took was to look for the source of the rumors, to ascertain their veracity. It was then when I obtained two new pieces of information which increased my curiosity even more.

First, I learned that all the Overlords of The Others, with the exception of one, whose identity still I don't know, wanted nothing to do with the Sol System — Why? I asked myself. Why would they abdicate their right to challenge, as is their custom, another Overlord who is exploring an unclaimed star system? I also discovered that all but one of the bosses of the Nostelat syndicates were afraid of approaching that system, and that he in fact was engaged in doing business there. At that point any doubt I had about visiting Sol vanished and went looking for the boss of this syndicate to ask for transport on one of his craft.

I wasn't expecting, however, the surprises were going to start during my first meeting with Econost.

"It would be my pleasure, Wanderer, to give you passage on our next craft to that system", he said to me in an uncharacteristic friendly voice as soon as I told him my request. "The crew is finishing preparations and should be departing in a few days."

No haggling! No curiosity about my reasons for going there! — I puzzled.

"You are kind, Econost. Since I don't want to be a burden to you or your enterprise, I can compensate you for your generosity."

"No need for that, Wanderer. Your presence is enough compensation for such a small favor."

"It isn't just me. I have some cargo with me... a gift from an acquaintance... an old and small hybrid solo-craft that I might use to explore the system while your people conduct their business."

"Don't need to be concerned about that either. I already know about your craft, and the crew has prepared room in a cargo bay for it."

Of course! I should have realized that before meeting with him, his network of spies had skulked around to discover my motives to see him. "May then the Light, Econost, make your ways smooth and abundant in that system!"

With a hint of a grin, he inclined his head.

Too easy — I then thought. *So the rumors are true. He is daring but also afraid of something, and he thinks I can protect his crew and craft if need be.*

I was about to rise from where I sat in front of his desk, thinking the interview had ended, when he said, "Your reputation, Wanderer, reaches many places; even my humble abode. I trust our business in that star system will remain... well... confidential... between us."

"Yes, Econost", I replied right away. "You can rest assured of it. We Wanderers take no sides."

My reply must have pleased him because he then leaned across his desk and whispered, "Between you and me, Wanderer — it hasn't been easy. Two craft I have lost in that system in the interplanetary anomalies it harbors, but the returns from my dealings there have been most favorable. There is a bounty of iron ore on the fourth planet — *Yfel* its inhabitants call it — that could rise my standing to the top among my people." He salivated at the thought of it. "I just need time. More time. If you or others of your Order require transport to that system, my craft are all available for you to use." He regarded me and added as if granting me a great token of wisdom, "Avoid the third and the fifth planets, Wanderer. They are of the darkness!"

With that warning I left his office that day. I kept my part of the deal and he his. We departed five days later with my craft stowed in one of the cargo bays. Econost had ordered his engineers to check each of its systems and to supply it for a thirty-day exploration. They even installed a direct Nostelat com-link with his craft — "Just in case, Wanderer... Just in case", he said to me before we departed. His crew was going directly to the planet Yfel, and I was going to visit as much of the system as I could manage in that short time.

The trip there was circuitous, avoiding standard routes, yet uneventful. So was entering the system. I decided to start my exploration with the star, followed by the planet on its first orbital harmonic, which at that time was on the same side of Sol as Yfel. After, I was going to make my way, one planet at a time, to the furthest planet. The Nostelat craft was going to wait for me outside the ös-sphere of the system once their dealings were finished.

I expected Sol to be an arrhythmic star — that would have explained some of the rumors — but no. The star is magnificent, with a song and light so beautiful and grandiose that my whole being felt expanded as I approached it.

After the star, a quick survey told me the first planet had nothing of importance to explore — a rocky terrain and strong light-fields; nothing unexpected for its position close to Sol.

It was in the ös-sphere of the second planet where I found the first anomaly. An echo of a long-gone Humanity sounded throughout it. The echo didn't sing of their death but of their ascension to higher light-fields beyond the physical. That finding alone, although it didn't explain the rumors, would have been enough to justify my exploration of that system. For long Wanderers have theorized that an entire Humanity could refine their bodies' light-fields to the point they could free themselves from Space, all of them together; although, evidence of this had never been found... until that moment.

The planet I next visited on the same side of the system was the fourth — Yfel. I explored it away from the area where the Nostelat crew was extracting the ore. Nothing, though, had prepared me for that civilization! Three days moving invisible to its Human inhabitants was all I could withstand. They were segregated in six major clans, each with lesser sub-clans, in a system of a cruel, life-or-death competition for individuals to ascend in status. Among the clans, war was their way — a military-religious war of intolerance to each other's beliefs and views, and with the purpose of destroying the other. The saddest part of all was that the beliefs and views of all the clans were based on an unnatural philosophy built upon a misperception of themselves and the Universe.

I couldn't accept, however, that the darkness of their ways was all born from their own Human heart — for Humans they were, proud and intelligent. Their bodies stood tall and slender, and moved with great agility. They were strikingly handsome, with deep black eyes, through which the light of determination shone. This was accentuated by their copper-red skin, which they adorned with geometric black drawings that marked them as members of a particular belief clan. Thus—

"What is the matter, mother?" Her mother had turned to look at Marshal Mhali with a face of recognition, which Mhali had returned with an Aha! expression.

"Finish your story first", her mother replied to her.

Looking at Laidé, who shrugged, she continued:

To me something more had to explain what was happening on Yfel. Thus, before leaving orbit, I searched for clues that could explain its inhabitants' psychology. I did find them. Yet, what I found is still a mystery to me: the core of their planet was ill! Threads of a dark light had contaminated the normal light encodings in it, as well as the core's energy links with the bio-sphere and with Sol. As a result, those Humans were handicapped to absorb the beneficial energies of their star and of their planet's core. But, what could explain such an illness in the core? It was unnatural in the extreme. We know darkness always retreats in the presence of light. And we also know that the core of planets where Humans and Amethen are born, is made of Light in its purest and fieriest essence. What was then the source of that darkness in Yfel? Alas, the only explanation that came to me was that Yfel was a battleground between a more primordial Light and a more primordial Darkness, whose existence my Order has theorized. What else could explain that illness?

Once more Soen noticed a reaction in her mother, but this time she continued with her story.

More recently, while I was on the planet Orphes with the delegation of Lughai, when the news reached me telling the Humanity of Yfel had destroyed itself, I became uneasy. Still I am — not about the fate of the mind-souls of that Humanity since the Universe will give them another opportunity, but by the question: *In the end, which of the two proved to be more powerful, the Light or the Darkness?*

She paused for a moment to compose herself. Every time she thought of that, it distressed her.

I had prepared myself for even worst findings when, next, I arrived to the sixth planet, a gas giant with four large moons and dozens of small ones — the largest of the planets in that system. Yet, to my surprise, that planet's music is a symphony of harmonies, pleasant and nurturing, and in its light-fields I sensed the evolving seeds of new and future bio-spheres.

When I left that planet, it was with the firm conviction that something unknown to our science and philosophy had to be the cause of the contrasting evolution of the planets of Sol. But what could that be? And, why that star system in particular? What is different or special about it? — The answers to these questions still elude me.

By then I had been in the system for nine days, and the nearest planet was on the other side of Sol. I directed my craft to it. It was the third closest to the star. As a turquoise jewel, inviting and seductive, it beckoned to me. But Econost's warning was in my mind, and I approached it with caution.

He was right. A sense of uneasiness gripped my heart as I came close. I felt I was trespassing on forbidden grounds and that it was better to leave immediately. But I also felt something oddly luring about that planet, personally. Thus, I decided to continue my approach with a greater caution, at a low speed and towards a large continental land that I saw on the dayward side of the planet. Then, time passed and I noticed my craft wasn't advancing, at all, in spite that every one of its systems and my inner senses were telling me we were indeed moving. Something was holding me away from the planet in the most strange way, as if I had entered a layer of Space with different laws. I checked the systems of the craft for malfunctions, yet every one of them worked fine. Afterwards, I attempted my approach through the nodal points of the planet's ös-sphere, including the poles. Every attempt had the same result.

During these attempts I witnessed the planet make three full rotations, while the instruments of my craft showed that my attempts had lasted only for less than one of its days. This observation confirmed to me that the planet was inside an anomaly. With reluctance, then, I was about to desist my efforts and visit the next closest one, the fifth, when on impulse I made one last try.

At that moment the large continental land was beginning to be shrouded by the night, and I directed my craft towards the day/night transition because it was closest. Astonishingly, nothing stopped the craft this time! I couldn't believe it. My eyes and the instruments showed that, indeed, I was approaching the planet's surface. My mind sought for an explanation. Why hadn't my approach worked in the previous attempts? Why that randomness? Was the planet surrounded by a variable anomaly?

I was engrossed in these questions when my craft suddenly accelerated towards the planet, out of control. The next moment it began to level up. Right then, it was pushed away from the planet, at an odd angle, at a great speed. Alarms began to sound in the cabin, telling me the hull was under too much stress. I attempted to slow down but of no avail — the main power drive was unresponsive. At some point, the automatic systems took over and the old emergency photon-driven engine brought the craft to a halt.

Although shaken, I immediately inspected the condition of the craft. The hull had held its integrity, but the photon-driven engine had exhausted itself and the main drive system was dead — its live-crystals had lost their cohesiveness and had vanished. Most other systems were operational, however. Then, when I was figuring out where I was, I discovered the greatest surprise of all — if the communication beacon of my craft was correct — which later I confirmed it was — ten standard galactic days had elapsed since my attempt to approach that third planet! Whatever force had ejected my craft from the planet, not only had sent it beyond the seventh orbital harmonic of the system, but had also propelled it into the future!

It took me some time to recover and to digest what had happened. The craft had approached the planet at the right angle of entrance and right speed to avoid the slingshot effect. Every maneuver had followed standard procedures. I had to conclude then that the cause of the incident had to be something in or on the planet.

Afterwards, any fix to the photon-driven engine I could imagine, I tried. Eventually I resigned myself that I was adrift, with only emergency power to maneuver. I then decided to use the com-link to call the Nostelat crew. They hadn't finished extracting the ore on Yfel, and I had to wait for them for eight more galactic standard days.

I used my time to study the interplanetary light-fields with my expanded perception and the working sensors of the craft. Curiously enough, the interplanetary light-fields near the third planet were unreadable, as if the planet was surrounded by a null-field of sorts. In contrast, those fields near to and in between the other planets, I could detect without any difficulty. In them I discovered that not just the planet Yfel but a few other regions of the system were processing the radiations of Sol with difficulty.

I was perplexed with these findings. To my knowledge, nothing in our science but something undiscovered could explain them. In my mind too, I reviewed all I knew about the Aïdin Planets of old and about the Blight of the Ancients. In a few legends it is told that the Blight affected only those star systems near the location of Aïdin Planets — Was the third planet of Sol an Aïdin Planet? Could all the anomalies of the system be explained by the reappearance of the Blight?

Laidé chose that moment to ask her, "You said to us earlier today that you don't think that planet is an Aïdin Planet. What changed your view of it, afterwards?"

"I think those anomalies in the Sol System have another explanation. Later, after my trip there, while studying the data I had collected, I discovered that the first planet does have an anomaly after all. The concentration of fifth-harmonic light around it is significantly higher than what is expected for its size and in the absence of a Humanity or of any other sentient race. This finding told me that Sol was responsible for that. That its output of fifth-harmonic light is higher to compensate for something happening in the system. What the nature of that is, I don't know. I do know, however, no one of the legends describe any of those anomalies."

No one spoke for a time. She knew it was an unusual story which had taken her two years to assimilate — and still she had questions. She was, however, curious about her mother's reaction, and Mhali's, when she had described the Humans of Yfel. Thus, she asked her the reason for it. Her mother answered that they wanted her help with something and, that for that, they needed to travel to the planet Lös. She had then added:

"You may help solve an enigma entrusted to the Rangers, which they haven't been able to penetrate. However, there is no need to talk about that now."

Soen questioned Laidé with her eyes.

"I know nothing of this", he whispered to her.

After this interchange they spent the rest of the afternoon considering the information they had in an attempt to understand the situation of the

Sol System. At some point it became plain to Soen something else was in her mother's mind.

"Mother, I told you all I know. What about you? Are you telling us all you know?"

"It's something which may not be related to this affair. It happened long ago and too faraway from the Sol System." Then her mother told them about her meeting with Councilors Ulhloom and Thaël, during which Ulhloom had mentioned an 'Ancient Darkness', and that at the end of that meeting, the only course of action they saw appropriate was to find more information on that Ancient Darkness. So far they hadn't found any.

"Your daughter's account of her findings in the Sol System, Chancellor," Mhali said after her mother finished, "adds weight to Councilor Ulhloom's view that we shouldn't blame The Others for the destruction of the Resistance's hideaway on Mal'ek. It may also explain the tragedy on Yfel." Pausing for a moment, he next added, "Everything in this affair is atypical, and the only thing we can do now is to remain vigilant. Very vigilant!"

Her mother nodded, so did Laidé.

"I have the feeling", her mother said while rising to end the discussion, "that the third planet holds the key to deciphering the whole mystery of Sol, and perhaps clues as to The Others' uncharacteristic behavior."

"You're thinking of sending the Rangers there, mother. Aren't you?" Then without waiting for her answer, she added, "I'm going with them!"

"A mission to that planet will raise a lot of eyebrows in the High Council", Laidé said before the Chancellor answered. "Most Councilors will object chasing down legends when the problem is with The Others on the fifth planet."

"We could send Rangers to both the fifth and third planets… quietly…" Mhali said with an innocent grin, "as part of the Corps routine of intelligence gathering; in that way we won't need approval from the High Council."

Her mother regarded him for a time, then sighed and addressed the three of them. "No, let's follow normal protocols. I want the smallest possible party of Rangers to travel to the fifth planet to find out more information as to the reason The Others are there — I will inform the other Councilors of this mission; they will understand it. I also want the Rangers to begin a stealth, continuous observation of the Sol System without entering it — we must collect all the information possible, including analysis of the characteristics of Space, inside and in the neighborhood of that system. I will present this operation to the other Councilors as a standard procedure in view of the circumstances and events. Meanwhile, I want you two, Mhali and Laidé, to travel to the planet Thel to meet with Issën Althesal and her team."

With pleading eyes she next addressed Soen. "I hope, daughter, you will accompany them. Issën Althesal and her team aren't your common Thelians. The knowledge and insights you possess will be invaluable." Looking at them all, she added, "I want you, with the Thelian team, to find a way to obtain more information on that third planet, without risking anyone's life and without starting a serious confrontation with The Others."

Soen nodded. Her experience dealing with Thelian Humans was minimal. It would be an interesting experience to visit their world for the first time.

"Tomorrow morning, however," her mother added, "we will travel, together, to Lös — you too Laidé. We have some guests with us who may provide some light on this affair."

14

The Crusade of Yfel

Planet Lös, Alcyone System

Laidé seldom visited the planet Lös, even though it was located next door to Esdänl. For its uniqueness, it housed the Ranger Corps training academies. Mountainous regions contrasted sharply with vast tundras, and deserts with rain forests and vast wetlands. But more peculiar was the planet's ös-sphere. Its fundamental light-field frequency shifted at random with the seasons, and regionally, between the second and the fourth ös light-fields of its star. These irregular variations in the electro-magnetic fields and light frequencies of the planet created an ideal setting for training new generations of Rangers, teaching their minds and bodies to quickly adapt to conditions they would find on a multitude of other worlds.

Yet, not all on Lös was about the training of Rangers. The Corps also had on that planet a division dedicated solely to the healing of illnesses caused by the undue exposure to the radiations of Space. It was to the Healing Halls of the Corps where the Chancellor and Marshal Mhali took him and Soen that morning.

During the short trip from Esdänl to Lös, Mhali had told Soen and him that on the same day when the Corps received the news about the tragedy on Yfel, a party of independent explorers had handed over to the Corps a Human woman and a boy, whom they had found adrift in interplanetary space. According to the explorers, the pair had been rescued in the vicinity of a planet of the Eridan System, drifting on a crudely built craft that could barely withstand the medium of Space. The woman and the boy had been unconscious and had severe radiation damage when they had been received by the healers. Now they were fully recovered in their bodies, but the healers wondered if their minds and psyches were also damaged. They were both withdrawn and refused to talk or to interact with anyone but themselves, and their behavior was unlike anyone they had knowledge of.

"Since the peoples of the only inhabited world in the Eridan System aren't Human," Mhali continued, "the healers suspected the explorers weren't telling the truth—"

"Treasure hunters!" Soen blurted. "They always disguise themselves as trade explorers and never reveal where they are coming from or where they are going to. Not even with Wanderers are they truthful."

"That's what the healers suspected", Mhali replied. "However, the woman and the child have body features that haven't been observed in the known worlds, and communication with the pair has been unsuccessful. Thus, we have been unable to discover their planet of origin."

"And their craft," Laidé asked, "did the Rangers go looking for it?"

"The explorers' account was that the craft was already disintegrating when they rescued them. A search party sent by us to that star system found no debris at all, confirming they weren't telling the truth."

⚡

"Their reaction is the same every time one of us approaches them", the healer told Laidé and Soen. "Although we have observed that with those of us who don't have a fair skin, their reaction is more relaxed — still cautious but not aggressive."

Laidé observed the pair. The last ones of their people — Soen had confirmed they were natives of the planet Yfel of the Sol System. The woman was approaching her middle years, while the boy was about to enter adolescence. They both stood in the center of a garden contiguous to the rooms assigned to them. Their stance indicated they were ready to fight. They held their gaze steady on the three of them. Both had refined bodies, tall and muscular, with black, long hair loosely braided. The woman had elaborated black drawings on her face, arms and legs that stood out on her tawny skin. The boy also had them, but different and of a simpler design.

"They are made of a crude iron dye, injected into the dermis, and we have observed the two value them dearly." The healer had explained.

"Do they speak at all?" Laidé felt the contempt in the woman's eyes as he and Soen spoke with the healer. Her defiant stance wasn't to protect the boy, but that of a predator ready to pounce upon a quarry. Yet, he was sure the hostility wasn't directed to him or to the healer, but to Soen.

"They converse between themselves only when they think they are alone."

"Have you attempted to communicate with their minds?" Soen asked.

"Yes, Wanderer. However, their emotions overrun their minds at all times, and in the few moments during which they appear to be mentally receptive, our mind contact elicits in them such a strong fearful reaction that we desisted from this approach. What's more — and you may too notice this, Wanderer, if you tune in to the thoughts they broadcast — they don't construct thoughts as most sentient races do. There is mind-light in them but heavily weaved with emotions in undecipherable patterns."

Laidé knew, from the experiences of his people with other civilizations, that sentient beings still confined to planetary development, and with no exposure to light-fields of Mind other than the one of their planet, usually rejected the idea of mind-to-mind communication and interpreted it through superstition. He then concluded that there was only one course of action to reach them.

"Do you have any recordings of their conversations?" he asked the healer.

"Yes, Advisor. All of them."

Next, Laidé spent the entire morning and part of the afternoon studying those recordings while Soen used her skills as a Wanderer to attempt communication with the pair. The Chancellor and Mhali had left them alone upon arriving and worked in a building nearby on operational matters of the Corps.

Soen hadn't been alone with the woman and the boy for long when she came looking for him. "I give up", she said with a grim expression. "Their hostility towards me is puzzling! All I gather is that their relationship isn't the one of a mother and her child. Yet it isn't either any of those I observed on their planet."

He nodded at her distractedly, and she sat down in silence, next to him, to follow his study of the recordings. After a while she left again, telling him she was going to visit other patients in the Healing Halls to give them some company.

At first, the language in the recordings baffled Laidé. It was syncopated and with many repeating syllabic sounds. However, by observing their gestures and facial expressions as the woman and the boy spoke to each other, he discovered their language was a mix of emotions given expressions as vocal sounds, and all having as a point of reference the speaker — as if their conversations were a stream of short phrases during which each participant kept saying, "I feel this about this…" — "I feel this about that…" — "You listen to what I feel…" — "I am listening to what you feel…" and so on.

By mid afternoon, satisfied his pronunciation matched that of the words he heard on the recordings, Laidé was ready to attempt communication with the woman and the boy. He didn't feel threatened by them and convinced the healers to leave him alone with the two. He knew, nonetheless, Rangers would be monitoring him close by.

On the recordings he had noticed that in all instances the woman sat at a lower level, as if the boy were of a higher rank in their social structure, yet the boy also listened to the woman with full attention and respect when she addressed him — which meant she was of a certain standing and of importance to him. These observations prompted Laidé to enter the garden where they spent most of their days, and to approach them, with a submissive attitude, then to sit on the ground, lower than the two.

As before, and for a reason he couldn't discern, they didn't regard him with aggression, although they had risen to an alert pose as soon as he had entered — *Is it the color of my skin as the healers think?* Thus, ignoring how awkward he felt with the pair towering over him while he sat, five paces away from them, he proceeded with his plan.

He too had observed water played a role in establishing or acknowledging the ranking order. The woman always presented water to the boy whenever she wanted to speak to him, but the boy never did so — *Their planet must have been a dry world,* he had theorized when he noticed this behavior on the recordings.

Thus, next, Laidé offered to the woman a bowl with water he had brought with him.

The boy immediately scoffed at him. For her part, the woman regarded him with a curious face, yet she made no attempt to accept the water.

Laidé was ready for this and said to her, "Tzalkal" — that was the name the boy appeared to use to address her.

Now it was the boy who showed surprise, while the woman frowned at him.

Not ready to give up, Laidé repeated his gesture of offering her the water and calling her 'Tzalkal' at the same time — he didn't know what the name meant but suspected it was a title.

Once more the woman ignored the water and his call.

A third time couldn't hurt. Almost unconscious of his gesture, he bowed his head and looked to the ground when offering the water and saying the word 'Tzalkal'. When he rose his eyes, the woman's face had relaxed and had an extended hand to accept the water. This time the boy just studied him with his penetrating dark eyes.

Thus began four long days during which he established communication with "the Tzal" and "the Tzalkal" — the clan chief and the priestess of a first rank clan of the planet Yfel — a time during which he became an 'accepted' of the clan but not 'blood' of the clan. The Tzalkal was the only one who spoke to him during their meetings. The boy followed their conversations with great interest, and at times, it was apparent to Laidé he too wanted to speak to him, though his rank prevented him from doing so. By the second day the boy had begun to smile, even laugh when Laidé made mistakes in his choice of words and expressions.

One thing was clear to him from the start: the two were starving for communicating with others and for answers to their situation; however, their conditioning culture kept them in a prison of silence and isolation.

It was on the fourth day when Laidé could penetrate the emotional wall that kept the Tzalkal silent every time he asked them about the catastrophe on their planet. A cloud of sorrow enveloped the woman, and she turned away from him. The boy too was affected, but his reaction was anger.

That day he had brought them their breakfast and was sitting on the ground eating with them by the small water fall at one corner of the garden, which they so much enjoyed. When they finished, he asked them the question once more. This time the boy immediately started speaking to the Tzalkal very fast, and he couldn't follow what they were saying. He could see, however, the boy was talking to her as the Tzal and using his authority on her. When their interchange ended, she stood up and took a step towards Laidé with a look of fury that made him recoil — he truly thought she was going to attack him! But before he could do or say anything, she cried aloud:

"The Fire of Yfel they deserve! — Specters from the abyss! — They brought death to Yfel!"

She had looked into the distance when she shouted those words. Now she regarded him. She seemed to be making an effort to regain her composure. The boy showed no reaction at all at her outburst. Then, after a deep sigh, she sat again in silence.

Laidé thought at that point that he had failed in his attempts to learn the fate of their people. He couldn't remain with them for much longer. He needed to return to his duties on Esdänl.

In the silence, however, the boy and the woman studied him with intent. Eventually the boy placed his right hand on the Tzalkal's shoulder, and she nodded. Turning towards him, the Tzalkal began to speak, slowly and making sure he understood. It was later when Laidé realized they had been measuring him up to assess if he was worthy of the revelation they were about to share with him — the Truth of Yfel.

Well until the evening the Tzalkal spoke, pausing to answer his questions when he couldn't follow their language expressions or the thread of the story. The boy listened with great attention to her, as if he was too listening to the story for the first time. When she finished, she and the boy appeared to be more relaxed and emotionally close to him.

And here is the story Laidé told afterwards to the Chancellor, Mhali and Soen — the story he pieced together from the Tzalkal's account of the fate of the planet Yfel:

> The Tzal and the Tzalkal are 'the man leader' and 'the woman leader' of the Fourth Clan of Yfel — the Tzalmacke Clan. Their Clan was the main clan among many for their skill in designing and manufacturing 'instruments of subjugation' to their Deity, whose name was also Yfel. In fact, the planet was named after their Deity, for the planet was the countenance the One Deity showed to Its followers.
>
> Since times immemorial all the peoples of Yfel were dedicated to their Deity in what they called "the Crusade for the Truth of Yfel" — and it was for this Crusade that the Fourth Clan built instruments of subjugation. In fact, all knowledge, all sciences and all creations in all the Clans were dedicated to it — that is, to make the Truth of Yfel prevail over everyone and in every land.
>
> No one of their people could remember how they had known of Yfel for the first time. Some said Yfel had come from the starry heavens to teach them the Truth. Others believed Yfel had directly spoken to the ears of the early inhabitants of the planet because they had been born devoid of the Truth — infidels. Still others knew, and the Fourth Clan so believed, Yfel had created all the peoples with the Truth already seeded in their hearts. On one thing they all agreed, however — the Truth of Yfel was never to be written or depicted on any material form, nor was Yfel Itself or Its name; only through the oral word could the Truth be communicated, and only to those who had proven their worth.
>
> Also since times immemorial, even though they all believed in the same Truth, each of the Clans claimed they were the only true bearer of the Truth of Yfel, and each regarded the other Clans as infidels, as untruthful to Yfel, and as those who needed to be subjugated — and that was what the Crusade was all about; that was what

their entire life was about.

Thus, throughout their history, clan after clan had appeared and had lasted for a while, to end being subjugated by other clans whose strength and military superiority made them claim they were the sole bearers of the Truth of Yfel. All the peoples of Yfel had always accepted that fact — that having military superiority meant Yfel was blessing them for being truer to the Truth than others.

Since no one was killed in the Crusade but subjugated, the Crusade had thus created a ceaseless intermixing of the peoples and a blending of knowledge and skills that made of all of them stronger as time went by.

Fifteen generations back, however, the Crusade came to an abrupt halt when it was challenged by severe changes in the seasons of the planet. In the span of one generation the planet abandoned its normal weather patterns and launched a fight against the peoples themselves — against all the Clans and not just the infidels. Next, the rains became scarce, and an unending thirst took hold of all the lands.

At first no one could understand why Yfel was testing all Its peoples in that manner. But after a time some of the Clans accused the others of being responsible for the war the planet had declared on the Crusade, and that the reason was their wickedness and their distortion of the Truth of Yfel. These accusations became more violent as the drought deepened and eventually led some of the Clans to conclude, and all the others followed soon after, that the Crusade for the Truth of Yfel could no longer be that of subjugating the infidels but that of purging the planet from them.

This change of objective became a major turning point in their history. At that time there were thirty-six major Clans, and the violent clashes that ensued reduced their numbers to six major Clans in the span of eight generations. Then, the fight leveled off because each of the surviving Clans developed the means to protect their cities and lands with energy shields, making thus ineffective the powerful light-rays and missiles each had used until then against the others.

The lack of rains, however, carried on the devastation the purge had inflicted, and the numbers of the peoples of the Clans continued decreasing as many perished of starvation and disease. The new objective of the Crusade also left most survivors exhausted in their hearts of the killing. Thus, in the last five generations direct physical confrontation between the Clans attracted few. Nonetheless, the Truth still had to be disputed and thus, of the six Clans left, only the Fourth and the Sixth continued quarreling for which of them was superior in holding the Truth of Yfel.

At that point, although the Crusade had been reduced to sporadic clashes between the Clans and to verbal animosity, all dedicated their efforts to be inventive in new ways to destroy the infidels without exposing their now-fewer people to the risk of death. This led to the development of more sophisticated and subtle instruments of destruction. Undetectable poisons for the air and the waters, and diseases for the body and the crops were the beginning of this new phase of the Crusade. But the Clans also became better at protecting their lands and cities from any incursion, and these new instruments of destruction did little damage.

This balanced hostile behavior lasted for a while, until more recently when the Sixth Clan developed instruments of destruction aimed to sever in the infidels the connection between their souls and Yfel Itself — "so that they would suffer as Truth-less wreckages, and for eternity, the pain of their wickedness." Those who were thus targeted with these new instruments became mad of mind and sick of body, and languished for many days until death claimed them. These new instruments of the Sixth Clan used sounds over large distances whose science principles and technology were unknown to the other Clans.

When the others Clans realized what was happening, the Tzal and the Tzalkal of the Fourth Clan knew then the Sixth Clan had renounced, forever, the right and dignity they once had to claim they were bearers of the Truth of Yfel — they had become empty; they had become what they attempted to do to others: Truth-less. The reason was that, in the ageless long Crusade, all Clans accepted that the plans and instruments of subjugation a Clan developed were to be done in such an open way that, eventually, through their spies the other clans would know of them and have time to prepare.

But these new instruments of destruction were unstoppable, and the other Clans knew not what to do to protect their peoples. Thus, the father of the current Tzal saw only one choice to protect the Fourth Clan — to contact the bloodless and soul-less creatures who were helping the Sixth Clan develop those unholy instruments, and to trick them into giving to the Fourth Clan the same instruments they were giving to the Sixth Clan.

Those creatures had come from the stars in powerful 'instruments of flight' different from those the Clans had developed in all their history. In their bodies those creatures resembled the peoples of Yfel, with two differences: their skin was pale and their hair was fair, revealing thus they had no true blood and no soul... revealing they were less than infidels... specters of the depths. Besides, they were tricksy and without honor, and all they wanted was the iron ore of their planet — the foundation of their civilization.

These were the type of creatures the Tzal chose to deal with in his sacrifice to save the Crusade. The Tzalkal herself advised him during those dealings, and thus the Fourth Clan avoided to be defiled by the soul-less ones, as the leaders of the Sixth Clan had been defiled. From these creatures — who called themselves *Nost'lt* — the Fourth Clan obtained knowledge and instruments to perfect their defenses against the Sixth Clan in exchange for a few of the secrets their Clan had developed to transform iron into a powerful emitter of light rays.

This situation worked well for the Fourth Clan because the unholy instruments of the Sixth Clan became ineffective. And soon after, through their spies inside the Fourth Clan, the rest of the Clans also gained access to this knowledge. Thus, with this the father of the Tzal achieved what he had wanted: to level the military strength of all the Clans to protect the Crusade.

But the wickedness of the Sixth Clan ran much deeper than what the father of the Tzal had first thought. His network of 'eyes' and 'ears' soon discovered that the real plan of the Sixth Clan was other, that the use of unholy instruments was just a start. The leaders of the Sixth Clan were preparing to take all their people to the sky in instruments of flight, and from there they were going to unleash upon the planet a new weapon to destroy all the other Clans at once. After accomplishing this, they were going to return and be the sole bearers of the Truth of Yfel. Such was their wickedness that they also knew they were going to destroy all plant and animal life, and thus their preparations included taking with them the minute seeds of life that would make possible for them to restore many species.

This treachery of the Sixth Clan, not only against the other Clans but against the countenance of Yfel, the planet, was soon confirmed by the spies of the other Clans.

No one knew what to do with that latest news, yet something had to be done. Thus, the Tzal, father of the Tzal, did the unthinkable. He called the other four Clans to join him to stop the Sixth Clan. Three accepted his call while one rejected it, and the Second, the Fourth and the Fifth Clans used all their weapons together against the Sixth Clan. Some damage they did but not enough, and the Sixth Clan retaliated with great force. But this was the new form of the Crusade, and the Fourth and the Fifth Clan held their ground because Yfel so wanted, while the First, the Second and the Third suffered great losses and became no more.

The Sixth Clan, however, remained strong and continued with their plans.

At that point the Tzal of the Fourth Clan and the Nzal of the Fifth Clan didn't know what more to do. Yet, they had found their strength together and sought to use it. Thus, to a joint meeting they decided to call their advisors. It was then when, after much debate, the decision was made to protect the Truth of Yfel in the only possible way left: to build instruments of flight to take to the sky above the planet as many of their peoples as they could, to wait there until the Sixth Clan would exhaust their wickedness. They reasoned that the Sixth Clan couldn't remain in the sky forever, and the Fourth and Fifth were going to prepare to remain longer than them.

Thus with great zeal, and fast, the peoples of both Clans worked together to prepare themselves to live in the sky, since no one knew when the Sixth Clan was going to be ready to depart and launch their weapon.

Seven seasons passed and the preparations of the Fourth and the Fifth Clans came to an end. They were ready to take all their peoples and to bring also the minute seeds of life of great many species to restore the planet, if it was needed. They too had prepared for any attack the Sixth Clan might attempt while they orbited their planet.

Thus, it came to pass that the Fourth and the Fifth Clans launched themselves to the sky before the Sixth Clan did. The Sixth Clan had known of the preparations the two Clans were doing. Yet, in their arrogance they had believed their people were going to launch themselves first.

With great rage the Sixth Clan reacted to this defeat and unleashed missiles of great power upon the instruments of flight of the two Clans. But the two Clans defended themselves well and suffered no losses, increasing the fury of the Sixth Clan. This too prompted the Sixth Clan to launch their instruments of flight before they were fully ready, and to bring with them instruments of destruction which they hadn't planned to carry.

Thus, the last Crusade for the Truth of Yfel took place in the skies of the planet. For days the Sixth Clan attacked the Fourth and the Fifth Clans. But it was clear their instruments of flight hadn't been made for combat in the high skies, and to the Tzal and the Nzal it became apparent that the Sixth Clan was weakening with every attack and counter-attack. But not all was good news for the two Clans, a number of their instruments of flight with some of their peoples were lost during these confrontations. To avoid losing more, the Tzal and the Nzal moved theirs away and to a higher orbit.

But the wickedness of the Sixth Clan hadn't been exhausted, and on the sixth day after the last Crusade had started, the Sixth Clan committed its last act of betrayal to the Truth of Yfel.

It began as a small fire in the upper atmosphere of the planet, not far from where the Sixth Clan had its instruments of flight stationed. Rapidly the fire became a conflagration of great proportion, enveloping the entire planet. Next, a blinding light came from this conflagration — from all places in the atmosphere at the same time — followed by an explosive force that struck with great might all the instruments of flight of the three Clans. Many of these were pulverized by the impact — mostly, those of the Sixth Clan. The rest tumbled away from the planet in all directions, colliding with each other. It was during this chaos that the instrument of flight of the Tzal, his family and his advisors, became separate from the others.

For days they tumbled towards the darkness of the sky, not knowing the fate of the others. In the uncontrolled rolling, sections of their instrument of flight broke apart. Most of the family of the Tzal and his advisors died during that mayhem, including the Tzal himself, the father of the current Tzal. Next, one by one the rest of the survivors perished, either of injuries or lost in the darkness as their instrument of flight disintegrated, until only the son of the Tzal and the Tzalkal remained alive.

Even at that point, the Tzalkal couldn't accept that everything had ended. Yfel had to have something else in Its plans. But neither the son of the Tzal nor the Tzalkal were in control of the Crusade anymore.

Thus, the last thing the Tzalkal did before surrendering to the darkness was the only thing in her power — she consecrated the son of the Tzal as the new Tzal of the Tzalmacke Clan, and asked Yfel to spare him from Its anger. As long as he would live, there was hope of restoring the Crusade for the Truth of Yfel since his seeds carried the Truth.

"And this is the sad story of the people of Yfel", Laidé finished, looking at the Chancellor, Mhali and Soen.

None of his listeners spoke for a long while. The great sadness he felt weighed down on his heart. The peoples of Yfel had been noble, even if their principles differed from his. He was unsure, however, if their path had been a natural one or had been influenced by an invading Darkness as Soen had suggested.

"The Light, indeed, triumphed!" the Chancellor said at some point, addressing Soen and startling him. "You had questioned that, daughter. Now we have the answer. The people of Yfel are gone, and their planet is uninhabitable, but in the end, the nobility of their heart won out. Those souls will never forget that lesson, and the trauma of the destruction of their world will drive them to be careful about militant beliefs when they return to physical forms somewhere else."

Soen assented in silence, though her face betrayed the emotions she felt — Laidé could see tears in her eyes.

"I am lost for words", Marshal Mhali whispered and rose from his chair to look at the Tzal and the Tzalkal through the wall-size monitor display. The two were conversing to each other in the garden. Their faces and bodies were relaxed for the first time. They sat by the small waterfall. "They are the most extraordinary Humanity I have ever encountered. Something dark, definitely, took over their civilization early in their history, but their hearts couldn't be poisoned completely… ever… and they made of that darkness a path to move forward."

"So, do we think", Soen managed to ask, "that it was a blight… a blight of the heart and mind that affected their planet?"

"We could see it as that", Mhali replied. "But was it the Blight of the Ancients? I don't know if we can answer that question. Of one thing I am sure, however. The Syndicate of Econost has a lot to answer for their intrusion in the affairs of that civilization. They violated a number of provisions in the Protocol of Union, and they will answer for that!"

"Agree", the Chancellor said. "This time Econost went too far." Then, addressing him she added, "Laidé, upon our return to Esdänl, inform Advocate Schelea to start a case with the Courts."

"I-I don't know, Chancellor, if the Tzal and the Tzalkal are ready for a process of that nature", he replied.

"The Advocate can work with your story and testimony, and those of others who—"

"Mother! As a Wanderer, you know I can't be part of that. I'm the only one who is supposed to know Econost had his hand in this affair."

Dismissing Soen's concern with a wave of her hand the Chancellor replied, "I know that, daughter. I am not asking you to testify. However, you also know we have never been able to bring to the Courts any of the Nostelat syndicates, even though they enjoy playing at the edge of all protocols and treatises. In this case they crossed the line, and the Magistrates must add this to their already-long dossier with the hope that one day they can be brought to face the consequences of their actions."

Soen nodded in silence, then asked Mhali, "What's going to happen to the Tzal and the Tzalkal?"

"They are free to go wherever they want, and that's going to be a challenge, for them."

Laidé had already thought about that. "With your permission, Chancellor, and yours, Marshal, I would like to bring here a small group of my people, including some youngsters. I can teach them the language of Yfel and introduce them to the Tzal and the Tzalkal, one or two at a time. More than any other thing, the two of them now need friends who can help them assimilate all the new experiences in which they find themselves. They are still uncertain of their situation, not knowing if they are alive or in an afterlife. They too are eager to know what happened to their planet and to the rest of their people. They still believe the Crusade hasn't ended."

"We could take them for a visit to their planet to see for themselves the devastation", Mhali replied. "This may help them close that chapter of their lives. As for the fate of the rest of their people, they must be told the truth: they are the only survivors!"

"And after that?" Soen regarded the two of them, still revealing in her voice how much their story had impacted her.

"As Mhali says," Laidé replied, "they can go anywhere they want; although it's clear they aren't the typical refugee and will need much support before they can make a decision of that nature. That's why I would like a group of my people to befriend them. They can serve as their guides in this new phase of their lives."

"Please see to it as soon as possible, and thank you." The Chancellor's voice was quiet when she spoke to him. Then, clenching her jaws she added, "That Sol System is calling to itself all sorts of guests — the Nostelat, The Others, treasure hunters… The list keeps growing the more we dig into this affair. We may end up truly finding a Darkness we can't explain."

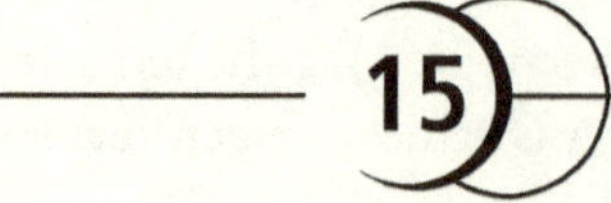

Null Time

What's happening to me? — The night hours slipped away and Althesal couldn't fall asleep. At times and without control, she felt soaring to expanded levels of awareness. The time loss during her encounter with the Asli troubled her. She had been feeling out of place since then. She felt aware of herself as Althesal and, simultaneously, aware of being someone else in a place beyond Time.

"You have more light in the head", Nesdil had said after examining her, two days before when she had mentioned it to her. "That would explain the enhanced neural activity we detect. But nothing appears to be wrong with you. On the contrary, these changes look similar to those Rangers and Wanderers experience when they cultivate the higher faculties of Mind-Soul."

It had been twelve days since their visit to the island. A question that hadn't left her mind either was the nature of the spark-looking phenomenon leaving the island in the vision the Asli had shown them — *Spark of Aïdin*, Daothel had said the Asli so called it. Why that name? Was it related to the Aïdin Planets of old? Was it the same 'spark of Primordial Fire', as the Master Chronicler called it, used by those Humans in the vision Nesdil and Daothel first saw? And where was it now? On that third planet of Sol? Could it be the reason for the anomalies the probe encountered there? And who was orchestrating all those events? Could it be possible the Manaï of the legends were still around? — While pondering on these questions, she felt again the urge to travel to that planet.

She turned on her bed once more — By the standards of her people she was an adventurous person. They were right. Exploring new horizons was her passion. It explained the urge she felt. She could at that moment walk to the transportation center and procure herself with a star-shuttle craft — no one would notice it and no one would ask questions. It was a type of craft she could easily pilot and that The Others wouldn't detect with their technology. She could be on that planet in no time, make a preliminary search for the Spark, and return home before anyone would miss her.

She turned again — No! She was a Thelian… Her people, above all others, respected Protocols and acted in accord with others. The fate of many was at stake in that affair, and every decision concerning it would be better if it was the product of a concert of wills. Besides, she couldn't ignore the political consequences of a Human entering a star system controlled by The Others if she was caught.

She turned to rest upon her back. The stars peppering the sky twinkled at her through the dome of her bedroom — She wasn't the only one who didn't know how to proceed. The High Council hadn't reacted well to the few answers and too-many questions raised by her report. Now several of the Councilors called for the original plan to send a team of researchers to the Sol System to find the true reason that had led the people of Yfel to destroy themselves. They needed to know if there was a risk to the Union. The term 'blight' wasn't used, but the undertones were clear in the demands of those Councilors. The irony was those Councilors were the same ones who had, at first, dismissed the Nostelat's logs and note as misinformation and had opposed the survey as a waste of time and resources. Now, she was refusing to answer their calls and had left the Chancellor to deal with them.

On Thel, some among her people, mostly from the Providing Guilds, wanted her to resign as Dean of the Exploring Guilds for having used the new probes without the right permissions. Of course, it was all posturing to impress those who didn't know the real use of the probes. She was holding her ground with the support of her peers in the Exploring Guilds, who respected the silence surrounding her decision. She hadn't expected these dynamics when she had accepted her responsibilities as Dean.

But her three friends weren't helping much either. Ethën and Daothel had already decided they were going to travel to that third planet, by themselves if no one else would want to go. And Nesdil insisted they should enlist the help of the various Exploring Guilds to understand what the Asli were doing to them and, of course, to explore that planet. For the three of them, as for herself, the initial possibility of that planet being an Aïdin Planet had morphed into a personal quest, and this too unsettled her.

"Why the rush?" she had asked them. "That planet isn't going to go any-where. Something much larger is occurring in that system, and we need more information to figure it out."

In truth, she knew Ethën, Nesdil and Daothel were right, and she told them so afterwards. The only way to find answers was to organize an expe-dition with researchers from the various sciences. The Synod of the Wise had already offered her support for that. But in this too she hesitated — deep in her heart she had the feeling that her role in this affair was other, and that it wasn't wise to involve others.

Thus, unable to sleep, turning on her bed, she felt standing at the edge of a precipice with a chorus of voices encouraging her to jump, in this or that direction, while she attempted to hold her balance. Yes, she needed time before she made any decision — but time for herself, to understand the changes in her and her role in the mystery of Sol.

⚡

She awoke in the early morning tired in mind and body. A strange dream had plagued the short time she had slept, and it had left a warning in her heart.

As all Galactic Humans, her people gave close attention to their dream life, which they consider as a temporary freeing of the mind-soul from the constraints of the body, allowing them to see a vaster horizon of their lives. Since early age the youth were educated to guide their dream life; other-wise, dreams would be a series of disconnected and incomplete experiences of no use to them. That was the reason Althesal was puzzled about her dream when she awoke. It had been disconnected and felt as if it had been someone else's dream.

In the dream, a multitude of shadowy creatures reached out to touch Humans… any Human… all Humans. They thirsted for their life-energy — that had been clear. But they harbored, at the same time, a great dread of Humankind. The shadows appeared from nowhere and moved as swarms, consuming on their path every world they touched. No one could find a way to stop them, and desperation took hold of many hearts. A mas-sive exodus of Humans from many worlds began. After this scene, the dream had shifted. She saw a people, also Humans, and she with them, standing on a planet looking towards an azure sky. Somehow they had gath-ered a fireball of concentrated light, not unlike a star, and had hurled it to an approaching swarm of the shadows — at the moment, when she had wanted to see more, she awoke.

Still lying down on her bed, she pondered on the meaning of the dream. She hadn't recognized the planet with the azure sky, but the first image coming to her mind was the third planet of Sol — the probe had shown a sky of that color. The most unsettling part of the dream had been the swarms of shadows. In their behavior they reminded her of a rare species of locus she had once read about, which jumped from planet to planet attracted by the blood of warm animals.

Is this a warning of things to come? Is this dream about the message the Asli are telling us, that a war upon Humans is coming? With a shudder she pulled the blanket closer to her. *No! This can't be from the Asli. I'm just imagining things.* And with that thought she leapt from her bed.

Her back and neck felt stiff, something she had never experienced, and a realization dawned on her. Since the moment of her appointment as Dean of the Exploring Guilds of her people and as Issën of Sciences of the Union, she had been losing control of her life — and now, apparently too, of her dream life! Before, her daily life had been straightforward and away from the turbulences created by those attracted to power. She missed that life! When she had been an apprentice in the Bio-Soul Sciences, she had researched and described the sound harmonics of thoughts and feelings in self-conscious beings, the principles ruling them, and the ways they affect the light-fields of the Human form, including the effects upon the nervous and endocrine systems. The education of children and young adults on many worlds had been transformed by her discoveries, and the new generations were already showing more refined bodies and minds. But her new job had removed her away from the field of Education, which she so much loved. She no longer had the time to mentor apprentices and to instruct new teachers. Not a day passed during which she didn't receive word from those who missed her.

"Enough!" she said aloud. "Time to retake my life!" And she knew right away where to start.

After a light breakfast she contacted her assistant and told him she was going to be unavailable for a day or two. All those research review meetings and conferences would have to wait — "No, Laeth, I'll be out of reach", she said to him at some point. "Even the Chancellor will have to wait until I return."

Next, with quick steps she went to the nearest transportation center to procure herself with a solo-craft for a trip to Othy, the small companion planet orbiting Thel. She was going to visit her friend and former mentor, Serenn. He would be pleased to see her.

Her skills piloting a solo-craft were rusty, but the fun of it distracted her. Thus, when she arrived to the unassuming spaceport on the small planet, she wished the trip had lasted a bit longer. No one was around, and everything was as she remembered. Inside the building all the bays were occupied with the small hover-vehicles — *Good! No one is visiting.* She wanted her visit to be quiet and relaxing.

She entered one of the hover-vehicles and left the port. It wasn't the most direct route, but she took the one her parents loved to follow in their outings to the mountain lakes when she had been young. Her destination today wasn't far from the lakes. She wasn't in a hurry and instructed the vehicle to 'touring speed'.

Othy was as magnificent as ever. "The Jewel of Thel", a poet had once called that small world. The harmonic interaction of its light-fields with those of Thel, together with its thinner atmosphere — which allowed a large amount of the radiations from their suns to reach the surface — created a much more exuberant bio-sphere than what was common for planets of its size.

By mid-morning she halted at the beach where her family had many a day bivouacked. The crisp mountain air caressed her body as she left the vehicle, and she took several deep breaths — "Unused air", her father liked to say. Next, she undressed and jumped into the cool waters of the lake for a swim. It felt invigorating. Soon after, a family of oolel [otter-like mammals] approached and welcomed her to their morning party. She wasn't going to refuse and joined them in their splashing and diving contests. The hubbub must have announced her presence to the forest because a small group of female deer came through the trees. They were proud to introduce to her their new offspring. The fawns were, of course, curious and eager to smell and touch with their sensitive noses a creature they hadn't encountered before. They too loved the feel of her hands stroking their backs and necks. When the mothers decided it was their time to move on, she sat on the grass contemplating the horizon and letting the mountain air and the warmth from Eir-1 dry off her body. It was as in the old times, and she felt content.

After dressing and indulging herself with wild berries, she continued on her way. The future, or rather Time itself awaited her.

Serenn was the head of the Time Science Research Institute on Othy, and he and his team were the only permanent inhabitants of the small planet. No one was allowed to visit the facility uninvited. This was Althesal's first visit to it, and his friend didn't know she was coming. Regardless, she pressed on towards it.

Time research was an area that only a handful of Galactic Humans were attracted to pursue, and Serenn's group was the only one from Thel doing it. Their research was based on the most accepted theory of Time, a theory that Althesal had heard her former mentor describe with passion. According to it, Time is a 'field' of actuality analogous, but not similar, to the one Space has, with its own laws, constants and motions. The theory went further and said that this field is the realm where Consciousness exists, and that this field interpenetrates Space at every point, not touching it but compelling it to follow its dictates — *"This is the reason"*, Serenn had said to her, *"observers inside Space misperceive Time as being a component of Space."*

But that theory posed a challenge: since Time was a 'field' made of something entirely different to the energies and forces of Space, it wasn't possible to study it and measure it with the same reasoning and tools used to study Space.

"If Space is an obstacle to understand Time, and because we don't have time-made tools, then let's bypass both; let's go beyond them and study Time from the 'outside'!" Serenn had proposed. His approach, which he called 'the Null-Time methodology', was so unconventional that it met with a lot of skepticism in the Trans-Galactic Association of Sciences when he had made it public. Undeterred, he had accepted the challenge and went even further: he took a path none had considered before — *"The only known factor transcending Space and Time is the Self. Therefore, if we find a way to observe Time from the perspective of the Self, we may grasp its essence, its workings and its laws."*

His research required facilities situated away from the mass impact of Human thoughts and feelings. Othy was an ideal place for it since no more than twelve visitors were allowed on the small planet at any one-time to protect its pristine bio-sphere. When Serenn had presented his plans to the Synod and to the Exploring Guilds, all had encouraged him to proceed, and no one had opposed the use of Othy for the experiments. Many in the Providing Guilds had also been delighted by the challenge of designing and building the research facility in a way that would have no detrimental effect upon its bio-sphere.

"So, you have come at last, dear one", Serenn said to Althesal while embracing her. "In spite of the silence of these walls, the news has reached me that you are ruffling many feathers. Good! Light knows we need more like you! You've always been a catalyst." Next, letting go of her and looking at her eyes, he added, "The rumor is that you and your team are doing research along a strange path — I like that! Many said the same of my project. Thus, since ours is a lone path, I knew it was a matter of time before you came to disturb me with questions… intriguing questions I'm sure."

"You know me well, Teacher, but the questions I bring are about myself. That 'secret project' of mine, many are talking about, is more about politics than any other thing— you and I aren't made for that."

"True enough", he answered with a laugh.

She then proceeded to tell him her experience in the Asli's chamber with the loci of Time and the change she was experiencing in her sense of identity, leaving aside the vision the Asli had shown them… "I don't want to know my future", she said after finishing her account. "With your wisdom, Teacher, help me understand the reason I am now living with aspects of myself as Althesal and aspects of another me, apparently in other lives in my pasts and futures, and also outside Time."

"There is a circularity in Time we have detected but don't yet understand", Serenn replied. "The data from my research hints it's the future, not the past, that conditions the present. I must say, however, it's rare to find someone as you, aware that other moments of Time affect their present. As you were telling me of your experiences, I thought you would provide an ideal test-case for my research — of course, that's out of the question. On the other hand, I doubt we can change what is unfolding in you. Perhaps you should accept that being aware of an expanding identity doesn't have to be a handicap but an asset."

"Then, help me see in another way what I'm experiencing. I don't want to have the feeling of losing control of myself. Give me some light for the present. That's all I ask."

Serenn hesitated before asking her for more details of her experience with the Asli. Eventually he said, "I can't leave you alone to face this situation — you were and are my favorite student. Perhaps we could do something after all. Come with me."

He led Althesal along a secluded walkway, spanning above the canopy of the vegetation, to a large outdoor exoskeletal structure, with the shape of a dodecahedron and suspended over a small lake. A sphere of a crystal-clear material, about seven lont in diameter [15 meters], hovered at the center of the structure.

"This is the Null-Time Chamber." Serenn pointed to the sphere. "It collects, focuses and combines the radiations of a dozen pulsar stars. In our earlier research we discovered that the radiations of pulsars aren't random, that they interact with each other in the vastness of Space to form five-dimensional patterns, following precise harmonic principles. For a time we studied these patterns attempting to discern their effects on Space. It turned out their main effects aren't upon other stars or planets but upon bio-spheres — more precisely, upon sentient beings — stimulating and speeding up their awakening to self-consciousness. I then theorized that these patterns were imprints of Time upon Space, created by the universal essence of Consciousness. That pulsars were outlets for these Time imprints, and that something analogous had to be happening between our individual Self and our body—"

"I should be on your team!", Althesal teased him. "That falls within my field of work."

Serenn nodded. "I know. But we haven't disclosed our findings to any one. Not yet." He then continued:

"Our research then is about the impacts of our individual Self — the non-spatial Self — upon the way the mind, the psyche and the body experience Time. We first discovered that in every incarnation, analogous to the work of pulsars, we as the Self impress Time — a pattern of Time — upon our body and its surrounding light-field. The study of these patterns, using volunteers, is the current focus of my research. We are finding that these patterns of Time aren't limited to the present incarnation, but that they accumulate in the light-fields of the body from incarnation to incarnation, forming an unfolding symphony of Time/Consciousness unique to the individual. We have learned to read these accumulated patterns — and from them we are learning to discern the laws, constants and motions that characterize Time."

Althesal regarded him with pride. Serenn had always been unusually bright and unconventional. That's the reason, when she had been an Apprentice, she had asked him to mentor her.

"In the Null-Time Chamber", he added, "we collect and focus the pulsars' radiations, and calibrate them to resonate to the unique light-energy signature of each test subject. This amplifies the energy-vortices of the person's light-fields in and around the head, making it possible to read the symphony of Time/Consciousness in them — that is, letting us read the evolutionary journey of the individual Self across Time."

Althesal gazed at the structure hovering above the lake. The exoskeleton around the Null-Time Chamber was made of a standing light with an emerald hue. Also hovering, but over the shore, were three small circular buildings, each crowned by a light spiral, white in color. The entire complex resembled a grand sculpture pleasant to the eye — "Beautiful and silent", she said to Serenn. "With this facility and with the opportunity to know one's life journey from a higher perspective, I see the reason you aren't short of volunteer subjects from many worlds."

Serenn grinned at her before saying, "True, but not everyone is fit to enter the Chamber. During the early stages of the research we observed that it's unsettling for Humans to experience themselves outside Time, even for a brief moment, which is what the Chamber does. A few of the first test subjects suffered, afterwards and for months, a psychological dissonance in their sense of self. Studying them we discovered that their sense of self was still strongly identified with the body and with physical living, and not with their mind-soul and non-spatial Self. Thus, we now accept only volunteers who meet the most strict requirements in this respect."

Before Serenn could form the question, Althesal answered, "I'll do it!"

"That's what I thought you would say", he replied with a smile. "We'll use the harmonies from the pulsars at their minimal potency, and it will be up to you to find the answer you are seeking — which is, I imagine, you will want to experience more of your expanded Self to confirm that you are still yourself."

After a short preparation and instruction, an assistant guided her along a shimmering and apparently insubstantial ramp projecting from the sphere. They entered the Chamber through its lower hemisphere, and she was directed to stand at the exact south pole of it. Then, the assistant donned her a pair of tight-fitting eye shields, asked if she was comfortable, and left the sphere after her reply.

Unable to see any trace of light and following Serenn's instructions, Althesal relaxed her mind and focused her awareness at a point in the center of her head. Not long after, she felt a slight shift inside and around her head. The sensation of rising from the floor came next. From the instructions she knew it wasn't just a sensation, her body was indeed floating towards the center of the sphere.

After a short time the sensation of floating ceased, and she became aware she was exiting her body through the top of her head. She next found herself in an infinite expanse of light, free from the burden of physical existence — pure awareness and pure joy, without the slightest trace of disharmony. Spiraling threads of a crystalline, sparkling light formed dancing patterns of indescribable beauty around her. As she studied this, a dissonance caught her attention, and a force pulled her towards its source. In an instant she found herself in a strange, large and vaulted space suffused by a reddish twilight — *This isn't right. Serenn's instructions didn't include this!*

Confused, she didn't know what to do. It was then when she saw *them* and flinched.

At first she hadn't seen much of her surroundings, only indistinct silhouettes moving at some distance from where she stood. However, as she had focused her attention, the figures became clearer and she recognized them — a group of The Others!

Her instinct was to flee, but some extraneous force kept her pinned to that place.

She counted six of them, all belonging to the Dreki race. They hadn't noticed her, yet. Strange shadowy creatures, more like specters, continuously shifting from view and not unlike those of her dream, stood with them. The shadows and the six Others' attention was engaged in handling reddish energy pulses. Althesal looked past them and saw they were using the pulses to push a small, rocky planet at the outskirts of a star system. It was clear to her, though, they struggled with it — its light-energy signature probably didn't match the harmonics of its new orbit, and the small planet moved along a slanted plane. They were attempting to stabilize it.

The whole spectacle was surreal. The amount of energy needed to accomplish such a feat had to be staggering! It appeared to come from the same reddish light suffusing the vaulted space surrounding her.

How did I end up here? Did the Null-Time Chamber malfunction? Or, am I hallucinating?

"You! — There! — What are you doing here?"

Alarmed, she looked around and saw two Dreki coming towards her from another direction — *I should have expected there were going to be more of them!*

She attempted to move away with no result. Something kept her fixed on the spot. Panicking, she looked at her feet to see what was holding her — *I don't have my body!* — It then dawned on her that her body was still in the Null-Time Chamber. She was now clothed in a diaphanous and luminous Human form, probably created by the impact of her mind-soul upon the surrounding light-fields of that place.

"You will tell us who you are!" Their words, spoken in Galactic Standard, left a harsh note on her mind.

Better not to tell them much — "Why have you brought me here?"

"Don't fake innocence, Human. You came to spy!"

Standing in their presence was like being next to something frigid and bone-chilling. It was true then, as cold-blooded creatures, needing an external source of warmth to live, some of these beings stayed alive by siphoning off the heat of other beings.

"I'm not a spy. I was conducting a science experiment when something transported me here."

At her reply, uneasy, the two Dreki looked at each other, grunted, and moved away from her. She still could see them, however. They were engaged in a discussion, waving their clawed fists to one another. She made one more effort to move — *What's holding me here?*

After a moment they approached her again. "What have you seen? Tell us, or you will suffer!"

"In this twilight, how could one see anything!" she retorted. She needed to buy time to figure out how to escape. "What is this place?" she asked them.

"Are you from Sol or from the Union?"

Their question took her by surprise, and her heart sank. The star system had indeed looked familiar — Sol. But how could the Dreki and those shadows be moving a planet? That was against the principles of spatial harmonics! And for what purpose?

None of that was, however, her problem at the moment.

"I am from the Union", she answered with boldness. Her suspicion was those two Dreki were subalterns and weren't altogether certain of how to handle the situation. For all she knew of The Others, by this time they would be using the techno-implants on their bodies to force any information from her. Instead, these ones moved around her, keeping a certain distance — with an evident fear of her — and asking witless questions that revealed their superiors' plans.

At this point one of the Dreki engaged with the small planet, by the looks a female, came rushing to join her interrogators. After a glance at Althesal and at the spot on the floor where she stood, she addressed her interrogators. She was much taller than them and towered over Althesal. Her facial saurian features had a permanent snarl, as if that were all she did in life. Her gestures and quick but indiscernible Dreki words directed to them told Althesal she was angry at them, very angry, probably for not having informed her of the intruder's arrival.

Her predicament was now worse. This Dreki had a stronger will. What could she use to oppose her? The way she had regarded her and the spot where she stood suggested to Althesal that she had probably fallen into a booby trap for intruders. That would explain why she couldn't move.

"You are now a prisoner of *the Dwellers*", she snapped the words at Althesal in Galactic Standard. "And you are going to pay for your stupidity by coming here." The harshness of her words felt worse than those of the two

Dreki, but they didn't obscure from Althesal the use of the expression 'Dwellers'. To whom was she referring? To those shadowy beings? It had to be since she and all Dreki in that place had the uniforms and insignia of Overlord Ankepum's dominion.

"I—"

"Shut up!"

"You cannot silence me! I am a citizen of the Union! I have not taken any hostile action against you. You kidnapped me, and you can't hold me against my will. Your people agreed to this and to respect the members and the territory of the Union when your Overlords signed the Armistice of Adhara. Besides, you are intruding into a star system with Human worlds."

In response, she spat at Althesal, then hissed to the two subalterns while shoving them towards her, "Grab her. The Dwellers will take care of her."

It was her action of shoving the two Dreki that made Althesal realize something didn't fit in the whole picture — all those Dreki had their normal bodies there, in that place… wherever that place was… but she didn't. That could only mean one thing.

The two Dreki approached Althesal with some reluctance. A brown-reddish glow had started to come out of the implants in their arms. Midway to her, however, they halted. She could feel their fear of her.

"Seize her, weaklings, or you will regret it!" The female Other snarled.

Even though the words hadn't been directed at her, Althesal felt the blow they contained. Regardless, she already knew what to do. Thus, she focused her attention at a point in her mind and waited for the two to approach.

The two gave a last glance at the looming figure of their superior, and this time lost their indecision. Next, with a quick move they reached out to grab her.

Althesal smiled to herself at their faces of surprise: they had found empty space! She had been right in her assumption. She was only an insubstantial light projection from her Self into that place, realistic in a way that probably made the Dreki think she was a Ranger since that was how Rangers looked when they were using some of their mind-soul powers. Somehow and for a reason — perhaps as an aftereffect of her exposure to the loci of Time — she had been brought to that place so that she could witness the actions of The Others to affect the destiny of Sol. But they couldn't harm her.

She had seen enough. She was done there.

Regarding the faces of astonishment of the three Dreki, in a sotto-voce she sang the fundamental chord of her being — that triple sound which every Thelian Human is guided to discover when entering adulthood: the fundamental chord of the three light-fields of the body, whose source is the non-spatial Self.

Upon sounding the chord, she had expected to return to the universal field of Mind-Soul in the same way she had been projected there. It didn't happen. Instead, the light-form she was wearing exploded in a myriad of sparks flooding that vaulted space. The three Dreki looked at her with horror as they were thrown backwards by the shock wave. The other Dreki in that place also collapsed. More surprising was the reaction of the shadowy beings. With an otherworldly wail they burst into flames as the light from her essential Self touched their forms. Next, the entire vaulted space disappeared from her view.

Unable to figure out what had just happened, Althesal remained standing at the center of a vortex of light. Not for long. Almost immediately she felt herself lifted by a mighty force and lost all consciousness.

She awoke lying on the floor of the Null-Time Chamber. Serenn and two physicians were at her side. One of them was speaking to Serenn:

"Her bio-signs are returning to normal, although her neural activity is still in a sort of electrical restart that I haven't seen. My guess is she experienced a momentary separation of her light-fields from her physical body and was born again into the body."

Serenn saw she was awake. "You're lucky, dear one. I thought I'd lost you."

Against her protests, they floated her to the infirmary on a gurney. The physician made a thorough examination and told Serenn that she was in perfect condition. Only then Serenn consented that she could stand up and walk.

They next went to the dining hall. She was famished.

"I am sorry that the Chamber didn't work", Serenn said. "I already have the engineers checking it to explain the malfunction."

"But the Chamber did work!" Althesal replied and proceeded to tell him everything that had occurred.

Serenn remained silent until she finished her account. "This is one more confirmation the mind-soul of Humans, and the Self, do exist outside Time", he said with the calm voice of those who have seen so much in life that nothing surprises them anymore. "You collapsed to the floor almost immediately after the Chamber matched your light-energy signature, yet you had a whole adventure in that instant."

"I understand that. However, Teacher, why was there such an intense re-action when I stated my intention to return to the Mind-Soul level?"

He took his time to answer, "We can only theorize. I am inclined to think that, when you sounded the chord of your being, you invoked the full power of your non-spatial Self. This then created an influx of light-energy from the level of Mind-Soul into the projected form you had at the moment, and the purity and power of this light-energy was something those shadows and the Dreki evidently couldn't withstand."

"To *when* did I go?"

"There's no way to know", he shrugged. "You could have witnessed something at any point along the Time field."

Althesal paused for a moment before saying, "The present — so my heart tells me."

⚡

Althesal returned late in the evening to her home in the aerial city of Ïthel. The lights and the warm air of the city felt welcoming after the perennial cold of Othy. Ethën had come looking for her and had left a warm dinner for her. The light-field surrounding it to keep it fresh displayed one of the happy pictures he loved to create for her since they were young.

During the trip back she had considered her next step. Serenn had been right. Having witnessed the effects of the power of her essential Self had re-awakened her self-confidence — she wasn't losing control of herself but becoming more of her Self. Still, she felt 'something' or 'someone' was pro-pelling her along an unknown path, and she had an inkling where to look for answers.

Tomorrow, I am going to visit the Asli… by myself.

As for the event she had witnessed, the more she thought about it, the more she was sure it was related to 'the power to see the patterns of Time' that Iolthel had spoken of — a thought that gave Althesal the reassurance she had experienced a real event and not a hallucination. Her only doubt now was the star system. One of the Dreki had implied it was the Sol System. Yet, there were countless systems similar to Sol, and she hadn't been able to hear the star's song from inside that vaulted space to be sure it was Sol. Thus, on this, the only thing she could do was to wait. Her quest, as Ciän the Wise called it, had only begun, and her intuition told her, more was to come.

16

Raider of the Peace

Planet Thel, Eir System

A sudden gust of wind buffeted Althesal. She looked in the direction it had come and saw an opening in the dense forest she hadn't noticed before. A path stretched beyond it. A dozen paces ahead of the opening, the path entered a lingering morning fog. The creatures of the land accompanying her had fallen silent. For an unknown reason her heart began to race with a feeling of anticipation. With cautious steps she walked towards the opening. Then, moved by an inner impulse she stepped onto the path. At that moment the wind picked up again and dispersed the fog ahead of her. It was then when she saw him…

When she had awoken that morning, she had decided to explore the Asli's island first. As a bio-soul scientist, the processes at work in that unique bio-system intrigued her. That's how she rationalized to herself what her intuition had prompted her to do.

Twice she had surveyed the island from above before landing the solo-craft. Nothing out of the ordinary had then become apparent to her keen sight. Rolling hills covered with luscious forests comprised most of the land. A few beaches stood out from the air for their whiteness. The rest of the coastline was made of rugged cliffs shaped by the relentless waves of the Meridional Ocean. A few small rivers and streams crisscrossed the island, with meadows and prairies adorning them at various points. The Asli's underground complex was located inside the tallest hill, towards the center of the land. She estimated it would take her about twelve days to walk the entire island from north to south, and seven days from east to west.

After her first trip to meet the Asli, with Daothel's assistance she had studied the available records of the surface of their planet. To her surprise, the island wasn't anywhere described, nor pictured on the detailed maps of oceans and continents. Their people hadn't given much attention to their planet's surface after they had moved to the aerial cities — since then, the planet's inner and outer natural processes were monitored in the ös boundary, outside the atmosphere, by autonomous instruments. Nonetheless, how could have such a large island remained undiscovered to a people who were masters of the land, the oceans and the air? How could that have happened when the entire planet, inside and out, had been extensively studied by generations of her people?

To start her exploration she had chosen a meadow next to the largest river, about one day walk, and north, from the entrance to the Asli's underground.

A few deer, a flock of large, colorful birds with striking crests and long tails, and a pack of the playful canidae species Nesdil called *doïel* came to her when she exited the craft. They were eager to greet her and be in her company. Soon too, smaller birds, butterflies and bees danced around her, some competing to settle on her arms and shoulders. She felt a great joy to be with them. In her travels to other planets she had encounter countless creatures friendly to Humans, but the joy she felt at that moment was unexpected.

How can one explain that a good many species of the fauna and flora of this island are unique to it? she asked herself. Yet, she hadn't come to study them but to sense and feel the music made by the island's soul — the cadences and harmonies of its song would reveal to her the processes at work in its bio-system. Thus, she set forth to wandering along the meadow, up river, with her inner and outer senses open to the song of life around her. As she had expected, the deer and all the doïel chose to accompany her. Soon, the symphony of the land and of the many species-souls reached her ears. It was lively and playful. Letting it suffuse her own soul, she became one with it.

After a while, however, her inner and outer ear discovered that, although allegro, the island's music was punctuated by a longing. She halted to listen to it more carefully, and her heart was then moved to sing aloud: "With all your beauty and harmony, what do you long for, oh wondrous island-soul?" In reply — perhaps to her winsome voice, perhaps that was how the natural world wanted to answer — group after group of land and air creatures came to greet her as she walked. She wondered then if the longing of the island was for Humans — *For how long did those of my people who followed the Source Path inhabit this island?*

The day was still young, and she ambled close to the river through a prairie of knee-high soft and undulating grasses — observing, listening, and opening trail as she went. As a bio-soul scientist she was trained to let bio-spheres and bio-systems speak to her while her mind kept silent. Every step she took, every smell, every sight and every sound filled her soul and senses with the flows and processes happening all around. Yes, the island was mag-nificent and with many unique species, but its processes weren't much different from those of other places she had studied. She continued, none-theless, moved by the need for answers to questions she didn't know how to formulate.

At some point, where the river took a sharp turn, she found herself at the water's edge. Kneeling on a mossy rock, she scooped up some water and splashed it on her face. It felt good and refreshing. When she next rose, she noticed the music of the land had, abruptly, entered a faster tempo and had changed its tune to a more solemn one — Was that the change Ciän the Wise and the others of the Synod had noticed a year back? While looking for something to explain the change, a rare formation caught her attention. Large slabs of stone, resembling a broad stairway of Human proportions, descended towards a natural pool at the bend of the river. They still retained some of their smooth surface and fit.

Searching around she found three other slabs not far from these. These were perfect circles, twenty paces across, close to each other, and forming a triangle. A fourth and similar slab rested on the ground at the edge of the forest.

It had been then, when she stood on that other slab to study the weath-ered lines etched on its surface, that the wind had picked up and she had seen the opening in the forest… and the path where she saw him…

She halted on the spot at the sight of the extraordinary Human who stood where, before, the fog had shrouded the path. His inscrutable face regarded her. A shaft of sunlight fell on him, highlighting his presence and accentu-ating the beauty of his looks. He was younger than Daothel, and taller. His clothing was striking — simple and elegant but all in green and brown tones tastefully combined to enhance his fair skin and short, wavy auburn hair. Auburn hair! — Only a few worlds on the outskirts of the Seventh Galaxy had Humans with red hair! What was one of them doing on the island?

"Greetings, Thelian", he spoke to her. "Have you come to escort me back to the Council? Have the Councilors changed their minds?"

The questions added to her astonishment. His voice was strong, deep and accented, in the language of her people, yet with some vocal inflections foreign to her.

"W-Who are you?" was all she could say.

In reply he strode towards her, halting three paces away from her. With a puzzled expression he answered, "I thought everyone on this planet knew of me. Aren't you from the Council? You dress similar to some of them."

"No, I'm not." Her heart still raced. She felt a magnetic force coming from him uncommon to Humans, and that disturbed her usual composure.

"Then, who are you?"

"I-I am Althesal…" Her voice had wavered in spite of her efforts to calm herself down.

He regarded her with his penetrating green eyes, as if seeking to read her soul, then he relaxed and said, "You don't behave as the others of your people. They are so full of themselves and uptight all the time! — I am Iain, from Ær. Do you live on this island?"

"No one lives on the surface—" Still attempting to calm herself down she asked, "I've never heard of the name *Ær* before. Is it a planet, a star system or a galaxy?"

The young man's perplexed face returned. "Of course *Ær* is a planet! How can you not know? Of all Galactic Humans, your people more than any other can't stop talking about my planet… though, mostly condescendingly." His voice trailed away with a note of sadness.

She was at a loss for words, and the young man noticed her confusion because he said matter-of-fact:

"Something isn't right. Could it be…?" He turned his head from side to side, examining their surroundings.

She mirrored him. There was only the forest. It was then when she noticed the morning light had changed. Now it looked as if it was already mid afternoon on a cloudy day.

"Yeah, something isn't right", he repeated, scrutinizing her from head to toe. "I hadn't expected this. Either you or I don't belong here, to this time, and we need to figure out who doesn't. In that way, when the convergence node appears, you or I will be able to exit this time." He next produced from a pocket in the left sleeve of his shirt a small, flute-looking cylinder and began to touch various points on it. As he did this, rings in the device rotated, shone lights of different colors, and sounded a series of notes of a changing song.

The situation started to make sense to Althesal — she had been transported to another time; although it was unexpected to encounter someone who was also aware of being in another time. What had triggered the experience in this instance? The Asli? The island itself?

"Yes, a Time anomaly. Here on the island", Iain said to himself while working the small cylinder. "And this means only one thing — the situation is getting worse!"

"What is getting worse? Can you explain yourself?"

Ignoring her questions, he spoke absently, still focused on his device, "Hmm! Strange! Neither of us is in a fixed node of Time... Unless..." He did something more to his device and looked at her with a puzzled frown. He took a step towards her and with a wave of his hand showed her the small cylinder. "Unless this thing is malfunctioning."

"Stop, young man!" She wasn't used to that behavior. "Answer my questions, and explain to me what is happening."

"I already told you more than I should have — your name is... Althesal... Yes? — The situation is, Althesal, people from two different times — you and I — trapped together in the same shifting node of Time, hasn't happened before, that I know of." He paused a moment with the look on his face that an idea had just come to him. Scrutinizing her again from head to toe, he continued, "You are a Thelian, so you must be good at either Science or Art. Which one is it?"

"I work with both. My people don't separate Science from Art, or Art from Science." The youth was testing her patience. She wanted to ask him some questions, but he resembled an ocean wave that you cannot stop but only ride along.

"Then, your time is in my past, when the Thelian civilization hadn't yet become polarized."

Althesal, taken aback, shook her head in disbelief. "How can you know of this? And how can you speak the language of my people, which most Galactic Humans find exceedingly difficult to learn?"

"We don't have time for stories now! We need to find the way to exit this Time anomaly before it is too late!"

"Too late for what? In my experience, the anomaly, as you call it, will resolve itself and we will return to our time and place."

His eyes widened in surprise. "This isn't your first time? — Those from my planet who have been trapped once in a Time anomaly return with changes in their bodies that somehow protect them from a repeat. Hmm... The anomalies must have begun in your locus of Time, and they aren't, yet, as strong as they are in mine."

"Locus of Time! Where did you learn that term?"

"You keep asking questions!"

"Please, I need to know."

He sighed, then said, "My people began studying Time about one hundred years ago — and those are our years, not yours — after our planet went through changes that forced us to re-think everything about us and life. The expression 'Loci of Time' was adopted by those who then began the new research on Time."

It had to be a coincidence. Did they know of the Asli? — "Why did you come to my planet?"

"The first time we discovered something wasn't right was a year ago, when a Time anomaly connected both our planets. Since then, more anomalies have appeared at random on my planet and neighboring space. At first we thought the source of the problem was there, but we couldn't find anything to explain it. That's when we decided to come to Thel."

"So you came to ask the Council for assistance to find the source of the problem, and the Councilors declined to help?"

"Not exactly. They rejected our presence on this planet from the start. They don't even want to listen to what we have to say. They call us *Nam~Sel* and have told your people to avoid all contact with us, as if we were infected with a disease."

"Nam~Sel?" — *Raider of the peace!* — Althesal felt a revulsion in her stomach. No one used that kind of expression in her time! Much less so to label another Human! Were her people in the future going to descend that low, deriding others? It was then when she remembered the question she had meant to ask next: "What are you doing on this island?"

"After the Council closed all doors to us, we came here because in our research we discovered that the first known Time anomaly bridged this island with a location on my planet. We looked into the data records my people have of this planet and found this island is clearly identified as a place of great importance to the Thelian people; although we don't know why this is so. But you cannot imagine our surprise when we discovered that your people, in my locus of Time, don't know at all of the existence of this island!"

"How do you know so much about my people?" The youth didn't stop surprising her. "You speak of data records… Have you been studying us?"

"Of course not!" He laughed. "That's what those of your people who took us to the Council believe — although they used the word 'spying'. The fact is the coming of my friends and I to Thel is the first instance when anyone from my planet has ventured beyond our star system. But we have—"

A soft clapping sound had struck close to where the two of them stood. Startled, Iain had stopped speaking to look in all directions.

"What's the matter?" Althesal found herself imitating him, in spite that the noise had sounded to her as a normal forest sound. Perhaps an animal had broken a branch.

"That's the sound made by a 'Time convergence node' when it becomes visible." He kept looking in every direction. "I don't see it. It should be right in front of us. A translucent opening."

The sound struck again, this time in the space between the two of them, but no opening appeared either. Instead, their surroundings changed. The forest path became a smooth, gleaming surface extending for about eighty paces behind Iain. At that point, it entered a wide pillar of a silvery light. High above that pillar, three iridescent spheres danced. Each sphere was as large as a solo-craft, and in their dancing they sang a short, yet majestic and ethereal tune that kept repeating itself. The sounds were barely audible to Althesal, as if their source weren't the spheres but something remote, in higher light-fields.

Iain didn't seem surprised by the change and gave a quick glance to the extraordinary structure behind him before he began, once more, to work the cylindrical device. After a moment, he addressed her with a frown, "We have moved to my locus of Time. Yet, you should have returned to your time when I returned to mine. Hmm… This is one more thing I didn't expect." After pausing briefly, he continued, "There are only two possibilities that could explain why you are still here. One, this place — this structure behind me — affected the behavior of the Time anomaly that trapped us. Two, you are the cause of this strange behavior. Which one is going to be?" Squinting his eyes, he asked, "Who are you, truly?"

Their eyes locked for a long moment. Then, he turned around and strode towards the pillar of light. It was then when Althesal saw that the surface where they now stood was a ramp spanning across a wide cylindrical chasm whose walls were covered with a polished, luminous surface, and that the pillar was its central axis.

"Wait!" She strode after him. "Tell me about this place."

Ignoring her, Iain kept his march. Only when they arrived closer to the pillar, he halted and turned to say to her with haste, "I don't have answers. I, too, need them. I don't know how to return you to your locus of Time. I don't know if this place is the cause of the anomalies. I don't know why we met. You affect me in ways I can't explain. I hope, as you said, the anomaly in which you now move will resolve itself and you will return to your locus."

"You too affect me as no other being has. I wish we could have more time to understand the reason. Just tell me one thing — In your time, why is it that my people and your people don't understand each other?" She then added something that surprised her, "I don't want that to be the case between you and me."

"My people see life with different eyes — it's that simple. Long ago your people decided who they were. Now, all they do is protect that. My people, in contrast, in all our history, haven't been able to settle that question, and we are still searching for the answer." He paused, looking at her with his first tender expression towards her before adding, "My heart whispers to me, Althesal, that there is no distance between you and me. Let's hope one day that will also be the case between both our peoples." Ending with a smile, he then said pointing to the chasm, "My friends are down there, figuring out the nature of this structure, to see if it has something to do with the Time anomalies. I must return to them. I feel time is short to solve the problem affecting both our planets."

He turned and walked towards the pillar of light. The large spheres high above kept humming their remote tune, and Althesal felt a knot in her throat seeing him go. Then, at the moment when she expected to see him disappear inside the light, Iain was thrown backwards with great force, landing on his back at her feet!

"Ouch!… That too is a surprise", he said and grinned at her.

She bent to help him stand up. But when she touched him, a jolt of energy shook the two of them, and her body jerked backwards. He then rose without her help and, to her astonishment, began to laugh.

"I'm beginning to think you are more of a 'nam~sel' than I am", he said still laughing. "You remind me of one of my friends — by the way, he is a Thelian, a most unusual one, and he is always placing us in the most awkward of situations."

Althesal didn't feel amused at his comment but managed to say pointing at the pillar of light, "What happened?"

"Don't know… When my friends and I discovered this place, we entered that light without any impediment. They all descended first through a doorway in it, to explore what's down there. I was about to follow them, when I heard the clapping sound of a Time anomaly. I exited the field and walked over to investigate. That's when the surroundings changed and I saw you."

He turned and walked to the edge of the ramp and, looking down, shouted, "Anyone there?" There was no reply. "Etele?… Anöthel?… Tau?"— No reply.

He came back to Althesal rubbing his lower back. Next, he produced again the cylindrical device to consult it. "Yes, this is my locus of time, or so it appears to be." Pointing it to her, he added, "The only odd factor here is you, which means you are the key to solve this riddle."

She was beginning to accept his audacious way to address her… some of it… and asked, "What can I do?"

He remained silent, absorbed in thought.

Althesal used the opportunity to study him. The light and song of his being were., remarkable, beautiful and unusual, yet also familiar, and his entire demeanor was relaxed. He was free and uncomplicated in ways she felt attracted to. Nothing deterred him. The unexpected was an adventure to explore: it gave him energy and resoluteness.

"I have an idea", Iain said to her after a while. "Something happened when you attempted to help me rise… when you touched me. We have observed on my planet that the Time anomalies have different and unpredictable effects on the surrounding Space. We have likewise discovered that all Humans, or at least those from your planet and my planet, have a localized Time-field of sorts interpenetrating each individual. It is because of the existence of this localized Time-field that anomalies can affect us. So — and this is speculation — what about if the anomaly that trapped us was affected by this place, creating an alternating polarity between the Time-field in your body and the one in my body? That could explain why at first we weren't in a fixed locus of Time and why I'm not fully back in my locus of Time."

She nodded, dumbfounded by his reasoning.

"Here is what I propose", he continued. "The two of us will walk together and enter the pillar at the same time. The thing is, the first time I heard the clapping sound it came from inside the light itself, and its polarity could have affected the Time anomaly, forming a sort of three-sound chord with yours and mine. Thus, if we enter it together, the possibility is that your body and my body will return to their normal Time polarities, and that each of us will end in its own Time locus." With a grin he next added, "If this doesn't work, each of us will have some backache."

The idea made sense to Althesal. Thus, in silence they approached the pillar of light, next to each other, but careful not to touch. It was right before they entered the light when she remembered the question she had wanted to ask him when they had introduced each other: "Iain, you never told me the name of the star system that your planet belongs to."

As the light washed upon them, she heard him reply with his musical voice, "Sol… We call it Sol… Farewell, Althesal."

⚡

A deer and two doïel stared at her from the forest's edge. Beyond them, she could see the river and other deer grazing on the open meadow. Iain was nowhere, and she felt an emptiness in her heart. She called to the creatures, and they leaped excitedly towards her — *I'm back!* she knew then. Taking quick steps towards the creatures, she embraced them as they joyfully greeted her.

When noon arrived, she desisted in her search for the strange structure Iain and his friends had found in that future time, even though she could still hear, combined with the island's song, the ethereal and remote tune of the three spheres.

Sitting under a large tree, surrounded by the creatures of the land, she spent most of the afternoon reviewing her life since the time she had been young. She had known at an early age that she was older, much older than her body. That certainty had never left her. Meeting Iain had awakened in her another certainty — that her non-spatial Self was also in other loci of Time, and perhaps in Iain's.

That must be what the Asli want us to remember! she realized. *That we are more than just our present identity… But, why? Why is it so important for us to remember that?*

She took a deep breath. Iain had made one thing clear: she was the odd factor in that entire affair. As the forest path had become the access ramp for that enigmatic structure, she had become a bridge between loci of Time, as well as a bridge between Thel and that other planet of Sol — *Ær*, he had called it. She couldn't control how affairs were going to unfold between both times, both planets, both peoples, but she was going to play her role to make things whole.

Humans, then, were going to people the third planet of Sol, and perhaps already had done so — Iain hadn't said it was the third planet, but in her heart she knew it was so. This thought gave her some peace of mind regarding the fate of the Spark of Aïdin, which she was convinced was now on Ær. On the other hand, being peopled by common Humans eliminated the possibility that Ær was an Aïdin Planet. Yet, that didn't decrease but increased its mystery… and Iain had made it clear that Thel was part of it. Was the real mystery not the planet but its two Humanities and the connection between them? Was Iain and his fellow Humans the descendants of those Thelians who had followed the Source Path? And what was the connection between her and Iain? It felt more personal.

There was only one way to find answers: she had to travel to Ær, and that wasn't going to be easy in spite of the support of the Synod. By all appearances the Sol System had already become the new theater of hostilities of The Others against the Union. There was also the possibility that a new and dangerous player had joined that game — those shadowy entities the Dreki called 'Dwellers'.

Nonetheless, in her heart she felt the urgency to act, and quickly — the time to travel to Ær was now! What was she going to do?

17

The Night Caller

Chancellor Vuensé, startled, turned on her feet to face her desk. Someone was requesting to talk to her on her private communication channel via the epi-net. Only her husband, her daughter and a few friends knew of it. She was at her house, and it was almost midnight. After long hours of work she was tired and about to go to bed. Thinking it was Selé, her husband, she rushed to reply. Yet, when the light beam resolved into the face of the caller, the thrill of excitement froze in her chest.

"A-Aldiarlim… What a surprise!"

"Vuensé, you look good", the caller said in a jovial, yet throaty voice. "The games of power have been kind with you."

She forced herself to smile to that strange-looking face. It had been many, many years since they had met during the Conference on the planet Adhara, where the Armistice between The Others and the Union had been signed. She hadn't yet been elected as Chancellor and had participated as the delegate of the Pleiades League of Worlds. Aldiarlim was the personal advisor of Ankepum, one of the eleven Overlords of The Others who had signed the Armistice. They had met informally a few times during the Conference and had struck good and polite conversation, each curious to know more about the other. Since then, she had kept herself informed of him as much as it was possible — something not that easily done of one who kept himself behind the scenes.

"Today, by chance," he continued, "I found among my records the calling information you gave me and decided to give you a ring."

Unlikely! — she thought. Aldiarlim was one the most brilliant strategists she had ever met. Nothing he did was 'by chance'. Once he had been Human — a prince of a remote world in the Cealaïs Galaxy. Early in his life he had renounced his title to roam the galaxies, and had eventually formed a friendship with Overlord Ankepum. He had then altered his body to fit in as a Dreki in Ankepum's clan. He was a malcontent and an idealist who disliked authorities and power structures, but didn't know what he truly liked. Why was he calling her now, after such a long time?

"I must confess", she said in reply and playing his game, "that you are in my mind from time to time, wondering if you have become once more a free man."

As she said that, it didn't escape her that for a fleeting moment the expression of his face changed from jovial to worry — *So, something is troubling him!*

"Nah, life gives me enough excitement as it is."

Now she had to be proactive. "We should meet and talk. Your informality is always refreshing. What do you think?" She had just told him that they could meet in secret, in a place of his choice.

It took him a moment to answer, and that told her that, definitely, something was bothering him, something contrary to his principles and ideals — *And my principles and ideals too! If not, he wouldn't have called.*

"The sails of my life are close to the wind!" he said slowly and with emphasis in reply to her invitation. Then, after a brief pause he added, "I will let you know… Talking to you, Vuensé, is also refreshing." And with those words, he broke the connection.

She stood there, looking at the empty holo emitter. *He remembers I love to sail!* — She too remembered he loved to sail, a hobby which the Dreki felt no attracted to with their dislike of bodies of water, and a hobby that gave Aldiarlim something to remember his humanness. By telling her that he was 'sailing close to the wind', he had just told her that his life was passing through a moment when all things were moving against his principles, but that he was, nonetheless, inching ahead — that he wasn't defeated, not yet.

All traces of sleep had left her. She then went to the kitchen. She had skipped dinner and so made herself a light snack. She needed to think.

She had recorded the conversation and played it several times. Aldiarlim was worried — the gestures of his Human-Dreki face confirmed it. Yet, if she knew him well, he wasn't going to actually meet with her. He didn't need to. The call itself, the time of it, and the carefully chosen sentences contained all he wanted to tell her — A warning! A warning that something was rising under the cover of darkness. The problem was it was a vague warning. He also knew that. Yet he also knew she would fit his call into a larger picture — into one of the affairs in her job that she was dealing with at the moment.

A warning about the Sol System? — It had to be. Aldiarlim had to know she was now dealing with the situation in Sol unleashed by the events on the planet Yfel. He was a man who kept himself very well informed on all happenings in the halls of power, and in the Underworld as well — that vast clandestine network of fringe groups, outsiders to the laws of civilizations, and opportunists, found on many planets, moons and asteroids. But what could his warning add to what she already knew? That his Overlord, Ankepum, was the one having dealings with the elite of the planet Mal'ek? — No, he wouldn't call for that; he was too loyal. Or was his warning about something much more ominous? — That could be; something that threw him into such an internal conflict that he had had to talk to someone: her.

She rubbed her temples. The tiredness was settling again in her body, and her bed called to her. Tomorrow she was going to order the Rangers to find out Aldiarlim whereabouts and to follow him wherever he went. It wasn't going to be easy, but she needed to know what his interests of lately were.

18

Legends, Politics and Science

"Thaël!" She rushed to stand up. "Welcome to my home." Althesal seldom had visitors that early in the morning, and this one had come unannounced and had let himself in.

The two stood facing each other for a moment before the Thelian Ambassador to the Union, Councilor Thaël, said, "Greetings, Esal."

He was the only one who called her by that name. Althesal returned his smile and said, "Uncle, I was about to have some breakfast. Would you like to join me?"

"I'd be delighted. It has been a long while since we shared a meal together. I miss the long discussions with my favorite niece."

"But I'm your only niece!" She laughed and embraced him tightly. He sighed in relief, and she felt that something weighed on her uncle's mind. As many of their people, he had chosen not to have children in that lifetime, nor even a long-term companion. During her youth he had dedicated his affection to her, treating her as his own daughter. That had changed when she had become an apprentice in the Bio-Soul Sciences and left their home city, Ïllal, to live in Ïthel, their capital city. Being alone, he had assumed more and more duties in the Providing Guilds. He ascended through their ranks in responsibilities and influence because of his nobility, great intelligence and command of the Power of the Voice. Both had made efforts to see each other regularly, but their paths and interests were now different.

Together they made breakfast, each knowing what the other was supposed to do to prepare the food both enjoyed, and talking about their family and the antics of Althesal's parents.

"Last time I heard from them…" she said, "let me see… thirty-one days ago, they were visiting a planet in a star system of Cealaïs. They are studying the music and folk dances of a Humanity which developed in complete isolation for most of their history because their system is inside a nebula. Father says their music is majestic, though peculiar, unlike anything we have heard."

"They haven't changed, have they?" Thaël said with a chuckle. "Good they are traveling! I've never told you this. When we were growing up, your father used to embarrass me every time he sang his unusual musical compositions in public. Some thought that, as his elder brother, I wasn't a good role model for him. The fact is, my brother has always been… unconventional… to the point that if our people ever had those attracted to be Wanderers, your parents would be Wanderers!"

"You miss them, uncle. Confess it."

"Of course, I miss them! The four of us are family!"

Althesal regarded him. There was something in the tone of his voice when he had said those words. Thelian Humans don't age physically in the way other Galactic Humans do, because of the higher content of light in their bio-cells and because of Thel's unique atmosphere. Instead, towards the end of their lifespan, 3,600 standard galactic years, they begin to feel tired of living until they arrive at the point in which, one day, they leave their bodies and, with their will power, dissipate the light-fields forming them. Was her uncle tired of life when he had lived only two-thirds of it?

"What's the matter, uncle? I sense something isn't right."

With a sigh he replied, "I wish we could still be close and free from the burdens and preoccupations life has imposed on each of us. You've always challenged me with your expansive thinking — I love that in you… At the same time you've always marveled at the ways of our people and have dreamed of seeing all Galactic Humans as happy and as prosperous as we are. Remember how we used to make plans together to help other Humanities learn and master the Power of the Voice… the very foundation of our way of life!"

Althesal still didn't know where her uncle was going with that conversation and played along. "Those dreams inspired me to explore the Principles of Thought and Sentientness, and to describe their effects upon the light-fields of the body."

"Yes, and I was proud of you when the Parliament of Life Weavers adopted them as the foundations for the education of our people." Thaël paused, then with hesitation asked, "Esal, why did you leave the Path of Life

Weaving for the Path of Exploring? As an Educator you were leading the younger generations of our people to greater heights. On the other hand, as an Explorer you are just one more researcher among many; and now that you are their Dean, you are doing something you don't feel comfortable with. I can see it."

She looked into his eyes for a moment, before replying, "Is this what is in your mind, uncle? You can't hide from me that something is weighting you down." When she had been offered the position of Dean of the Exploring Guilds, she had hesitated for only one reason: it would place her in opposition to her uncle's role as Dean of the Providing Guilds. "You know well the reason I accepted the office", she continued softly. "Both the Life Weaving and the Exploring Guilds are displeased with the ideas and manipulations of the Providing Guilds. Exceptionalism and political control were never the ways of our people."

"I don't like what's happening either, Esal. But you need to understand, since the moment our civilization was discovered by Galactic Humans, the Providing Guilds have been the vanguard in establishing relations with other civilizations. We took the brunt of the cultural shock and the need to open ourselves to others. We've adapted but at a price. Many among the Providers were deeply changed. There are some of us, however, who want to offset this. We are working to heal our Path and restore the wholeness that should exist between the three Paths. We are a small group but respected by all, and some are already listening to us."

"Why hasn't your group brought this to the Council of the Paths? You will receive support from the other two Paths."

"Oh Esal, you don't know how deep the changes are! Those who sponsor the idea that our people are special, and who justify our policies towards the Union, are influential among many from the other two Paths, not just with the Providers. A direct challenge to them could bring a split in our people. Even the Synod of the Wise is concerned this may happen, and one of the Wise Ones is in contact with us to give us guidance on the steps we are taking."

Her uncle's revelations explained to her some behaviors she had observed in the last assembly of the Parliament of the Explorers, and a connection came to her mind about something Iain from Ær had said to her — in the future, her people were going to be less holistic, split in their pursuits, and some would even harbor xenophobic attitudes. Was this the beginning of that? Had the Wise Ones seen that possibility in the future of Thel, forcing Them to speak Their minds?

"You wish for me not to be the Dean of the Explorers. Yet, I don't understand. Isn't a strong voice from the other two Paths good to balance the voice of the Providers? At the least, I will distract them from the quiet work your group is doing to make matters right."

"Yes, your strong voice is good, and I don't want to talk you out of your current role — That's not the reason I've come today."

"Then, what is weighting you down?"

He regarded her in a way she knew he was going to say something he rather didn't have to.

"The news is out, Esal — You have found an Aïdin Planet!"

Althesal hand froze in mid air, spilling some of the food in the dish she was going to pass to her uncle. She lowered the dish to the table and leaned back until she felt the backrest of the chair.

Her uncle continued speaking, his eyes locked with hers:

"Late last evening someone posted on the epi-net the data of the entire survey of the Sol System, including the probe's findings on the third planet and the annotations and comments made by you and your team. Everything is out. By now the entire Union knows the whole lot of the survey. By tomorrow The Others will know of it too. In a few hours Humans and Amethen in all the known worlds will have heard that you've discovered an Aïdin Planet."

Althesal took a deep breath. Secrecy in the affairs of the Union was explicitly repudiated in the Protocol of Union. It was thus expected that the entire data of the survey would be made public at some point, but not in this way and not with the personal annotations made by her researchers and by her. Mustering all the calm she could find in herself, she said the only thing she could say:

"The data on that planet is fragmented and incomplete, and is still being studied. That planet has some oddities, but no one can claim it's an Aïdin Planet. The annotations of my team are no more than a discussion of possibilities for other scientists to join in the conversation, and as scientists we shouldn't ignore any reasonable avenue to understand the unusual. For our people Aïdin Planets may be non-sense, and may open old wounds, but for most scholars in the Union who study the old legends, they are still a subject worthy of research."

"I know that, Esal. I'm also aware that a large number of our people disagree with our official stance on the matter of the old legends. That isn't the issue. It is—"

"Who could have posted the data?"

"It was easily traced to our planet. An apprentice in Planetary Harmonics Sciences saw the data Ethën sent to one of the scientists there and thought it was for publication since it arrived together with some data packages for publication — a careless handling of sensitive data and a simple clerical mistake, that was all. That's why secrecy never pays. The unexpected always happens. Chancellor Vuensé contacted me earlier today and told me the news. She wanted me to hear it from her and to explain why the data of that third planet hadn't been shared yet with all the Councilors. Of course, I told her I was surprised at the news but that I would do all in my part to help her and the High Council move through this."

Althesal realized her uncle was hurt by the fact she hadn't shared the data with him in the first place. After all, he had defended her in the Providing Guilds for her use of the new probes without official endorsement. Thus, taking his hand in hers, she said, "Uncle, you know, in this affair I'm not in control. The entire operation has been and is under the authority of Chancellor Vuensé, and it's in her mandate to decide to inform the High Council when she sees it opportune. Any conclusion drawn from the annotations of my team are premature. The data spans only twenty standard galactic minutes of transmission, and some sensors didn't even work. There isn't enough information to say what we found there."

"I understand that, niece, but you have also to think about politics, because that's what this affair has become. We have differences of views on many subjects and that's fine. I also know you aren't the type of person to chase fables blindly. Nonetheless, on most worlds of the Union people don't know you, and as of this morning you have become a symbol many will praise and many others will rebuke. Be ready for both."

Her uncle was right, her life had become more complicated. It was one more thing she would have to deal with. But her mind was on something more pressing. "The reaction of The Others is what concerns me now. They will see the operation in Sol as an invasion to a star system they already control, and as violation of the Armistice of Adhara."

"Well, we'll see to that. I contacted the other two Councilors who are, with me, the liaison with the Armistice Inspectorate. We are working on a strategy to deal with the situation. So that you know, officially The Others haven't claimed the Sol System, which means they have no case if they present a complaint to the Inspectorate. I don't see them going to an open conflict with us for this issue — our capacities to move and to communicate through Space, and to shield entire systems from them, are far superior. In the latest intelligence gathered by the Rangers, it's clear their Overlords are becoming desperate for finding something to match our advantages. Thus, they may become bothersome for a time but will calm down again. We may expect, however, that soon they are going to surround the Sol System with an entire fleet to keep everyone else out — after all, their alliance with the Humanity of the fifth planet gives them that right in the absence of other Humanities in the system."

Althesal took another deep breath, trying to relax her mind. "Then, the possibility to clarify the nature of that third planet has been reduced to zero."

Thaël nodded while observing her carefully.

The niece in her wanted to tell her uncle all the experiences she recently had had. But she couldn't. Daothel was right. Now more than before she felt and knew that their experiences, and what that third planet concealed, were part of a personal journey through unusual paths. Until the four of them had a better grasp of the situation, it was better to remain silent. As for the fate of Ær now that its existence was known to all, her encounter with Iain had told her that Humans, not The Others, were going to have a civilization there, at some point — this thought eased some of her tension; although she still felt the urgency to travel there.

Her uncle may have mistaken her silent pondering for hesitation because he said, "This isn't the time for the Explorer and Life Weaver in you, Esal. No, you need to do something to straighten out this situation by going public, and I'm here to help."

"I know, uncle. I want to start by telling our people everything my team thinks about that planet's data. I have the feeling they are going to show a more reasonable attitude than other Galactic Humans."

"Good! Let it start with me. I want to meet with your team and, together, analyze the entire data from that planet. The more I know of your minds and of the findings, the easier it will be for me to help you… and those who may be upset by this affair."

Althesal couldn't believe what her uncle had just said! She nodded to him and said in a whisper, "This morning we can start, if you have the time, uncle."

"This is a priority now. Let's meet at your offices right before noon." Thaël rose, kissed her on the forehead and departed.

Althesal was left speechless. Thaël was full of surprises lately. First, his strong defense of her use of the probes, and now this. He had never shown any interest in seeing and experiencing her work directly. She had the distinct impression that, like her, he was deeply affected by this affair.

19

Unconventional Thinking

Naleean hesitated to open his eyes. His left leg felt cramped. Flexing it slowly, he readied for the pain. It never came. He opened his eyes and took a deep breath. He next sat upright, turned off the protecting body shell, and removed the safety harness. In the dim deck he saw the others doing the same. He was their leader, and they needed him now. He stood up and asked if anyone was hurt. No one was, but he could feel all were shaken by the rough landing. He helped the younger ones unfasten themselves while speaking to them with encouraging words.

He wasn't the oldest among the twenty-seven of them, two others were. None of them, by the reckoning of their people, the Nauthians, had yet reached adulthood. They had passed adolescence and were in 'the questing age' — when one chose a life path. They had chosen voyaging through the stars to experience anew the soul of their people and thus renew the search for the source of the legends of old. Appointing him as their group leader had come as a surprise to him. He had pledged to himself that he wasn't going to be less than their hopes and dreams.

Their craft was old, a salvage, from the time when the trans-photonic technology had been hybridized with Thelian live-crystals. A few were still in use, mostly by fringe people. Theirs was small for a transport but enough for their numbers and needs. It had been gifted to them by a traveling bard who had befriended them while visiting their native planet. But on entering the new planet they had rushed to reach, the craft hadn't fared well. Its drive system was now dead. They were stranded. Perhaps it was fate. They had reached their objective, nonetheless, and now were the first and only Humans on that planet so much yearned for in songs and tales. They could claim it as their home. Twenty-seven Human inhabitants wasn't enough to ask for a membership in the Union. Nonetheless, galactic treatises would protect their claim.

He had no doubt the planet would feed and provide for them. Later, when they would want to continue their voyaging, something would come along their way to make it possible. For now, it was going to be as in the pre-settling times when their people used to travel through the stars, from world to world, in search for the source of the legends — living simple, communitarian fashion, and unencumbered by protocols.

The soft light of an early morning poured through the vaulted, transparent hull, illuminating their faces. It was then when the enormity of what they had done dawned on him — there was no turning back! He didn't know exactly how to feel about it, though his heart started racing. They were about to step on a planet of mysteries. He sensed the others' anticipation too. They all surrounded him in silence, waiting for his next move. Their people had collected stories of those planets for thousands of years. Yet, in truth, no one knew what to expect if one was found. "It's a place of boundless possibilities", the elders had stressed during their schooling.

With effort, manually and unaided, he opened the main exterior hatch — it was the duty of the leader to do so upon arriving to a new world. Fresh, warm air swept inside the cabin carrying a sweet scent, and he heard some exclamations behind him. In no time, everyone scurried to crowd around the opening. However, the angle of the hatch was such that only a patch of ground covered with green grasses alien to them was all they could see. It was inviting. Naleean jumped, then took a few unsteady steps and halted — he felt lightheaded. The others were observing him, and he motioned them to jump. Standing on solid ground was new to them. They hadn't traveled for long, and their bodies hadn't forgotten the ceaseless motion of the floating islands on their native world. Some had thus to sit on the ground to avoid falling. After a few minutes, however, everyone looked better and eager to do something, their eyes drinking to the last drop the panorama stretching all around. But it would have to wait. They all had decided to follow the old traditions of their people, and gratitude was now their duty.

Thus, while Naleean was still recovering, the others moved to form an arc facing the rising sun. He joined them, and in the silence of their hearts they all gave thanks to the Unseen Source of All for the gift It had bestowed on them. Their gesture was enhanced by the awe they felt looking at that beautiful azure sky, and by the choruses of birds in the distance welcoming the new day. None of them had ever seen or imagined such a sky, and if he knew them, they were thinking what he also thought — that sky was the perfect setting for 'the luminous beings' who dwell on Aïdin Planets to appear to them.

A long moment passed and no 'beings of light and song' came to greet them. It didn't matter. They had time in abundance to wait or to look for them. Thus, Naleean ended their ceremony by picking one of the small yellow flowers that grew in profusion among the grasses; it had the color of the planet's daystar and a faint, pleasant perfume. He next placed it with care through a slit on his shirt, close to his heart. The others followed his lead and started inspecting their surroundings. Their home world was a planet with little vegetation and land animals, mostly aquatic plants and sea creatures. During schooling they had experienced live projections of other planets and had studied the great variety of bio-spheres their multi-galactic environment harbored, but nothing had prepared them for the lavishness of that world. Naleean's senses were overwhelmed — so much to see!… touch! … smell!

They had landed on a large glade. The herd of antelope-looking creatures that had been dispersed by the commotion of their craft's arrival were returning in small groups to continue their grazing. When they saw the visitors, all of them approached curious. A few came to Naleean, to inspect and smell him. He patted the closest one on its head, between its curved horns: its coat was soft and wooly. The creature then became still, and Naleean's senses expanded beyond his body to encompass the ground, the trees, the sky, everything around him. Without control, he crossed a threshold where he felt the creature's species-soul greet him. His heart was immersed in pure joy, and he wanted that moment to last forever… Then, the creature moved when another of its kind, also wanting his attention, nudged it on its rib cage, and Naleean lost the magic of the moment.

Shaking his head he wondered — *How that happened?* — By the look of his companions, he saw they too were having a similar experience — *Is this normal with land animals? Or is it only on this type of planet?* — He patted a second creature but felt only its friendliness and the warmth and softness of its coat.

He continued exploring and found his way to a small stream where schools of multicolor fish swam at leisure. He knelt down, touched the water, and tasted a few drops of it. "Fresh water!" — his cry rose unconfined. On their native planet the only fresh water came from the demineralization distillers. It was an auspicious sign. They had made the right decision!

At that moment someone called his name and he rose.

As he had requested of the others, none ventured inside the forest, but three of the youngest ones came to him carrying a type of nuts and a few spherical, yellow fruits that the sparse trees in the glade were loaded with. They were elated with their findings and wanted to try them all — the fruits had a honeyed aroma, and the nuts a palatable look; besides, the birds and the antelopes were eating them. He laughed at their enthusiasm and asked them to wait until they could analyze their composition. With stubborn faces the youngsters stared at him, unwilling to give up so easily, so an idea occurred to him. He told them that, from then on, it was going to be their contribution to their new community to discover, analyze and classify all the edibles on their new world. Everyone had to follow their lead on this, even him. The youngsters beamed at him and at each other, next bolted to continue their exploration, discussing aloud who of the three would do 'this' or 'that' in their new role.

Exclamations and shouts coming from everywhere told him the others were likewise exhilarated. He felt proud to see them content and joyful, and ready to start a new life on a world that until two days before was unknown throughout the multi-galactic expanse where Humans and others of the Young Races lived. It was theirs now, and with the magic of its lavishness it had already started to enhance their souls. What more did it have in store for them?

During their trip to their new planet he had given temporary assignments to each one to start organizing the rhythm of their new community life as soon as they would land. Later, once their needs would become better defined, each could choose their area of contribution. Thus, after each felt satisfied with their initial exploration of the glade, they took to their tasks. Naleean did the same. It was almost noon, and he and two others — the 'engineers' among them — set to inspect the condition of their craft and their supplies. He wanted to finish before darkness. Tomorrow, he was going to organize parties to explore the forest. They had brought three small hover vehicles, and he was eager to try them.

During the rough landing the hull had held its integrity; although the bottom of the craft had sunk in the ground when the landing gear hadn't deployed. Nonetheless, the decks were almost level — that was a relief since the craft was going to be their home until they could build houses in the fashion of their ancestors. To their surprise, some of the craft systems were inoperative, although no damage was apparent. Food they had in abundance until they could identify those plants, nuts and fruits that their bodies could consume — it was going to be a major change for them since their bodies were used to a diet of aquatic plants and a few aerial, cereal crops. Tools they had also brought. Most of them were undamaged. Some of these, however, when they inspected them, couldn't tap into the light-fields of the planet to power on while others did — the two 'engineers' scratched their heads wondering at the reason for that.

"It must be the same force that affected the drive", one of them said to him. "We need to study their mechanism to find out what makes some work. We can start tomorrow."

Naleean assented with a murmur — he was feeling lightheaded again. Of course, none of these things they might need if the legends were true that on that type of planet there were places where Humans could precipitate everything one wanted from the omnipresent light-fields, just by using their thought power. But Naleean was a realistic individual too, and, everything considered, it was good to know they weren't going to have hardships because of the provisions they had brought. However, the systems of the craft that didn't work worried him, specially communications. They had to contact the Office of the Chancellor on Esdänl to state their claim of the planet. A delay could place their lives at risk if The Others decided to claim it first. Earlier he had asked his new friend Nadé to figure out what was wrong with communications. She was the 'expert' among them in all matters concerning Thelian crystal technology — her skills controlling the live-crystal of the main drive had spared them of a catastrophic and perhaps fatal landing.

"Naleean, I need to talk to you", Nadé said to him with her silvery voice. He was helping open the cargo exterior hatch to improve the craft's ventilation. It was taking four of the strongest ones to force it open.

"Is communications working?" he asked while wiping sweat from his face.

"I'm not sure", Nadé replied. "Everything looks fine. The crystals are whole, their arrangement is correct and the light-field around them is doing its work. Nonetheless, I can't contact any of the beacons in the nearby star systems. In fact, I doubt we are reaching the second ös harmonic light-field outside this planet. The feedback I am receiving is off-phase by one hundred and twenty-four seconds, and that doesn't make sense. It should be instantaneous."

"So, you're saying we are cut off from the Union!" Naleean failed to suppress a frown of frustration. "What do you think the reason is?"

"I think it's something about this planet — probably the same force that affected our entrance; it must be all around us. However, if my guess is correct, this force has a periodicity, with ebbs and flows… or something like that. I first suspected it when we lost control of the drive's live-crystal upon approaching this planet's ös boundary. The crystal stuttered but with a clear rhythm, almost musical. All I did then was to recalibrate its fundamental chord to that rhythm, and it worked. But that trick isn't working with communications."

Naleean knew where she was going. "Yet the drive's live-crystal worked only until we entered the atmosphere, which we did at an angle from the night side towards the daylight side of the planet, and this could mean the rotating folds of this planet's ös-sphere may be affected differently by that unknown force."

She nodded, her eyes and face sparkling at him — It had worked, he had impressed her!

"And what you are also saying", he continued, "is that communications might work at some point, when that force will again be weak or absent in this location."

"That's the possibility since we don't have a way to detect it and study it." She continued regarding him with her sparkling smile.

"Good enough. I don't know what *I*… w-what *we* would do without you." He smiled at her. "Please, stay close to communications and let me know when it connects."

She wheeled on her feet and walked away singing a happy tune he couldn't catch. He sighed seeing her go, and turned to continue helping the others open the hatch. They were waiting for him and had witnessed the entire conversation in silence. As he turned, he caught them exchanging conspiratorial looks and sniggers. He scoffed at them and said, "Come on, lads! Let's finish this job."

By the end of the afternoon everyone had finished their tasks and sat on the grass, under the shadow of the craft, to eat their first meal on their new world and to exchange impressions. Nothing could dampen their spirits, and they all agreed the experience was far more exciting than in the stories told by their people. As the daylight faded they sang songs which filled the glade with their sonorous voices and the melodious notes of their flutes and strings.

That night the first signs of trouble appeared. Most of them had felt lightheaded throughout the day, and they had attributed it to the small differences between the electromagnetic fields of their new planet and Lyaty — "The composition of the atmosphere also has some differences," the two 'healers' among them told Naleean, "although minor ones." But early in the night some of the older ones started complaining of headaches and of seeing sparkling lights. By daybreak only him and four others were still spared of the symptoms. Nothing the healers had done had worked. Their people had eliminated diseases thousands of years before their time, and this added to the anxiety he felt. Had they made a mistake coming to that planet? As soon as he had read on the epi-net the report, he had rushed everyone to come without following the proper protocol for new planet exploration. Perhaps Humans were no longer fit to walk on the planets of legends.

He had been awake most of the night helping the healers, yet he didn't feel tired when the dawn arrived — the evening before they all had made that same observation: none felt tired and were little hungry in spite of all the work they had done that day. He rose quietly and left his bunk in silence to avoid rousing others. Yet, as he tiptoed out of the cabin, a yell made him trip over a pair of boots someone had left around. The next thing he knew, Nadé was racing towards him and shouting:

"It's working! We're connected!"

He darted and shouted to the first one he saw on his way with her to the upper deck, "Hurry, awake everyone. I need all with me on the communication concourse."

Within minutes he had everyone standing next to him. They didn't look as cheerful as they had been the day before, but all knew the importance of the moment and tried to appear so.

Nadé had already established a communication link with the Offices of the Chancellor. Someone there had just replied they were ready for them.

Naleean had rehearsed several times during the night what he was going to say to the Union authorities — now he couldn't remember any of it! It didn't matter, he could improvise. Fussing with his clothes one last time, he nodded to Nadé. She then proceeded to rotate one of the crystals. The light in the concourse shifted, and the twenty-seven of them were surrounded by an elegant communication chamber in the Chancellor Offices. A woman and a young man dressed as dignitaries stood looking at them. When the man saw them, the blood drained from his face and his mouth dropped.

⚡

Laidé had never been so busy in his life as in the last two days. The leaked report of the survey of the Sol System had elicited all types of reactions on a multitude of worlds. Eighty-two aides he had had to call, so far, to help him deal with the many who wanted to speak, personally, with the Chancellor. From heads of state to ambassadors, from scholars to simple folks, everyone wanted more information. There was none, and this made the situation harder for him and for his aides because the requests then turned into conversations and, sometimes, into a lecture on the reasons the third planet of Sol was or wasn't an Aïdin Planet.

It was early evening. He was tired and ready to quit for the day, and directed his steps towards the Chancellor's private office. He was about to announce himself, when one of his aides came trotting to him:

"Advisor, I am receiving an urgent request to talk to the Chancellor—"

"Don't they all claim to be urgent!" he snorted and immediately regretted it when he saw her face.

She smiled at him with understanding and replied, "This one is different. The request is coming from the Sol System."

"W-What? Are you sure?"

"I checked the signal five times. It's coming from a mobile beacon, probably a craft, inside that system."

Laidé searched in his mind for an explanation, but she continued:

"I could be missing something. The signal is weak…" She paused, thinking, before adding, "It could be a hoax. We have had a few… The strange thing is, the signal has the signature of our people."

As him, she was a Nauthian. In fact, the aides he had called to help him were all Nauthians, experts in multiple languages and cultural protocols, and capable of dealing with the crisis the Chancellor sought to contain.

She was right, none of their people would ever think of making a hoax call to the Chancellor Offices. Then, a foreboding took hold of his heart. He didn't know why.

"Let me handle it", he said softly. "Direct the signal to the main communication chamber. I will enhance it and see what we have."

She inclined her head in respect and left for her post in a hurry.

He was about to hasten towards the main communication chamber when the door to the Chancellor office opened. A voice said to him from inside:

"Laidé! Never before you had a conversation with others in the lobby of my office, much less so if you needed to raise your voice. Let's hope it isn't something unwelcome!"

He went in while the Chancellor asked him with a frown, "What else is now demanding for attention?"

He didn't excuse himself for his behavior, and quickly told the news to the Chancellor. Only one exchange of looks was all it took for the two of them to rush to the communication chamber.

When they arrived, the signal had already lit the chamber. Live projections of two communication beacons stood in mid air. The first one was in the Sol System, the second in their city, Llën of Esdänl. The signal was weak to the point that the system was unable to pinpoint the exact location of the beacon inside Sol.

Laidé ordered the chamber to enhance the first beacon. It improved slightly but still didn't identify the location of origin. There was also a fluctuation in that beacon, and he became afraid they were going to lose connection with it.

The Chancellor was probably thinking the same thing because she ordered him, "Start as it is!"

He sounded a word, the light in the chamber shifted, and the two of them were surrounded by the communication concourse of an old transport craft. A group of Human youngsters of about the same age looked at them. The filtered light of a morning sky gave them an otherworldly look. He felt the blood drain from his body. Next, with a hoarse voice he managed to say:

"You!… Impossible!"

"Who are they? — Laidé! Speak!"

Before he could reply to the Chancellor, one of the oldest youngsters took a step forward and said in clear Galactic Standard with a ceremonial cadence:

"Greetings, Chancellor Vuensé, Keeper of the Charter of Rights of the Union and of all galactic treaties. In the name of my companions here with me, we claim the third planet of Sol for us and for all Nauthians. We petition you to file this official claim in the records of the Union and with the Armistice Inspectorate of the Order of the Wanderers. This transmission contains encoded the names of the twenty-seven of us and seals thus this lawful claim. Likewise, as it is accepted, all the parties engaged in this communication are witnesses to the claim."

The other youngsters around him nodded in pride, some had a defiant smile.

Laidé, his mind blank, turned in slow motion to the Chancellor. She held a deadpan expression. Her mouth opened but no words came from it.

Before the two of them could recover, however, that young man he knew so well continued, this time in an informal tone:

"Greetings, cousin Laidé. Good to see you! Please, let all our people know of our new planet — an Aïdin Planet! All are welcomed here… the

Chancellor and you likewise."

"How… how did you arrive there?" The Chancellor whispered.

"Madam, we were traveling in the vicinity, in the Seeërer System [Sirius System], when the news of the report reached us, and decided that visiting Sol was an opportunity we couldn't miss." The young man beamed to them.

"Some of you don't look well!" Laidé burst out. He was infuriated with his cousin. "Naleean, what's happening? Tell us the truth!"

Naleean looked taken aback by his demand and said with halting words, "We had trouble entering the planet… a bumpy landing, but we managed… The drive system of the craft is now dead—"

"Is anyone hurt?" Councilor Vuensé hastened to ask.

Naleean hesitated before replying, "Not during the landing, but something is affecting us. We all are lightheaded, and some have headaches and—"

The projection stammered, and when it resumed the two of them heard him saying, "… progressing."

"Have you been outside the craft?" The Chancellor's voice trembled.

"Y-Yes, Chancellor, but everything is fine… It's beautiful. The air is fresh and invigorating." Naleean took one more step towards them and resumed with a more steady voice, "We think there's a force or field of some type all around us. It's affecting only the craft's live-crystal systems. Our bodies may be adjusting to it…" He paused to think, then added, "We encountered land animals, and they are normal, healthy and friendly. The planet too feels welcoming. Whatever is—"

The projection stuttered again, and before the transmission broke off they heard him saying, "… temporary."

"Reconnect!" The Chancellor commanded the chamber.

Nothing happened. The beacon in Sol was gone.

"Rangers!" she said aloud.

The chamber lit with a spacious room nearby where Rangers were engaged in their work. All the Rangers stood up when they saw her.

"I need a team of you, experts in communication. Right now! Here!"

"Yes, Chancellor", one of them replied.

"And tell Marshal Mhali to meet me in my office. Now!"

"Yes, Chancellor."

Next, she turned to Laidé and said, "From now on, this chamber is to be used only to communicate with those youngsters. I want a team of Rangers day and night here, doing all they can to reconnect with that beacon and keep it live. I will be informed immediately of any development."

Laidé nodded. He was afraid that if he spoke his annoyance would show. Those youngsters had placed themselves at the center of the looming confrontation between the Union and The Others. What short-sightedness! And they were his people! He was living a nightmare.

At that moment two Rangers entered the chamber with quick steps, and with disconnected words Laidé explained to them the situation. The Rangers gave a subtle bow to him and set to work. One of them opened an access panel on a wall, while the other commanded the chamber, "Triangulate with beacons R-467 and Arthaï-390, then project to beacon Seeërer-681." The chamber's light shifted and the beacons appeared. "Initiate communication protocol Rangers-001 and look for a Nauthian beacon within the Sol System."

No beacon appeared.

"Look for any communication beacon within Sol."

Still nothing.

"Look for any type of beacon within Sol."

No change.

The Ranger looked at the Chancellor, and she said to him, "Keep doing your best."

Next, she grabbed Laidé's arm, whispered, "You come with me", and strode out of the chamber.

⚡

"Apologies, Chancellor", Laidé broke their silence as they entered her office. Laidé and Naleean had each been the only child in their families, and their relation had always been one of older to younger brother. Thus, he felt responsible for Naleean's behavior and well-being. "My cousin and his friends don't know what they are doing."

"*Don't know*, you say? To me, they are very much in control!" She sat heavily on her chair and shook her head, "You don't have to apologize for them."

For a time neither one spoke. The Chancellor, lost in thought, with her back to him, gazed through the large panoramic window behind her desk. Alcyone was setting, and the magnificent play of lavender lights in the horizon didn't ease what Laidé felt. He couldn't sit and began to pace noiselessly.

When Soen and him had been on his home planet recently, Naleean and his friends were about to embark for their new life. Many of the elders had shaken their heads at the youngsters' naiveté and had commented that in no time they would be back. Laidé hadn't been so sure about that. He knew Naleean. He was a practical dreamer, of the type who makes his dreams come true. He also felt a change was unfolding for all Humans, that events were forging new ways, and that his cousin too felt that. But a life of voyaging! That was a thing of the past. Their people weren't the same as in the old times. Soen, on the other hand, had been delighted with their decision and had encouraged the youngsters not to give up when they would encounter challenges. She had suggested places and peoples they could visit, and had talked to them for hours. Laidé hadn't been present during most of those conversations, engaged as he had been in handling the archeological artifacts of Lughai to the leaders of his people.

Did she encourage them to visit Sol? — No, she wouldn't do that. She wanted to keep Galactic Humans away from that system.

Why did the elders allow Naleean to accept that old craft? — None had ever heard of that strange, visiting bard before. "He filled the youngsters' heads with heroic twists of the old legends that our people never heard before", his aunt had told him.

Marshal Mhali's quiet entrance interrupted his thoughts. The Marshal inclined his head to the Chancellor, who next said to him, "Laidé, please, play the communication for the Marshal."

Laidé waved a hand to the wall next to him and a communication photo-sonic field lighted up. He then said a word, and they were immersed in the recording. When it finished, the reaction of his friend wasn't the one he expected:

"Ha! Those youngsters just made our lives much easier!"

"How can you said that?" he said, irked, to Mhali. "They are stranded, sick and unreachable. Besides, The Others are going to accuse the Union of having schemed their claim. Any chances we had with their Overlords to manage the damage made by the leaked report have evaporated. They are going, not just to blockade the system, but to isolate it completely as soon as they are notified of the claim. Then, we will have a confrontation unlike any other we have had with them in a long time. Tell me, how are we going to rescue those kids?"

"You aren't getting it, my friend." Mhali's voice was calm. "From the beginning this affair has been anything but conventional. I'm almost certain The Others are struggling even more than we are in grasping what is going on in that system— they always have a hard time thinking outside the box. On the other hand, that's not a problem for those youngsters. That's why they have taken all of us by surprise. Besides, they've already given us invaluable information that even my Rangers couldn't have provided."

The Chancellor remained silent, listening to their interchange. For the gravity of the situation, Laidé couldn't avoid noticing she was much calmer than he would expect from her.

Then, addressing the Chancellor, Mhali added, "I suggest their claim be filed with the Armistice Inspectorate, right away. They too are going to be surprised, but I have the feeling that more than one Wanderer is going to be pleased with this outcome. They also will read in the youngsters' communication more than what is apparent."

To Laidé's astonishment, the Chancellor replied to the Marshal, "I've already decided to file their claim. I want you to do it, personally, as soon as we finish here. But I want the news of it to remain among official channels only… for now."

"It will be done", Mhali said.

Next, the Chancellor addressed Laidé: "I would like you to delay informing your people. The least thing we need next is an entire fleet of daring ones following those youngsters' steps. Is this acceptable to you?"

Laidé nodded, "Yes, Chancellor." Mhali and the Chancellor were right, yet he still wished the situation didn't involve his people.

"The youngsters' health and safety concerns me, however." The Chancellor signaled to the two of them to sit. "Tell me, Marshal, what did you mean when you said they had already given us invaluable information? Would that help us reach them if need be?"

"Nothing in their appearance told me they are ill", Mhali replied. "Their breathing was rhythmic and normal, their pupils responded properly to the light, and their posture was full of energy. There is some wavering in their bodies' light-fields, but minor. Their leader may be right. It is a temporary situation. Their bodies are probably going through a normal adaptation process to that world. They are Nauthians, and they will do it quickly. They always do. They haven't lost the capacity to adapt their people developed during their former life as voyagers.

"Their safety is another matter", he continued. "We don't have enough information about that planet to assess an internal threat to their safety. As for an external threat, that's a possibility. The Others may attempt a landing if they are serious about that system, especially now when they know of our visit there. But I doubt they will attempt it. They have known of that planet for a long time, yet they have ignored it. A powerful reason has stopped them from taking possession of it and of the other planets. This reason is something we still need to discover. My Rangers—"

Laidé was forcing himself to focus on the positive side of the situation but didn't hesitate to interrupt his friend. "It doesn't matter if the potential risks they are exposed to are known to us or not. If we don't do anything and something happens to them, many are going to condemn the Chancellor for her inaction. Already some voices are requesting audits for the way the whole affair of the Sol System has been handled."

The Chancellor was staring at him, then addressed Mhali once more: "You haven't finished describing the information you gathered from their communication. What else?"

"Their transport made it intact to the ground and is still with them. In contrast, the Thelian probe sent to that planet had all sorts of trouble and vanished after a few minutes inside the planet's atmosphere. Wanderer Soen's craft also entered it and remained intact. The ejection her craft experienced was caused, probably, by its proximity to something that, we can surmise, is either a powerful source of energy or a defense system unlike anything we know. The common factor in the case of the youngsters' craft and your daughter's is that both craft were able to enter the planet's össphere without vanishing, and both craft were old technology, equipped with hybrid drive systems that don't depend on live-crystals. On the other hand, the Thelian probe was entirely built of densified light-fields and crystal technology — which tells me that whatever that planet harbors affects that type of technology."

"Then, when we go there," Laidé said, "we now know how to prepare better for it. Don't we?"

Mhali smiled at him as if saying — You said it, friend, not me!

"No one is going to go there… at least not yet." The Chancellor rose and went to a side dispenser to pour some scented water for the three of them. While giving a cup to the Marshal, she asked him, "What news do you have of the three Rangers sent to the fifth planet?"

"We are in contact with them daily. As we noticed during the survey operation, The Others aren't keeping a watchful eye on that system, and the Rangers reached Mal'ek six days ago without difficulty. Since then, they have been moving among the population, blending with them and seeking for information to explain the presence of The Others on their world. But the common people are reluctant to say much. The regime has them so afraid that they are suspicious of anyone who asks questions. Nevertheless, we have gathered a few bits of useful information. Mostly, that The Others haven't shown themselves to the people since their initial introduction by the Elite three planet-years ago."

Laidé raised his eyebrows — that was also uncharacteristic of The Others — while Mhali continued:

"They do visit the planet regularly, but limit their visits to one place. What's curious is that the native people, in fear, avoid that place. This is a remote place where a large clusters of towers to collect the energy of the core of the planet is located, built about one hundred years ago. Strange events began to happen there not long after they were erected. That's the reason the natives fear the place. But for us the question is: What is special about this place that The Others are so interested in? — To find the answer, the Rangers began moving towards that location, yesterday."

"Have The Others made any movement to blockade the system?" Laidé asked him. "I mean, yesterday or today, since the report of our survey of Sol was made public?"

"No, they haven't, and that's puzzling. We have no doubt they already secured copies of the report. We have observers in all their bases in this region of the galaxy, and there isn't any activity to indicate the movement of a fleet or anything unusual. Although, there may be an explanation for their inaction. My Rangers have recently gathered information that reveals the Overlords are having serious disagreements with each other, beyond their usual bickering. Something that's kept very secret is making the Overlords uneasy and stirring them to dissent loudly."

"So you think the reason for their inaction is something they fear in the Sol System, don't you?" the Chancellor said with a frown. "That's also what my daughter told us."

"Yes, Chancellor. However, our long-range mapping and monitoring hasn't discovered anything abnormal, not yet. That system has so many moons, asteroids and small bodies that my Rangers are still working in a detailed mapping of it."

"Then, The Others could be there," Laidé said with a sinking feeling, "somewhere other than on Mal'ek, and we haven't seen them yet." The Others were attracted to using small bodies in Space to hide their bases.

Mhali assented in silence.

"Are you sure the health of the youngsters is fine and they can manage on their own, for now, as long as The Others don't change their minds and decide to visit them?"

The sudden shift in the conversation, back to the youngsters, didn't pass unnoticed to Laidé. Was the Chancellor concerned they could be affected by the same malady that had affected the Humanity of Yfel? — She had mentioned to him, unofficially, that she feared the Blight of the Ancients was back, explaining the catastrophe on Yfel.

"As I said," Mhali replied, "they show good health and good spirits, at the moment, and I think they are capable of dealing well with their situation and the unexpected." With a quick glance to Laidé, he added, "Nauthians have an inner resolve and a resourcefulness which surprise even them. However, if in your judgment, Chancellor, you see the need to give them assistance or protection right away, we could order the three Rangers on Mal'ek to go to them — their shuttle craft isn't powered by live-crystals. Once they are there, we will know for certain the conditions and the environment the youngsters are experiencing."

The Chancellor murmured, "That's a possibility…" then sat in silence.

That idea had also occurred to Laidé, and he had discarded it. Even if in his heart he wanted to move those kids away from that system, to know what The Others were doing on Mal'ek was of vital importance to clarify the stance of The Others on Sol. There were also the other parties of Rangers monitoring the system from the outside. But these were of no help. They were using craft not suitable for planetary landing. Besides, those craft were all built with Thelian crystal technology.

"No!" the Chancellor said after a moment. "The Rangers stay on Mal'ek until they finish their mission. It is of supreme importance that we know what is happening there. However, Marshal, order your strategists to start planning for a rescue mission, in case we need it to bring those youngsters home in a hurry. As for the two of you, I don't want to postpone more your trip to Thel. I want you and Soen, if she still wants to accompany you, to leave as soon as your affairs here permit it. You must meet with Issën Althesal and her team. I want you all to come up with viable options to know more about that third planet without risking any one's life. If we can re-establish communication with the youngsters, I want you to include them in all your deliberations. After all, they are now the rightful inhabitants of that planet."

20

Paradigms in Collision

She didn't have a name. Not for this mission. 'Number One'— so the others called her.

For thousands of years her people had lived in peace. Their isolation in the outer arm of the Laïs Galaxy, in a group of four star systems that didn't offer the best of conditions, had made of them a resourceful Humanity. They had even managed to develop a space-drive technology that had made possible the formation of *Bastal* — a modest federation of six planets. The first change to their quiet lives came when they were discovered by Rangers seeking out new Humanities. Life had then become easier in many respects with the few new trade routes and the assistance provided by member-worlds of the Union. Not long after, however, The Others had come on the heels of the traders, and her people's life was now exposed, for the first time in their history, to the threat of an external aggression.

The Others had observed them for a time, until six years back when they had made their first move and seized the only uninhabited star system of their federation. They had next built an automated depot base on its sole planet, designed to supply their craft in the vast expanses of the outskirts of the galaxy. But for how long was that going to be before they decided to capture the other star systems of Bastal? Her people had asked for protection to the Union, but the politics and wording of the Armistice of Adhara had prevailed. The High Council had then declared The Others weren't a present threat to their federation and nothing could be done until they became one. Many among her people disagreed, and the moment had arrived to make a point of it.

She had been recruited because of her ideas that Humans had had enough of The Others and that the leaders of the Union were cowards by not using their power to eliminate them. The leaked report of the survey of the Sol System was one more proof that it was imperative to take action to rein in their threat. It had come as an unexpected boon, at the right time to reinforce their resolve and to make other worlds receptive to their cause.

Every chance of succeeding was now in her hands.

The dark alleys had concealed her presence in the circuitous route she had followed to arrive at the destination. The map, painstakingly memorized, hadn't been enough, and twice she had had to retrace her steps. Now, crouched inside the shadow of an abandoned land vehicle, with her enhanced night vision she studied the featureless façade of a large building looming in front of her. It had to be it. No sounds or lights of any kind came from the massive structure, contrasting with the noises and lights in the surrounding buildings.

She had been assured that the entire base was deserted that night, but the presence of security bots patrolling the streets and alleys couldn't be ruled out. Everywhere discarded machinery and refuse littered the passageways between buildings. An omnipresent acrid stench irritated her eyes and nose in spite of her face-gear. She was recording and broadcasting, live, everything with multi-sensors to demonstrate to other Galactic Humans that The Others hadn't the dignity of most of the Young Races and treated worlds with disdain.

Her two companions weren't far behind. She sensed them approaching in silence. Each had taken a different route in case something went wrong. None of the three had known or seen each other before that night. They had first met upon boarding the craft that brought them to that dismal and lone planet.

When the two arrived, she moved aside to let them in under the cover of the shadow. The satchel she carried pressed against her rib cage. It felt heavy, even though it contained only a glassy sphere that fit in the palm of her hand. Her companions also carried, each, an object needed to fulfill their mission. Each of the three objects could easily purchase one-year supplies and food for the entire population of her home world. They had been obtained in the Underworld through an untraceable chain of agents until they had reached the operation's core group.

She nodded to one of her companions as soon as she felt sure it was the place and that they were alone. He nodded back, rose silently and approached the featureless building. A small disk strapped to the palm of his right hand gave a pale reflection when he raised it and rested it on the façade. It took a few seconds for the molecular structure of the wall to shift noiselessly, and for a dark, round opening to appear. It was large enough for them to enter, one at a time. She went in first, followed by her second companion. The one with the disk remained behind, guarding their escape.

Inside the building it was even darker than the gloomy night outside, yet she could see ahead a red glow and the supports that held its source high above the floor. It took them longer than she felt comfortable to navigate the obstacles before they were almost beneath that source. It was jet-black and had an octahedral shape. Through its upper vertex it captured and concentrated a narrow band of the spectrum of radiations emitted by the brown dwarf star at the center of the system. She had seen only drawings of it. It was a near-infrared photonic condenser designed to power the large supply depot and its landing port.

This is it! — she told herself. It had taken her more than two years to prepare for that moment. The entire operation had been, several times, on the verge of collapse, but the core group had managed to keep it going. Her heart was running so fast, she felt it wanted to jump out of her chest.

Her companion waited for her move. She dug out the small sphere from her satchel. It was a Thelian live-crystal, by itself harmless. Nonetheless, with slow, calculated, almost-reverent movements, she placed it on the floor. A faint glow shone from it, barely enough to illuminate their boots. It had taken many minds and two years of experimentation to shield the enormous amount of light from the first ös light-field that it contained.

When she released it, the sphere rolled of its own in slow motion, away from them. She tensed up ready to snatch it back. She didn't have to. One handspan from where she had set it, the sphere found a resting place. At that moment her body forced her to realize she had been holding her breath.

Without delay her companion knelt. In his right hand he held a pocket-size tuning fork with a circulating, bluish light in the interior of its five prongs. It was the most expensive of the three objects, made of a crystal-metal alloy known only to the Thelians. How its existence had become known, what its intended use was, and how it had left the Thelian home world, she still couldn't guess.

His companion struck the largest prong of the fork with his other hand. A soft, low hum came from it — it was all she could hear of the multi-level harmonics the fork was sounding. Next, he rested it on the sphere. She knew then he had begun to count. She did the same. Thirty seconds applying the sounding fork would unleash a slow and controlled unraveling of the standing sound pattern that held the light contained in the sphere.

At the thirty-second count her companion removed the fork and rose. They turned and retraced their steps with brisk but noiseless strides. Upon exiting, their other companion nodded to them — the alley was clear.

It took them much less time to navigate together the convoluted, dark and narrow ways to exit the base. It wasn't going to be that easy, however. Thirty paces before they reached their craft, a slow moving bot that hadn't been there before forced her to halt their run. A coldness spread inside her — the bot was inspecting the hull of their craft! She was about to abandon hope of leaving that planet before the conflagration started when the bot decided the large containers nearby were more interesting. She then sprinted towards their craft, and her companions charged next to her.

The hatch gave way when her hand touched it. Still in complete silence, she took the controls and maneuvered the craft away from the planet as fast as its power-drive could manage.

Before they entered the sole bay in the transport waiting for them outside the system, a blinding light erupted on the planet. The near-infrared photonic condenser had augmented the power of the released ös-light of the sphere, and the entire base of The Others had been reduced to a molten mass. She turned off the recording-transmitting device attached to her forehead. Only then she spoke for the first time to her two companions:

"Our message has been sent!"

⚡

Ethën sat alone in the garden surrounding his home. The fountain, which he had designed and crafted to enliven it, sang today a sorrowful tune. It had never before. It mirrored the feeling in his heart. He was the one who had sent Althesal's report to his friend in Planetary Harmonics Sciences. He too was the mind behind the principles and techniques to create the sphere of concentrated ös-light used by the Bastal rebels.

How can the unexpected arise in a Universe so precise in its laws and principles? he asked himself. There was no explanation he could think of except the presence of free-will choice — the central characteristic of Humans and of all the others of the Young Races.

"I guessed you would be here." Nesdil's voice reached him from behind, and right away the fountain changed its sad tune into a joyful one. Her heart radiation was stronger than his. Even the fountain's lights and the flow of water became lively. She approached, kissed him on the forehead, and sat at the edge of the basin.

For a time no one said a word, and Ethën felt her studying him. Then, she spoke with her soft voice: "I went to your lab looking for you. Everyone there is wondering if you have really disappeared from Thel — as you told them you wanted to — and went to a place beyond the reach of politics."

"I wish such a place existed!" He sighed.

"But it does! Our Aïdin Planet in Sol." She smiled at him.

"It wouldn't work", he replied biting his lip. "Our going there would make of it a place of politics." He would rather be silent but couldn't stop himself from following the thread of her thought. It happened every time. Her mind and voice moved with such an unsurpassable grace that it compelled all who listened to dance at her tune.

"Try some may," she countered, "yet it will never take hold there. The music of that planet is an uncontrollable wave, and nothing extraneous to its theme can last for long."

He knew then where she was going. Thus, unable to contain a smile he said, "You are still studying the recordings of the Asli's island and of the probe to that planet, aren't you?" When her only answer was a grin, he added, "Forget it! There is no way we can travel to that planet now." When still she didn't answer, he said, "Anyway, I wouldn't be surprised if at this very moment the Council of the Paths is deciding to exile the four of us to a remote galaxy."

"Come on! Lighten up! This isn't the Ethën I know! You know well the Council hasn't that type of authority. Besides, you heard and witnessed Thaël's interest in the findings of that planet. We have done nothing wrong with our musings about it being an Aïdin Planet, nor has any of our people — and that includes you — done anything unwise by sharing with others our wonderful creations. Our weakness is that we expect others to use them as we do. Out there, however, reality is other — our people better learn to see it in that way. Besides, we live in a Universe that, thanks Light, loves to surprise us at every step of our journey."

Ethën shook his head. "That reasoning is what brought us to this crisis. The fact is that our people keep dancing between sharing with others and restraining from sharing, not truly deciding which one is the right one."

"Well, then, it's time we look at this affair in another light!" She paused when a group of eos came to the fountain attracted by their presence. "In this matter, there is no right or wrong way. Our commitment to participate in the Union, and see others rise to a greater flourishing, is and should be our only guiding light."

One of the eos alighted on her lap, and she broke her intense gaze upon him to caress the creature. Ripples of colored lights flashed through the creature's flower-like translucent body, and in the process it emitted a soft, joyful music.

So much has our people learned from its kind — Ethën couldn't evade the thought, admiring the creature's striking body. *Why can't others do the same with all the marvelous creations the Universe offers? Why do they focus just on themselves? On their likes and dislikes?*

"Have you heard from Althesal?" Nesdil asked, still caressing the eos.

"Not a word since she went this morning to the emergency meeting of the Council... But let's not change our subject. Assuming we stay in the Union, according to what you say, what should be our contribution to the Union? Our sciences? Our arts?"

"Those shouldn't be the choices", she replied with a grin. "Our contribution should be *us!* — The fullness of us!"

He gaped at her. When she didn't elaborate her answer, he said, "If you mean our philosophy, we are already doing that. We have offered to all our view of the Universe and of life's journey. That they are free to accept it or reject it is also part of our philosophy. There is also the fact that our science and art in themselves are direct outcomes of the Song of our life."

"Ethën! On this very day most of our people are repeating those same words! Science... Art... Philosophy... They aren't who we are! We aren't a mere song for others to hear. We *are* also a heart that loves and suffers, that aspires and has disappointments, that has successes and failures, all at the same time — and this is what we should share with others... that we are Humans on a journey to discover more about us, others and the Universe... Many beyond our planet fail to see us in this light and have us on a pedestal."

He shifted on the bench and lowered his eyes. Nesdil and Althesal talked like that. Yet, that didn't help him with the burden he felt at that moment. "I thought we are already doing that", he murmured. "Sometimes I wonder, if the Åh truly existed, how they would answer that question — how they, having more to offer, would decide what to share with those who are less evolved."

"Perhaps that question itself should be the sole motivating force of our journey through Time as a people."

Ethën stared at her. There it was again. It was the second time in recent days that Nesdil had brought him to look at the journey as the best answer to one's questions. He loved to reach to the answers immediately, dismissing the journey. With a sigh he rose and walked to the oleesia tree near the fountain. It was loaded with fruit, bite-size, of a rosy color and a sweet aroma. He picked two handfuls of them and returned to his bench, gave a handful to Nesdil and started to eat the rest.

"In the past two days", she spoke when she finished the fruit, "many from the Exploring and the Life Weaving Paths, and some from the Providing Path, have contacted me to encourage us to continue to study the mystery of the third planet in Sol. Some offered to help us. They see this as an opportunity to break the taboo our people have on the legends. It doesn't befit our Song to close our ears and eyes to them — they too form part of the Song of the Universe… And who knows? We may end living on that planet one day."

Her last words startled him — she really wanted to go there! Nesdil was changing from the person who liked to play safe to one who felt comfortable with taking risks. Had he become attached to his ways and to playing safe?

A few minutes passed during which none of the two felt the need to speak.

Strangely enough, their conversation had relaxed his mind for the first time in days, and he let it muse on the possibility of living on another world, with a whole new future in front of him. Would he be able to really let go of everything, and focus on a journey that would be a question in itself?

"I don't want you to give up now", Nesdil said softly to him. "I'm sure Althesal feels the same. Our path is together. Besides, I'm liking that we are shaking everyone up. I feel we have just started." After pausing to gauge his reaction, she continued, "I bring some news. Last night the Asli communicated with me through a dream once again. They want us back there. I felt an urgency in their desire to see us."

Ethën's initial enthusiasm for unraveling the mystery of their experiences with the Asli had waned with all the turmoil of late. He still couldn't make sense of them, but pursuing that path would only create more trouble for the four of them.

"Going there now isn't wise", he whispered. "Too many eyes are upon us. Using an atmospheric craft would raise a lot of questions. We need to wait until the situation settles down."

Nesdil laughed. "You continue imagining things! Our people haven't had so much excitement in a long time. Even coming here, to your place, was an adventure. Everyone on my way here wanted to talk to me. For what I am gathering, our people aren't ignorant at all about the legends, as everyone assumes." With a chuckle she added, "Some, however, still want to be discreet and call them 'remote history' — can you believe it?"

At that moment a commotion, by Thelian standards, in the front of his dwelling halted what he was going to say about that. The two of them rose at once and strode around the house towards the many voices. It was then when Ethën recognized Althesal's voice saying:

"I know, you all want to know what the Council of the Paths decided." She was talking to a small group of people gathered around her. "Before this day is over, the Secretary of the Council will release the minutes and the conclusions of the meeting so that all those who couldn't attend in person will be informed."

"But, Teacher, we want the Council to know you have done nothing wrong, and that we support you", a young man said with a taut voice.

Ethën saw their faces and realized they all were Althesal's former apprentices in the Bio-Soul Sciences.

"No need for that, Dalsil", Althesal replied to the young man. "Our Council is wise, and a good plan has emerged from all the unsettling news of late. If you hear the call in your heart, you could be part of that plan."

"What do you mean by that, Teacher?" A girlish woman asked.

It was then when Althesal turned and saw him and Nesdil witnessing the unusual gathering at his doorstep. Turning back to face her former students she said, "Why don't you go and wait for the release of the minutes and the communique from the Council. Then, we can talk again if you want… but at my office. Tomorrow."

In silence the group dispersed in twos and threes. Althesal wheeled on her feet and, shaking her head, said, "What a day!"

↯

Althesal was exhausted. She sat alone by the fountain. Ethën and Nesdil were preparing dinner inside the house after she had answered their many questions regarding the meeting. The fountain's song soothed her, and on her lap two eos creatures warbled at her with soft notes.

Her people were going to continue as members of the Union, sharing their knowledge, their sciences and arts, and their technology, in the same way their ancestors had decided — progressively, from the most advanced civilizations to the less advanced ones, and according to their commitment to live by the Protocol of Union of the Laendänl. The system worked, and many worlds had grown wiser because of it. Missing in their contribution was the Human touch, the contact of close friendship with others. Without it, many remained in the darkness, not truly knowing the way her people understood and lived life and the manner they regarded their creations. That was a contribution the Council was going to ask next of all Thelians — to ready themselves to befriend all those from other worlds to whom they would encounter along the ways of life.

In her heart she hoped a new era would come for her people with this new step, an era that could change the future Iain of Ær had presented of them.

Her uncle had become an enigma to her. Thaël had made a speech so compelling about her team and their work in making possible the survey of the Sol System, that everyone had agreed the issue of the legends of old and of Aïdin Planets was not a matter for the Council but for each Thelian citizen to decide. That too was how their ancestors had opted, but most had forgotten it. It was time to remind everyone of that.

Yet, she couldn't stop wondering, why was her uncle acting different? Why was he wanting to be closer to her now, after so many years of traveling different paths? Why his interest in the minutia of the work of her team? And why had he asked Daothel, an apprentice he had just met, to accompany him to the Library of the Explorers, not once but several times? What was he looking for? Did he know Daothel was Ciän's successor in the Synod?

21

Winds of Change

Planet Esdänl, Alcyone System

"Overlord Ankepum has ordered a blockade of the Bastal Federation, Chancellor", the Ranger in charge of the patrol reported. He stood with his two companions on the communication concourse of a scout craft. They were young, probably recent graduates from the Academy, but his voice and demeanor told her he wasn't intimidated by the situation.

"He is enraged", the Ranger continued, "and has vowed to give a lesson to every one of the six federation worlds. For what we have gathered, the base destroyed wasn't just a supply depot. A secret research facility lay beneath it. No one was there when the conflagration took place; however, the small planet no longer offers conditions of any use to the Overlord. According to the conversations we intercepted, the research had to do with the energy of the core of the dwarf star around which the small planet orbits, but no details were mentioned."

Chancellor Vuensé shut her eyes for a moment. She could feel the tension in those present in the meeting. The twelve Marshals of the Ranger Corps sat with her around the conference table. By a coincidence they all were on Esdänl for the biannual assessment of the work of the Corps. She had been awoken in the middle of the night by a call from Marshal Mhali, informing her that a small party of Rangers, on duty in the systems of the outer arm of the Galaxy, had requested a communication priority-1. The two of them had immediately suspected trouble in the Bastal Federation. She had been expecting it but not that soon.

"Where are you, exactly, and how long has it been since the Overlord's fleet arrived?" she asked the Ranger.

"We are in the vicinity of the dwarf star. We arrived two standard galactic days ago to the Federation space, not long after the broadcast of the destruction reached Headquarters. We received orders to be on alert for a reaction from The Others and to report any development. Less than one standard galactic hour ago we noticed a disturbance in the light-fields near the star. That's when the fleet arrived, with Ankepum's personal craft commanding it. Immediately we moved closer to study their intentions and to intercept their communications. The first order the Overlord gave was to send a small landing craft to inspect the remains of the base, but it had to return because it couldn't land. The surface is still too hot. Soon after we intercepted his orders to his commanders to prepare to form a blockade around the six worlds of Bastal."

"Has anyone detected your presence?"

"No, Chancellor. We are sure that not even the peoples of Bastal know of our presence here. They may have been expecting a retaliation because no craft has left or arrived to any of their planets since we came into their space."

"How many craft does Ankepum have there now?"

The Ranger activated the visual sensors of their craft, showing in the distance the Overlord's fleet.

"They have twenty-six, of various types and capacities, plus Ankepum's personal one. As you can see, five of them are large transports, of those used to carry troops and small landing shuttles. There is another craft, from this angle partially hidden by the transports, that is of a design and type we haven't seen. The curious thing about this fleet is that all the craft arrived at the same time."

"That's more than enough power to lay siege to those six worlds", one of the Marshals said. "How did they manage to assemble that size of a fleet in that remote region in just two days? At the speed of their fastest craft, the nearest bases are five standard galactic days from there. And you said they all arrived at the same time? That's more unusual."

The Ranger remained silent, acknowledging that he and his party didn't have answers to those questions.

Since the start of the affair of the Sol System, Chancellor Vuensé had ordered the Rangers to heighten their alert status for any unusual behavior in The Others, anywhere. Now that she had heard the news, a blockade to a small federation of worlds, where no valuable resources of any kind were found, and for a remote outpost base — research facility or not — and a blockade led by Overlord Ankepum himself — wasn't what she had expected. Something more had to be happening to explain the behavior of Ankepum. The Marshals were probably thinking along the same lines but waited for her to proceed.

"Please, describe to us this new type of craft", she asked the Ranger. It was the only observable new element in the situation.

"It has the dimensions of a mid-size transport, Chancellor, but perfectly spherical and with large and narrow spikes protruding from its hull at various points — these are as tall as the diameter of the hull. When the fleet arrived, a reddish energy field surrounded that craft beyond its spikes. But it must have been powering down because this field was contracting, and in less than a minute… it disappeared…"

The Chancellor saw the change in the face of the Ranger as his voice trailed away while finishing his last sentence. In his rush to inform Headquarters about Ankepum's arrival, it was clear to her, he hadn't had the time to digest all they had observed — until that moment. Some exclamations coming from the Marshals told her they too had figured out the same thing that she and the Ranger were thinking. One more thing was all she needed to confirm her suspicion: "Where was this craft located with respect to the others when the fleet arrived?"

"At the very center of the formation, Chancellor", he replied pursing his lips.

She took a deep breath and regarded the Marshals. Their faces were grave with the enormity of the discovery they had just made.

"How, in the name of the Light, haven't we heard of this before!" one the Marshals said. "Are we asleep in complacency? This is too big to have missed it."

"Something isn't right here", another of the Marshals said shaking her head. "With their research capacity, the development of a mobile power to translocate an entire fleet through the higher ös light-fields would have taken Ankepum's people decades. To keep that kind of development secret for that long isn't The Others' strength."

"They had help", Marshal Mhali said. "It's the only reasonable explanation. The question is, from whom?"

He was right, the Chancellor thought. She then said slowly and addressing everyone, "Nothing in the recent years tells us The Others have been investing in research capacity. On the contrary, all along these years they have intensified their efforts to steal knowledge and technology from us and from others. This leads us to Marshal Mhali's conclusion: someone is helping them, and this new ally is more powerful than them."

"If that's the case," one of the Rangers on the scout craft said, "this new ally must be from beyond our Seven Galaxies, because we would have heard of them."

Some of the Marshals nodded in agreement. Mhali and others appeared unsure. She looked at him.

"That may be the case", Mhali replied to the Ranger. "However, some considerations don't fit with that possibility. For one, a craft able to create a displacement field through the highest *intra*-galactic ös light-field wouldn't be able to operate in a *trans*-galactic displacement — it either had to be built in our galaxy, or brought inside a large trans-galactic transport; which leads to my other point. The Tharans near the core of this galaxy and the Mæl would have noticed the coming of a new race through the galactic Portal and through one of the Portal Stars, specially a race so technologically advanced. The Tharans and the Mæl may be neutral in their stance regarding our stalemate with The Others, but they dislike anything that upsets the order of the galaxies — and we know well nothing escapes their watchful eyes."

"So, what are you saying?" one of the Marshals asked — her Islnom was contiguous to Mhali's. "That this new ally is from our own galaxy, or that it has a way to travel outside normal Space?"

"I don't have an answer to that", Mhali replied. "But, that's what we must find out, and soon. We need to redouble our observation of The Others, be on maximum alert everywhere else, and ask for help to the Order of the Wanderers — they have eyes and ears everywhere and will not hesitate to collaborate with us in this matter when so much is at stake."

"Could the recent events in the Sol System be related to this new ally?" another Marshal asked.

Mhali sighed, then answered slowly, not hiding his uneasiness, "Let's hope they aren't. If they are, then a powerful threat is already in our midst and we can't see it. It would also mean Overlord Ankepum is the one interested in that system, which wouldn't come as a surprise. Of lately, he has been testing how far he can go without violating the Armistice."

Mhali's words were met with silence, and the Chancellor took a deep breath. She next surveyed each of the Marshals. Now many things made sense. Ankepum with a new ally that powerful explained some of the happening in the Sol System. But who could be that ally?

"Let's redouble our observation of The Others", she told them all. "I will inform the other Councilors of these events. We can't keep a lid on the news of the blockade of the Bastal Federation, but let's manage with discretion the discovery we made of this new technology in the hands of Ankepum. However, let's not reveal yet the possible existence of this new ally of his — we don't want to alert Ankepum, or any of the other Overlords, that we know of it. I will myself contact the Wanderers of the Armistice Inspectorate and request their help. You too can contact all your Wanderer friends and work with them. They all will realize the gravity of the situation and will be discreet about this new threat.

"As for the blockade," she turned towards the Marshal in charge of the Islnom that included the outer arm of the galaxy, "I want you to implement an emergency shielding of the planets of the Bastal Federation. How soon can your Rangers be there?"

"The emergency protocol for this type of situation is already active, Chancellor, and all the preparations began when we heard the news of the destruction of the base. My Rangers can be there in less than one standard galactic hour. The shielding of the planets will be in place before The Others finish taking positions and before they notice our presence."

"Good!" she said. "Let's hope Ankepum's response will be the same as in other instances and order a retreat when he realizes his blockade is futile. I don't need to tell you this, but gather all the data you can about that new craft… No heroics, please. Ankepum is showcasing it with intention, and we don't know if he has other surprises in store for us."

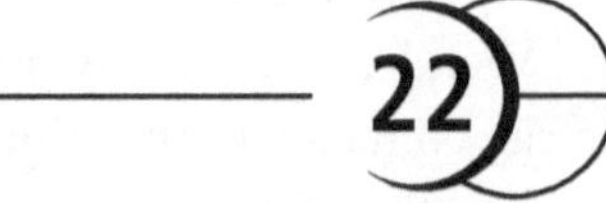

The Seven

Planet Thel, Eir System

Marshal Mhali walked next to Althesal along the central promenade of the administration complex of the Exploring Guilds, in the city of Ïthel on Thel. Everything around them was a living work of art — gardens of colorful beauty blending with each other in a symphony for the eyes, water works with sounds affecting one's mood in a certain way, and sculptures of lights and sounds with ever-changing shapes. Everything fitted in perfect harmony with all the other elements around.

This was Mhali's third visit to the planet Thel, and in each instance he marveled at the sophistication of its people. The origin of Thelian Humans was a mystery. They had become a highly evolved civilization almost overnight, in terms of evolution. All other mature, enlightened Human civilizations had a long history of struggles to arrive to their present standing. The Thelian themselves didn't have a satisfactory explanation for this difference. They reasoned, and others agreed, their planet was a central factor in their development. Its ös-sphere and bio-sphere were remarkably harmonious, and it processed the radiations of the two stars in the system, and those coming from the rest of the galaxy, with an efficiency and balance that some thought unnatural.

The others in the group strolled ahead. Soen and Nesdil, in spite that they had just met, whispered and giggled — about what? Mhali couldn't imagine. They had taken to each other as if they weren't a Wanderer and a Thelian but two school girls from any Human world. Laidé and Ethën conversed with each other, probably about more serious themes, although they too laughed at times — they were old friends from the time Laidé had lived

214

as a student among the Thelians.

Soen, Laidé and him had arrived early that morning. He hadn't been sure if he was going to have the time for this visit with all that was happening with The Others, but the Chancellor had insisted that meeting with Althesal's team was of utmost importance. As soon as they had met, the three of them had shared with the Thelian team the news of the claim of the third planet of Sol by the young Nauthians, Soen's account of her visit to Sol two years before, and their present understanding of what might be happening there.

Each of the Thelians' subtle reaction to the news had told Mhali that Althesal, Nesdil and Ethën knew something the rest of the Thelian research team didn't. With discretion, he had made Althesal aware of his observation. He had noticed she too had been studying the three of them since their arrival from Esdänl. In reply to his observation she had suggested for the six of them to visit a 'Nomöe of Minds' that afternoon. He didn't know what that was but went along with it. She had also mentioned one other — "He will meet us at the Nomöe."

"A Nomöe of Minds", Althesal explained to him as they directed their steps towards it, "is one of the technologies my people consider unwise to share with others civilizations. It is simply Sound Science combined with geometry, and its operation is straight forward, but it could harm those unready. We have eight of them on Thel. Laidé has already experienced their working during his time with us. However, few off-worlders are ever taken to visit a Nomöe. A precise control of one's mind is necessary, otherwise the experience can confuse the identity of the person. Among our people they have no major importance, only mentors and teachers use them to share with their apprentices particular areas of knowledge that otherwise would be incompletely understood."

The Nomöe was located in a secluded area adjacent to the promenade. Majestic evergreen trees towered at a certain distance from it, cloistering it completely from the city life. The place was open to the sky, resembling a small amphitheater. However, instead of series of seating tiers, it had a single semicircle, made of a seamless white crystal, where twelve small pentagons were etched. Where the stage would be located, a central circle was seen. Two gradual ramps spiraled down from the promenade level to the floor level, ending at each side of 'the stage'.

A young Thelian, dressed with the distinctive clothing of the Exploring Guilds, waited for them at the top of the nearest ramp. When they approached, with decisive steps he came to him bearing a broad smile, taking him by surprise.

"Mhali, Marshal of the Rangers," the youth said to him with a musical voice while placing his right hand on his heart, "with the Song of our world and our stars, I welcome you. I am Daothel, apprentice in the Bio-Soul Sciences."

The youth next looked deeply into his eyes, and Mhali felt a strange thrill. The force of Mind-Soul in him was unlike anyone he had encountered before — he felt as if the youth was measuring up the depth of his being. He then ended the greeting with an approving smile, again surprising him.

Afterwards, Daothel addressed Laidé and Wanderer Soen in the same formal manner. Laidé returned the greeting in the Thelian language, eliciting a slight bow and a grin from the youth. Yet, Soen, in response to the greeting, kissed him on both cheeks. Taken by surprise, the youth, beaming from ear to ear, said to her, "It is true then that Wanderers charm others with their grace and manners! I will have to learn to protect myself from you; otherwise I will become a Wanderer myself!"

Everyone laughed with mirth at that reaction, except Nesdil who shook her head while saying with a contained chuckle, "He's always acting sweet and warmhearted. But I warn you, it is he who will bewitch you if you aren't on guard. He already has a large following among the other apprentices and mentors, as well as among the many creatures of our world that cross his path."

Daothel gave them all an innocent look and shrugged his shoulders. He then became serious and addressed Althesal by her Thelian title: "Dean, as you requested, the Nomöe is ready. No one will disturb us for the rest of the afternoon."

"Excellent!" she replied. "Thank you for taking care of this."

She then said to all, "What I am about to share with you happened to me thirty days ago during a visit to the Time Science Research Complex on the small companion planet of Thel. Only my former mentor knows of it, but the time has come to share it with you. Its relevance to what we now know of the involvement of The Others in the Sol System will become apparent to you."

Turning to Soen and Mhali, she added, "The spoken word has no place inside a Nomöe of Minds." Next, with a gesture of her hand she invited everyone to descend along the ramp.

Daothel took the lead. Mhali descended next with Soen at his right. As they went down, a deep silence began to settle all around, and a sparkling, luminous, bluish mist, that wasn't visible from above, enveloped them. Mhali understood right away that the amphitheater-looking structure was an amplifier of the universal light-field of Mind. They were immersing themselves in this field and, once on the floor level, the outside world was left behind — not even the sky was visible.

Without speaking, Daothel directed Soen, Laidé and him to stand, each, inside one of the pentagons on the floor. Then, Ethën, Nesdil and the young apprentice did the same while Althesal entered the central circle.

With a voiceless voice that sounded inside his head, Althesal directed him and the others: "Focus your attention on your mind, yet think of nothing, and close your eyes."

Mhali, curious, observed everyone. The mist had begun to move. It swirled around each in a distinctive pattern, easily recognizable and with sparkling hues unique to the person. After a moment, bands of this mist became more numerous around Althesal, and the pentagons where they stood lightened up with a soft sapphire light.

The awareness of being in the Nomöe faded as soon as he closed his eyes. Immediately in his mind a moving picture took form. He was entering a large sphere, hovering over a small mountain lake. The images next turned to real sensations, and he could feel the cold air buffeting his skin. It felt good. Somehow the thought came to him that the sphere was a Null-Time chamber. He then realized he was inside Althesal's memory of the event she wanted them to witness — re-living it in detail as it had happened to her.

Mhali lost track of time as the memory unfolded, and he became engaged in the bizarreness of the event. He/Althesal found himself in a large, vaulted space suffused by a red twilight. Yet, when he/Althesal saw the group of Dreki surrounded by strange, slithering shadows, his concentration wavered a bit — seeing a group of Others so close compelled his training to take control and do something about it. However, he knew well he wasn't there, and let the memory continue.

Mhali was also able to focus on the minor details that Althesal's mind had recorded. He suspected they were inside a craft of some type, and recognized the insignia of Ankepum's Dominion on the Dreki uniforms. The slithering shadows with them appeared to be alive and intelligent — Were they Overlord Ankepum's new allies? — The craft had no partitions on the spacious deck, and the hull's inner walls appeared to be made of a rough, dark brown, mineral material. Lumps of a foul substance were scattered along the periphery of the floor — the reddish light inside the craft came from these. But he couldn't sense or identify a drive system, nor the source of power to move the small planet they maneuvered. Through the twilight that surrounded him, besides the two subaltern Dreki and the six ones working with the shadows, he also observed three other Dreki standing at the center of the deck. They appeared to be semi-conscious and had a sickly look. Behind each of them, touching the Dreki's head with an appendage, loomed one of those shadowy beings.

The event ended when Althesal returned to the Null-Time chamber. Then, abruptly, as it had started, he was free from her memory and aware of the luminous mist of the Nomöe and of his companions. Questions crowded his mind, and a feeling of apprehension weighed on his heart.

He took a deep breath to relieve the tension. Where had Ankepum found such bizarre entities? He needed to ask Althesal more about the circumstances of that experience. A quick look to the others told him they too were full of questions — all regarded Althesal with grave and inquiring faces.

⚡

Althesal opened her eyes. Marshal Mhali and Wanderer Soen had met her expectations. Their minds were disciplined and free from emotional clutter. She hadn't had the need to support them during the experience as she had, at times, done it with young apprentices. Of Laidé she already knew he could match any of her people in mental capacities. His weakness was his all-embracing love, which felt too deeply the plight of others. During the experience he had felt sorry for the two underling Others when they had been punished by their superior.

But there was another reason for her to have brought the three of them to the Nomöe of Minds — to have a better understanding of the harmonics of their mind-souls. Were they the other three of whom the Asli had spoken? For days she had wondered who they would be. That morning, meeting Soen, Mhali and Laidé together, and observing the camaraderie that flowed between them and with Ethën, Nesdil and her, her intuition had told her they completed the seven. She needed a confirmation of this. She had hoped the soft blending of her mind with theirs during the sharing would provide it — teachers and mentors, when they used a Nomöe of Minds with groups of apprentices, could easily assess the harmony of their minds with each other, or the lack of it.

Her observation that morning had been right. There, in the silence of the Nomöe, she now heard and felt clearly the beautiful song made by their seven minds.

It wasn't yet the sunset when, from the Nomöe of Minds, Mhali and the others walked to Althesal's house — "The best and most elegant in the neighborhood, and the food is excellent!" Ethën told everyone with a teasing smile.

"Don't pay attention to him", Althesal said to Mhali as she guided him into her home. "He's uncharacteristically giddy. My home is a simple dwelling."

Of course Mhali didn't see it as 'simple'! It was a magnificent place, as all Thelian buildings were, great and small. But Mhali too felt different. Throughout that day he had felt a growing connection with the four Thelians, not unlike the close friendship he now had with Soen and Laidé — Had Chancellor Vuensé foreseen that? Her insistence on having the three of them meet with Althesal's team at a time when other issues were more pressing wasn't like her.

They partook of a simple dinner, Thelian-style — prepared by Laidé of all people! Yet his Nauthian friend had claimed the right to be the cook. During the meal — which was delicious — they shared with each other those intuitions that had moved their lives along their current paths. It didn't surprise them how similar those inner promptings were for them all. Each also told the others how they had felt of recent, being at a turning point in their lives.

The highlight of the evening, at least for Mhali, was the story of the existence of the Asli and the energy resonance of their island with the biosphere of the third planet of Sol. Laidé had listened to this telling with the fascination of a Nauthian for new stories. At the end of it, he had wondered aloud the reaction of his cousin, Naleean, when he would learn that Thel could well be a twin planet of the one they had claimed — Althesal had been surprised by that comment, which led her to disclose to them the possibility that those of her people who had followed the Source Path could well have traveled to that planet.

Soen, for her part, couldn't hide her enthusiasm when she heard of the Asli and their power to work with Time. Mhali noticed, by the questions and comments she made, her mind connecting many pieces of knowledge regarding Time she had learned as a Wanderer.

To each of them a new horizon of possibilities appeared to be opening up with those revelations.

But notwithstanding those feelings, Mhali was unable to shake from his mind the images of those strange, viper-shaped shadows in Althesal's experience, and their power to move a small planet. Thus, with a calculated decision, when the conversation quieted down he told them of the recent discovery made by the Rangers that Overlord Ankepum had a new and powerful ally who was providing him with advanced technology.

"The shadowy beings I saw!" Althesal cried out. "It has to be them."

"So I think they are", Mhali replied. "But then, this ally is even more powerful than I had imagined. With your permission, Althesal, I must inform the Chancellor, tonight, of what you witnessed. I must also tell the commander of the Rangers monitoring the Sol System to look for that small planet on a skew orbit."

"Yes, of course", Althesal said softly.

"Who are those Dwellers?" Ethën asked. "I mean, they appear to be made of dissonant light-fields… dark presences, really… and in their forms they differ from each other to such a degree that it suggests unnatural processes at work."

No one said anything to this, but everyone shifted uneasy in their chairs, as if speaking of them was in itself an ill omen.

"Althesal's experience gave us only a glimpse of them", Mhali said after a moment. "However, one thing is certain to me. They aren't the typical sentient being, and we must assume their plans and actions aren't typical either." Then, bending over he asked Soen, who sat at his left, "What do think of them?"

Soen shuddered before answering, "Never heard of them, not even in the legends… I feel a revulsion in me, as if they are the antithesis of what we, the Young Races, are. I too find puzzling the Dreki call them 'Dwellers' — Dwellers from where?"

"Well, whoever they are," Daothel said with his easy-going manner, "we have the advantage we already know of their existence, while they aren't aware that we know. We too know they can't withstand the light of Mind-Soul and of the higher light-fields. This knowledge has to count for something."

Mhali looked at the youth with renewed admiration. "You are right, Daothel. Moreover, that too hints at their origin: a place of twilights and shadows. Although I can't think where such a place would be. Outside the normal light-fields of Space?"

"What are we going to do", Althesal asked him with concern on her face, "if your Rangers confirm that the small planet has already been moved to a skew orbit?"

"That will fall to the Chancellor to decide…" he answered quietly. "My Rangers will start, however, by figuring out what that planet houses. If it's a base of operations, we could neutralize it. But then, this may mean an open confrontation with Ankepum and his mysterious allies, and I doubt their technology is limited to moving planets and entire fleets."

His words must have carried his growing apprehension because they all regarded him with a worried expression.

"We must not forget", Laidé said slowly, "there is also the politics of the situation. Chancellor Vuensé can't make a decision for herself to engage The Others in a direct confrontation. She needs the backing of the High Council. That won't be as easy. The Councilors from Human worlds will probably support an engagement to eliminate the threat. On the other hand, the Councilors from Amethen worlds will be divided. Some will vote for restraint and for finding non-confrontational ways, while others will want, not the Union itself, but the more powerful members of the Union to deal with the menace. And, then we have Councilor Thaël who is constrained by the ways of your people to use any form of destructive power." He shook his head. "This isn't an easy situation. The Councilors will have to be told of those Dwellers, and that means soon after everyone in the Seven Galaxies will know of them — Can you imagine the reaction to that?"

Mhali regarded his friend. He was right. The Union didn't shift easily from its established ruts to new paths. Ankepum knew of this and was probably counting on it in his plans for the Sol System.

At that moment he noticed that Althesal, who sat across him, still regarded him with a questioning face. It then struck him that she was waiting for an answer from *him*. She had asked what *they* were going to do if the small planet had already been moved — not what the Rangers or the Union would do, but the seven of them. Thus, he forced himself to speak aloud the thought that had been forming in his mind since they had left the Nomöe of Minds:

"Dealing with this affair by following established ways and protocols won't work. This is all a new territory. My intuition tells me we need to find a new way. For days I have wrestled with this. After this afternoon, however, I feel the seven of us may be the ones having to find that new way to deal with the menace."

She locked her eyes with his and gave him a sign of assent. He then understood — that was the answer she had wanted, that she could count on him!

Ethën had been quiet during most of the conversation and startled

Mhali when at that moment he shouted, "Of course!"

"Of course, what?" Althesal asked, frowning to him.

"An idea just came to me. Planetary Harmonics isn't my field, but I know enough to say that one doesn't move a planet, no matter how small, without a clear knowledge of the harmonics of the entire star system. If it is done, it has to be with the intention to produce a particular effect in the system. So, here is my idea: let's engage the help of those of our people who study this science and ask them what this move may mean for Sol… That could give us a hint of Ankepum and his allies' intentions — What do you think, Marshal?"

Until that day Mhali had known Ethën only for his reputation as the mind behind the live-crystal technology, and had never interacted with him. Thus, his idea and reasoning took him by surprise, and for a moment he didn't know what to say of it.

Althesal, on the other hand, reacted with eagerness. "That's a great idea! In this way too those in Planetary Harmonics Sciences will redeem themselves for having leaked the report of the survey. The first order of day is to chart the harmonics of the system, which the Rangers can easily accomplish tomorrow with the normal sensors of their craft. Then—"

"Wait! Wait! Let's not involve my Rangers in this… Not yet." Mhali knew the Thelians were over-enthusiastic about any scientific inquiry, but he hadn't expected for them to start giving assignments to his Rangers! "Let's start at the beginning. Are you suggesting, Ethën, that the small planet isn't for a base but for something else?"

"It's a good probability", Ethën replied, unfazed by his reaction. "Moving a planet would require tremendous planning and energy. Establishing a base can be achieved with far less effort on any moon or asteroid anywhere in that system. No, I think Ankepum and his allies must be after some other outcome. To get an idea of this, first, we simply need to confirm that the small planet has been moved; then, we need to identify the effects that, in its new orbit, this planet is having in the harmonics of the system — there must be one effect that will stand out as the most advantageous to them."

Mhali, again, was left speechless. The Chancellor had been wise in sending him to meet with the Thelian team. They were carrying him from surprise to surprise. Ethën made him realize how much he himself was approaching the entire affair from the established mindset of the Rangers. On the other hand, that's what the Chancellor wanted and needed now, and she knew it — unconventional thinking!

"I will order, tonight, the commander of the mission monitoring the Sol

System", he said to Ethën, "to look for that planet, obtain its exact orbit, and gather the data on the harmonics of the system. As soon as we have this information, I will forward it to you. They can collect all this data from their current position at the ös-boundary of the system."

Ethën nodded in reply and rested his back on his chair with the characteristic air of simplicity of the Thelians. A scientist from another planet might have felt smug for having scored a point with a Marshal of the Rangers. For a long moment, no one said anything more, giving Mhali the time to make a mental list of all the tasks he needed to do before the night was over.

"I keep wondering", Althesal interrupted his thoughts, "on Overlord Ankepum and the Dwellers' interest in that system. For what we know, with the exception of the enigma of the third planet, there isn't much there that isn't found in other star systems — and I don't think they suspect that the third planet could be an Aïdin Planet. My understanding is The Others treat the legends with contempt."

"It may have something to do with the planet Mal'ek", Laidé answered. "That appears to be the only planet in the system that absorbs Ankepum's attention."

"Ankepum may be seeking to acquire alternative sources of energy", Mhali added, "to gain some advantages over the Union. For what the Rangers intercepted, that was the subject of his people's research in the dwarf star of the Bastal Federation. As for the role of the Dwellers in this relationship, I have no idea."

Soen, who was following the conversation while inspecting the artwork and the plants and flowers around the living room, came back to sit. "I hear what you three say. I suggest not to jump to conclusions. Ankepum isn't the typical Overlord. I wouldn't be surprised if he is attracted to the legends. The rumors tell that he likes to collect ancient artifacts."

Mhali had heard of those rumors too. Besides, Ankepum had become the most powerful of the Overlords of The Others by going against the established ways of the other Overlords.

"No! It isn't energy sources", Nesdil said with a taut voice. "He's interested in that third planet — I know it in my heart. We must move soon to find out what's there. But, since we can't use any of our craft to go there, couldn't we ask for help to Laidé's cousin and his friends?"

"We haven't been able to re-establish communication with them", Laidé replied, knitting his eyebrows. "That planet is surrounded by something erratic that shields all communications."

"Then, let's find a different way to travel there!" Nesdil didn't want to give up.

"Traveling there is becoming less and less feasible." Mhali had already thought of that. "And more dangerous with every news we receive and every discovery we make."

Ethën rose from his chair, went to one of the broad windows, and rose his gaze to the starry night while the others mulled in silence. Mhali observed him, wishing that he would come up with an idea of how to go to that planet. Ethën, definitely, wasn't the common Thelian. He had an impulsive trait that made him spontaneous and unpredictable, in a good way — Mhali liked that.

As if sensing that he was thinking about him, Ethën turned around and, facing him, asked:

"Marshal, I'm sure you have your science teams studying the data and information we have of that third planet. Which explanation do they have for its oddities?"

"It's only a conjecture. They think a technology of an unknown origin shields that planet — a technology not unlike the ös-boundary phase-shifting generators that we Rangers use to shield entire planets from The Others. They too add, this could be for one of two reasons: either to protect something on that planet from falling in the wrong hands, or to protect outsiders from something dangerous housed there."

Returned to sit in his chair, Ethën said, "Nesdil is right. If there is a risk that Ankepum and the Dwellers are interested in that planet — and the risk is real — we must go there before them. To me, and to a friend in Planetary Harmonics Sciences, the anomaly of that planet appears to be in the way its ös-sphere interacts with the inter-planetary and extra-systemic light-fields, as if the planet's internal light-fields are off-phase with respect to the rest of the system and the galaxy. This would be the reason any device operating with, or built from galactic-light frequencies, like live-crystals, doesn't work there. Thus, to enter that planet safely and be able to return, we need a craft that is either inert to all ös light-fields, or that it can rise above them — I don't know of such a craft. Do you, Marshal?"

"No, I do not… However, I'll ask the other Marshals and my strategists and commanders to make inquires. Perhaps the Tharans have such a technology. If they do, it will take some time and a lot of effort to convince them to listen to us. They may even side with us if they learn of the presence of those Dwellers in our galaxy. Besides them, I don't—"

"I have an idea", Daothel rushed to say, and Mhali looked at the youngster bracing himself for another Thelian surprise. "We haven't asked the Asli if they know anything about Sol and its third planet. If there is a connection between their island and that planet, they must know something… Who knows? They could have visited it!"

Her face brightening, Nesdil added, "Yes, let's go to see them, the seven of us—" She stopped herself when her eyes rested on him. "Although taking the three of you to the surface of our planet, if we are discovered, would land us in big trouble."

"Teacher," the youth said, "don't worry! No one will find out. Besides, this is the only option we now have to know more about that planet."

"Ær…" Althesal said softly. "Ær is its name."

Mhali gave her a quizzical look.

"Ær is the name of the third planet of Sol", she said louder.

"You know, Althesal," Soen halted pouring herself another cup of Thelian tea, "you could be a Wanderer. A good one. You are a bag full of surprises — How can you possibly know Ær is that planet's name?"

"I-I… There is one more story I haven't told you", she replied. "But I don't know if you want to hear it now. It's late and it has been a long day for us all. You must be tired."

Everyone spoke at the same time in protest, and Mhali couldn't contain a laugh.

"Well… if that's what you want," Althesal said grinning at them, "here is." She rose from her chair to take a pillow from a recessed cabinet in the wall, then sat again and placed it under her feet. With the voice of one who is used to tell stories, she began:

"It happened the next day after my experience in the Null-Time chamber. My heart and mind were full of questions, and I decided to visit the island of the Asli, all by myself. But I found there more than I had expected. I met there a young man from the third planet of Sol—"

"What!" Ethën said. "How can that be possible? Here? On Thel?"

"Patience! You will understand how it happened when you hear the story… His name is Iain…"

23

Corridors of Power

Planet Esdänl, Alcyone System

"This news you bring to us, Chancellor, is troubling indeed." Thaël fidgeted with his sleeves as he spoke.

"I have never heard that before…" Councilor Ulhloom muttered. "Moving a small planet! Not good! Altering the natural harmony of Space is a dark art — so my people think."

"Why didn't we notice its presence before?" Thaël asked. "Planets on skew orbits are rare, and usually as a result of a cataclysmic event affecting the normal orbital harmonics of a system."

"The Rangers did record its presence when they mapped the Sol System during the survey operation," the Chancellor answered, "but it's rather small, and the finding was unrelated to the objective of the mission. Now that it has been identified, however, no structures or anything on it has been found to indicate it's used as a base."

"And you said news of its existence and connection with Overlord Ankepum came from Althesal?" Thaël struggled to understand how his niece could know that.

"Yes, Thaël. Marshal Mhali informed me of Issën Althesal's 'remote witnessing experience' — as he calls it. And the Rangers found the planet in the orbit she described. I must say it is an unconventional way to obtain information of the movements of The Others, and I don't understand how she did it, but it worked."

"Only the presence of the small planet was confirmed", Ulhloom said. "We still don't know if it was moved as the Issën described it."

"I don't doubt the rest of her story!" she said sharply. Worry was on her face, something that Thaël seldom saw in her.

The afternoon light was waning, and the broad panoramic windows around the room gave the three of them a magnificent view of the city of Llën. The Chancellor's offices were the highest in the towering building that housed the High Council. In the floors below, the twenty-four offices of the Councilors of the High Council formed the spindle-shaped body of the tower. Above her offices, at the apex of the spiraling tower, was the perennially lit dome of the High Council Chamber. The entire structure resembled a lighthouse of vast proportions, and it was held together and in place by the harmonics of its form and its materials interacting with the planet's light-field harmonics. It was a fit design for the type of decisions the High Council made — more so for those the three of them considered: to guide and inspire the delicate balance needed by a union in friendship of thousands of peoples and races.

"Although we have no direct evidence," the Chancellor resumed, "it is a strong possibility that Ankepum has made an alliance with those beings Issën Althesal calls 'Dwellers', and that they are the ones who gave him the new craft." Then, pausing to think for a moment, she next addressed Ulhloom, "Could those beings be in any way related to the Ancient Darkness you investigated?"

Ulhloom halted his customary pacing and instead of a reply asked, "Are you concerned, Chancellor, Ankepum's new associates are that old enemy?"

"Yes, I am. We don't know who those Dwellers are, Ulhloom, and Marshal Mhali's description and analysis of them reminded me of your words — *'agents of the Ancient Darkness'*. They do appear to come from a place where light, as we know it, doesn't reign."

"Hmm… I see your point but don't have an answer… Besides what I already told you two, nothing more is mentioned of that Darkness in the Stream of Lhool."

"Then, we truly don't know who or what that Ancient Darkness was!" The Chancellor regarded the two of them with a downcast look.

"Well… Yes… That may be the case", Thaël said after clearing his throat. "However, I don't want us to make of it a supra-natural, all-mighty power — that's not the nature of the Universe. It is for this reason that, after our last meeting, I engaged the help of a Wanderer friend who likes to study the old legends from a pragmatic perspective… more like a historian. According to his research, a few of the legends tell the Blight of the Ancients was a disease seeded by beings 'with a dark heart' out of spite for not being able to control the Aïdin Planets. These legends also tell these beings came from beyond our group of galaxies."

Ulhloom nodded to Thaël.

"Has this friend of yours found anywhere if the Blight of the Ancients affected also the fabric of Space and the flow of Time?" The Chancellor asked him.

"No, Vuensé. I asked him the same question. He's as puzzled as we are about the anomalies in Sol."

"And what do you know of this, Ulhloom?"

Ulhloom took his time before answering, "For what I know, neither Space nor Time were affected then. My people's far-memories make it clear that only sentient beings suffered the affliction. All of them were from the Young Races… Amethen, if you want… Humans hadn't yet appeared. Those affected were the ones who brought destruction upon their own worlds and neighbors."

"Thank you, Ulhloom", she replied. "My concern is that we have in our hands a situation that clearly echoes various elements of the old legends. On one hand, the Humanities of Yfel and Mal'ek could be described as suffering from something similar to the Blight. On the other hand, it appears the Sol System has spatial anomalies and has attracted beings such as the Dwellers who bring to mind the aggressors of the ancient War of the Kskiln."

Thaël had noticed in their last few meetings that when they spoke of those old events, there was an undue sense of defeatism in his two friends, as if the causes of the Blight and the War were beyond the capacities of mortal beings to address. Thus, he said to them:

"Vuensé. Ulhloom. Unless we consider rationally and pragmatically the information we have of the Sol System — and these bits of similarities to the past — we are going to continue moving in circles and unable to deal with the present threat. I thus propose for us to let go of this gloomy mood."

When the two silently assented, he continued:

"Let's make sense of what we have. We know of psychological changes in two Humanities, and of anomalies in the ös-sphere of the third planet and in the core of the fourth planet. We also know of the possible presence of those beings, the Dwellers, in Sol. Question one: I understand that during the ancient War of the Kskiln anomalies in interplanetary and interstellar space also appeared. Is this true?"

The Chancellor gave a look to Ulhloom who in turn replied:

"Yes, Thaël. During that old War some thought the Åh had gone mad and were responsible for the spatial anomalies. Yet, in truth, in those dire times no one had the opportunity, or the audacity, to study them."

"Question two — also for you Ulhloom: What was the connection between the Blight and that War?"

"Many versions of the legends speak of them as one event, but our people remember well the Blight happened first, and no one ever understood what or who caused it. It took place many, many millennia before the War. The War again, when it came, affected only the Young Races, and the aggressors were beings no one had seen before. From that War our people remember only suffering, destruction, and heroic efforts to elude the swarms of attackers which nothing we did could deter. Then, to answer you: we never connected the two events."

"Well, then," Thaël said to Ulhloom, "if the aggressors in the War were new to everyone at a time when already our group of galaxies had been explored extensively — as you told me before — one could assume they probably came from another region of Space."

"That's what most who lived through those times thought." Ulhloom nodded.

"And," Thaël continued, "it's possible, if they acted with such a viciousness, some could have considered them as 'agents' of the same Darkness, or unseen enemy, who brought the Blight at an earlier time... My point is, Ulhloom, those two events could indeed be connected, and we are now confronted with the same ancient enemy of the Young Races — a race of beings from outside our galaxies."

The Chancellor shifted in her chair. She now looked even more uncomfortable. "Are you implying, Thaël, the Kskiln are back, that they are Ankepum's new partners, and everything we are witnessing in the Sol System is the resurgence of that Ancient Darkness?"

"That's a possibility, Vuensé. Yet, calling that threat 'Ancient Darkness' is just a name."

She pursed her lips unable to say anything to his comment.

Ulhloom was also visibly troubled with that possibility and said, "I don't agree with that reasoning. The likelihood those two events are connected with each other, and with the present events in Sol, is extremely remote. The War happened millions of years ago, and the aggressors — which, I want to point out, some called 'Kskiln' but no one truly knew their real name — were eventually destroyed by another, also unknown and mightier race. This other race came out of nowhere, and then left our region of Space right after they brought the war to an end."

"And this last piece of information is also part of the old legends, I assume!" Thaël said raising his eyebrows. That was the reason he disliked the legends. It was all accounts of a circular nature, with some legends used to validate other legends.

His friend locked his mauve-colored eyes with his.

"Yes, Thaël", Ulhloom whispered with intensity. "Yet, know the Blight and the War did happen — the Stream of Lhool preserves those memories! I was there!"

"I know that, friend. I am only attempting to make sense of this muddled affair, and to identify who our real adversary is. Now!"

The Chancellor had risen and had her back to them. The more they talked, the more she appeared mortified by something.

"What's the matter, Vuensé?" Thaël asked. "Share with us what is in your mind."

Without turning to face them, she spoke:

"Regardless of the ultimate identity of Ankepum's new partners, the fact is our Union is facing a threat we haven't encountered, ever. My concern is that we are too attached to our protocols, customary ways and capabilities… We are stuck in a rut and won't be able to react fast enough to deal with it." She turned and added, "This is the warning Aldiarlim wanted me to be aware of when he called me recently. His Overlord's doings are destabilizing the order of our galaxies, even for The Others. Aldiarlim wouldn't approve of this. He's a malcontent, but his personal principles are towards harmony, not towards chaos."

Thaël nodded slowly. The inertia of the Union was too in his mind.

Ulhloom had stopped pacing and just stared at her. Thaël knew that look. His friend didn't grasp the full extent of Vuensé's concern. His people were so old and had seen so much that they seldom registered the need to change, or to act fast. Yes, they adapted, but at their own pace. And the People of Lhool weren't the only ones in the Union who had difficulty adjusting to new circumstances. Most of the Amethen races were like the People of Lhool. Many, too, among Humans, had become complacent in their ways and expected the Union to protect their customary ways.

"If that ancient enemy is back," Ulhloom said, his body rapidly changing hues, "we are doomed… All of us. It won't matter how fast we react. My people confronted it with all types of offenses and defenses… Everyone did… I remember… It was futile, and it all ended in a desperate escape. The home planets of the People of Lhool were destroyed then, and with them many perished, their lives and memories lost forever. Today we are a fraction of our previous numbers, and the planets we now call 'home' are the worlds where we hid at the time… The intervention of that other mightier race that ended the Kskiln was, perhaps, a stroke of luck. We still wonder who they were… The only thing that might save us this time is a similar type of intervention."

Thaël shook his head at his friend but said nothing. He wasn't going to wait idle for peoples to awake, or for a savior to appear.

⚡

Later, at his ambassadorial offices, Thaël rose to prepare himself some tea, then sat again at his desk. He had work to do of a nature he had never imagined he would. After the meeting, the Chancellor had invited him to dine with her at her residence — she had noticed his reaction to Ulhloom's last comment. There, they had talked alone and undisturbed, and had made plans. Now it was time for him to send invitations to several acquaintances in the Order of the Wanderers to meet with him as soon as possible. It was time for old favors made to be repaid.

The Matchmaker

Planet Thel, Eir System

Thaël placed his hands on both temples, letting the light and warmth in them soothe the fatigue he felt. He had returned to Thel, to the quiet of his home, where he had been formulating strategies and working on a plan for a whole day. Two hours of rest was all he had before going to the Transportation Center to receive the Wanderers. He had been surprised by their prompt acceptance to meet with him, even though some were traveling in remote regions when the invitation had arrived. It told him something worried them.

Wanderers had no fealty to anyone nor to any authority, but they were sincere, matter-of-fact, and acted with impartial wisdom. Since his earliest involvement in galactic politics, Thaël had felt a deep respect for them and had sought to cultivate their friendship. He had succeeded where others had failed, and now he had the reputation with the Order that he wasn't going to exploit them for his purposes — not that Wanderers allowed to be taken advantage of, but there were those who tried.

The number of the members of the Order of the Wanderers was a mystery. Not even the Wanderers themselves knew it. They maintained and increased their ranks through the apprentices that most of them instructed at some point in their lives, but no one kept a tally of this. The common people believed there were hundreds of thousands of them, but Thaël had calculated nine thousand was closer to the truth. They were a loose group, all of them Humans, without any structured organization or hierarchical order. They simply recognized the wisest among them and met informally from time to time to share information and knowledge, and to seek counsel from each other when need arose. The five Wanderers who were coming to Thel to meet with him were considered wiser than most, and their views were influential in the life of the Order.

This meeting is going to be more than interesting! Thaël told himself as he walked towards the concourse for trans-stellar craft. Never before had he met with more than two Wanderers at the same time, and he knew from experience Wanderers were more comfortable working companionless. He could have met with them at his ambassadorial offices on Esdänl but had chosen his old lake-side family residence on Ïllal — the aerial city on Thel where he grew up. This visit was the first time on Thel for them all, and he wanted these reserved individuals to experience his planet and his people in an unassuming setting.

⚡

"What you ask of us is most unusual, Councilor", Eleaph, the oldest of the five Wanderers, said to Thaël. "You know well we don't take sides in the stalemate between The Others and the Union. However, the information you just disclosed to us is disturbing, and we understand the reason for your request. This information sheds light on recent observations made by some members of our Order, which suggest that Overlord Ankepum is consider-ing abandoning his pledge to uphold the Armistice of Adhara. He may be preparing to take a more aggressive stance."

Wanderer Eleaph paused and made a slight nod to one of his compan-ions, who in turn continued, "Your request requires a decision that none of us can, alone, make — not even the five of us together can. We will need to consult with others of our Order. By the end of this afternoon we will have an answer for you."

Thaël knew, as he had been talking to them, the five Wanderers had ex-changed mental impressions of what he was telling them. They had done it subtly. Nonetheless, he had sensed it at the periphery of his mind. The five of them had probably already arrived to a decision but wanted it to appear otherwise. He attempted to read their faces once more without success. Wanderers were good at hiding any intention or feeling, and sometimes even Rangers were at a loss with them.

"I understand. Thank you for considering my request", Thaël replied. "From this room you can communicate with anyone you wish in the Seven Galaxies who is within range of a communication beacon — I will send one of my aides to assist you. Your apartments are ready if you need some rest or quiet, and the dinning room is in the building next door to this one. If any of you prefers to eat alone, that can be easily arranged. Anything else you may need, please let me or any of my aides know." Then with a smile he added, "I suggest a stroll along the lakeshore. Its beauty inspires the soul to soar."

The two women and three men in front of him returned his smile — of course, as good Wanderers, uncompromisingly.

Thaël rose from his chair, bowed slightly to them, and left the conference room. What he had proposed to them was daring. It asked of them to abandon their neutrality, and more. The Chancellor had hesitated when he had told her of his idea. So was Ulhloom's reaction later when he had been told. Yet in the end they had given him their support to proceed. Bringing Rangers and Wanderers together on a mission hadn't been done before, ever. Both groups treated each other with utmost respect, but their methods and objectives were different. The main challenge to his plan was that Wanderers never acknowledged they had certain powers. More so, they never used their higher faculties as a group. Yet, as far as his plan anticipated, they were going to use them together and in coordination with of a group Rangers also using their higher faculties.

He strode to the small building that served as his temporary office when he was at the family residence, and contacted his deputy at the Administrative Offices of the Providing Guilds on Ïthel. He wanted her to start selecting a group of trusted members of the Guilds who would participate in a special mission with a group of Rangers and a group of Wanderers. If Ankepum had powerful new allies and were now operating in the Sol System, he and his people weren't going to stand idle while this happened. Whatever Darkness was behind them, it had to be contained.

After talking to her, he sat quiet for a time, reviewing in his mind the plan he had designed. No one could know if it would work. Better it did. Next he contacted, one by one, several members of the Council of the Paths and the Director of the Thelian Trans-Civilization Relations Commission. He was going to need the support of the other leaders of his people. He was going to step outside certain protocols and use technology created by his people probably to inflict damage. What is more, if he received the support he expected, his people's role and influence in the Union would never be the same.

25

A Bridge across the Stars

The underground gallery took a right turn that Nesdil didn't remember. Puzzled, she looked at Daothel. He glanced back at her and shrugged unconcerned. The seven of them walked in silence. Similar to her previous visits to the island, the walls had lit up as soon as they had entered the tunnel, and the light shepherded them towards their destination. She also realized they had walked longer than the time it took before to arrive to the Asli's chamber, and that the floor continued descending with a gentle slope. Soon after, however, the gallery leveled out and began to widen.

"This isn't the route we used before", she told the others. "We should have arrived there by now."

"I noticed that too", Ethën said. "What are the Asli up to now?"

"They knew we were coming", Nesdil answered. "Last night, once more, they were present in my dreams. Our experience in the Nomöe of Minds two days ago affected them, somehow, but I couldn't understand their other imagery. They gave up their attempts to explain it to me, disappeared, and I woke up."

"Can they read our thoughts?" Soen asked.

"No," Althesal replied before Nesdil could answer, "the seat of their intelligence and self isn't in their mind, which appears to be undeveloped. However, there's no doubt they are aware of us and of the natural world in a profound way."

The appearance of the arched gallery changed at that moment, silencing everyone. Until then its walls had been smooth and emitting a uniform, radiant, soft light. Now they were peppered with sparkling points, playing a soft hum as they lit up in forward-moving waves. Ethën rushed to inspect them with Daothel and Mhali following him. Soen, Laidé and Althesal halted and resumed talking to each other.

Nesdil slowed down her march with some reluctance. She felt an urgency to arrive at their destination, yet she was puzzled — *Where are the Asli shepherding us this time?*

Looking back and forth along the gallery, she attempted to picture in her mind its layout in relation to the one they had used in their other visits. Also, as in that other gallery, this one had branches that weren't lit as they walked by. She was now twenty or so paces ahead of the others, forced herself to also stop, and turned to see what they were up to. At that moment Mhali's sonorous voice came to her as clear as if he were standing next to her:

"Did the Asli build this complex of tunnels?" Mhali's two hands rested on the wall. "This material can't be natural", he added.

"They didn't", Daothel answered him. "I asked them this same question, and their reply was that it was already here when they were born."

"Born? Are they biological beings?" Mhali now had his left ear against the wall. "If I am not mistaken, I hear music… a song."

"You can hear it!" Daothel replied in awe. "It took me longer to make out the sounds of a song!"

Mhali turned with a grin on his face and patted Daothel on the shoulder. When the youth didn't say anything more, Mhali repeated his question.

"Sorry, Marshal. You surprised me… The Asli, when you inquire them about their origin, use an imagery that elicits the idea of both 'born' and 'made'. In truth, they are impossible to define within the current classifications of bio-souls. To me, they are Time-beings using a diaphanous biological form to interact with Space."

"Then, who built these tunnels? Although I shouldn't call them 'tunnels'. They are such a marvel of design and engineering that they remind me of the underground glittering cities of some of the older worlds near the center of our galaxy."

"The Asli don't know, and we don't know either." Daothel answered. "The only thing the Asli say is that this complex was built by a group of luminous beings using the same 'Power' that made them. But they are unable to describe those beings and that Power. What is curious, they insist that Power is still here, with them."

They all resumed walking and, when they caught up with Nesdil, Althesal was saying to the others:

"It's better not to make sense of their form of communication with our reasoning faculties. The way I see it, they use a language of Time while we use languages of Space. The closest language we have to a language of Time is music, with its tempo and harmonies, as these move our awareness in the intended direction and with the steps conveyed by the music. That's the reason their communications with us resemble a music they play upon the DNA of our biological cells, and which our brains and minds translate into mental constructs."

Nesdil thought for a moment about this and said, "Then, as music does it, the Asli could be moving us to see ourselves in another light."

Althesal nodded slowly back to her.

The gallery was now a broad throughway, twelve paces wide and as much tall, with a slight curving towards the left. Its walls and floor were again changing. These were becoming diamond-like in appearance, with countless minute facets, polished and sparkling. More surprising was that the light emitted by these facets formed delicate 3D flows intertwining with each other as they extended into the open space. The seven of them slowed their pace to admire and play with these strange light formations, swirling around their bodies as caressing waves.

Nesdil was more concerned about meeting the Asli, and after a minute she again marshaled everyone to continue. If her sense of direction was right, the gallery was taking them beneath the central chamber.

Abruptly, the gallery widened to form an open space whose boundaries appeared to extend into infinity. She stopped in her tracks as the floor, likewise, had vanished. The others approached her from behind with caution. At that moment the intertwined flows of light in the gallery vanished, and a deep darkness enveloped them.

Unable to understand what was happening, she looked through that darkness to see if the Asli were there.

No one was.

"Ouch!" An intense, bright light had flashed ahead of them, blinding Nesdil. When her eyes adjusted again, she gasped.

⚡

The flash of light had sounded in Althesal's ears as a call, and with it she felt herself expand into infinity, as if a memory from deep within, too large for her mind, had awakened with it. It didn't last, though. With a shake of her head she cleared her mind. It was then when she saw it — an ethereal and alluring sphere lay at the center of that vast space. It gave off a soft, yet intense light. There was more. Constellations of stars, with their planets and moons, were all around it. But the light from the sphere, instead of eclipsing the stars, intensified their intrinsic radiance.

She took a tentative step in its direction and felt a solid surface under her feet in spite that the illusion of the depths of Space extended likewise downwards. The others followed her, and all began to march towards the sphere, unable to stop themselves but avoiding touching the stars and planets on their path. To Althesal it was a strange feeling, though not altogether unfamiliar somewhere deep in her, to apparently walk in outer Space as colossal beings to whom the stars were playthings!

The call she heard became more pressing the closer she approached to its source. Quickening her pace, she arrived ahead of the others.

The sphere was five handspans across and hovered in mid air, at chest level. But it wasn't a sphere. It appeared to be a bubble of no-Space, and its radiance came from a dimensionless spark of intense luminosity at its center. The spark didn't appear to be there, with them, in that chamber, as the stars were. It was faraway.

"This must be the Power that made the Asli! — The Spark of Aïdin!"— she whispered in awe. Then, as her lips sounded the name *Aïdin*, for an instant a vision of a beautiful and exotic garden with the Spark at its center flashed in her mind.

She turned to the others to ask them if they too had seen that garden, but they were enthralled by the Spark.

A long moment of complete stillness passed before it was interrupted by Daothel and Mhali shifting on their feet. Next, of a common accord the two of them began to walk around the sphere with their eyes fixed on it.

"I wouldn't do that", Mhali said softly.

Daothel's right hand was entering the sphere. "It feels warm… and I sense a vibration — faint and distant", he replied to Mhali.

"Daothel!" Nesdil called him. "Is that wise?"

The youngster withdrew his hand with a jerk, flexed his fingers and studied them with a grin on his face. "I've the feeling nothing here can harm us."

Althesal had no desire to touch the sphere in spite of the strong attraction it exerted upon her. But Daothel's action awoke in her a recognition.

She examined the sphere once more. It truly resembled a window into a remote place. Turning around she directed her attention to the constellations and began to walk among them, searching for something recognizable. She found it — her native star system, Eir, with its two stars and her planet. Next, one after another, she recognized the neighboring stars.

"Amazing!" she said aloud. "All these stars and planets here are at the exact positions where the actual stars and planets are at this moment in Space."

The sound of her voice brought the others' attention to her. She then repeated what she had said.

It took Daothel a moment to react before he too began to walk among the stars. Soon he started pointing: "Arthaï… Procyon… Seeërer…" Then, when he walked to the next star, he studied it for a moment before exclaiming, "Dean, this is a sky-map! A live sky-map of our region of the Galaxy, with Sol—"

"No! Look well", Althesal said to him. "The star there is Sol, and the sphere lies in the position of its third planet!"

A thrill ran through her body as the magnitude of what the Asli wanted them to see sank in. The creators of that underground complex had left a map of the Spark's new location. Wheeling around to take in the magnificence of that place, she realized, because she felt it, that the map wasn't just a map. It showed the power of the Spark extending far and wide into Space. That was the reason she could hear its call there, in that chamber.

"This place…" she whispered to the others, overcoming a sudden inability to find words. "This sphere is a bridge across the stars! It connects this island, and Thel, with the Spark in its current location."

"Of course!" Daothel rushed to say breaking the spell she felt. "That's the reason the Asli say the Power that made them is still here!"

"What kind of power are we talking about?" Mhali asked softly. "To me this sphere resembles the trans-dimensional portal in a Portal Star, albeit very small."

"A Space singularity?" Soen asked.

It didn't seem so to Althesal. "My suspicion is the Spark has more to do with Time than with Space. The nature of the Asli themselves, and their capacity to work with Time, point to that."

Ethën had been quiet all this time. When no one said anything to that, he spoke not hiding his frustration. "Space! Time! It doesn't matter what type of singularity that Spark is! At this moment all I know is that one doesn't go about drawing power from the singularities we know of as if they were playthings. Do you know of anyone who can use any of the known singularities as the Asli tell us some beings did? — No, we don't! — Can you imagine what it would take to move the portal from a Portal Star to another star? — No, we can't imagine it because it can't be done! — Yet, that's what the Asli showed us, a singularity being moved from this planet!

And here we all are thinking, mere mortals, that our destiny is somehow connected to it! — Aren't we missing something big in this picture?"

Althesal stared at him — *Leave it to Ethën to place things in perspective!*

"Well…" she spread her arms to break the tension Ethën words had created. "We wanted to ask the Asli if they knew anything about the third planet of Sol, here is their answer!"

"And where are they?" Laidé asked. "I want to meet them."

"There must be a way to go to their chamber from here", Nesdil replied. "Let's look for it."

They all began to move in various directions, except Althesal who remained next to the sphere. The many questions that had been in her mind for days came back with force. Ethën was right. Those flaming beings who had removed the Spark from Thel had to be beings of untold power. She didn't think they were a group of the Åh — all the Åh had disappeared more than 600 millions years before. Could those flaming beings be the Manaï of old?… And where were they now?… More so, why had the Spark been moved to the Sol System?… Had her people truly failed someone's plan, as the Mæl had told her?… Above all, what was the nature of the connection the seven of them had with that Spark?

Unannounced, she felt a light touch on her left arm. Looking down, she only saw the small hand that had touched her and an almost-Human face floating close to it. Slowly, the rest of the Asli's body became visible. She knelt, feeling a surge of joy, and the creature grabbed both her hands, gentle and caressing. A thrill spread throughout her arms and chest, and her brain translated — "Friend, together again we are!" — The Asli regarded her with a twinkle and nodded with his beautiful head; the golden color of its fur reflecting the light of the Spark of Aïdin.

"Greetings, dear friend", Althesal replied. "Yes, our paths cross again, and our togetherness fills my heart with joy."

The others had rushed to her when the single Asli had appeared. Now they surrounded the two of them. Nesdil and Daothel beamed. Everyone else was enthralled at the sight of the Asli conversing with her.

The Asli released her and went to Soen, gliding more than walking. Before he arrived, Soen had already knelt, and Althesal saw tears of joy rolling down her cheeks. The creature greeted her in the same manner, grabbing both her hands, but Soen couldn't contain herself and ended embracing him.

At that moment Althesal realized some of the extent of the Asli's power. Her body could 'hear' what the creature — just one of them — quietly communicated to Soen through his touch.

Next, he went to Laidé, who had also knelt. This time the creature touched Laidé's left cheek and communicated to him something puzzling to Althesal: "Your eyes haven't changed, storyteller." Laidé must have understood a deeper meaning from this because he grinned with affection to the Asli and bowed his head.

After, the Asli welcomed each of the others in the same manner; although with Daothel the creature ended placing one of his delicate hands over the youngster heart and communicated something that Althesal didn't 'hear' — What the creature said to the youth she wanted to know! A shadow of sadness had momentarily crossed Daothel's face. Something was going on between the youth and the Asli.

It was then when she also noticed the creature looked more diaphanous than what she remembered of them in her previous visit.

With the welcoming finished, the Asli returned to Althesal, grabbed her right hand and began to lead her, gesturing with the other hand for everyone else to follow the two of them. They soon exited the sky-map chamber through an opening near the gallery they had come through, and which they hadn't seen until that moment. The opening led them to an anteroom, also with glittering surfaces. A broad shaft, made of crystal-clear light, rose at its center. It reminded Althesal of the shaft of light at the center of the structure where she had met Iain.

The Asli next shepherded them, one by one, to enter the shaft of light, where they disappeared once inside. He and Althesal were the last ones to enter it. She gasped as soon as she went in. She was expecting to be inside the light but instead they were immediately standing on the ledge around the large spherical chamber of the Asli. The creature still held her hand, and the rest of his kind hovered in mid air, smiling at the seven of them.

⚡

Daothel hadn't disclosed to any of them that he had recently visited the island, three times, with Ciän the Wise. During the third visit he had noticed the Asli were becoming more insubstantial. He had then asked them about the change, and they had been enigmatic in their reply — "To the NOW beyond all nows we return, to see the song of a new beginning."

Today they were even more translucent, and the iridescent light emitted by their bodies had a faster tempo.

Daothel looked at his six friends. The group of Asli hadn't communicated anything yet to them, but he had a suspicion — he had felt it when the one Asli had touched him in the star-map chamber. Thus, unable to stop himself, and feeling a knot in his throat, he cried to the others, "They are leaving!"

"What! Why?" Ethën asked. "How do you know?"

"Because they have finished their mission with us", Nesdil answered for him. "That's the message they attempted to communicate to me, in my dream, last night. Now I understand it."

"But we have only started to know each other!" Ethën sounded devastated. "I have—"

"It must be this way, Ethën." Althesal whispered to him while resting a hand on his arm. "I know it too, in my heart. I had the feeling they were here only for a short time… to be with us. It has been difficult for them to be here. They don't belong to Space anymore."

When Althesal finished speaking, a swirling light issued from the Asli's bodies, accompanied by their music-words:

> "The Spark of Aïdin sees a new light and sings a new song — that's the
> beginning to which we return — to be whole. Seeing we are. Singing
> we are not. To be whole, Singing and Seeing must together be."

After this communication the Asli remained surrounded by the swirling light, and Daothel felt they were waiting for something, *from them.* He then repeated to himself what they had just said, seeking to decipher their meaning. Soon he made the connection. Turning to Althesal, he asked her:

"Dean, do you remember Iolthel's last message?"

She nodded with a puzzled expression while the others regarded him with questioning faces.

"I'll explain it to you later", he said to the others with a wave of his hand. "Dean, Iolthel said in her message these words:

> *'As our skill and mastery of the Power of the Voice has grown in*
> *us, the Power of the Eye has faded… Yet, as Sound and Light are*
> *the two halves of Space, so are the Voice and the Eye the two*
> *halves of the wholeness of Human…'*

"Dean," he continued, "both, the Asli and Iolthel are talking about the same thing. Listen…

> "Iolthel tells us in her message that Humans aren't whole anymore
> because no longer we can *see* into the light of Time, while the Asli say
> to us that they aren't whole either because they can't *sing* to Space.
> "We Humans *sing* to Space. The Asli *see* into the patterns of Time.
> With our singing we make creations of Space. The Asli show us that

their seeing is about the patterns the loci of Time create.

"But the implication is clear — We both need to return to the Source from which we came to be whole again!"

Althesal beamed at him. "Once more, dear, you are right. This completes their message to us through all our experiences with them—"

"That we have a journey ahead of us to find our Source to be again whole", he added.

"And it all points", Althesal ended, "to the third planet of Sol, where the Spark of Aïdin waits."

They both turned to look at the Asli.

The creatures smiled and nodded in confirmation, then communicated: "Friends, our shepherding is done. Yes, the Spark of Aïdin waits. Although we depart, we meet again… in your tomorrow that is a beginning."

Without giving them time to react, with these last words their forms quickly dissolved into the light of Time enveloping them. Next, this light contracted to become a point at the center of the spherical chamber. It flickered twice and disappeared.

The chamber remained illumined by the light emitted by its walls, and the seven of them stood there, alone, by themselves, at the start of their journey.

Who the Asli had been — neither Daothel nor the others truly knew the answer.

Why had the Asli chosen the seven of them — they could only guess.

One thing was clear, though — the 'shepherding' was now their responsibility, from then on.

⚡

When they exited the underground complex it was past noon. The vacuum left by the Asli worried Althesal. Their loss could affect in unforeseen ways the island's many bio-souls. Yet more disturbing was the fact that the island and the underground complex, with all the secrets it housed, were now in their care. That was a responsibility she hadn't expected and didn't know how to handle — *Perhaps the Synod can help in this.*

Ethën and Mhali had attempted to explore other galleries after leaving the central chamber, but these hadn't lit with their presence and the darkness had been impenetrable, even for a Ranger. Only the one that led them to the surface still had light. Then, as the seven of them had crossed the exit to the open air, the entrance to the complex had mysteriously vanished. It had been replaced by a continuation of the hillside, covered with undisturbed vegetation. She and Daothel had felt a shift of sorts as this had happened. None of the others had.

"A veil of Time has now, not only shrouded the Asli from us, but also everything under our feet", Daothel had said to them, and it was the best explanation Althesal could think of.

Yet the somber mood in them was about to change.

Mhali and Ethën marched in the front when they entered the clearing where they had left the craft, and they were the first to be assailed by a rushing wave of unstoppable friendliness. The family of doïel that had greeted them in the morning had invited relatives, and their numbers had swollen to twenty or so. The creatures were overjoyed with their return. One of the youngest puppies came running with small leaps to Althesal and begged her with soft musical barks to pick it up. She lifted the creature and cradled it in her arms — by its size, the pup was probably the newest member of the family. The creature was delighted, and its cries of joy had an effect on all the other pups. Soon, all the young ones wanted to be cradled by Human arms; nothing else could satisfy them.

Then, when everyone, Humans and creatures, had had enough merriment, the doïel settled down on the soft grass around the craft for a siesta. Nesdil asked everyone if they were hungry, and they too sat on the ground to eat a light refreshment among the resting creatures.

"They, for sure, need some discipline", Mhali said while eyeing Daothel with a frown. "Someone has been spoiling them."

Althesal nodded with a grin to Mhali.

"My Rangers would have them under control in no time, as they do with unruly cadets", Mhali added wickedly. "They have methods... effective ones..."

Soen and Nesdil looked at Mhali with horror on their faces while Laidé burst into a laugh. Althesal winked at Ethën, who had his mouth full and was chuckling. Daothel, however, didn't rise to the bait and continued eating his food with an air of innocence and ignoring them all.

When she finished her food, Althesal said in a more serious tone:

"We should keep the existence of this island to ourselves. Neither our people nor any others are ready to understand what's happening here."

They all assented.

"That won't be difficult." Ethën stretched his legs and rested his back against the hull of the craft. "I did some research and found that our planetary monitors can't detect the presence of this island. That tells me that somehow the island is veiled to any type of instruments. I'd thought it was the Asli's doing, but after the entrance to the underground became sealed, I'm inclined to think it's the technology of the place itself that's responsible."

"It could be an automatic system left by its builders", Mhali offered. "However, it's still possible the Asli were the ones responsible for it."

"I will check the monitors as soon as we return", Ethën said.

"But, if the island is invisible to instruments all the time, how was it that our craft's PI found its location this morning?" Soen asked him.

"I piloted the craft manually", Ethën answered. "Every time one of us has come here, he or she has done the same. Nesdil was the first one to observe this."

"Wouldn't that mean anyone can see the island upon approaching?" Laidé asked.

"Probably…"

"Then, we must assume the island is accessible to anyone", Mhali said matter-of-fact.

"I've the feeling", Althesal said shaking her head, "something more is at work here to protect this place. For one thing, although the Asli are gone, the power of the Spark of Aïdin is still present. I feel it."

Daothel had finished his food and rose, indicating thus to the others that he was ready to leave. "I must add", he said, "that whether the island is visible or not to Human eyes, it's protected. None of our people will venture to the surface of the planet or will survey the Meridional Ocean, and no off-worlder will be permitted to do that either for any reason. Besides, the Synod of the Wise will also continue Its vigilance of the island, and that means—" He paled when he realized what he had just said.

"Why did you say that about the Synod?" Nesdil asked with suspicion. Althesal knew she was aware of Daothel's involvement with Ciän the Wise, but Nesdil didn't know the Synod had discovered the island the previous year.

Daothel regarded Althesal with an apologetic face, and she said to him:

"It's fine. Tell them. They too should know what the Synod knows. After all, the seven of us here are now the stewards of this place."

The young apprentice sat back on the ground and began his account of what Ciän the Wise had told him, including the story of Iolthel. He left out, of course, his training under the Wise One. Although Althesal saw that Ethën made the connection but said nothing of it.

When Daothel finished his account, and after Althesal and him answered questions from the others, they all rose. It was late afternoon and Althesal wanted to return to Ïthel before darkness.

Mhali, Ethën and Laidé helped Daothel to clear the place. Meanwhile, Soen and Nesdil strolled around the clearing, conversing with each other; the two had expressed their desire to return to study the island and to walk it from end to end to explore its mysteries. Althesal could see that a strong friendship now bonded, not just the two but all of them.

The doïel awoke with the activity around them, and somehow the creatures knew they had to move away from the craft. They hadn't changed their natural behavior in spite of the absence of the Asli, and that gave Althesal hope. She wanted the uniqueness of the island's bio-souls to continue developing.

Before they entered the craft, Laidé asked Althesal the obvious question she knew was in everybody's mind:

"Now that we know the Spark of Aïdin is on the third planet of Sol, what are we going to do about it? For what Nesdil and Daothel witnessed, its power is beyond anything known. However, if we ask the Chancellor for help, she will want to know how we obtained the information, and that's out of the question. On the other hand, we can't just do nothing and risk that The Others, or any other race, will take control of it."

"The answer is simple", Althesal replied. "We must go there before anyone else does."

"How?" he asked.

"That's what we need to figure out next", she replied.

⚡

The daylight was beginning to fade when they returned the craft to its bay in the Transportation Center. The concourse for atmospheric craft was usually quiet since few Thelians ever utilized it, and they had counted on that. The place was deserted. The only activity came from the maintenance bots that approached them noiselessly to serve the craft they had used.

It wasn't going to be that easy, however.

As they exited the concourse, Althesal was the first to see him. Her heart skipped a beat. She halted. The others had been conversing with each other and fell silent too.

Thaël was alone, looking away from them, but with a deliberate slow motion turned to regard them. His face was unreadable.

Althesal took a deep breath and walked to him with uncertain steps. The others followed rather meekly behind her.

"Uncle! You surprise me."

He nodded to her with a disarming smile, and then said to those around her, "Welcome to Thel… Wanderer Soen… Marshal Mhali… Laidé…" He then added courteously, "Good evening to you all."

"What's the matter, uncle?" Althesal knew his only reason for being there had to be them.

"Well… It's obvious, isn't it, niece? The daughter of the Chancellor of the Union and a renown Wanderer, the Marshal of the Rangers for this region of our galaxy, and the Chancellor's personal advisor come to our planet and I am not informed of their visit. Don't you think that's strange? In addition, they came to meet with the four of you, the troublemakers. That's even more curious!"

Someone behind Althesal suppressed a laugh. Her uncle had winked at her when he had said 'troublemakers'. She opened her mouth to say something but nothing came out. Her uncle was teasing her while being genuinely intrigued with the seven of them.

"And 'No!'" he added. "It isn't what you are thinking. I don't have spies following the four of you. By happenstance, my deputy saw the seven of you this morning when you arrived to the Transportation Center. Her first thought was that my secretary on Esdänl had forgotten to inform me that the Marshal was visiting our planet. Laidé, she knew, is an adopted son of our people and visits us regularly. Wanderer Soen, she had never seen before. Thus, she concluded that, since the Marshal seldom comes to our planet, his visit had to be for an important matter."

It was Mhali who came to Althesal's rescue. "My apologies, Councilor Thaël. You are right. I should have informed you of our visit, which is an official one. Matters concerning the unexplained data obtained during the survey of the Sol System brought us here. It was the desire of the Chancellor that we meet with the Thelian team to find ways to clarify those findings."

"Then, Marshal, my guess was correct. Have you made any progress? I'd be interested in what you have come up with so far." Grinning to Althesal he added, "But my real reason for being here, at this moment, is to invite you all to dine with me this evening, at our family residence on Ïllal. I want you to enjoy my hospitality. Besides, I've a feeling you are going to need my help with the trouble you all are probably planning to make."

Before Althesal reacted, the others laughed and followed her uncle.

26

A Message from the Past

Planet Thel, Eir System

Thel's only moon hadn't yet risen, and the evening was dark and cold in the city of Ïllal. Sitting close to the fire, on the cozy terrace overlooking the lake, Laidé gazed at the waters. Flocks of eos performed aerial acrobatics near the water surface, and in their wake attracted schools of fish and other aquatic creatures which jumped out of the water in vain attempts to imitate them. The faint warbling and singing of each eos was amplified by their numbers. Everyone around the fireplace listened in silence to their concert.

Thaël had invited the seven of them to remain at his family residence after they had dined with him the previous evening. It had started slow at first, from both parts. However, as dinner had progressed, it had become evident to everyone that each had information and knowledge essential to make the decision each party needed regarding the affairs of Sol. Thus, they had spent that evening, and the day which was now ending, speaking openly of what was wise to tell.

Yet, Laidé still held something back, something that could be important and that no one but a few of his people knew. The discovery of the Dwellers made by Althesal, and Thaël's account of 'the return of an Ancient Darkness' had shaken his soul.

Outside the circle of leaders of his people, no one had ever suspected the Nauthians guarded a secret. During the Voyaging Age of their history his people had been known as 'the Nauthé'. Now only those initiated as leaders retained that name. In the course of that long-gone age the Nauthé had visited strange and remote planets and had befriended races still unknown to the Union. There, among one of those races, they had encountered a civilization to whom the passage of Time had left untouched. And on that planet his people had been entrusted with something destined for a future age. That 'something' had disturbed them so much, however, they had decided to keep it buried in utmost secrecy.

On that evening, when everyone around the fire felt the anxiety of an impending, yet unseen fate, Laidé asked himself — *If a secret is never used for its intended purpose, of what value is it?*

He was a Nauthé among his people, not because of his age, since he was still young in seasons, but because his people had seen wisdom in him at an early age. He wasn't unique either, since it wasn't uncommon for young adults to be initiated as Nauthé when they showed capacity. Simply, they had trusted he was wise. Was his wisdom enough for him to decide, alone, to disclose the Nauthé's secret?

The flocks of eos ended their evening games, and most moved away towards the heights. A few, however, came to the fire to dance around it. Against the flames Laidé could see in their translucent bodies the delicate interior geometry of their organs that made them resemble crystalline flowers — and the creatures' bodies reminded him of the nature of his people's secret. Without forethought, he extended an arm towards them, and one of the creatures came to alight on it. The creature's warbling changed then, and he felt its singing was directed to him.

"In a mysterious way", Nesdil had told him once, "eos sense our feelings, and when these are pulling us down, they will approach and sing a song to give us relief."

When the creature finished its song, it rose towards the heights to join its kind. The silence they left was replaced by the music of the leaves stirred by the evening breeze coming from the lake. Laidé then knew the moment had arrived to tell others of the secret of the Nauthé.

He cleared his throat — the others looked at him — and he began:

"Friends, not everything we know has been disclosed on this day. I've something more to tell you."

Everyone shifted in their chairs, and the waiting silence gave him more courage. Using the storyteller tone of his people, he then began:

"There was a time when my people spent many a night around campfires in the company of those who also loved stories, songs and plays. That time is long gone, but the stories, the songs and the plays remain with us. When we abandoned our voyaging ways, these all were committed to record and made available, broad and wide, to those who wanted to learn them... Thus, everyone assumes we shared all we knew. In truth, friends, some stories we kept for ourselves."

Soen sat across him, on the other side of the fire pit. He saw her smile and nod to him. "What…?" he asked her. He still felt hesitation, although he had already committed to disclose the secret.

"I had sensed it…"she said softly. "There are elements in your culture and behaviors in your people indicating you steward a profound knowing. But, please, continue."

The others murmured in encouragement while Thaël moved his chair closer to him. Laidé gave him a quick nod. On that day he had discovered the Ambassador regarded him with great respect and considered his advice with great attention.

Once more Laidé cleared his throat before resuming:

"In their travelings my people met races and civilizations which wanted to remain unknown and isolated from all involvement with other worlds and races, for diverse reasons. A few of them rejected us up front when we approached their planets, but most befriended us, perhaps eager to know and have a glimpse of what lay beyond their isolation. It was among one of these races that a surprise awaited us — *Aenrelm*, the people of this race called themselves; which in their language means, 'Cloud People'.

"My people had heard from other travelers and explorers rumors of the existence of the Cloud People. Some of these rumors told that they were mighty and dangerous beings, and destroyed any and all who attempted to enter their star system. Other rumors suggested they were descendants of the Åh. It was for this later reason that my people decided to search for them. It wasn't easy, however, and many years they traveled following clues as to their whereabouts. Eventually, in the Cealaïs Galaxy they found a system that matched some of the descriptions given to them.

"As some of the rumors had hinted, entering their system was perilous, yet not for the reason that was told. The system had an overactive ös-sphere that generated continuous ionizing and magnetic storms traveling between its three stars — storms which were mighty enough to damage or destroy spacecraft. And in a rare orbital path, never touched by the thunderbolts that crossed between the stars, there was a lone planet with a thriving bio-sphere.

"When my people landed on that planet and met its inhabitants, the Aenrelm, they found they were nothing close to what the rumors told. They are, or were, since we don't know if they still exist, a humanoid race — taller than us, slender, graceful, and with a copper-colored skin that gave them an air of nobility since they dressed mostly in shades of blue. They were friendly and intelligent, yet innocent in their hearts and with a civilization that, although ancient, hadn't progressed beyond the agrarian stage. Their world was, for the most part, covered with oceans of fresh water and populated by countless species of friendly creatures. On the equatorial latitude there was a ring of mountainous islands encircling the planet all around — and these islands were the only dry land and the home of the Aenrelm. More unusual was the motion of the light-fields that made the planet. It was such that a continuous layer of high clouds covered the ring of islands, protecting their inhabitants from the intense radiations of the stars and thus creating a lush paradise.

"The Aenrelm welcomed my people with a great display of friendship, as if they had been waiting for their arrival. And so they had been! When the initial communication gaps were bridged, they told my people that, indeed, they had known of their coming — *'We expected the return of your kind'*, their elders told Rïal, who was then the leader of my people. *'Long our wait has been, though not in vain.'*

"These words astonished Rïal and those of my people who heard them. But what emerged on the subsequent days of our visit was even more amazing. It began with the telling of the story of a visit, generations back.

"In their story the Aenrelm told my people that only in four instances before had outsiders visited them. In the first two visits, only single individuals, non-Human, had visited. However, on the third visit — more than one hundred seasons before Rïal — a small group of Humans had one day appeared on the island next to the main one. *'We come from beyond the clouds, from the starry vastness that lies all around your world'*, these Humans told the Aenrelm, and then asked for permission to live among them.

"The Aenrelm knew of the starry vastness, and in their innocent nature they were delighted to have among them beings who were from there, and who had such a wonderful musical voice and friendly disposition as the Humans showed. Thus, these Humans, who amounted to nine and were since then known as 'the Nine', lived with the Aenrelm for twenty seasons, which is about eighty standard galactic years — *'They lived with us without aging, without disease and without dying'*, so the Aenrelm told Rïal.

"During that time a deep friendship developed between both parties. The Humans taught their hosts many practical ways to improve their lives. For their part, the Aenrelm told their guests the many stories they knew about the Åh — and many they knew — *'For...'* and this is what the elders told Rïal, *'when we were seedlings, every season the Åh, groups of them, visited us, our islands and our waters.'*

"It was from the Åh that the Aenrelm learned of the many galaxies of stars and worlds beyond their clouds, and of the many beings enriching the Universe. It was from them too that they heard stories of events — some strange, others wonderful— happening elsewhere.

"Life went on in that idyllic paradise during that visit until one day the nine Humans requested a gathering of the elders of the Aenrelm. In that gathering they told the elders it was time for them to return to the stars — *'We are needed there.'* From this, the Aenrelm understood that someone in the stars was in need of help, while they weren't. Thus, with this simple reasoning, they accepted the decision of their friends, thanked them for the gift of friendship, and bade them farewell. The Humans then created a sphere of light as an extension of their own bodies, stepped inside and departed.

"No one among the Aenrelm expected the return of the Nine, and the memory of the time with them was weaved into stories and recorded in works of art. Thus, when a dozen seasons later the nine Humans reappeared on the starting day of their harvest festival, they were overjoyed.

"This time their nine friends remained with them only for the duration of the festival, which was eighteen of their days. They had many celebrations together, with dances and storytelling, and the Humans were granted the honor of naming the children born since the last harvest festival.

"When the festivities were over, the Humans asked the Aenrelm for a favor. *'Of course'*, they replied — for the Aenrelm this was a great honor, to help each other. Then, the Humans invited the elders of the Aenrelm to follow them to the island where they had first arrived. Once there, they said to the elders: *'One day, many, many seasons from now, a group of our people will come from the stars to visit you and enjoy your friendship as we have enjoyed it. To them, we would like you to give this message.'*

"Before the nine Humans departed, their final words to the Aenrelm were: *'Friends, a burden we may have placed in your care, but we know of the kindness of your heart and of the blessings of your world. With you, the message is well protected. The survival of our people may depend on receiving this message. Farewell... We shall see each other again at the Gathering, at the end of Time!'"*

Laidé paused his tale at this point and took a deep breath. This was the second time he had narrated it, aloud. The first time had been when he had been initiated as a Nauthé of his people. He was repeating it now, word for word, as he had been required to memorize it. His listeners around the fire regarded him with expectation on their faces.

Daothel, who was sitting next to him, leaned forward and narrowing his eyes said to him, "Well... What are you waiting for? What was the message? That can't be the whole story!"

Everyone laughed at the youth. Laidé patted him on the shoulder and said, "Patience, friend. More is to come."

All shifted in their seats, and he continued:

"After the Aenrelm told Rïal and the others of my people the story of the nine Humans, they were invited to visit the island where the Nine had arrived the first time. By then none of the Aenrelm lived there anymore. They had made of the entire island a place to honor the memory of the Nine, and, of course, they had made of it the place where the message was kept.

"To go to the island, my people, who at the time were about twelve hundred, were led on foot by the elders of the Aenrelm along a broad avenue lined with majestic, tall trees. During the march others of the Aenrelm joined my people, mixing with them and offering each a sweet drink flavored with the nectar of flowers. The avenue went straight to a rocky cliff on the shoreline and continued through a suspended bridge spanning between the main island and the memorial one. The bridge was also wide, made of the strong woods that grew on their islands, and it was adorned with a beautiful lattice-work — *'Our friends, the Nine, taught us how to build this type of bridge'*, the elders of the Aenrelm told Rïal with pride in their voices.

"On the memorial island the broad avenue continued until it ended at a plaza where the ground was covered with a light-blue-colored sand. At its center, a short flight of steps led to a platform made of stonework, and a round column, with strange symbols etched all around and made of the same wood used to build the bridge, rose from it. A crystalline object rested on the column. *'This is the message entrusted to us'*, the elders of the Aenrelm told my people when everyone had arrived and surrounded the platform. *'We now deliver it to you. We hope it will help your kind in the hour of need as we were told.'*

"Rïal, as the leader of our people, alone approached the object. Everyone was silent, and the sand on the ground was so fine that Rïal couldn't even hear his own footsteps. He walked with his eyes fixed on the object while his heart raced. He had never seen anything like it!

"The object was three handspans in height, and as much wide. It was made of a material resembling a fluid crystal and had the shape of a regular dodecahedron. Inside it, flame-like flows of multi-color sparks could be seen, dancing in a rhythmic motion. He could also hear a faint song coming from it.

"For a time he stood in front of the object, unsure what to do next. Then, with hesitation and some fear, he touched it with both hands. Startled, he quickly removed his hands and took a step back — the object had begun to rise!

"Slowly the object ascended, to stop at a height about twice as tall as Rïal. Everyone in the plaza could then easily see it. Rays of a bluish light now came from it, and these became brighter when the object started to rotate on its axis. Rïal hastened to descend from the platform to step outside the object's radiance, and to have a better view of it. Then, to add to everyone's astonishment, a woman appeared inside this radiance! A murmur immediately filled the plaza, and my people heard the elders of the Aenrelm repeat the name *Stïel* several times — the name of the woman. When Stïel spoke, her voice was clear and musical, and all understood every word she said in spite that her language wasn't the language of my people, nor the language of the Aenrelm. This is what she said:

"Welcome Voyagers! The patterns of Time foretold of your visit
to the world of the Cloud People. As they were keepers of this
message, so we ask of you to also be its keepers until the time
when it will be needed.

"Listen well Nauthé! — An age is coming when 'Voyagers'
no longer shall your name be. At some point in that Age, that
which should remain sealed beneath Space until the end of
Time will be stirred awake by those unaware of the danger, and
a door they will open into Space. Unless their efforts are

thwarted, all that breathes on this side of the door will be crushed by a Darkness for which none is ready.

"The flaming crystal you see here contains a key to close fast that door. It is attuned to that which is most Human. Those who know, will use it!"

"Stïel said no more, and for a long moment regarded those present. Then, her form became indistinct, blending with the radiance of the flaming crystal.

"Later the witnesses to her appearance were divided. Some of my people thought it was a recorded projection, encoded in the flaming crystal. Others believed she had been there. A few of the elders of Aenrelm who had met her in person agreed with these last ones — 'She came again... one of the Nine,' they told Rïal, who during the rest of his life couldn't make up his mind about this.

"After Stïel disappeared, no more light came from the flaming crystal, and slowly it descended to rest again on the column. Rïal then knew what to do. With decisive steps he climbed the platform and approached it, then lifted it with his hands. He had expected it to be heavy. It wasn't. As a rose blossom its weight was, and as hard as a sapphire it felt to his touch. It too felt as warm as the Human skin. The sparkling flames were still dancing in its interior, but no song came from it anymore.

"Rïal then, carrying the object, headed a procession back to the main island of the Aenrelm. Once there, at the suggestion of the elders, he placed the flaming crystal in the assembly hall of the Aenrelm on the same short column where it had rested before — someone had brought it with them. This hall was a large space under the canopy of large trees, with no walls but many decorated columns all around, and in that hall each of my people had the opportunity to inspect the object in the days which followed. On the same day the most skillful of the Aenrelm began the task of making a beautiful carved wooden box to transport *Stïel Key* — as the flaming crystal came to be known since then.

"My people remained with the Cloud People for five seasons, and a deep friendship developed. From them we learned much about the Åh, as the nine Humans had done before. From us they learned many stories and plays, but not songs, since the Aenrelm's vocal apparatus wasn't made for singing.

"The memories of their friendship is one of the most cherished among us. Many a time Rïal and those after him wanted to take my people to visit them again, but in every instance they were unable to navigate through the dangerous turbulences in that trinary system. As the years elapsed those of my people who knew the exact location of the planet passed away, and subsequent attempts to find it came to naught."

Laidé finished the story looking at the flames of the fire. He had done it! However, instead of feeling regrets, he was now sure Stïel Key was going to play a role in the days to come. He thus finished disclosing his people's secret:

"When my people settled on Lyaty, upon abandoning voyaging, Stïel Key, in its original wooden box, was placed in a secret location that only the Nauthé of my people know of. There it rests until the time when this mysterious key shall be needed to close a door to a realm beneath Space. But none of my people knows where or what that 'door' is, nor how to use the key. Those of us who are initiated as Nauthé are pledged to be on alert for the signs which might presage the dire time spoken of by Stïel has arrived."

Secrets and Revelations

Althesal awoke before dawn. Many thoughts were in her mind. She needed a quiet time for herself and decided to go for a walk along the lakeshore. She dressed for the chill air outside, left her rooms quietly and exited the house through a side door. Her eyes adjusted to the twilight, and she took an unkept trail through the woods surrounding the lake.

The house had been in her family for several generations, each generation making changes to it to accommodate their tastes and needs. Her parents had passed it to Thaël when they had decided to embrace a life of traveling and research. Among her people no one owned anything, yet each and all enhanced the quality of the spaces and objects they used. Thaël was an outstanding steward. He had kept unaltered some of the spaces in the house, including the rooms that had been hers when she was growing up, and had added more to accommodate guests and gatherings. But he had also mirrored his soul in the building by connecting it to the light of the stars adorning the Thelian sky. Thus, at a turn of the trail from where the entire house was visible, Althesal saw it as a multifaceted jewel glowing bright with the symphony of the reflected starlights.

After a twenty-minute walk through the dew-covered trail she knew so well, she came to an outcrop projecting over the lake. She climbed to its highest point, stood looking towards the east, and took several deep breaths. The vista was magnificent in the growing rose-pink light announcing the morning.

The resourcefulness and creativity of her people never ceased to marvel her. They had left the planet's surface to allow the natural world of Thel to thrive and evolve without Humans encroaching it. In exchange, they had built the aerial cities with abundant spaces resembling that natural world. According to the stories, most of these spaces were copies of similar ones found on the planet's surface. By the time Althesal had been born, the twenty-four aerial cities had become an intrinsic part of the bio-sphere of their planet. They had their own ecosystems, with a balanced diversity of plants and animals, yet all in tune with the planet's song. Initially, the diversity had been less but, as time passed, many species of plants were sown by the winds carrying their seeds from the surface. Many birds and insects also found their way from the lands below; and, of course, the eos felt at home on the massive aerial structures right from the start. All these migrations had added to the harmony that was the natural characteristic of Thel. To Althesal there was no doubt that Nature, in its ceaselessly drive to be more, had followed her people to the aerial cities as if telling them, "We still want to be with you!"

She next sat on a shelf of the outcrop to let the surrounding life fill her soul and mind. The birds were already singing their morning rituals to the nascent day and awakening other forest creatures from their slumbering. Some were early risers, and a group of nïal [small wombat-looking creatures] found their way to her. When she greeted them, they didn't hesitate to climb onto her lap and legs. It had been the same when she used to live at her parents' house: the forest creatures followed her wherever she went — "So much for wanting a quiet time this morning!" she scolded the creatures while caressing the soft and thick wool of their bodies.

The sound of muffled steps through the forest told her someone was approaching. By their rhythm, she knew who was coming.

"I am here, uncle", she said aloud, in the process startling one of the creatures making attempts to climb to her left shoulder. When her uncle appeared, the creatures knew it was time to look for their breakfast. Thus, they left Althesal alone and began to descend from the outcrop with their unhurried, waving gait.

Thaël climbed the outcrop with the agility of an adolescent and sat next to Althesal. None said a word. The sun Eir-1 was rising in the horizon, and the display of light announced a clear and beautiful day.

After a long while Althesal broke the silence: "You and the Chancellor are planning a move on the Sol System. Aren't you?"

Her uncle remained silent.

Regardless, she was going to have an answer and continued:

"When you retired early last evening, the seven of us talked for a while and concluded, from the observations and stories you told us yesterday, you are thinking a powerful Darkness is rising in that system and it is a menace to worlds everywhere."

Without answering her question and gazing into the distance, Thaël asked, "What do you think of the story Laidé told us?"

"Laidé feels, strongly, there is a connection between that object his people keep and the happenings in the Sol System. Although Soen told us, after you retired, she has seen two similar objects to the one described, smaller in size. These objects are in the hands of peoples who use them for healing. The Wanderers think these objects are ancient, from the earliest times of Humans, perhaps gifts from the Åh."

"But, what do *you* think, Esal?"

She considered her answer for a moment. "After the experiences I recently had, I think there are Powers in our Universe we aren't aware of, not even through the legends — they could well be our future, more evolved selves… or they could likewise be other beings, ancient and mighty. There is also the fact that story after story among the Amethen speaks of higher beings who are benevolent and protectors. Let's add to this that, for an unknown reason, our people… our planet and the third planet of Sol are linked to each other. Those unknown Powers could well be responsible for that connection. They too could be responsible for that mysterious singularity the Asli call the Spark of Aïdin. At the same time I feel — as you do — something unexplained… dark… is lurking in Sol, and The Others are attracted to it. It's thus reasonable that whoever hid the Spark on planet Ær, they also wanted to be sure it didn't fall in the wrong hands. And this takes us to the story of Stïel Key. It fits well with that intention."

She paused and looked at him before adding, "I doubt, however, we would obtain a straight answer if we were to tell the Nauthé the 'key' entrusted to them is now needed. It would take time, even for Laidé, to convince them to acknowledge that such a thing is in their hands!"

"Agree with everything you say," Thaël replied, "and this is why we must be proactive in this affair and use the means we have at hand. Since we learned of the catastrophe that befell the Humanity of Yfel, we have done nothing but to fear a confrontation with The Others. We have been dancing around that system, hesitant not to overstep the terms of the Armistice. Yet, we can't continue on this path. The consequences could be disastrous. The difficulty is, there is much that remains inconclusive. If we were to bring what we now know to all the members of the High Council, we will enter into endless debates while The Others dig themselves more in the Sol System and that Darkness grows in strength."

As her uncle spoke, Althesal realized what he was going to do, and it made sense to her. Thus, she said to him, "Then, the move you are planning isn't an official one. Your plan is for us… our people… to go there, to Sol. Isn't it uncle? In that way the Union won't be accused of violating the Armistice. At the same time, if I know you well, you will not dare make such a move unless you have the support from the highest echelons of our people—"

She rose her hand to her mouth in shock. She had been so blind!

Slowly she turned to face him. "Y-you… You are working with the Synod in this. Aren't you?"

"You know me well, Esal", he replied with a grin.

"Yes! I should have suspected it when I saw you and Daothel together several times entering the Library of the Exploring Guilds… You and the Synod think the Darkness arising in Sol is interested in its third planet, don't you?"

He shook his head. "That's what the Synod thinks, not me. They are of the mind, as you are, that those who were of the Source Path of our people are on that planet. Thus, they think it's imperative to protect it. My way is other, however, and the mystery of that planet has to wait. What the Synod and you think might be correct, yet we need to be pragmatic and act on the facts we have. Containing Ankepum's new allies is the priority. We must find out where those dark beings are coming from — which it doesn't appear to be that third planet — and close that door. The Chancellor, Councilor Ulhloom and I are waiting for the return of the party of Rangers sent to Mal'ek to gather intelligence. Once we have their report, we will act."

Thaël took a stick from the ground and began to dig the soil from a small crack on the large boulder where they sat. He waited for her reaction.

"Knowing you well," she said, "you are going to send to Mal'ek a group of our people, probably with a group of Rangers, using one of our craft. That isn't going to be enough, uncle — I tell you. Dealing with those Dwellers is going to be a great challenge. They are unlike any race we've ever encountered. The Rangers will be in for a big surprise — Marshal Mhali can tell you this too. You need those who can act and react in the most unexpected of circumstances… Those who aren't the product of a formal training, as the Rangers are."

"And who would they be, Esal?"

For the briefest moment Althesal thought that she and her friends could accompany the Rangers. However, remembering those shadows she knew even she would flinch in fear. "Wanderers!" she blurted. "Wanderers would be the ideal partners for the Rangers. Many of them have seen and interacted with the most unexpected of beings, and they too have mastered higher faculties."

Her uncle nodded and replied with a grin, "I already have them."

They locked their eyes, and Althesal understood at that moment the two of them saw life in not so different ways as it appeared.

"We are sending", Thaël continued, "twelve Rangers and five Wanderers on a special new craft manned by a small group of our people. They will assess the situation in the Sol System and take all necessary actions to contain any threat to the Union, which is probably on the planet Mal'ek."

Althesal took a deep breath before asking, "Are we too late, uncle?" At that moment more than before, she felt powerless and paralyzed by the circumstances and events. The urge to go to Ær was now with her all the time.

"Let's hope it isn't so. The Rangers monitoring the system report no activity, at all, in its interplanetary spaces. However, we know nothing of those Dwellers. They could have the means to travel in ways we aren't aware of. That's why the intelligence report from the Rangers sent to Mal'ek is so important before we act."

"Can't the Synod help with this? After all, the Wise Ones have higher faculties you and I are still developing"

"No, Esal… They are as surprised as we are about those Dwellers."

At that moment a ray of the morning light shone upon the outcrop. Althesal stared pass the lake and the forest towards the horizon. Without waiting for Thaël to say anything else, she said:

"Uncle, this much I know in my heart: the number one priority for your mission to Sol should be to protect the third planet!"

Her uncle said nothing to that, and she thought their conversation was over when he rose to descend the outcrop. She followed him, and the two started walking in silence along the trail bordering the lake. It took them away from the house. Other houses were nearby, but no one was outside at that early hour. They had thus the quietness for the two of them. At some point a thrashing noise came from the woods at their left, and a string of five ponies appeared. Althesal thought they were coming to drink from the lake. It wasn't so. To her surprise, they rushed straight towards her uncle who took a handful of honey bites from his pocket and began to feed one to each.

Althesal was speechless. That was so unexpected of any of her people, much so of her uncle! Regaining her voice she asked, "Have you also given each of them a name?"

He nodded in reply with a sheepish smile, and she shook her head to him in a teasing reproach.

When the honey bites were finished, two of the ponies came to Althesal, digging with her noses in the folds of her clothing. She stroked their heads and said to them, "I have none. I didn't know there was going to be a party."

The two of them resumed walking, and the ponies left them, this time to drink from the lake. When they arrived to the turn on the path that was going to take them back to the house along the opposite shore, her uncle spoke:

"I understand the reason you want to go first to that third planet. The Synod wants that too. I'm not ignoring your reasons. It's a matter, however, of what to do first. I'm balancing my actions to make things happen in a way that the greatest good for all can come from this complex affair."

"And, on what do you and the Synod agree regarding this affair?" she asked him. She hadn't had any contact with any of the Wise Ones except Ciän, and in truth she didn't know of what they thought.

"Well..." he answered. "Most historians concur that the original alliance of races that became known as The Others first came from beyond the seven galaxies where we Humans appeared, and that they came with the sole purpose of eliminating Humans. But Humans outsmarted them and a stalemate ensued. For an enigmatic reason, our people are latecomers in this saga, but we bring the capacity to eliminate the threat of The Others, once and for all. Then, think Esal! What better way to give a serious blow to Galactic Humans than to cripple our people.

"The Synod thinks, based on some personal stories and records from previous Synod members found in their archives, that we were indeed the target of dark Powers early in our history, right before we were discovered by Galactic Humans. In fact, this discovery by Galactic Humans may have been encouraged by those same dark Powers, since those who first found us were marauders, pirates — we knew not then anything of that and were glad to meet other Humans, yet brigands and outcasts they were. But discovering us was premature. We weren't ready for it, and a great time of turmoil for us came from it. Fortunately, we recovered our senses fast and retook control of the song of our life. Nonetheless, a damage was done. Those of the Source Path may have left for that reason, and the current attitudes of pride and exceptionalism in many of our people may well have their origin in those times too.

"As I was saying," he continued. "the Synod has reason to believe the attempts of dark Powers to thwart us began early. They have records showing a number of species of animals and plants suffered a disease — a blight we may call it — and that a few of those species became extinct. This happened three hundred and sixty years before we were discovered by Galactic Humans. But Nature or someone, not our people, stopped it, and the balance of the bio-sphere was restored — that's why we don't see signs of this blight today.

"Thus, it you fit the pieces together… First, it was the appearance of The Others threatening all Humans. Next it was an offensive against us, the Thelians. Now, for a yet-to-be-discovered reason it's a push against the Sol System. It's then clear we Humans are still the target of dark Powers — and this is the reason those Dwellers must be contained at all costs."

The magnitude of these revelations shook Althesal. The Master Chronicler had told her their planet had failed, but he hadn't said why. Could it be because it had been discovered by dark Powers before it had matured enough to fulfill a destiny? Which destiny?

Trying to find her voice, with a whisper she asked, "Why… Why don't our people know of this?"

"Because it is only recently that I and the Synod have been able to connect the threads weaving this picture."

"Then, I assume you knew of the island in the Meridional Ocean even before we told you about it. That's the reason you weren't surprised when we told you of it. Moreover, that's the reason you were at the Transportation Center waiting for us two days ago. You knew we had gone to visit the island."

Thaël nodded. "It is true I knew from the Synod about the island, but I'm not following your movements. I waited for you at the Transportation Center because my deputy truly saw you that morning. You just gave me the opportunity to bring your quest and my plans together. The Synod knew of Nesdil's trips to the island, and these prompted the Wise Ones to find out the reason she was going there. That started them on the trail of this entire affair. Next they contacted me, knowing I had the position and means to work out their plans without stirring others' curiosity."

"So much for wanting to keep the situation quiet!" Althesal sighed. The secrecy had been her idea, and she now realized how laughable it had been. From the moment when she had decided to use the undisclosed probes to study the Sol System, she had called upon herself the attention of each of her people. She could well have told them aloud: "I'm doing something secret and interesting. If you want to know of it, follow my trail."

"Esal, rest assured," Thaël said while gently grabbing her right hand with his two hands, "once we secure Sol and contain the situation, you'll be able to go to that planet, unimpeded, and discover what's there for you."

28

Dark and Eerie News

Althesal closed her eyes at the sight of the two Rangers, wishing she could alleviate their pain. She sat listening to the conversation between Mhali and the Rangers who had returned from the planet Mal'ek. Her uncle and the others, including Mhali, were with her at a communication chamber at Thaël's offices in the administration complex of the Providing Guilds on Thel. The eight of them had returned to the city of Ïthel the previous day from her uncle's residence. That morning they had had a long meeting with Chancellor Vuensé to inform her of what they knew. Althesal and the others had agreed they would be helping Thaël with the preparations for the mission to the Sol System. It was after the meeting with the Chancellor when Mhali was informed of the return of the party of Rangers to Headquarters.

"How is Ranger Ewis doing?" Mhali asked the leader of the team.

"He is now in the hands of the healers, Marshal", the Ranger replied with a shaky voice. "They foresee his recovery is going to be long and difficult. Although he received burns in his skin and lungs, the injuries aren't serious. It's his psychological state that's damaged. No weapon was used against us but something else. We felt the impact right away… We still do. Ewis took the brunt of it and just froze there — and I mean it literarily. His body became cold, with patches of frost all over; and he wasn't there anymore, as if he had vacated his body. It was… eerie…"

"Our healers are wise and skillful like no others", Mhali said. "And you and I know of Ewis' strength. Let's trust he'll recover."

"Yes, Marshal, you are right. Excuse my outburst."

Althesal regarded the woman with admiration. Talking to her superior gave her strength. Mhali knew this and was using it to help her — Althesal could also feel Mhali's heart energy flowing between the two of them in spite of the distance between Thel and the planet Esdänl.

"It's all understandable, Ranger Solvi", Mhali said. "We are dealing with something… 'eerie' you said… Yes, that's a good way to describe the situation. Now, are the two of you in a condition to report on your mission?"

"Yes, Marshal", the Ranger answered weakly. Then with more strength in her voice, she added, "Besides, it will help us unburden our minds of the memories we carry and, perhaps, free us from what we feel."

Mhali nodded at her with an understanding smile.

Althesal could see in the eyes of Ranger Solvi the fear haunting her. If she was in such a condition, Althesal couldn't imagine the state of Ranger Ewis — What had happened to them?

Mhali had sent to Mal'ek three of his best Rangers, veterans in infiltrating the most guarded bases of The Others. They had arrived to that planet eighteen days before. For the first seven days the three had communicated regularly with the support team stationed outside the Sol System. After that they fell silent for nine days, and any attempt to contact them had been in vain. On the tenth day, Solvi, the leader of the mission, had used her mobile emergency communication beacon, instead of her mental telepathic power, to send a distress call and request for an immediate extraction. When they were extracted from Mal'ek, they didn't look like Rangers anymore. Their bodies were emaciated and with multiple burns and frostbites. One of them was unconscious, and the two others were in state of great distress for no apparent reason.

The two Rangers were in a debriefing room on the planet Lös, accompanied by Chancellor Vuensé and a group of Mhali's deputies. The woman and the man looked pale, haggard and tired, and Althesal wondered if the two were truly fit for a debriefing.

The second Ranger walked to sit next to the Chancellor, who for a moment grabbed his hand with a reassuring motherly gesture, while Ranger Solvi remained standing. She then began her account:

"As we reported in our last communication to Headquarters, and following information obtained from common Mal'ekians and from three mid-level government officials, our next step was to travel to the location visited regularly by The Others — which is the largest array on the planet of towers collecting the energy of the core. Most of those to whom we talked concurred that was the only place the off-worlders visited. We had decided not to use our craft since we anticipated to encounter a heavily guarded base.

"We started in the evening of our seventh day and traveled all night through a savanna. When the morning arrived, the land became progressively emptied of vegetation and animals. We were, of course, cautious and let no one know of our presence. By then we had expected to start seeing Mal'ekian government troops, or commando units of The Others, patrolling the land. Yet we saw no one and began to think our informants had been mistaken. Nonetheless, we kept going, following the only lead we had to fulfill our mission.

"By midday we approached the target coordinates and saw, in the distance, the group of black towers. The usual faint, ground tremors shaking the land everywhere felt stronger there.

"A different picture began to emerge the closer we moved to our destination. First, the savanna changed abruptly into a broken terrain, covered with a layer of dust which didn't resemble soil, and with fissures and fractures making our progress difficult. It all looked as if the land had received repeated hammer blows from a mighty hand.

"When we arrived, early in the afternoon, the panorama became even more strange. We had been told the cluster of towers was arranged on the hills surrounding an agricultural valley. Instead, a barren crater lay in front of us, making us think no native of Mal'ek had probably visited that region in a long while.

"The story of that place was as strange as the vista in front of us. Eight years ago, the vegetation started dying and the domesticated animals became aggressive and unpredictable. Also, people began to lose their sleep for no apparent reason, and many of them complained of shadows and monsters lurking in their minds. Some became sick in the body with unknown diseases. Then, after two years of this nightmare, most of the inhabitants of the three villages fled the valley fearing for their lives."

Ranger Solvi pause at this point and went to stand at the center of the room on a large and flat circular crystalline material. Seconds after, the circle lit up with a soft blue glow, and her body became immersed in it. At the same time, both, the debriefing room and the communication chamber where Althesal and the others sat, began to out-picture what the Ranger was seeing with her mind's eye.

The debriefing technology was another gift of the Thelians to the Union, for the exclusive use of the Ranger Corps. It used the same science principles of a Nomöe of Minds, yet out-picturing only the mind of the one who stood on the amplifier and blocking the intrusion of the minds of the observers.

For a reason Althesal couldn't grasp, she felt deeply disturbed when Ranger Solvi began to show what the three Rangers had found there, as if a dark miasma wanted to suffocate her soul. Thus, moved to understand better what had happened to them, she did what teachers on their planet did, at times, with apprentices — she tuned in directly to the thoughts and pictures broadcast by Ranger Solvi, to live the experience as she had lived. And this is what she experienced:

A chill ran through Althesal/Solvi. Besides the desolation of that place, she felt an unwholesome presence all around. It felt primeval and violent. From her/Solvi's position she could see near the center of the crater a series of buildings and a large space port. There was also a strange mirror-like platform at the other end of the base, re-flecting the sunlight. The place was deserted, and no craft or vehicles of any kind were in sight.

"We need to rest", she told the others. "Let's wait until darkness to explore this place."

Ewis and Cai nodded. Next, she and Ewis lay down between two boulders to sleep while Cai kept guard, sitting close to them. When she awoke a couple of hours later so that Cai could rest, he said quietly to her to avoid awakening Ewis:

"We're cut off. I haven't been able to communicate with our support team. It must be the weirdness of this place. When the Marshal was stranded on this planet, he didn't have this problem."

"We'll manage."

The rest of that afternoon they took turns to sleep in spite of the constant humming of the ground. The towers continued doing their work, collecting the energy from the core and sending it straight up towards the upper atmosphere. The spectacle was beautiful, but Solvi felt death all around and wondered about the fate of that planet.

When evening came, they moved to explore the buildings. Indications the place was an active base were everywhere, yet no one guarded the place — not even mobile or fixed bots. The first buildings were for warehousing and servicing the port. The curious thing was they were powered up, as if expecting a craft to arrive at any moment. Further in, they found the barracks for a small contingent of forces that hadn't been used recently.

"I don't like this", Ewis broke the silence. "Why isn't anyone guarding this base?"

Solvi had been feeling the presence of an unspecified danger the whole time, but didn't want to alarm the two others and just looked back at Ewis.

They came next, not far from the mirror-like platform, to a large windowless building of a rectangular shape, resembling those they had seen in the towns of that planet. A straight, broad ramp connected it with the platform, yet no door or opening was visible in it.

She felt a growing dread as they approached it. She also noticed something inside clouded her extended senses. Regardless, they needed to investigate. Taking the lead she jumped to the ramp and went to inspect the wall where the door had to be. Placing a hand on it, it went in without any resistance.

Ewis came to help her while Cai guarded their backs. Soon they found the three of them abreast could easily walk through that wall. "I can't sense what's inside? Can you?" she asked Ewis.

"Not a thing", he whispered. "I'll go first."

"Careful!"

He nodded and went in.

It seemed like a long time — she couldn't sense the deep, normal connection Rangers felt with each other — but it was only a couple of minutes before he came back.

"There aren't any partitions, and no one is inside. But, you have to see it."

Cai signaled to her that all was okay, and she and Ewis went through the wall.

A foul smell, a gloomy twilight, and waves of fear hit her as soon as they were in. The odor and the light came from chunks of a reddish material scattered at random all over the floor. The waves of fear came from strange fluorescent, greenish bubbles floating in mid air, elongated and much larger than a Human. There were about two dozen of them in that large space. They were filled with a gurgling gelatinous substance. She became nauseous and panicky as she approached the closest one. Instinctively she retreated, and the thought came to her: *If there is evil in our Universe, these things are of it!*

At that moment Cai rushed inside and said to the two of them, "The beams from the towers are changing direction!"

They exited and wasted no time jumping from the ramp to the

ground to take cover behind a group of abandoned construction bots. Nothing was visible at the center of the base, but something there was forcing the beams to bend towards it. In fact, after ten minutes all of them converged onto a single point, about ten lont [22 meters] above the reflective platform. Slowly, this converging point expanded.

"Let's move closer", she told the others. "There." She pointed to a partly demolished wall. It was about midnight, and she sensed no one around.

Once there, at a dozen paces from the platform, with a better view of it, and crouched down in a trench, they saw the convergence point of the beams become an opening — to where? she couldn't see much through it. The opening was about twenty lont across [43 meters], hovering right above the platform. Soon after, they noticed greenish flashes inside it.

"I don't know about you, but I feel we are in grave danger!" Ewis whispered — his eyes wide open, his body tense.

"Agree. Let's move back", she said.

They didn't have the time. With astonished eyes they saw amorphous, brown-red shadows emerge from the opening at a great speed. Once out, these halted as if they had hit a wall. Within seconds the shadows condensed into a group of bizarre and malformed entities with a remote resemblance to stubby serpents, yet of great size — about twice the length of a Human. Dark-brown scabs covered them all over, from which shifting, flame-shaped shadows issued. And they had multiple eyes in places where they shouldn't be! After this sudden transformation, they started to slither with difficulty along the platform towards the ramp.

Solvi had thought the fear she had felt inside the building was at a level of 10/10. She had been wrong! With the appearance of those entities, the radiations of fear of that place had now more than doubled.

"S-Seventeen, I count", Cai stuttered. He looked as if he was about to bolt from that place.

Two or three minutes passed, and once more they saw greenish flashes through the opening. What came next added to the weirdness she felt. Something or someone pushed a train of five large rocks towards the already crowded platform. These were irregular in shape and about five paces at their widest point and four at their narrowest.

As soon as these were out, the opening contracted fast. In less than a minute it was gone, and the beams of energy snapped loose, becoming straight with a boom that startled her. Meanwhile the bizarre entities slithered along the ramp as in a trance and didn't even react to the thunderclap the freeing of the beams had produced.

It took the entities the great part of one hour to reach the building, a distance that would have taken her two minutes walking at a normal pace. The three of them used the time to study the entities. There wasn't, however, much new to see. In the artificial illumination of the base, their features looked blurred. They also appeared to be unaware of the surroundings and showed no concern that someone could be observing them.

All sorts of questions crossed Solvi's mind during that time: Who were these beings? Where had they come from? What were they made of? Were they sided with The Others? What was their intention? Was the ruling Elite of Mal'ek aware of them? Regardless, of one thing she was sure at that moment — they didn't look capable of much; least of all, they didn't have the appearance of an invading army.

Eventually the entities arrived to the wall and entered the building in the same way the three of them had done it.

"Shouldn't we follow them in?" Ewis asked.

"No, the risk is too high", she replied. She knew they felt the same she felt. She doubted any Human could withstand for long, and keep the mind sane, the waves of fear coming from those entities. "Let's inspect those 'rocks' first."

To all appearances the 'rocks' that had come through the opening were just large rocks of an unrecognizable type. They were dark-brown and chunky, and nothing on their surfaces revealed anything else. They hovered over the platform and could be pushed with little effort. After a time, the three of them gave up on trying to figure out their nature and purpose.

"Something must be inside them", she told the others. "If not, why to bring them here!"

They next debated what to do and concluded they needed as much information as possible of those creatures. Since nothing was heard from inside the building, after a couple of hours had passed

Solvi decided Ewis and she were going to enter the building while holding themselves invisible to the lower light fields. They did so with a greater effort than was normal, but found the precaution wasn't needed.

The entities were each inside one of the greenish bubbles and appeared to be unconscious. For a reason they couldn't think of, with the reddish illumination of the place their bodies revealed more details. They had no orifices at all — no mouth, no ears, no nose, no any other. Only black, featureless eyes, of difference sizes and shapes, protruded through their scabrous skin. And what they had seen as flame-shaped shadows were now multiple appendages, all different and resembling nothing remotely similar to arms, legs, tentacles, antennas or claws.

"Where in our Universe could Nature have produced them?" she said to Ewis.

"A symphony of chaos, that's what they are", Ranger Ewis replied.

After exiting the building, the three of them retired to a secluded spot to share impressions. It was clear they had stumbled on a mystery, but half of it was still unknown. They too concluded somebody would eventually come since those bizarre creatures weren't going to bask inside those bubbles forever. Thus, they decided to wait and keep a watch.

One day passed and nothing changed. Several times they inspected the entities, and these remained unconscious. During the daylight they also inspected the rocks, looking for a way to open them, but couldn't find any. They too renewed their attempts to mentally communicate with their support craft.

Two more days elapsed without any change in the situation.

On the fourth day since they had arrived, and the third since the entities had entered the bubbles, some of the greenish gelatinous substance had fused to the entities and the scabs were gone. By that afternoon, they looked less solid, and their bodies undulated inside the bubbles; yet they were still unconscious.

The following morning they heard rustling noises inside the building, as if something was moving at a fast speed, and decided not to enter it and wait hidden outside observing the situation. As the day progressed, the noises increased in volume and frequency. No other change happened until the night came.

Sol had already set, and the night was dark when the noises inside suddenly ceased. For a long while all was silent. Then, the sound of many grating, cacophonous wails, all at once, broke aloud. It lasted for fifteen seconds. A minute or so passed in silence before it all began again. This pattern was repeated for about one hour.

"A call", Solvi told Ewis and Cai. "They are calling someone."

She was right. Close to midnight, a large flying object approached in the direction opposite the way they had entered the base. The three of them rushed to hide behind a group of crates near the port to have a better look.

The craft descended with an erratic course, and it almost crashed as it landed.

"The pilot must still be learning the basics", Cai snorted. "And look at that craft!"

It had the size of an inter-planetary spaceship, with an irregular, bulbous shape, as if it had been assembled by those who didn't know what they were doing. It was made of a rough dark material. More strange were the wart-like protrusions that covered it at certain points, and which resembled the rocks that had come through 'the door'. Its hull also had openings underneath, stained with reddish streaks.

Solvi felt her anxiety rise to a new height. She had lived through many dangerous situations before, but never with the feeling of a malevolent presence watching them. By the way Cai and Ewis looked, they weren't faring better than her.

After two long minutes a hatch opened. It was large enough for sizable equipment to pass through it. Then, a group of Others heavily armed descended — six Dreki in all. As soon as they were out, they rushed to cluster together at a certain distance from the hatch, their weapons ready.

"Ankepum's elite forces!" Ewis whispered. "What's going on here?"

Next — making the three of them jerk backwards in their crouched position — dark brown shadows came out of the craft at a high speed. They approximated those inside the building in their last state of transformation, but with a shadowy body now fluid, covered with phosphorescent red blotches, and phasing in and out of their field of vision. The transformation was unbelievable. These weren't the slow, semi-conscious entities that had spent one hour crawling along the ramp. No, these ones slithered fast and wild but through the air, and had a threatening aura all around them. They couldn't stand still. Feelings of fear, rage and aggression, all at the same time, came from them as an uncontrolled flood, to the point that Solvi thought the weapons the six Dreki carried were for self-defense in case those shadows decided to attack them.

"I count eight, but I'm not sure", Cai whispered to her.

At some point the entities appeared to organize themselves and moved towards the building where the others of their kind waited. The six Dreki remained on the landing platform clustered together.

"Ewis, watch them. Cai, come with me", Solvi told them.

Cai and she followed the entities, as fast a they could, hidden by the dark night and by the many discarded bots and containers scattered everywhere in that base.

When the entities entered the building, the two of them heard repeated thuds followed by many rustling noises. Solvi had to summon the best of her will not to bolt from their observation place, and to give assurances to Cai. She felt the presence of an evil she didn't know existed.

After ten or so long minutes the entities came outside. At first, the two of them couldn't identify those that had arrived on the craft from those that had come through the opening. Soon though, it became evident that those which came on the craft were herding the others towards the craft. The spectacle was that of a wild group of beasts being rounded and herded by a smaller group of other wild beasts!

The two of them followed from a distance and eventually joined Ewis. By then most of the entities were inside the craft with the exception of two which went to the reflective platform. These then came back to the port pushing through the air the five rocks. All this time Ankepum's people hadn't moved from their position; however, once the rocks were inside, they too entered the craft.

Solvi was expecting the hatch to close when she heard a commotion inside the craft. Shouts from Ankepum's people also reached her ears. Next, three or five shadowy entities came rushing out through the hatch. They were mad, wailing and slithering through the air in complete chaos, colliding with one another at times.

"Let's retreat! Fast!", she whispered to Ewis and Cai when one of the entities moved in their direction,

They sprinted towards the barracks where they knew of a place to hide. Ewis ran in front of Cai, and Solvi was last. By then they knew well the base and every obstacle that could be on their way. They were approaching the barracks when she saw through the corner of her eye a streak of phosphorescent red pass by her right. At that moment Ewis took a sharp left turn, and she knew then they had been discovered!

Before she could react, however, a frigid wind passed through her body and a sudden sharp and unbearable pain shoot through her spine. She lost control of her body, stumbled and fell towards Cai. Ewis had turned towards them, and with horror on his face he looked at her before collapsing to the ground.

Cai had also turned and grabbed her shoulders. The look of terror and pain on his face matched hers — she had never felt so afraid in her life, and she felt no strength at all.

What happened next became blurred in her memory. The two of them dropped to the ground, covered with frost, drained of all energy, and unable to think. Soon after, she lost consciousness.

"Solvi! Solvi!" She heard her name and felt a hand shaking her shoulder. When she opened her eyes, Cai knelt next to her regarding her with concern. At that moment all came back to her. With a great effort Cai helped her sit up.

It was mid-morning. The entire base was silent, and there was no sign of anyone.

Ewis lay on the ground close to them. He was unconscious, and his body had burns all over.

"I can't awake him", Cai said weakly.

The two of them next managed to stand up, supporting each other. Like Ewis, they had lost body mass and their Ranger suits were ragged. Walking was an act of supreme effort. Nonetheless, Cai went to fetch some water, which fortunately was close by, while she went to the port ignoring the aches she felt. The strange craft was gone. The three of them were alone in that desolation of a place. Nothing had been taken from them, which told them Ankepum's people probably hadn't known they were there.

"We have food for several days", Cai said to her when they returned to Ewis. "But I don't see how we can make it to our craft on foot."

"I already thought about that. I'm going to call our people. I don't think anyone on this planet or nearby will intercept the sub-eth call."

Cai nodded and closed his eyes in exhaustion.

Ranger Solvi released the field of mind, and the debriefing chamber became silent.

Althesal's hands ached. She had been clenching the arms of her chair the entire time. But the turmoil she felt in her heart dwarfed the aches. Like Solvi, she had never thought that kind of evil could exist. The Dwellers were truly a force she doubted anyone could stop.

"Excuse me, Marshal", Ranger Solvi said before anyone could react to her extraordinary report. She looked war-weary. "One thing is clear to Ranger Cai and me. That base is so isolated and unguarded that if the Chancellor decides, it could be made inoperable quite easily." She paused before adding, "The thing is, Sir, that door must be closed!"

Mhali nodded to her with a thoughtful expression, then he addressed Chancellor Vuensé: "Chancellor, do you have any questions for Ranger Solvi and Ranger Cai?"

"What can you tell us of the rulers of Mal'ek?" the Chancellor asked.

Ranger Solvi looked at Cai for help, and he answered:

"The common people of Mal'ek are less inclined to talk about the Elite group that rules them than about the off-worlders. However, for what we could piece together, these rulers are also surrounded by a mystery. They rose to power from within a consortium of engineering groups that was formed to build the energy-collecting towers, one hundred and eighty Mal'ekian years ago.

"Before them, and for more than two thousand years, the Mal'ekian civilization was run by cooperatives and stewardships in charge of supplying all the needs of the people. Anyone could become a member of them, and most citizens were affiliated with one. Their government was a simple council of regions elected by the cooperatives and the stewardships. All businesses were then transacted through a medium of exchange which they called 'money'.

"The establishment of this consortium changed all that.

"At first, the Consortium — and this is how it came to be known — was formed as just another stewardship. But, once it finished the construction of the system, one hundred and twenty years ago, those in the Consortium argued against accepting new members since their work was too specialized. Thus, they became a closed stewardship and took control of the energy supply of the entire civilization. With this step they started to accumulate more money than it was normal for a stewardship. Next, with their wealth came an undue influence over the leadership of the regions everywhere.

Later, the Consortium gained more influence with the governing central council than any other group. Eventually its members dominated the council and began to pass laws to make them even wealthier and more influential.

"This ascendancy of the Consortium made of it an elite in a civilization that had been egalitarian until then.

"Eleven years ago a sudden change took place within the Elite. Something happened behind the scenes with the twenty-six groups that had formed the Consortium since its beginning, and power passed to the hands of a new group. At the time rumors surfaced telling that this New Elite had risen to power by making a pact with a powerful ally, but no one could know what it really had happened nor who this ally was or where it had come from.

"Immediately after, this New Elite built a citadel near the administration city of the civilization, where the governing Council had its headquarters. Only the most trusted vassals of this Elite were allowed to enter and work in that citadel. New rumors then arose saying that some of the New Elite members suffered a disfiguring disease and that they never showed themselves to anyone, not even to their servants. The fact is no one has seen the faces of this New Elite, ever, and the exercise of all their power has been conducted through a deputy — a man who calls himself 'the Spieler'.

"Then, six years ago, with a swift display of power, the New Elite took control of everything. Their move didn't surprise anyone, however, because for a time they had been openly organizing a military-style force with presence in all the regions. The Elite then dissolved the Council of leaders, the judiciary, the cooperatives, the stewardships, and all other institutions of government, and declared themselves sole owners of the resources of the planet. Everyone else, from then on, worked for them. The Elite called this, *The Entitlement*, because, according to their Entitlement Manifesto, '*They have a superior intellect and know better how to run the civilization than any others*'.

"It was only three years ago when the common people saw for the first time spacecraft in their skies. Soon after that, and through an organized event all people had to watch, the New Elite, through the Spieler, presented a small group of off-worlders as their friends. According to the descriptions we obtained, these off-worlders were Dreki and carried the insignia of Overlord Ankepum's Dominion.

"The mystery in all this, Chancellor," Ranger Cai added, "is that, as we all know, The Others, and more so Ankepum, don't forge alliances with other civilizations, especially with those less advanced — they openly take over them. Also the dates don't indicate Ankepum was behind the consolidation of the original Elite, since this event happened eight years before his craft were seen for the first time in the skies of Mal'ek. Besides, the Corps own reports show Ankepum was actively engaged elsewhere during that time. Who then was the powerful ally that helped the New Elite oust from power the twenty-six groups of the Consortium? No one among the common people can say."

Ranger Cai ended with a nod to the Chancellor.

None of those present spoke for a time.

"*Dwellers…*" Althesal said softly, still unable to shake the feelings she had.

The Chancellor and the Rangers gave her a questioning look.

"The allies of the New Elite, and of Ankepum, are those shadow entities", Althesal repeated louder. "The ones Ranger Solvi showed us — *Dwellers* the Dreki call them. They are the same ones I witnessed moving the planetoid in Sol." She looked at her uncle, and he nodded with a frown.

One of Mhali's deputies, shaking his head, spoke:

"This entire affair is becoming darker and muddier the more we dig into it. For instance, the partnership between those Dwellers and Ankepum is perplexing. How are those beings able to give him technology, or the knowledge to build new technology? It's clear his underlings fear them in the extreme, and I don't see Ankepum himself having a friendly talk with them either — if the Dwellers can't even remain still for a second, how can Ankepum communicate with them? And where is the Elite of Mal'ek in this partnership? Based on what Ranger Cai describes, they aren't the type that will surrender control of their planet easily."

The Chancellor regarded the deputy, shifted in her chair, and then signaled to Ranger Solvi. "Come sit next to me. Standing there doesn't look comfortable at all."

When Ranger Solvi sat down, the Chancellor rested her hand on the Ranger's arm for a moment, before addressing all those present:

"We are confronted with two enigmas: Enigma one is Overlord Ankepum's partnership and the benefits he is gaining from it. Enigma two is his ultimate intentions, or theirs. With the information we have, we know Ankepum isn't rebuilding his fleet or his military capacity — Yes, he made an isolated display of one new craft in the Bastal Federation, and this other craft on Mal'ek doesn't seem capable of much; but that's all. This tells me something else is in his mind; which brings us to the question of his real intentions. We know he covets power and will do anything to gain more. Then, with the picture we now have, what is it that can give him more power? Tell me… I would like to hear from all of you in this conference your thoughts on this."

The Chancellor regarded everyone present, waiting for any comments.

Daothel sat next to Althesal. She had learned to recognize the youth's moods and now sensed the restlessness he exhibited when he wanted to say something but didn't know if it was appropriate. She rested a hand on his arm and gave him an encouraging nod.

The youth then rose his hand and said:

"Chancellor… with your permission… regarding your question… I don't have the training of a Ranger nor knowledge or expertise in multi-galactic politics. However, it's obvious to me Overlord Ankepum has to know, by now, that we, the Union, the Rangers, have been gathering intelligence about the Sol System. Yet, it doesn't bother him — he has no patrols or permanent craft in that system. Why? Perhaps, because what he desires isn't there, or cannot be detected by any means we have, or is guarded in such a way he knows it is secure. The same could be said of the Dwellers. They don't care to conceal their movements; but they are there for a reason. There is no doubt of that. Yet, it doesn't appear to be an invasion either. Similar to Ankepum, they must want something. I am inclined to think both partners want the same thing — if not, that bizarre partnership couldn't have happened. Thus, the key to unravel this mystery is to figure out what they *both* want."

Everyone, but Daothel's friends, was looking at the youth with wide eyes when he finished, to the point that Soen couldn't contain a laugh. "That's Daothel, and you better get used to his surprises."

"Young man," the Chancellor said with a broad smile on her face, "I want you to work for me. You could easily replace several of my advisors."

"I hope I'm not one of them", Laidé said, feigning concern.

"Oh yes! It's you he'll replace", Mhali said with mirth. "Better start looking for another job."

The Chancellor winked at Laidé.

Everyone was laughing, including Ranger Solvi and Ranger Cai, and Althesal knew at that point they were on their way to healing.

When the silence returned, with a more serious tone the Chancellor asked Daothel, "Do you have any inkling of what Overlord Ankepum and the Dwellers may both want?"

Daothel shifted in his chair regarding the Chancellor with his deep blue eyes.

Althesal patted him on the shoulder. He had dared to speak his mind in a meeting of the powerful, now he needed to finish what he had begun. He looked at her showing his hesitation, and she said to him, "Go ahead, tell them what you think. There aren't secrets here anymore."

"For our people," Daothel began, "when we are confronted by a mystery, we don't jump to conclusions based on what we know. Instead, we make the effort to rise above the mystery itself and attempt to see it within a larger context. In this way the mystery becomes a piece of a greater reality. Understanding the place the mystery has in this larger context makes it then easier to unravel it.

"Having said this, to me all that is happening in the Sol System, with the various enigmas it presents and with all the strange and not-so-strange players interested in it, all this constitutes a mystery that is part of greater whole. Could this greater whole be the relationship between the Union and The Others? It doesn't appear to be so — this isn't about controlling one more star system. What then is the larger context of this mystery? If it isn't about control of Space, what is it about?

"I see only one answer to this question, Chancellor — this larger context has to do with Time. By this I mean, everything we are witnessing in Sol has to be part of a chain of events that is moving along Time, a chain that began in the past. And it's in the far past, because this mystery evokes memories of Aïdin Planets, of the Blight of the Ancients, of the War of the Kskiln, and of a Darkness clouded in the mists of Time. What, then, are Ankepum and his partners looking for? It's obvious they haven't succeeded yet, but all they are doing is directed to it. I ask myself: What is it they desire from the far past that it's now within their reach? What is it they desire so much they dared to move a small planet to reach it?"

As Daothel phrased these last questions, Althesal knew right away and without doubt what Ankepum and the Dwellers were after. Her intuition had been right, and the young apprentice had placed it in the right context — they wanted the Spark of Aïdin! She immediately turned to look at her uncle and saw that Thaël was regarding her with intent — he had also grasped what Ankepum and the Dwellers wanted!

"I don't have an unequivocal answer to this question… not yet, Chancellor." She heard Daothel finish in the manner of the Wise Ones of their people. "But I've no doubt, what they want is going to surprise everyone. As you may know, there are large gaps in what is known of the earliest times of Humans, to the point some scholars suggest the only explanation for this is that someone systematically destroyed all reference to events they didn't want others to know about, or to remember. I think what Ankepum and the Dwellers want is going to be something of which no memory remains."

29

Corridors of Power

"What do you think of Daothel?" Thaël asked Chancellor Vuensé. He had traveled in a hurry from Thel to Esdänl as soon as the debriefing of the Rangers had finished. Now he met with the Chancellor, discussing how the new information from the planet Mal'ek affected their plans.

"He is refreshingly insightful" she replied. "He made me realize how absorbed we are in the direction set by the politics of the Armistice. The youth is right. This affair transcends The Others and our Union. I now understand why the other Overlords are disturbed and quarreling with Ankepum — they must suspect his dealings with the Dwellers and feel greatly threatened. I too now understand the inner conflict Ankepum's advisor, Aldiarlim, is having, and his need to let me know of it."

Just before the meeting the two had attempted to contact Councilor Ulhloom, but His aides didn't know where the Councilor was, which wasn't uncommon for Ulhloom.

The two of them had started the discussion by agreeing the Dwellers and the Ancient Darkness spoken of by Ulhloom had to be one and the same threat. Now that they knew where the door to their realm was located, to close it was much easier than what they had imagined, at least technically. However, politically it was another matter. Its location on a planet of Humans, and the fact that the door was powered by the energy system of that civilization, made direct action unworkable.

"I'd expected that door to be in interplanetary or interstellar space!" Thaël said, clenching his jaw. "What are we going to do, Vuensé? Most members of the Union will object to any move on an inhabited planet without due consideration and debate, yet a public debate will certainly lead to more reactions similar to that of the Bastal rebels. On the other hand, my people won't approve us going there to destroy the power supply of a civilization. We can't use the power of the Rangers to do that either, unless we alter their mandate, which is out of the question. In any of these options the political fallout could tear the Union apart. We would be violating its foundational principles. And on top of that, it will destroy the gains the Armistice has accomplished."

She nodded regarding him. Then, with a heavy sigh she added, "We don't have time either to establish open relations with the civilization of that planet. Besides, in most respects that Humanity isn't ready. Just to replace their planet-wide energy system with one that matches their present level of development would take years of work and a lot of adjustments in their way of life."

They both knew well they couldn't just give up, that something had to be done. The Chancellor turned her back to him to gaze at the horizon. Thaël already suspected, however, the course of action they were going to commit to. He felt frustrated and powerless.

After a long moment, with her hands on her back the Chancellor turned to face him again. "A planetary quarantine will at least contain those shadows. The High Council will understand the reasons for sending the Rangers to blockade that planet. The Humanity of Mal'ek won't notice it. And to contain Ankepum, let's turn up the heat on him with the Armistice Inspectorate. The Order of the Wanderers will call him to answer for all the violations in the Sol System. If that isn't enough, we can complicate his life in other fronts."

"And for how long will that quarantine remain in effect, Vuensé?"

The pain on her face told Thaël of her answer. Regardless of what they did, the Union was never going to be the same. An endless planetary blockade was likewise going to challenge the principles of the Protocol of Union, strain the Rangers, and take the stalemate with The Others in another direction.

Unaware, with his right fingers he began to drum on the conference table. They were living a crisis of dire proportions, and he saw no way out of it.

For a time none spoke. The Chancellor faced again the panoramic window while Thaël wished Ulhloom were with them. His friend's wisdom would point to elements in the situation that the two of them hadn't seen. Thinking about his friend reminded him of something Ciän the Wise had said to him when he had explained to him their plan to settle the affair in Sol. Ciän had said:

"Thaël, Space is a vast continuum, and there aren't walls separating one level from another, or a dimension from another, or stars from another — it's all in how we see it. A dimension of Space limits only our bodies, but no force in this Universe can limit the distances our consciousness travels and the dimensions it can visit. Thus, you can close that door, but you can't change the fact the Darkness can reach out anywhere. It is then only a matter of time before another door opens into Space somewhere else. To truly deal with that Darkness, you'll need to take action that isn't of Space — and for this, you will need to follow the heart, not your mind."

He took a deep breath. He wasn't, after all, much different from what many of the Providers of his people had become. He had been convinced he knew better, that he could eventually craft the perfect solution to deal with the menace in Sol. In his pride he hadn't considered that someone like Althesal, Ethën, Nesdil and Daothel could be right in matters which on the surface appeared to be political and involving inter-galactic relations. Yet, the fundamentals of existence were all the same for all beings, everywhere — Ciän had reminded him of that... that Politics and Diplomacy couldn't exist in isolation... that Politics and Diplomacy without the soaring flights of the heart were nothing more than brute and meaningless forces doomed to fail.

He closed his eyes and sighed once more, then he whispered, "My niece, Althesal, was right all along. So too were the members of the Synod of the Wise of my people. They insisted the third planet of Sol was the key to decipher this conundrum — and I brushed aside their intuitions."

The Chancellor turned to face him. "I too am guilty of the same error. I chose to ignore the promptings in my heart. However, right now my heart tells me this affair isn't over." Then, with a puzzled look she added, "I didn't know Issën Althesal was your niece! But then, you Thelians are so reserved about your personal life! — I'm glad I have the two of you with me right now."

Thaël bowed his head slightly. "Vuensé, although we can't close that door, I now know what Ankepum and the Dwellers want is on the third planet of Sol. Althesal and her friends suspect it to be an ancient power source unlike any other we know, and in this light, it makes sense that Ankepum covets it greatly. Why shadowy beings from another spatial dimension are also interested in it, I don't understand. But we have to act, nonetheless. We must protect planet *Ær!*"

30

Stïel Key

Planet Lyaty, Nauth System

Later, on the same day Althesal witnessed the debriefing of the Rangers who went to Mal'ek, she traveled to Laidé's home planet. No one on Thel knew of her trip there. She had acted on her intuitions when doubts about her uncle's plan began to assail her.

Water everywhere was an unfamiliar experience to her. The light breeze felt hot on her face, and her clothing wasn't balancing enough her skin temperature for her to feel comfortable. The rocking motion of the island also challenged her, even though it wasn't as strong as she had imagined it would be. No one on Lyaty knew she was coming either, yet the few passersby greeted her with respect — some using her title and name. That was a surprise since she had never visited that planet. This told her Nauthians were more interested in the official affairs of the Union than most other Humans were.

She knew, by name, the island of her destination on that world of floating islands, and from the spaceport she walked to the transportation center located in the next building. There, she spoke the island's name as she stood on one of the dozen translocation pads available, and a young woman who was studying her, probably because she had never seen a Thelian Human, covered her mouth to suppress an exclamation.

"Only the Nauthé go there!" she next blurted to Althesal.

"I know!" Althesal replied with a smile. "Yet, a Voyager also I am." And with these words she disappeared inside the oblong opening in front of her.

The island of the Nauthé was never pictured nor described in any form anywhere. She didn't know what to expect. She arrived to a lone translocation pad at the center of a rustic space open to the sky and surrounded by a low hedge. The midday sun shone bright upon her, making her squint. Beyond the hedge she saw plants and trees of exotic species unknown to her. They all grew as if the wind, and not the hand of a gardener, had planted their seeds.

A footpath led from an opening in the hedge to somewhere. As far as she could see and sense, she was alone, and the absence of maps or information displays told her that indeed no one came uninvited. But she had brought with her winds of change, and with determination she stepped on the path.

For many days she had let the events in Sol and in the Union play themselves out. She had observed them, and how everyone who was touched by them reacted. At the same time, almost unnoticeable, a transformation was happening in her. Yes, she was Althesal of Thel… but she was likewise more. It was from this sense of being more than her Thelian identity that she had felt the call to visit the Nauthé — that select group of Nauthians who were the leaders and the stewards of the traditions of the Voyagers of old.

She didn't know what she was going to say to the Nauthé. Laidé had already informed them, only them, of Naleean's claim of the third planet of Sol — their reaction had been one of complete silence, something which had puzzled Laidé. But she hadn't come to their island for any of that.

Not far from the translocating pad, the footpath became a trail, meandering through wild and unkept grounds. At the first turn, it started to branch off. After having to retrace her steps twice from dead ends, she realized she was in a labyrinth — *Good!* She liked the challenge. Thus, with a quick focusing on her heart sense, she next sought to contact the island's soul. She sensed it, strange and exotic as the planet itself. But Nature's soul everywhere in the Universe loves the touch of the heart, and Althesal let the island's soul guide her steps.

Soon she was walking fast, and not once again had she to retrace her steps. The rocking movement of the island under her feet felt stronger than at the spaceport, but she was becoming used to it. Birds from several species flew by her at times, and creatures scurried through the thick underbrush invisible to her eyes. At some turns she saw open spaces with unlit fire pits in their middle — *For storytelling under the stars,* she guessed.

Her solitary march continued for close to one hour, following the twists and turns of the labyrinth. Still she saw no one. She didn't know how many Nauthé guided the Nauthian civilization. Of course, most of them didn't live on the island, but two did as its keepers. According to Laidé, these were the eldest and wisest of all Nauthians — *The Song Keeper* and *the Story Keeper*, he had called them.

Then, after a tight turn of the trail, she arrived to the center of the island. A large and tall conical building stood surrounded by eight smaller, also conical structures. They all were white, windowless, and had a smooth surface. Pebble-covered walks stretched between them. Well-kept flower and vegetable gardens nestled among them.

A man and a woman, old in years, stood at the entrance to the place, regarding her with astonished faces — the Song Keeper and the Story Keeper, Althesal knew. They were dressed with long, white tunics, enhancing the olive hue of their skin and their glossy, still jet black, long hair. At their waists, a belt made of colorful feathers broke the uniformity of the white.

Althesal approached them with respectful steps. Then, after bowing in the manner of the Nauthians, she spoke to them. The words that came out of her mouth surprised not only them but also herself:

"I have come guided by Stïel of the Nine. The Key is needed. The Door has been opened, and it must now be closed before the Ancient Darkness engulfs us all."

The Song Keeper and the Story Keeper, at first, were visibly shocked and didn't know how to react to her claim and presence. However, when they she told them she had traveled the labyrinth in less than one hour, they marveled at her, saw it as a sign, and accepted the claim of her words.

"For those who come to the island for the first time to be initiated as Nauthé, it takes them at least two of our days to voyage through the labyrinth to arrive here", the Story Keeper told Althesal. "Stïel has truly guided your steps, Althesal of Thel."

Immediately after the Keepers summoned to the island the other Nauthé present on Lyaty — four of them. A mix of doubts and excitement filled the air during the afternoon and evening as they debated with the Keepers, around an outdoor fire pit, the extraordinary claim she made. But their doubts won out, and they arrived to the conclusion that only a Nauthé would know if the Door had opened.

They all nodded in silence at her as the Song Keeper voiced their decision: "Althesal of Thel, your presence here is a sign. We don't doubt that. It calls us to look to the stars and to listen to the sky for other signs. We shall determine if the Door has truly been opened. This we pledge to you."

Althesal said nothing, but in frustration raised her eyes to the starry vault above them. She had expected her very presence alone would prove to the Nauthé the Door was already open. Regarding once more the six of them, she was about to thank them before departing when a male voice spoke behind her:

"I suspected you might be coming here!"

Turning, she saw Laidé approaching. He beamed at her with one of his friendliest of smiles, then greeted the Nauthé in the fashion of his people. After sitting next to her, and with a whisper just for her, he added, "You will need my help. They forgot voyaging!"

Thus, it was only when Laidé told the group of fellow Nauthé of the events unfolding in the Sol System, and of Althesal and the Rangers encounters with the Dwellers, that all doubts and hesitations vanished in the custodians of Stïel Key.

Althesal had sat quietly all this time. Although Laidé had convinced the six Nauthé of the momentous need, it was clear to her none among the past and present Nauthé had ever planned what to do in the event that the Door to the Darkness spoken of by Stïel had been opened.

The discussion had then continued until midnight when it was agreed that Laidé and two more Nauthé would travel with Althesal to Thel, to eventually accompany her to Sol. They would carry Stïel Key with them until the time when its use would become apparent. Although no one knew who would use it, nor how to do it, the Story Keeper assured all: "It will be revealed when the time arrives." With all the decisions made, the gathering then adjourned until the following day.

In the morning of that next day, Althesal witnessed a ceremony which no one outside the tight group of the Nauthé had ever witnessed. The Song Keeper had explained to her that every seven years all the Nauthé gathered in the island to re-enact the ceremony which Rïal, the first Keeper of the Key, had designed in detail following directives from Stïel herself. According to the story, he had received these directives through dreams while still on the planet of the Cloud People. To re-enact the ceremony, seven were chosen from all the Nauthé gathered. Because at that moment only Laidé and six others were present, the choosing wasn't necessary.

The ceremony started with the seven Nauthé entering the central building reciting a poem in an ancient language new to Althesal. It was musical and beautiful to her ears, and its cadences evoked in her images of the planet of the Cloud People. Once more Althesal marveled at the language skills of Laidé and his people. With them, they linked in friendship a multitude of worlds with each other as they did their unassuming work of intercultural diplomacy.

She followed them in their procession. They were all dressed in the same white tunics of the Keepers, with a sash of colorful feathers at their waist, and feet shod with moccasins made of a strong, but soft and pliable tree bark.

The large conical building had no partitions inside. Its interior was also white, with the exception of an all-around mural depicting Rïal and his people receiving from Stïel the strange flaming crystal Stïel had called a 'key'. Even the column where the crystal had originally rested was there pictured with glyphs from, presumably, the Cloud People's language. On the floor of the building, seven stars were etched, forming a circle around the center. That was all. There weren't furnishings of any kind.

Once inside, each of the seven Nauthé took position on one of the stars, and their recitation continued for a good while. When it was finished, the Song Keeper left his place and took a few steps towards the center. He then halted and chanted a word in the same ancient language of the recitation. Slowly, a cylindrical column, about three quont in diameter [1 meter], rose from the floor. It was made of a glassy material, and inside it Althesal saw a rosewood box. Esoteric glyphs similar to those on the mural stood out on the sides of the box, and two metallic silver bands were strapped around it, encircling it from top to bottom. At the top, a seal of the same metal clasped each band secure.

Next, the Song Keeper returned to his place, and all the seven began to chant a sequence of words Althesal didn't recognize. The Story Keeper had told Althesal that, after this chant was finished, the box was lowered back to its vault and the re-enacting ceremony ended. This time, however, both the Song Keeper and the Story Keeper approached the box, each carrying a small hammer in their hands to break the seals. Anticipation was on their faces, yet their hands were trembling so much it took them a while to fracture them.

According to the oral tradition of the Nauthé, the box seals had never been broken since Rïal had clasped them on the planet of the Cloud People, many thousands of years before.

Once the seals were broken and the bands carefully removed, the two Keepers proceeded to open the box, their hands still shaking. No one since the time of Rïal had laid their eyes on Stïel Key, and Althesal sensed the excitement in everyone. Yet, instead of wonder, the faces of the two Keepers revealed horror as they looked inside the box.

"It's empty!" the Story Keeper cried, turning to look at Althesal before fainting.

Althesal froze, her mind refusing to acknowledge what just had happened. So had the others.

Laidé was the first to react, and he rushed to help the Story Keeper. Althesal jumped to help him, and between the two of them they carried the old woman to her quarters in one of the small buildings. When the Song Keeper came to stay with her, the two of them returned, in a hurry and in silence, to inspect the box. The other Nauthé had already done that, and Althesal would never forget the look on their faces. Nothing in the box, the bands or the seals indicated someone had tampered with them. Even the wooden box, in spite of its age, was still strong and sound, without the slightest sign of deterioration.

Althesal didn't know what to make of the loss. The devastation on the Nauthé's faces broke her heart. She too felt shocked. She had precipitated the discovery of it, and the words of the Master Chronicler came to her — *Change you are. It travels with you…*

Laidé appeared to have taken the situation better than the others, although he too was noticeably shaken. Knowing that the box wasn't going to tell them anything more, the two of them left the building together and in the open air talked for a long while.

What had happened to Stïel Key? Its disappearance added one more mystery to the strange happenings in Sol. Laidé had no doubts Rïal had placed the flaming crystal in the box, and that none of his people would have, ever, tampered with the box — knowing the Nauthians, Althesal believed that too. For her part, she had no doubt the threads of destiny had intended for her to visit the Nauthé and lay claim to Stïel Key. That was clear in her heart, even after the unexpected outcome. At the end, of one thing the two of them were sure, and with dread in their hearts they acknowledged it to each other: the two of them had trusted the Key would give them an advantage over the emerging Darkness in Sol. Now they had none!

After their conversation, Althesal left the island alone, with a heavy heart. Only Laidé bade goodby to her — "I will be here for a day or two. They need me now." She understood. The leaders of his people had a long voyage ahead of them. This time not through Space as in older times, but through their own souls.

On her way home she kept playing in her mind the message those mysterious nine Humans had left with the Cloud People. Could the key be something more than a physical key? Could the words spoken by Stïel to Rïal and his people mean something more than what was apparent?

31

Corridors of Power

"We should have guessed we were too late!" the Chancellor said to Thaël and Ulhloom with a strained voice. Furrows crossed her face.

Eight days had passed since she had ordered the Rangers to enact a quarantine around the planet Mal'ek. During that time neither Ankepum nor the Dwellers had shown their faces anywhere in the Sol System. Long-range planetary sensors directed to the base revealed no activity, with the collecting towers operating as they were designed. However, by chance, a patrol of the Rangers had seen with their own eyes — because their craft sensors hadn't detected it — a large patch of no-light, or shadow, traveling from the northern polar regions of planet Ær towards that planet's only moon. Upon touching the moon's surface, the shadow had resolved into a bulbous craft similar to the one the Rangers had seen at the base on Mal'ek. To make matters worse, that craft wasn't alone. Three similar ones rested close to it.

To add to this, Ethën and the Planetary Harmonics Science group's discovery that the Dwellers were altering the ös light-fields of the system had stunned even the usual serenity of Ulhloom. The findings indicated the Dwellers had moved the small planet to a new orbit to weaken the orbital harmonic of the third planet and, specifically, to weaken its ös-sphere. More than any other thing, this data provided support to the thesis that not only they wanted the power source hidden on Ær but also wanted to alter the bio-sphere of Ær, perhaps with the intention of settling in the Sol System.

"Now we have the proof that Althesal and her friends were right all along!" Thaël said while slapping his hand on the conference table. He felt angry with himself. He should have paid more attention to Althesal's intuitions. He too should have pressured the Chancellor into sending a mission to Ær after the Rangers' intelligence report on Mal'ek. But he had acquiesced when she had pointed out the risk of sending anyone there before assessing the effectiveness of the quarantine of Mal'ek.

"Don't blame yourselves, dear friends", Ulhloom said shaking his head. "Nothing done differently would have changed the situation. Overlord Ankepum and the Dwellers have been in that system for years, while we just arrived there. You two should also know you were right when you told me we needed to do something unconventional, and because of the preparations you already made, we will be ready to move quickly in our next step."

After a short pause Ulhloom resumed:

"I wasn't here during these past days because I went to meet with the other members of my government. I told them of your concerns regarding the lack of readiness of the Union to deal with this new threat. It appears others of my people are also hearing and seeing things, here and there, indicating many races and worlds feel something is coming. No one knows what that could be, but many fear the return of the dark times. The source of this uneasiness is The Others' latest behavior. Some of their Overlords are preparing underground strongholds in the most remote worlds of their dominions. Thus, with news coming from these two different fronts, my government has decided to use all its power to strengthen the Union and support your efforts — Chancellor and Councilor Thaël, tell us how we can help?"

"Thank you, Ulhloom", the Chancellor replied. "Let's first decide our next move, and then we will see what each can do."

⚡

Thaël left for Thel immediately after the meeting ended. He had much to do. The three of them had agreed, in a teleconference with Mhali, Althesal and Ethën, that the best course of action was a stealth operation, small and fast acting, focused on finding and protecting that mysterious Spark of Aïdin — they all too agreed, including Ulhloom, the primary objective of the Dwellers and Ankepum was, most probably, to take possession of it.

The first thing he did on his way to Thel was to contact his five Wanderer friends to invite them to be part of this new operation. They were going to accompany a group of Rangers, led by Marshal Mhali. He didn't have to persuade them. They had immediately accepted. They understood the gravity of the situation and had heard the same rumors Ulhloom had spoken of.

As Thaël traveled to his planet, Marshal Mhali was ordering his commanders to deploy a stealth fleet closer to planet Ær to prevent anyone else from approaching it. That's all they could do, for now. The mysterious anomaly surrounding that planet, affecting all live-crystal-powered craft, limited them to stay in an orbit beyond that planet's moon — a limitation the Dwellers' craft stationed on that moon didn't have.

Ulhloom's people were, for their part, going to activate the intelligence network of spies they maintained, with their many Amethen friends, throughout the Underworld. Any unusual happening among The Others, and elsewhere, was going to be immediately reported to Councilor Ulhloom. Besides, this move would give those races and worlds that felt uneasy about a potential threat, a means to act in support of the Union without compromising their own independence.

Thaël's job was a race against time. No one knew when the Dwellers' next move was going to be. They and Ankepum appeared to be waiting on that moon for something. Ethën had insisted during the teleconference that the only explanation had to be they were waiting for a window in the harmonic fields of the system to then land on planet Ær; but no one could figure out the nature of that window.

As soon as he arrived, Thaël traveled directly to the city of Ïnthil, where the main manufacturing facilities of the Providing Guilds were located. He needed to meet with the team of Providers that he had entrusted with the newest demonstration of Thelian science and creativity. The search for the door where the Darkness dwelt wasn't their mission any more. It was an expedition to retrieve and defend, if needed, a source of power from the Age of Legends.

32

Spaceblazer

Planet Thel, Eir System

Ethën stood still, staring at it. "So, this is what Thaël wants me to see!" he said, mostly for himself than for his companion.

He had rushed to the city of Ïnthil after an unusual meeting that morning presided by Ciän the Wise. During it Thaël had accepted, reluctantly, that Althesal, Nesdil, Daothel and him were going to be part of the expedition to the third planet of Sol — the Synod of the Wise felt the four of them were crucial elements for the success of the mission; the Synod too wanted a confirmation that those Thelians who had lived by the Source Path were living on that planet, and they thought Althesal, Nesdil and Daothel, with their expertise in the Bio-Soul Sciences were the ones to do that job. Althesal, for her part, had insisted that Soen and Laidé should also accompany them for the sole reason her heart so told her. Ethën had never seen Thaël so displeased, but it was understandable. It was a dangerous mission. Besides, including the six of them required additional preparations, and time was something they didn't have aplenty.

"Yes, Teacher, we wanted you to see this beauty of a craft!" Ethën's companion, Lyel, answered with pride in her voice. She was the team leader of the Provider group that had constructed it. "We started working with the schematics and ideas on the Në-Light material you presented at the last conference of the Materials and Engineering Guild. We wanted to confirm it could be manufactured. It was going to be a surprise for you. Then, Dean Thaël came to us, a few weeks ago, to recruit us for the operation to the Sol System. Since then we have been working day and night to finish it. Do you like it?"

At a loss for words, in reply Ethën gave her a slight bow. She had been his most enthusiastic student, ever, in his course on Light Dynamics. That had been twenty years back. After that, she had distinguished herself in the Providing Guilds for her talents. No longer could she be considered an Apprentice. However, the Guilds hesitated to appoint her as Teacher because of her youth.

The craft was a tear-shaped ovoid — twelve lont at its longest axis [26 meters] and nine across at its widest [20 meters]. It occupied one-third of the enclosing building. A soft yellow glow emanated from it, but he couldn't hear the music sounded by its light. He took a few steps towards it, mesmerized by its beauty, and began to walk around the hull to inspect it. Lyel followed him in silence. Others of her team lifted their heads for a moment to wave a hand and to smile to him — their faces were radiant, proud of their accomplishment. He too was proud of them and returned their greeting. All of them were busy and went back to work right away.

Ethën halted to touch the crisscross light threads forming the numberless trabeculae of the outer hull. He felt no vibration and turned towards Lyel with a grin — it explained why he didn't hear any music coming from the craft!

"You were right, Teacher." She returned his grin. "It is stable and vibrationally neutral." She couldn't contain her excitement: "This material is going to have so many applications, I already have a long list of possibilities!"

"It's more transparent than I had imagined it", he said. Now he was the one who felt proud. He had worked for more than three decades on the principles of standing light, free from polarity, that made the Në-Light material possible. What he hadn't considered was that it could be used to build a new type of spacefaring craft. Contemplating the elegant lines of the craft, he realized it could be used to travel through any type of environment, even through the most hostile ones. Thaël had been right when he had envisioned this craft could take the Rangers and the Wanderers to explore the Sol System, safe and undetected. It was impenetrable to any known force and energy. Now they were going to use it to penetrate the mysterious anomaly around planet Ær and to land on it.

He placed his left hand on the hull and closed his eyes to better feel the texture of the material — *What am I touching?* — The spaces in the trabeculae were minute regular octahedrons filled with a type of light whose origin, he had theorized, was beyond the ös light-fields of physical Space — 'Në light-fields', mathematicians were now calling it, a more subtle type of light. It was going to take many years to discover its origin and what it meant for physical Space. The main challenge was going to be how to detect it since no physical means but the mathematics of harmonics and the principles of light dynamics revealed its existence — *And here is that light, as a building component of something physical, yet still utterly remote!*

He opened his eyes, removed his hand, and continued inspecting the craft. On the other side of it they came to the ramp extending from the main hatch. It was made of the same trabeculate material. With hesitation he laid one foot on it — it was solid, though slightly pliable. Next, he stepped fully on it and jumped on his two feet. The material absorbed the landing force without deforming. He looked at Lyel, feeling like a child playing with a new toy. She was smiling, and he beamed back — she had probably done the same thing!

They entered the craft. There weren't any partitions on its sole deck. Two groups of monitoring consoles, made of the same Në-Light material, formed partial circles midway between the periphery of the craft and its center — some weren't yet finished. In the middle of the space, three members of Lyel's team stood around a small dome, three quont across [1 meter], protruding from the floor. They smiled as the two of them approached. At that moment he made the connection: *This is a prototype craft, and we are going to use it to conduct a most dangerous expedition!*

Shaking his head, he refused to continue that line of thought.

Halting close to the three pilots, he said to Lyel while pointing towards the small dome, "So, you equipped it with one of the prototype trans-dimensional riser-drives. Good match! They are made for each other. Have you tested it?"

"The riser-drive, yes, but before we installed it on this craft. That's why we want you here today, to go for the first ride!"

"We need a better name for it", he said. "I mean, for the riser-drive. 'Trans-dimensional riser' is too descriptive and long. The name should be musical, as… hmm… *Ïnm~Ah*… Yes, it sounds good."

"Spaceblazer!" Lyel cried with her usual excitement. "Great name! It's appropriate for the drive but more so for the craft."

"You're right… Well, what are we waiting for. Let's test this Spaceblazer!"

"Where do you want to go, Teacher?"

"Let me see… Othy is good for a start. We can land on the port but not for long." Smiling at the three pilots he added, "We don't want anyone to think we are using Othy as a testing field. After that we could go to Eir-2 and come back. That would give us enough feedback data."

Lyel gave a nod to her three team mates. They were ready. The hatch closed, and a four-dimensional, photo-sonic map of Space, with the planet Thel hovering over the small dome, appeared all around the pilots. It showed an area of Space about thrice as far as the distance to the star Eir-2. Ethën next sensed in his mind the connection and work of the three pilots with the Spaceblazer riser-drive — with their joined minds they gave instructions to it, triangulating physical and trans-ös Space. Then, fast, in less than two seconds, the map shifted to have Thel's companion, the small planet Othy, at its center.

"We have arrived!" Lyel beamed to him.

The map disappeared, and Ethën felt a rush of fresh and cold mountain air entering the craft. It came through several open windows that had appeared on the hull at the command of the pilots. He then saw the familiar spaceport of Othy. "This is excellent", he said to them. "I didn't feel anything when the craft rose beyond the first ös harmonic light-field. What about you all?"

Everyone shook their heads.

"Eir-2." Lyel nodded to the pilots.

The windows vanished, and the map of Space reappeared with Othy at its center.

Three seconds after, a strong bright light with soft bluish hues was all around the craft, and Ethën knew they were now inside the corona of Eir-2. Before he could react, a photo-sonic display appeared in front of the two of them. It showed schematics of the craft and the streams of data coming from the sensors in the hull and inside the craft. While he and Lyel studied them, she said:

"We tested the Ne-Light material in the lab with the highest possible vibrational light and sound found naturally in physical Space. As you can see, the light energy potential of the hull remains neutral and unaffected by the corona of the star. This is one more proof that, in its stationary and neutral state, light contains an almost-infinite stability which physical forces can't breach — You were right, Teacher!"

⚡

"Thirty-two of us only! That's your plan, Thaël?" Ethën had come from the hangar directly to Thaël's office to report on the Spaceblazer test. "And only twelve Rangers to deal with who-knows-how-many of Ankepum's forces… well, thirteen Rangers since Mhali is also going with us."

"You shouldn't discount the five Wanderers and the Chancellor's daughter", Thaël replied. He was calm and in a better mood. "They are as capable as any Ranger of dealing with the unexpected. Besides, since this is a stealth operation, we expect you aren't going to have a direct encounter with Ankepum and the Dwellers."

"Yes, but if Ankepum comes after us, he isn't going to invite us to have a picnic with him. He'll bring weapons!"

"Ethën, since when have you become a military strategist? Trust that you aren't going to be there unprotected", Thaël said to him with an assuring smile. "An entire fleet of the Rangers will be surrounding that planet, invisible to The Others but ready to act immediately if Ankepum brings his own. And there is also the fleet engaged in the quarantine of Mal'ek. Any one coming through that door will be contained."

"Hmm… I would feel more comfortable if the entire fleet of Rangers landed with us."

"You know that's not possible. The risk is too high to use craft powered by live-crystal technology. Time is short and we can't build another… 'Spaceblazer' you called it… right now. Lyel tells me it takes twenty days to weave just one-tenth of the Në-Light material needed for one craft of that size. Besides, this operation is about stealth, and the first one of many. We want to be sure we can land there with this type of craft and secure that power source. The Chancellor has also decided to take the first steps to establish a sizable and permanent colony of Humans there; for this, some of the Rangers will remain on that planet with the Nauthian youngsters."

"I hope you are right, Thaël… I do trust you have accounted for every detail. By the way, are you coming with us?"

"That's not my place. I have to be on Esdänl for any eventuality. The Chancellor, Councilor Ulhloom and I are going to need all our power of persuasion to obtain an emergency consent from the other Councilors if we need to destroy that base on Mal'ek while you are on Ær. Just know that, regardless of what happens, when you return, the Union won't be the same as when you left."

Yes, Ethën thought. *And I have the feeling that none of us is going to be the same, either.*

33

A Message from the Future

"Another 'urgent' meeting!" Laidé clenched his teeth in frustration.

The day before Althesal and the Chancellor had informed him that he and Soen were going to accompany the expedition to Ær. He had expected it. However, he had so many pending tasks to delegate to his aides before he could leave that he had turned off all incoming communications to his office. Now a messenger stood by his desk.

"All I know, Advisor is that the Chancellor requests your presence and that of the Marshal", the messenger replied.

Trying to calm himself down he strode to the Chancellor offices to be told there by her secretary that the meeting wasn't there but in the main communication chamber — "Naleean!" he cried and broke into a run. When he entered the chamber, Marshal Mhali was already there and Chancellor Vuensé was asking one of the Rangers, "Are you sure the message was sent from the youngsters' craft?"

Upon hearing the question he rushed towards the conference table where they sat. Holding his breath and unable to sit, he looked at the Ranger.

"Yes, Chancellor", the Ranger replied and gave a nod to Laidé with a grave face. "It is a voice-only communication and has the signature of the beacon of the young Nauthians' craft on that planet."

The Chancellor took a deep breath.

The large communication chamber suddenly felt crowded to Laidé, even though its only occupants were, beside him, the Chancellor, Mhali and the two Rangers assigned to monitor any attempt from the youngsters to contact the Union headquarters. After Naleean's first communication, thirty-two days previously, other attempts to reach him had failed. The beacon on Ær had become active a few times since, but nothing had been received from it, until today.

"And how can you explain that the encoded date in the message is nine standard galactic days into the future from today's date?"

"We can't, Chancellor."

It was too much for him. "Excuse me, Chancellor, since some of us came late into the meeting, could we hear the message?"

"Oh, I am sorry, Laidé", she replied. "Please, do it."

He could see the distress on her face, and he feared a terrible catastrophe had happened to the youngsters.

The Ranger sounded a word, and a voice filled the room. It was a remote, indistinct voice, mixed with the noises of a poor transmission. Some of the words were inaudible. It said:

> *"... send Rangers. Shadows and Dreki landed ... ... mad ... ... a*
> *darkness ... They want something. We ... ... in the forest ...*
> *dancing ... ... help!"*

"It's Naleean!" he said while grabbing the back of the chair in front of him to steady himself. "I know that voice anywhere." Then, the content of the message sank in: "What? They are under attack and they are dancing!"

No one said anything to that. He plunked down in the chair, and with his eyes questioned the two Rangers.

"The date is correct, Advisor", one of them said to him. "The relay communication beacons used by the transmission — in Seeërer, in Arthaï and on this planet — all have today's date. But the mobile beacon on planet Ær which the sender used has an encoded date nine days ahead. As you may know, no one can alter a communication beacon since its encoding light-kernel naturally resonates to the fundamental wave-frequency of the galactic core. Attempts to modify it will render the beacon useless."

"There has to be a logical explanation", he turned to say to the Chancellor. "We should—"

Marshal Mhali motioned to him to calm down and said, "I think, Chancellor, we aren't asking the right questions. Both the content of the communication and its date speak of an event that hasn't happened. It hasn't happened because my Rangers are monitoring that planet and the entire system, and no one has made any attempts to penetrate Ær space. Not yet. The four craft of the Dwellers, at this very moment, are still on that moon, and nothing moves there. The message sounds bizarre, at first; however, it must be one more of the anomalies of that planet. What we need to notice is that this is a confirmed instance in which Time is being affected there, on that planet, which is something we haven't taken into account in the planning of the expedition."

Laidé turned in his chair letting Mhali speak, realizing at that moment others were also attending the meeting, tele-participating from a conference room on Thel. There, his friends and Ambassador Thaël sat surrounded by Rangers, Wanderers and a few Thelians — these had the distinctive clothing of the Providing Guilds. Everyone looked puzzled but not as unsettled as he felt.

"Which questions do you have in mind, Marshal?" Eleaph, one of the Wanderers on Thel, asked Mhali.

"To start…" Mhali replied, "is this what is going to happen in nine days, or is it one possible outcome out of many? A next question would be, how are we going to deal with the Time factor in our planning? Is there something that we should prepare for?"

"And how can we answer your first question, Marshal?" the Wanderer replied. "Based on what? We don't have any means to ascertain if the future is a fixed path or an infinite spectrum of possibilities. Philosophers and scientists have spent countless lifetimes attempting to answer that same question."

Mhali hesitated and was about to say something when someone of those on Thel said softly:

"We could answer that question if we look at it from another perspective — one that can provide us with a better sense of what is in store for us."

Looking for the source of the voice, Laidé saw those on Thel staring at Nesdil.

Nesdil's voice rose: "We could obtain an idea of what is in store for us on that planet if we set aside the concept that Time is a component of Space."

She paused to regard everyone. All eyes were fixed upon her. "There is another way to see Time — one that recent experiences tell me would provide a better explanation of what the future is about. In this other way, Time can be understood as the building action of Mind, or Minds, upon the forces and light-fields that constitute Space. Thus, a future is nothing more than the joined action of Minds, in the present, upon a combination of forces and light-fields in Space that those Minds want to see organized in a particular way."

She halted again. Laidé and everyone's full attention was now upon her.

With a smile she resumed, "What I'm saying is, the future is neither a fixed path nor an infinite spectrum of possibilities. Instead, it's an ever-emergent horizon born from the activity of Mind. At this present moment we have the minds of Ankepum and his partners, plus the minds of all of us here... all working to see their own particular outcome materialize on the third planet of Sol. Each party in this affair is thinking, visualizing and taking steps to see their own plan or mind-construct succeed. Thus, we are now in a competition with Ankepum's mind power, and that of the Dwellers, to see whose outcome is going to fully materialize."

Laidé saw right away the implications of what Nesdil was saying. Still, that way of seeing Time didn't explain how a message from Naleean had come from a future that hadn't yet happened.

Nesdil must have read everyone's puzzled expression because she added, "The future of Ær that we are contemplating is still in formation... Some future events, such as Naleean's message, have already taken shape; others are only taking shape as we speak; and still others are yet to take shape based on the decisions we, and Ankepum, are about to make... It is a dance — some steps we create, other steps are created for us by others."

Althesal, looking at those on Esdänl, said, "I'd like to think Nesdil is onto something. I too have had experiences, recently, that make me think we need to change our understanding of Time. However, all we can say at this moment is that Time appears to play a key role in the enigma of planet Ær. We know already of at least one other case in which Time was affected there — when Wanderer Soen visited it. At this very moment we can't explain Naleean's message; but I suggest we take it at face value and read from it that Ankepum and the Dwellers are going to be there, on that planet, nine days from now."

"In that case," Laidé rushed to add, "we must go there before that time!" Then, it dawned on him: "Although that only means the outcome might be different to the one in Naleean's message, and still Ankepum and his partners could succeed in their plan."

Several of those present sighed, others shifted in their chairs. He felt the frustration most had. They were truly digging for explanations where none were to be found — Althesal was right, they had to take the message as a warning and leave the explanations for later.

"All this talk is just ornate theory", a younger female Wanderer spoke. "If we now know that in nine days those shadowy beings and Ankepum are going to attack, inflict a lot of damage, and take possession of that planet —

should we still continue with this small expedition? Because small it is! This is the question we should be asking ourselves now. We are hardly a military force. Shouldn't we consider alternatives?"

"I agree!" Another of the Wanderers said. "Why, Chancellor, don't you send the Rangers in full force, shield that entire planet and take control of the entire Sol System? That would be the most direct and effective way to deal with this entire affair. We already know Overlord Ankepum violated the Armistice in more than one clause and has an alliance with a partner whose intentions can't be anything but hostile. I doubt the Armistice Inspectorate will object if the Union so acts. Besides, the other Overlords will thank the Union for having eliminated the menace they fear."

The tension in those present rose higher at these words, and Laidé saw more than one of those present nod in approval. He also suspected most of the Councilors in the High Council would agree to that. But events were happening too fast, and he knew Chancellor Vuensé was walking a tight rope. Those four craft on that moon were already beyond the Rangers reach. Besides, Ankepum and the Dwellers could have other types of craft and weapons the Union didn't know of. If they defeated the Rangers in a direct confrontation, the psychological and political consequences of such a defeat would be enormous throughout the entire Union, and beyond.

He regarded the Chancellor, waiting for reply and wishing once more that Naleean and his friends weren't there. At that moment, though, he noticed that a silent glance passed between Mhali and the Chancellor. Next, Mhali, clearing his throat, said to all with a tired voice:

"We already tried that… We already tried to shield planet Ær, and the light interference patterns to create a shield didn't form. In fact, none of the technology now available to the Ranger Corps works within a spherical boundary sixty times the radius of that planet. What is more, we had a difficult time rescuing one of our scout craft that lost all power when its pilot ventured inside this boundary. Yes, we can shield the planet outside that distance, but then what? What do we do next? Witness as silent spectators when those four craft land on Ær carrying Ankepum and the Dwellers?"

Mhali studied everyone's reaction before continuing, "I was going, tomorrow, to tell you this news, when Laidé and I will be there, on Thel, for the final preparations of the expedition. You should also know that on the same day when the Nauthian youngsters laid claim on that planet, the Chancellor instructed me to plan a way to rescue them and to secure that planet. Well, I never thought I was going to say these words: the Rangers' capabilities are not sufficient to the need in this instance. Councilor Thaël's plan is the only option we now have."

In the silence that settled no one moved. Laidé hadn't known of the Rangers' attempts. Mhali had probably decided to spare him from any additional anxiety until the final preparations.

"Well… It's clear", Daothel broke the silence, "we have no other choice but to travel there in the Spaceblazer, and better if we do it before nine days from now. If we choose not to, the consequences of our decision could be dire for many. Could we live with such a decision knowing this? I can't. I'm going there."

"I'm too", Althesal said.

Then, one by one all stated the same. The younger female Wanderer, Laidé noticed, was one of the first ones to agree with Daothel.

"Councilor Thaël," the Chancellor spoke when everyone became silent again, "when do you expect that new craft of yours to be ready?"

"My people are doing all they can, Chancellor, to make it ready as soon as possible. Confronting the Dwellers directly has now become a higher probability than before. The expedition must be ready for this. Thus, we are testing the enhanced generators and finishing the modifications in the three planetary vehicles they might need. I am assured that in five days everything will be ready."

"Good… That will be four days before the date of this strange message. I am assuming there is enough room in the Spaceblazer to bring back the twenty-seven youngsters if the circumstances so dictate."

"N-No, Chancellor", Thaël replied. "There isn't enough room even if the expedition leaves all the cargo on that planet. Marshal Mhali and his strategists think that a quick trip of the Spaceblazer to one of the Ranger transports waiting beyond the moon of that planet, is the only solution to the lack of space in the craft. Quick trips to the transports are part of the plan, anyway. These will ferry the supplies, equipment and the personnel needed for establishing the permanent Ranger outpost — of course, once Marshal Mhali decides it is safe and doable."

"Let's hope the expedition won't have to leave that planet in a hurry!" The Chancellor's heaviness of heart was in each of her words.

Laidé's anxiety was at a new height. He took a deep breath. He too had expected the craft would be large enough to bring everyone back together. For the thousandth time he wished Naleean and his friends were voyaging somewhere else.

34

Through the Veils

The hectic days that followed were something none of the members of the expedition had ever experienced. "Perhaps the Rangers are used to this rhythm", Althesal replied to Soen after she mentioned some of the Wanderers felt strained. "Although, I sense the Rangers are being challenged too", she added with a consoling grin.

Marshal Mhali, as the leader of the expedition, subjected everyone to rigorous rehearsals of the role each would play in various scenarios. In addition, they reviewed again and again the information they had on planet Ær. It frustrated Mhali that his Rangers couldn't detect from their monitoring position the location of Naleean's craft, or of any unusual source of energy. Nonetheless, the Rangers had confirmed Soen's description of the planet's four continental masses. The largest one of these was rich in vegetation, while the others had extensive barren areas. It was while flying over the largest continent, on the equatorial region, when she had experienced the catapulting force that had expelled her craft from Ær two years before. Based on the available data, they had decided the larger continent was the place to land. All agreed the Nauthian youngsters had probably landed there, seeing that their first communication had shown a verdant landscape.

Althesal didn't complain about the intensive preparations, nor did any of the other Thelians in the group. For them the entire experience was a new opportunity to learn. Curiously enough, the team of the Providers led by Lyel, who were going to be the manning crew of the Spaceblazer, felt an enigmatic kinship with planet Ær and looked forward to traveling there. Their excitement contrasted with the circumspect attitude of the rest of the expedition members.

Everyone was, nonetheless and in spite of the risks, eager to venture to a planet where some of the occurrences described in the legends could be real. When the training allowed, they met in small groups to share their thoughts and to make plans for what would happen after the mission was completed — for instance, the Wanderers mused about establishing on Ær their first formal school, ever! This led Althesal to wonder if they knew something about the legends that wasn't recorded in the stores of common knowledge and which they expected to find there.

During those few days of preparation it also became evident to her the Wanderers weren't the only ones who had different goals and expectations of the expedition:

The Rangers and Laidé carried the official mandate of the Chancellor — to secure the Spark of Aïdin and prevent the Dwellers and Ankepum from taking possession of the planet. If everything unfolded as planned, the Rangers were going to help the Nauthian youngsters establish a permanent colony of Humans with the goal of integrating, at a future point, the entire Sol System as a full member of the Union.

The Wanderers, including Soen, besides musing about a school, had an unspoken purpose, which Althesal could guess from a few comments they made — to ensure the first Aïdin Planet to be discovered remained politically neutral and welcoming to all sentient races and civilizations.

The manning crew of the Spaceblazer worked for her uncle, who had his own purpose — Thaël wanted Ær to be a sister world to Thel, and to remind everyone it was the Thelians who were making possible the operation. Her uncle wanted for their people to be the true and direct link between planet Ær and the rest of the known worlds.

As for her, Nesdil, Ethën and Daothel, they had a more realistic attitude. They didn't know what to expect — Yes, the Spark, could be there. Yes, descendants from the Source Path could be there. But a broader destiny could be waiting for them.

Thus, Althesal felt in a strange space. She was stepping onto a mysterious path, and nothing was going to be the same for her — probably not the same for anyone else either. Twice during those days she had had the same dream, and she didn't know what to make of it. In the dream the Asli showed her, and her friends, a garden with light-made spiraling sculptures surfacing from a large reflecting pool. These changed in shape and moved from place to place at the rhythm of series of mysterious moving glyphs born at the center of the pool and marching towards its periphery. Hovering above the reflecting pool, she could see the Spark of Aïdin. The Asli urged them towards it but with a warning — not to touch it! However, no matter how they attempted to approach it, the moving sculptures blocked their path.

The moment of their departure finally arrived five days after, as Thaël had estimated.

Althesal felt calm and ready for the unknown when she entered the large hangar housing the Spaceblazer. Everyone was already there, clustered in groups and all dressed with Ranger-mission suits. She was also wearing one and felt comfortable in it. It toned her muscles and made every movement an effortless act — "The mission suit is designed to enhance the connection between the body and its subtle light-fields", a Ranger had explained to her. "Thus, the muscles and all other organs will receive, not only neural will-energy, but the full life force of the inner being at your command."

Her uncle and Mhali stood, at that moment, talking to each other on the ramp to the main hatch of the Spaceblazer. She halted when she saw them. Thaël moved his hands in the way he always did when he was upset. She knew right away a new development had happened.

"I was just informed," Marshal Mhali said to all the expedition members as they gathered around the Spaceblazer for their final briefing, "the four craft were seen, a short time ago, leaving that moon and moving towards planet Ær at a high speed. No other movement has been detected anywhere in the system, outside it, or in the nearest star bases of Overlord Ankepum."

For days the Sol System had been quiet, and Mhali had hoped the expedition was going to unfold as planned. Yet, in this affair, the unexpected had been the norm since the beginning.

After he made his announcement to the group, he glanced at Althesal. She had been right. She wished some of her other intuitions weren't going to materialize. The previous evening she had invited the six of them to her house. Everyone had been astonished when she and Laidé revealed to them the disappearance of Stïel Key. But Althesal had invited them for another reason. She felt in her heart something much greater was at work on planet Ær. They were going to need to work together. A change was coming for all, and she had meant both personally and for the many groups of beings from the Young Races in the known worlds — "The Call coming from that planet is reaching far and wide, not just to us", she told them. "And this is only the beginning."

"You must hurry!" her uncle said as soon as Mhali finished speaking. "You each know your instructions for this eventuality. May the blessings of all that is Good in our Universe and beyond give you success and bring you safely back home." Next, taking a step towards Althesal, Thaël hugged her while saying, "Esal, be careful!"

"Our paths are together, uncle, regardless of the distances", she whispered back. When she said that, unexpectedly she felt soaring to a place where she saw herself journeying beyond Space and Time. It didn't last, but it had showed her the journey started on planet Ær.

She next kissed her uncle in the forehead, looked into his eyes, and turned to board the Spaceblazer to meet her destiny.

Once on board, she took her position. The Spaceblazer hadn't been fitted with seats for a trip that short, and everyone not assigned to a specific task was standing around the central area. The twelve Rangers with Lyel and her team were in charge of monitoring the various displays, some for tactics, others for science, and still others for the craft systems. The three pilots stood forming a triangle and facing the navigation dome. A partition on the rear of the craft had been erected to secure the cargo. It included shelters and provisions for several days, since no one knew the time it would take to locate the Spark of Aïdin and the youngsters.

Their plan was to enter the planet's low atmosphere and, from there, search for the communication beacon of the youngsters' craft and for any energy anomaly. Then, they were going to land next to their craft. That was going to be their base of operations. From that place they were going to use the vehicles they carried to find the Spark and the youngsters, and to choose a suitable location for the new outpost of the Rangers.

Daothel, Nesdil, Soen and Laidé were clustered together next to Mhali and across from Althesal, who stood with Ethën. The Wanderers, as it was their custom, were by themselves, somewhat away from everyone else.

Mhali looked at everyone in the eye, gave a last glance to Althesal, and order the pilots to proceed.

Not three seconds had elapsed when flashes of memories began to assail her, one after the other and following no discernible pattern — her childhood with her parents, her meeting with Iain, visits to other planets, and some that apparently she hadn't yet lived. Her fellow expedition members looked bewildered and were probably having the same experience. She then forced herself to focus on the present moment and on the craft.

"What's happening?" The cry of the voice of one on board reached Althesal.

Time appeared to have dilated, or perhaps compressed — she couldn't figure it out. The three pilots were in deep concentration, doing their task. Their eyes were closed, but she could see strain on their faces. The craft should have by now arrived to its destination.

Next, the Spaceblazer shook several times as if by penetrating force-fields that resisted its presence. Voices in strange languages and unidentifiable sounds were heard inside and outside the craft. Insubstantial shifting shapes appeared, some with Human faces, moving around them. At the same time, the light coming through the hull changed from color to color before it settled in a neutral bluish radiance. Then, the voices and ghostlike shapes were gone, and all became silent and still.

The pilots opened their eyes, and Althesal could see relief on their faces. The stellar map around the navigation dome showed the Spaceblazer now situated inside Ær's atmosphere. The trip along Në Space had lasted about seventy seconds. It should have taken no longer than five.

Someone behind her sighed. Others shifted on their feet.

"Well… that was a… grandiose reception!" Mhali said with his sonorous voice, undisturbed. "Is everyone all right?"

No one was hurt, and the cargo and vehicles remained secured in their places.

"We're hovering over the planet's surface at an altitude of two ont [5.6 kilometers]", Lyel said while working with the photo-sonic display in front of her. "The large continental mass is directly beneath us. We can't detect any feature since the long range sensors are offline — we're working to fix them."

At a nod from Mhali, one of the Rangers standing in front of another display said, "There is no other craft activity that we can detect, and we aren't receiving any signal from the target beacon. Likewise, the tactical sensors have some glitches."

"Modulate the search frequency as planned."

"We are already on it, Marshal…" the Ranger replied. "You should also know we are unable to detect the beacons of our transports, nor do we have mind-to-mind communication with our people on them."

Mhali looked with a questioning face at the group of Wanderers, and they all shook their heads while Wanderer Eleaph answered, "No contact with them, either."

"Marshal…" another Ranger said. "Unless our beacon has been damaged… we have moved four standard galactic days ahead!"

Althesal's eyes locked with Mhali's — They had arrived on the day

Naleean had sent the message! Her mind wanted to cry out that they were already too late, but in her heart she knew everything was going to be fine — In response she gave him a reassuring nod.

Mhali turned and said to all, "Well, we are on our own. For now. Let's hope once we land, our communications will improve. Let's keep searching for the youngsters' beacon and for any energy anomaly — and let's fix those glitches in the sensors!"

The twelve Rangers didn't need to be told this. They were already busy at their stations. So were Lyel and her team. As planned, the five Wanderers closed their eyes, as did Soen, to study the planet's light-fields and to look for the eddies in them caused by the Spark of Aïdin, by the Dwellers' craft, and by the presence of the youngsters.

"We need to learn the way they reach out to sense the light-fields of an entire planet", Althesal whispered to Ethën.

In reply, he gave her a quick look with his skeptical face and turned back towards the console that Lyel worked on.

At that moment large panoramic windows appeared on the hull. Althesal didn't hesitate and strode towards the nearest one. Glancing back when Ethën didn't follow, she saw Nesdil, Daothel and Laidé move towards other windows.

Althesal's heart raced with anticipation as she peered through the window — *Is Ær truly an Aïdin Planet?*

A tall mountain range, far in the distance, stood majestic and beautiful as the light of Sol, rising in the east, illuminated its slopes. Multiple shades of green were revealed to her wanting eyes — that's all she could see — and the colors reminded her of Iain's clothing. Far to the north, a blue ocean spread through the openings in the cloud cover that hung above it. She needed to see more, but the Spaceblazer was too high for her to distinguish any details.

"What can that possibly be?" Ethën asked loud enough to startle Althesal.

She turned and rushed to him. He and Lyel were studying a display showing six bright lights on the planet's surface, almost directly beneath the Spaceblazer. Lyel spoke a word, and the 4D photo-sonic field expanded to fill the center of the craft for all to see. The sensors zoomed in to those lights. The quality of the images were poor but enough to show the contours of their sources.

Nesdil gasped and with a hand reached to touch the image that had appeared near her. "Those lights aren't reflexions of the rising sun", she said softly. "They radiate from multiple angles."

Everyone else was dead silent, mesmerized by the lights.

Althesal moved around the images of the strange formations where the lights originated. She had never seen anything similar. "Ethën," she said without looking at him, "scan for the presence of mind-souls on the planet."

Wanderer Eleaph came next to her and, with a slight bow of his head, let her know his impression was the same as hers — those weren't natural formations.

"Well…" She turned towards Ethën after a moment. "What does the scan show?"

"Strange," he said in response, his eyes locked on the display, "something is jamming in a most uncanny way both the bio-soul sensors and the sensors to detect self-conscious beings. They are working but aren't detecting anything specific on the planet's surface… not even animals or plants. Instead, they are showing the energy signatures of bio-soul life and mind-soul all around us, right outside the craft!"

"There, that should do it!" Lyel said before Althesal could react to Ethën's observation.

The resolution of the images improved significantly, and Althesal froze on the spot. Of all the possibilities she had imagined were going to happen, that one wasn't on her list.

The six formations created a perfect hexagon. According to the telemetry, the entire array was one hundred lont across [216 meters]. Each formation was a cluster of gigantic crystals of various sizes, standing upright, clear in color and arranged around a central one, this one taller than the others. They all had the shape of six-sided obelisks. Light came from each crystal, in sequence and with a rhythm. The light of each of the six clusters played at a different rhythm, but all attuned to the same apparent song.

"Zoom to the center of the hexagon!" Mhali said with urgency in his voice.

Nothing. The area inside the hexagon was void of any feature. Althesal had expected to see the same thing Mhali had thought — the Spark of Aïdin!

"By the shadows we can tell that whole area slopes towards its center," Daothel observed, "and by its color and texture, it may be covered with the same type of grasses we saw in Naleean's first communication."

"Are we looking at the Spark?" a Wanderer asked Althesal. "I meant, is the whole array it?"

She shook her head slowly. "No, but those crystals could be generating a field to make the Spark invisible. The only way to know is to land there.”

The light coming from the crystals was too perfectly synchronized and rhythmic to be a natural phenomenon. She had seen before natural light-fields colliding with each other to create perfect and symmetric geometrical shapes. However, natural physical formations were another matter. During their development they were normally exposed to factors that prevented them having a regular, perfect and symmetric geometry.

“We need to land there”, she next said to Mhali. “Even if those formations turn out being natural, the play of those lights isn’t.”

Others assented. It was a logical place to start their search.

“Any news of the youngsters’ beacon, or of the four Dwellers’ craft?” Mhali asked his Rangers.

“No, Marshal. The target beacon could be inoperable, and those craft have probably landed by now. Unless they take flight again and we see them, we won’t know their location.”

Mhali sighed, and looking to the pilots asked them, “Is there a place to land outside the perimeter of those formations?”

“Yes, Marshal. We already identified one. It’s adjacent to the hill where the formations are located, but close enough.”

“Then, let’s land this beauty.”

35

Evolutionary Awakening

Planet Ær, Sol System

It was early morning when they landed on that new world. The air smelled fresh and sweet. It carried a faint perfume of flowers unknown to Althesal's senses. The Rangers had exited the Spaceblazer first, after they had confirmed no known danger awaited them. Still, Mhali wanted caution — he and his Rangers, as well as the Wanderers, sensed the presence of undefinable energies in that land. He and she followed next. The array of crystal formations was to their right, behind groups of trees and thickets, and on the highest point of the terrain.

Holding her breath, she stepped down from the ramp. The short grasses felt soft under her boots, and the lavishness of that new world delighted her eyes with an exotic spectrum of colors that surpassed in harmony those of her planet. The air was mild and comfortable, and a soft breeze caressed her face and played with her hair. After a few watchful steps, her body told her it felt at home. She then knelt down on one knee and touched one the flowers that grew intermixed with the grasses. At that moment a bee chose to alight on her hand before it continued its busyness with the flowers. She had to smile at the creature and at the fact that Thel also had the same species of bees.

By then all the others had finished exiting the Spaceblazer. They looked as dazzled as she probably did. Two of the Wanderers walked unsteady and had to stand still to adjust their bodies to the conditions of that planet. Just like the Rangers, they were good at that and were going to be ready for any eventuality in no time. Similar to her, the other Thelians felt at home as soon as they left the craft, confirming Ethën's observations that there was a good number of similarities between the ös-sphere and environmental conditions of Ær and those of Thel. Laidé's experience was different when he descended the ramp, she could see it — after all, his planet of origin was a watery world much lighter than Ær — he briefly leaned on Soen when she offered to help him.

Everything around them revealed the hand of a mysterious Master Gardener, and Althesal couldn't stop herself in reaching out with her heart to the soul of that world, as she normally did when she visited a new planet. This time, besides saluting it, she asked the question, *Are you of the lineage of Aïdin?*

She hadn't expected an answer, yet one came — a group of five small, playful birds flew to her. They were dressed in blues and violet feathers and greeted her with melodious chirps. They had an intelligent curiosity that reminded her of the birds they had found on the island of the Asli — *Is this a 'Yes'?* her mind asked the planet's soul because in her heart she felt so it was.

She wasn't the only one being welcomed. Daothel approached her with one of the little birds resting on his hand. The little fellow scrutinized the two of them in silence and approved of their presence with short chirps, then it flew away joyfully joining the others in their singing. Daothel and she regarded each other with glee in their eyes.

"I'm liking this world already." The youth laughed before darting to catch one of the many butterflies delighting in the flowers. Of course he wasn't quick enough, and Althesal patted him on his back in consolation.

Against Mhali's instructions and without noticing it, the two of them began to move away from the rest of the group. They were absorbed in making observations to each other regarding the similarities between the island of the Asli and the bio-system around them. At some point, when Daothel was saying to her that he wouldn't be surprised if a pack of doïel came to them, a short cry was heard.

They both froze on the spot. It had come from the thicket to their left, about twelve paces from them.

"That was Human!" Daothel whispered.

She nodded. To their Thelian sense of hearing that call had been unmistakably Human, although it had been sounded to imitate an animal call. She turned around not making any sound to see what the others of the group were doing, and it was then when she realized the two of them were alone. They must have walked around a bend in the thicket because neither the craft nor the others were visible. She was about to tell Daothel they should return to the others, when he made a slight movement of his head indicating the thicket — branches were moving as if something large was coming. Fast!

Next, three of the most strange beings charged towards them with long pikes pointed at the two of them!

Before she or Daothel could react, however, from nowhere one of the Rangers jumped at a high speed in front of the assailants and rendered each of them asleep with adept touches to their foreheads.

Althesal was unable to speak, her heart jumping in her chest. All she could do was grab the Ranger's shoulder to steady herself. She should have known Mhali had instructed his Rangers to guard each of the other expedition members while on the ground. She slowed her breathing and gave him thanks.

Daothel had taken the incident better than her. After a quick nod to the Ranger, he had knelt to inspect the attackers. They had fallen forward, and he was attempting to turn them over. Each was so heavy the Ranger and she had to help him. Next, in silence, the three of them stood contemplating those peculiar faces and bodies.

"How can they be Human?" Daothel asked with a deep frown, looking at the hairy, coarse and bony shapes lying at their feet.

⚡

The news of the encounter with the primitive Humans took Nesdil by surprise. It also created a stir in the other expedition members. Not all were convinced they were Human. They resembled a species of advanced primates, stocky and long-limbed, and with a body so dense, it veiled their inner light-fields. Everyone, however, respected Althesal and Daothel's observation that the cry they had heard was a voice with the range of harmonics only a Human could vocalize.

Nesdil was fascinated with the three 'Children of Ær' — as she had already named them. In their induced sleep they had a peaceful countenance in spite of the roughness of their faces and bodies. But more so, as she had pointed to those who doubted their Humanness, their breathing had a rhythm and followed a pattern of harmonics that was Human. That told her their mind-souls were fully immersed in their bodies. That wasn't the case with other primitive Humans she knew of, and this suggested to her the Children of Ær were developing at a fast pace, moved by an evolutionary force absent in other worlds.

Galactic Humans knew of the existence of evolving Humanities whose phenotypes, psyches and minds were rudimentary, and whose light-fields were sluggish and integrated of lower light frequencies. Both Rangers and Wanderers had had the opportunity to observe some of these in close proximity. Yet, their origin was an enigma since most of the known Humanities had a history dating back to the time when the legends had been born. It was an accepted theory among Galactic Humans that they had been the direct creation of more advanced beings — who the 'creators' had been, no one knew. However, countless records from a multitude of worlds, Human and Amethen, supported that theory. But, why the Universe was also bringing forth Humans through a long evolutionary path, was a question no one had been able to answer.

A temporary shelter was erected next to the Spaceblazer to give protection to the three Children of Ær. They were going to be asleep for a time, and it was possible the land had animal species that needed the bodies of other lifeforms for their sustenance — the known worlds where primitive Humans were evolving had these, adding to the mystery of the evolutionary force behind those Humanities. Thus, Nesdil had felt relieved when Althesal and Mhali had decided not to leave them unattended while the expedition inspected the hexagonal formation up the hill. Three of the Rangers were going to guard them and the Spaceblazer. Everyone else was going.

"You know that the existence of those Humans completely alters the status of this planet", Laidé said to Mhali and to Althesal when they were about to start walking up the hill.

Nesdil moved closer to listen to his words. So did the others.

"This is their world by rights," Laidé continued, "and neither the Union nor The Others can come here uninvited... We are, technically, trespassers... Naleean and his friends are too, so their claim of this planet has no legal basis. And this also means we have no right to start a colony of Galactic Humans here — it doesn't matter how important to us this planet may be."

Mhali, with a thoughtful face, said nothing to that, and Nesdil regarded Althesal waiting to hear her view on the matter.

"You are right Laidé", Althesal replied, "in pointing out to us these matters. However, for what we already know, neither this planet nor the Sol System truly fits into any of our standards, protocols and views. We are walking along an unknown path by coming here. Let's then keep moving with our mission and be ready to change our plans as the planet tells us so. That's the best we can do under the circumstances."

"And if not, what else is there to do?" Soen asked Laidé, fixing him with her gaze.

Something unspoken may had passed between the two of them because Nesdil saw Laidé soften his face to Soen before he replied to all those who were listening: "All I am saying is for us to be aware that our plans now have to take into account the native Humanity of this planet… and for the record. As our friends here can attest," he added indicating the group of Wanderers, "the Overlords of The Others will use our trip here as an excuse to do the same on other worlds if we impose ourselves on the Children of Ær. Thus, from this moment on we need to be careful with any decision we make regarding this world. I also think, on the other hand, Althesal's guidance is what the Chancellor would also ask us to do — that is, to let the flow of events guide our decisions."

"Then, friend," Mhali said to Laidé with a broad smile on his face, "with that settled, let's move to explore the array of crystals. Who knows what else we may find on this world that is going to alter the way we normally think and act!"

Nesdil observed everyone's reaction, and all agreed with Mhali. To her, these concerns were dwarfed by the mystery she felt all around. She was now more convinced than before that no one could control or alter the destiny of Ær. Its music was its own, and it dominated all other songs.

36

The Eddies of Åkhas

Nesdil surveyed the hill. It had a broad conical shape with a distinct flat top, and although it was the tallest feature in a land of rolling downs and savannas, calling it a 'hill' was generous. As she and the others climbed its easy slope, trees and shrubs became scarce, and the panorama of the land around unfolded to their eyes. In the distance, here and there, clusters of dense woods broke the monotony of the open landscape. Not far away from the hill, a sizable river meandered — it stood out as a silvery turquoise ribbon stretching over a sea of deep-green grasses. Herds of animals of various quadrupedal species grazed on the openness. Far to the north, a tall mountain range of snowy peaks stood as sentinels guarding the lowlands. No recognizable settlements or villages were visible anywhere.

They found no paths or trails, nor any other indication revealing the place was visited by the Children of Ær. As she and the others gazed at the natural wonder surrounding them, Mhali had conferred with Wanderer Eleaph on the side. "We don't sense the presence of the Dwellers, nor The Others", they next told everyone. Nesdil felt relieved, for now. They had time to search for the Spark of Aïdin without the worry of danger lurking close by.

The crystal formations weren't visible from the slopes. Regardless, as they climbed up the hill, she began to hear their music. It was allegro and compelled those who heard it to participate in it. Though, listening carefully to it, she realized something was missing. The song was incomplete. She knew then Nature couldn't be the author of that music. The missing chords intrigued her so much that she turned and grabbed Daothel's arm — "Let's climb ahead of the others. I want to listen in silence to the song." By the look on his face, she knew he heard the music in the same way she did. They quickened their pace and went past Althesal, Mhali and Wanderer Eleaph. One of the Rangers, Fejhl was his name, darted to match their speed, and with a look told them to be cautious.

The three of them continued together and reached the hilltop well ahead of the others. A perplexing vista met their eyes. The hilltop was crowned by a broad flat rim surrounding a large concave basin covered with the same short grasses found on the hillside. The six clusters of crystals were positioned on the rim, equidistant to each other, forming a perfect hexagon.

Next, in unison, the three of them directed their steps towards the nearest cluster, attracted by the subtle emanations that came from it.

The crystals sprung upright from the ground as if they were tree trunks, and nothing indicated they had been transported there from another location. The cluster had nine crystals aligned to form, with their positions and heights, an equiangular spiral, both horizontally and vertically. The tallest crystal was about five lont in height [10.8 meters] and three quont in diameter [1 meter]. Those around this tallest one were sized smaller, following perfect, proportional geometry. Even in the daylight, the play of their lights was visible. The short grasses that grew all around their bases were healthy and unaffected.

To their surprise, the humming song and the light of the crystals didn't come from their shafts: they came from their pyramidal apices, which were regular and uniformly faceted. It was then when Nesdil discovered that the interference pattern of the sound waves emitted by the six clusters created a dome-shaped field covering the entire hilltop — she could hear the convergence of the waves and their sotto-voce song. The entire composition was so beautiful it made her conclude the builders of the place had a science and skills beyond those of her people and of any other known sentient race — *Could they be those of our people who left our planet?*

A most puzzling question to Nesdil was the source of the light the crystals emitted. "They probably gather, condense and channel light from the light-fields of the planet", she told the others while touching with both hands one of the crystals. It felt cold, even though it was already a warm day.

"Quartz!" Daothel said sliding a hand over one of them. "Although of a purity and size Nature doesn't produce. Their lattice structure must have some uncommon atomic arrangement, tuned to the planet to behave as the strings of a musical instrument. That may explain their power to take in and condense light."

There wasn't much more to see in the crystals, and Nesdil's curiosity of the purpose of the whole array grew with every moment. The music it sang called to her.

"Let's descend to the center of the basin", she said to Daothel and Fejhl.

The rest of the expedition party had already arrived to the top of the hill and were on their way to the cluster the three of them had just inspected. Waving a hand to Althesal and Mhali, Nesdil pointed to them the direction they were going.

There weren't any animals, or their dwellings, anywhere on the hilltop — not even birds or insects, nor any trails or paths to indicate the place was visited regularly by anyone. But to Nesdil that didn't rule out it wasn't used. Her people on Thel trod the ground lightly, so did most animals, and seldom they left tracks that lasted longer than a day. Fejhl may have been making the same observation because he knelt to touch the grasses with the palm of his hand, testing their elasticity to pressure. When he rose again, she smiled to him. He smiled back. He was young and friendly, from the Merope System, as Mhali was.

The entire pattern of harmonies sounded by the crystals became clearer the closer the three approached the center of the array.

"This place resembles and sounds as a resonator of sorts… a musical instrument", Daothel said. "For what purpose?"

"Whatever energies or forces it works with," Fejhl replied, "it appears it's harmless to us and to the natural world. The entire structure is so self-contained and isolated from the surrounding land that it could well be a star observatory, if I may venture to add."

"You both could be right," Nesdil said to them, "and I have an idea how to activate it." The thought that the array was the perfect setting to hide the Spark had been in her mind when they were climbing the hill. She was less sure now.

They reached the center after a few more minutes of silent descent during which Nesdil studied the music she heard and identified the missing chords. A flat circle, about forty paces across, indicated the location of the center. It too was covered with grasses. No other feature was visible.

"Could this entire array be the defense system of this planet?" Fejhl asked with a touch of anxiety in his voice, revealing he hadn't thought of that until then.

In reply, Daothel burst into a laugh. "If it is, we are in a big trouble… and I mean, big! If it becomes active while we are inside it, we may be hurled into Space as Wanderer Soen was!"

Nesdil didn't laugh. She hadn't thought of that possibility. Fejhl could be right, and that would mean it could be dangerous to bring the array up to a more active level. Would they be able to control its power? She was now standing at its center and turned around slowly. She felt, however, no danger. On the contrary, she felt welcomed — *No! The array has to perform a harmless function.* Besides the music, the view of the entire place was entrancing. Beyond its rim, only a blue, cloudless sky was visible, with Sol at its mid-morning position in the east. The music of the crystals was full, clear and pleasant. Its volume was surprisingly muted, telling her that the grade of the concave slopes had been precisely designed and shaped — *Who were the creators of this place?* she asked herself again. *It can't be the Children of Ær!*

"Do you hear the music of this place?" she next asked the Ranger, who was observing her with anticipation.

"Yes. Although probably not with the complete gamut of sounds you Thelians hear."

"I can tell you this. Something is missing in the song to make of it perfect music. But more interestingly, if I am not mistaken, the missing parts can be sounded *only* by the Human voice. As someone trained in the power of the voice, you know well the Human voice cannot be fully reproduced by those who aren't Human, or by any artificial means."

Fejhl nodded.

At that moment Daothel shifted on his feet. "What are we waiting for, Teacher? Let's test it. It's a straightforward composition. Any musician can identify the chords that must accompany the others to make it whole!"

"We should wait for the rest of the party to arrive", Fejhl said while regarding Daothel. "We don't know what may happen once it's activated. If the Spark is hidden here, for all we know, its power may be beyond our control. I suggest we wait for the Marshal and for Issën Althesal, and tell them of your findings before a decision is made."

"Fejhl is right, Daothel. Let's wait for the others."

Her young apprentice stared at her. Then, he turned to see how far the rest of the expedition members were, and stomped on the grasses as he moved a few steps away from the two of them.

After a moment, still observing Daothel and wondering about the reason for his sudden impatience, Nesdil had to blink. At first she thought it was a reflection of the sunlight forming a faint halo around the youth's upper body.

Fejhl was also observing him.

"Can you see it?" she whispered to Fejhl.

"Yes. It has to be this place answering to the music he is probably playing in his mind. Which means, we should be even more cautious because this place is finely attuned to Humans."

Fejhl was right. She could also read from Daothel's bearing that he was singing to himself, at the rhythm of the music of the array, the short series of chords needed to activate the place. Nesdil walked to him and placed a hand on his arm. "Let's be patient. The others are almost here." He turned towards her with a face of resignation, and the glow around his body vanished.

The others came soon enough with excitement on their faces and expressing how good they felt since landing on the planet. Nesdil had been so much focused on the music she hadn't noticed the well-being bathing her body. They were right. An energy was all around them, gentle, welcoming and harmonious, and affecting both the body and the psyche.

She then explained to everyone their findings and thoughts about the array. All the Thelians among them also sensed no danger and were eager to discover if the Spark was hidden there.

"Well," Mhali pointed out, "it's also possible, as Fejhl suggested, we are standing inside the defense system protecting this planet. If that is the case, it isn't wise to risk activating it with us standing here. Let's wait until we explore more—"

"No! It isn't a defense system!" Daothel blurted out with a force that surprised Nesdil and Mhali. "For all we know, the thing protecting this planet must act automatically, on its own. This place, on the contrary, needs the sounding of the Human voice to come to life, and not just a simple command but a series of complex segments of a song."

"He is right", Althesal said. "Nothing here indicates the purpose of this place is to concentrate and radiate large amounts of energy. I think this is a place for science, or for art, or for both." Next, cocking her head, she added, "And a good place to hide the Spark!"

"I concur with them", Ethën said to Mhali. "The sounds of the crystals create a cavity or chamber on this hilltop — not a focused stream like the one Soen must have experienced. Activating this array should produce a volumetric phenomenon of some kind, perhaps by altering its standing resonance. The fact that it needs to be activated by a Human or Humans standing here at its center, indicates it poses no danger to us. Most likely, the result will alter the light-fields within the array, which would be consistent with the idea that its purpose is to hide something here."

Lyel and the other crew members of the Spaceblazer expressed their agreement with their fellow Thelians with nods and short exclamations, arousing with this a laugh from one of the Wanderers.

"All right. All right!" Mhali said raising his hands. "Who am I to argue with Thelians on these matters? However, I want only one of you to sound the missing chords, and everyone else silent, even in their minds, and standing back there, outside this central area."

"I'll do it!" Daothel hastened to say while stepping forward, surprising once more Nesdil with his impatience.

She looked at Althesal and Ethën to see what they thought of that. Althesal was already regarding the young apprentice with a fixed gaze, while he in turn held a pleading look to her. After a quick nod to him, she turned towards Nesdil and whispered:

"Let him do it. I have an inkling of why he wants to do it. The song of this place isn't unfamiliar."

Ethën just shrugged, and she consented with some hesitation, still puzzled by Althesal's comment. She didn't find anything familiar in the song!

Nesdil and the others moved away from Daothel as he took up position at the geometric center of the array. At Mhali's orders, three of the Rangers quickly climbed back to the rim of the hill. They were going to stand outside the hexagonal array of crystals, and in continuous mental communication with Mhali and the rest of the Rangers, including those guarding the Spaceblazer. Fortunately, once they had landed, they could communicate with one another of those on the ground — although not with those on their craft beyond the planet's moon.

⚡

Daothel wasted no time and began singing the missing chords in tune with the array's song. At first, nothing happened. Then, when the song came to its end, the clear and sunny blue sky shifted to a deep indigo color, and the darkness of midnight enveloped him. He could, nonetheless, see every detail of his surroundings. The ground and the clusters of crystals had disappeared, replaced by a level surface that resembled still water extending into infinity. He could also see his companions around him standing on the still water-like surface. They were all wonderstruck.

This wasn't what he had expected; although in truth he didn't know what was going to happen. He hadn't been mistaken about the song. Dean Althesal had also noticed the similarity.

He then took a step to go to his friends, yet what happened forced him to stop — the movement of his body created luminous, outward-going waves all around him, not unlike ripples on water. They didn't last as long, however, as wavelets on water normally did. These, as they drifted away, soon elicited a sparkling resistance from the surroundings, which quickly ended their existence. He next moved his left hand, to and fro, in front of his eyes. The spectacle was mesmerizing. The light waves were ethereal, shimmering and multicolor, and sang a faint tune.

His companions were also testing the nature of the strange waves, most of them with a grin on their faces. Dean Althesal was the exception. She regarded him with intent, and her face told him something wasn't right. Next, she came marching towards him. The others followed her.

As he watched the motion of their bodies, he couldn't contain a laugh. The light waves their steps created were chaotic and collided with each other. "This place would be a good dancing hall for us to learn to dance and sing together", he said to everyone as they came close. "We would see right away how bad we do it!" His voice and his laugh also created light waves, but these were well proportioned and formed a colorful multi-funnel-like pattern issuing from his mouth.

"Be silent and still!" With a commanding voice Althesal said to him and to everyone else. "And control your thoughts!"

Everyone obeyed with a start, and the glee some had shown was replaced by a questioning face. Her words immediately resolved into a series of concentric, outgoing spherical waves enveloping them all. When the last of the waves moved outwards to include those standing at the periphery of the group, it halted and didn't vanish. They were now standing inside the shimmering dome created by her command. She next waved a hand in front of her, and no light waves formed.

Daothel knew then she had created with her mind power a stable and controlled space for them inside that strange realm.

"Excuse my rough intervention," she spoke to all in a softer tone, "but our group isn't trained to work together as one mind, and Mind is the power that works this place. The Spark isn't here, evidently. However, if I am not mistaken, this array must be an entrance into the *unlit light* that is the background of physical Space — the realm where thought takes shape before it manifests physically. The Time Seers of old called this unlit light *the Waters of Åkhas*. We need—"

"You are perceptive, Issën", Wanderer Eleaph said. "I wouldn't have thought of this watery light-substance as the Waters of Åkhas. But now that you say it, it has to be it. I'd have expected, however, for it to be so fast in reacting to intention and thought that one wouldn't see its waves and eddies."

"But then, if it is Åkhas, how are we able to see it here?" Soen asked Althesal. "For what I know, because of its high frequency rate, it should be invisible to the physical eye and undetectable by any physical means; only through a complex mental exercise to still the mind, one may see it with the eye of the mind, and only in places located far away from the impact of any thought or psychic activity."

"I don't have an answer for you", Althesal replied. "It may well be this place was built as a controlled environment for one to learn to work with Åkhas. We also must assume there are rules to enter here and to work with it, and this is what concerns me — that we don't know the rules and may become lost in imagined realities."

As Dean Althesal spoke, Daothel could see Ethën using a finger to poke the boundary of the dome. Luminous ripples formed on its surface with each touch. At one point he pushed his entire hand right through it, and waves of light also formed outside the dome. He withdrew the hand and turned to the Dean.

"Then, let's test it", Ethën said. "If it's a place for learning, it must have safeguards."

"For sure this place is the product of an advanced science", Mhali was quick to reply. "However, our primary objective is to secure the Spark. It isn't here, and we must continue our search for it. We can return to study this place when there is more time."

While Mhali had been speaking, Daothel had been thinking on the implications of what Dean Althesal had said. He knew he hadn't been mistaken, nor the Dean, about the familiarity of that place's song — it was one of the songs Iolthel the Wise had recorded, and that meant only one thing. Thus, ignoring what was passing between Ethën and Mhali, and feeling a rush of adrenaline in his body, he spoke to her, louder than what he had intended:

"Then, Dean, on this planet there must be eleven other places comparable to this one since Iolthel recorded twelve songs. And there must be Humans advanced enough that they can benefit from visiting them. We should expect it, shouldn't we?"

The Star-Born

Mhali wasn't surprised at the explanation Althesal and Daothel gave the group to clarify Daothel's startling statement. He had already accepted that Ær and Thel were mysteriously linked through the Spark of Aïdin. This new connection spoke more clearly of the Call this strange planet sounded in Space. Iolthel had heard the Call and had answered it. With her powers she had discovered the song the crystal array played. She had recorded it, together with the songs of eleven other places — all probably as enigmatic and all as uniquely attuned to Humans as the array was. The Spark could be hidden in any of them.

Althesal continued holding the controlled space in Åkhas where all of them stood, revealing a strength of will and mind power Mhali didn't know she had. Some in the group were still asking questions to her and Daothel regarding Iolthel and the Source Path of the Thelians. Ethën, Lyel and a Wanderer were more interested in the present moment. They all had their hands outside the dome, apparently playing with Åkhas. The patterns of light the two Thelians created by moving their fingers were works of art, and the Wanderer was attempting to imitate them. Mhali could see, however, that wasn't idle play. They were learning as much as they could of Åkhas in the unique opportunity presented to them.

But Mhali hadn't forgotten Ankepum and the Dwellers. The silence of the three Rangers he had left outside the array, and of those guarding the Spaceblazer and the Children of Ær, concerned him. With the unexpectedness of their immersion in Åkhas, he hadn't had the opportunity to attempt communication with them, until then. He wasn't sure if they weren't hearing him because the Waters of Åkhas in that place formed a barrier to mental communication with physical Space, or because something had happened to them.

He was about to tell everyone they needed to return to normal Space, that nothing more was for them to see in the array, when Soen addressed Daothel once more with a question that gathered everyone's attention: "Do you think Iolthel eventually came to this planet after recording the songs? Was that the reason for her disappearance?"

"That's the most logical conclusion", he replied. "Although we are talking of events that happened forty-five thousand standard galactic years ago."

"She could have left clues to confirm her presence here", Soen added. "The reason for her to record those songs may have been to leave a trail of her quest in case someone would have wanted to follow her steps."

"But where would we start looking for those clues?" The youth asked her with a tight voice. "We need to find the Spark and Naleean — they are our primary objectives. Iolthel's fate isn't our mission. Looking for clues of her visit would only delay us more."

"You sound disappointed", Soen replied with a soothing voice.

"I-I'm… a little. When I first heard the song of this place and recognized it, I had hoped to find clues right here of what happened to her. There aren't any, and we must move forward with our mission. We have new leads, though — those other eleven places — and we should look for them."

"Do we know how to return to normal Space?" Mhali hastened to ask Nesdil before anyone would object to Daothel's suggestion. That question had been in his mind since the moment they had entered the realm of Åkhas. Under other circumstances, he would have proceeded differently in the exploration of the array and would have ordered the return of the group to normal Space as soon as it had been activated. However, he was dealing with two groups of strong-willed people who had never worked together — and both, Wanderers and Thelians were known for never listening to Rangers! Thus, he didn't feel entirely in command of the expedition and knew well he needed to lead them by consensus.

"I though of it", Nesdil answered him. "The song of the array is still around us, in the background — I can hear it — and the law of symmetry is everywhere in this place and in the song. I think by completing once more the missing chords of the song, we will return to physical Space."

"Do it."

"I'll release my thought of this enclosing space when you tell me", Althesal told Nesdil.

Everyone took a step back to give Nesdil more room. Mhali hoped she was right. He wanted to leave that place as soon as possible; although, he too felt disappointed the Spark wasn't there. He had expected the grandiose design and make of the crystal array would have unveiled it.

He observed Nesdil. Her eyes were closed. A faint glow around her upper body was visible, telling him she followed the song in her head and was about to sing the chords. Everyone was silent, and he could also sense the same tension in others that was in him — no one wanted to be trapped in that place! Yet, at the moment when he thought she was about to open her eyes to indicate to Althesal to drop the control on Åkhas, a shout startled him:

"Wait!"

All around him people shifted and sighed, Nesdil face contorted in pain by the sudden interruption, and Mhali felt his patience being tested.

"Now what?" He asked Ethën when he identified the origin of the shout.

"Well…" Ethën said unapologetically and with grin on his face. "It just occurred to me, if my understanding of Åkhas is correct, we could use this array to see those who used it last. That ought to tell us something about this planet. It may provide us with more leads for our mission. Don't you think it would be worth a try?"

"And how do we do that?" Mhali was unconvinced. He was beginning to think the Thelians' insatiable scientific curiosity was becoming a liability for their mission.

"A thought… All we need is the right thought to make it work. We know Åkhas records the patterns impressed upon it by all thought-intentions, and that these light patterns are permanent, although so subtle that only another thought can access them. For instance, the Mæl read the recordings in Åkhas inside the Portal Stars left by the mind-souls of those who travel through them." Extending his arms he added, "This place provides access to a contained portion of the universal Åkhas. Therefore, reading what has been impressed upon it can't be much different from what the Mæl do, or — if you want — it can't be much different than using the mind technique we Thelians use to access a memory and share it with others in a Nomöe of Mind."

Mhali nodded back to him, though still uncertain. Turning to Althesal, he asked, "What do you think of that?"

"It makes sense to me. And the examples of the Portal Stars and of the Nomöe of Mind are not the only ones that come to me right now. Åkhas is the universal light-substance or light-field of Mind upon which the Universal Thinker leaves the records of Its thoughts and intentions. In a sense, the light-field of mind that each of us possesses acts no differently from the ocean of Åkhas — it is just smaller and contained within our all-enclosing mind-soul field — and we do regularly retrieve our memories from it. We could explain the validity of his idea further, but my intuition tells me it is the right thing to do."

As Althesal spoke, Mhali felt she was touching his mind with the thought behind her explanation in a way he hadn't sensed before — it elicited images which made understanding her words easier. Also, for a reason he couldn't discern, the disquiet he had been experiencing about his Rangers and the mission had disappeared, and the feeling that everything was all right came back to him. Something was different in Althesal since their arrival to that planet.

Shaking his head slowly and unable to contain a smile he said, "You Thelians! You are… You are a good surprise at every turn… Now we need to decide who will do it."

"I'm doing it!" Ethën stepped forward. "If you all want to stay inside this protective dome, it's fine. I'll walk outside and see if my theory works."

"And if I say 'No', you will do it anyway. Won't you, friend?"

"Yes, Marshal. I am glad we understand each other." Ethën's hearty smile was echoed by those of others, together with exclamations of "Let him do it."

"Dean Althesal," the youngest Wanderer was quick to say next, "you can now release this protective sphere. I can see it is taxing your energy. It's good of you to have created it, and we are thankful for it. But now that we know the nature of this place, we will control our minds."

Mhali nodded to Althesal. "She's right. We need you strong and alert."

It took but a moment for them to be surrounded again by the unlit light of the Waters of Åkhas.

⚡

Ethën didn't wait. Using his thought power, he commanded Åkhas to show the last use of the array in the same way he had learned to out-picture a memory in a Nomöe of Mind. At once, the Waters of Åkhas resolved into a new scene that took his breath away.

It was noontide, bright and sunny. About 150 Humans were on the slopes, all around him and his fellow expedition members, yet oblivious of them. Some were descending along the slopes, others sat quietly on the grass around the central area, and a few were standing conversing among themselves. Since the scene was intensely real, it took him a moment to reacquaint himself with the fact he was witnessing the thought-pattern left upon the Waters of Åkhas in the array.

Those Humans, however, weren't just any Humans. His first thought was they could be those of his people who had left his planet. Upon a closer look he realized only a few of them had a resemblance to Thelians, yet not entirely — still, they could be them; after thousands of years that planet could have changed them.

It too amazed him those Humans were of ten different phenotypes, contrasting with Galactic Humans in each of the known worlds, which were of one phenotype per planet. Their bodies were almost as dense as those of the three Children of Ær, with one difference — similar to Galactic Humans, their inner light-fields shone through their flesh, bright and strong, with a soft golden glow, making the outer characteristics of skin, hair and eye color almost indistinguishable. They were all remarkably beautiful, with a noble countenance, graceful in form and movements, and of various heights.

They all were relaxed, even playful in their manners. Their ages were impossible to establish, not unlike those of Thelians. If Ethën could guess, none had yet reached their middle age. They dressed with multicolor, elegant clothing in various styles with one thing in common: a jewel with a large sapphire clasped on the left side of their chest.

Those conversing among themselves used a musical language. Their minds and hearts were fully engaged as they talked, making of their communication with each other a sharing of souls and not just a sharing of thoughts and words. The thought-flow accompanying their conversation was clear and easy to understand, though their words weren't. Some of these had a Thelian-like structure, adding weight to the possibility that one of their ten groups could be those of the Source Path. They also used some modulations and sounds resembling those of his people. But there were differences, and these shocked him — these people were more masterful of the power of the Voice than his people! Some of the harmonies and sounds they made were even beyond the Thelians' capacity to vocalize!

When those Humans finished sitting on the grassy slopes, two men and a woman who had been sitting near the center of the array, the three dressed in a similar fashion, rose and came near to where Ethën stood. Immediately they began to sing together a glad song. In his mind Ethën translated the thought behind it without effort — it was a welcoming greeting to all those in the gathering. Still singing and after glancing at each other, the three briefly closed their eyes. At once, a large sphere made of the Waters of Åkhas, about thirty paces across, appeared hovering high above them.

Movement next to him called Ethën's attention. It was Althesal walking away from the central area for a better view of the spherical projection those three had created. Ethën followed her, and so did the other expedition members.

Once the three individuals ended their greeting, the indigo watery light-substance inside the sphere resolved into a series of moving images, sounds, textures and smells that quickly became a live scene — a scene that astonished Ethën even more: it portrayed the young Nauthians' transport craft! The craft rested on the clearing of the forest where Ethën knew it had landed. Naleean and the other youths were also visible, outside their craft, exploring their surroundings in small groups.

The sight of the youngsters and their craft caused a stir among those Humans sitting on the grass. All conversations had ceased, and Ethën sensed the relaxed attitude with which they had arrived to the gathering was now one of disbelief.

When he had projected the thought upon the Waters of Åkhas to witness the last use of the array, the Nauthian's craft hadn't been in his mind. So, that had to be the most recent recording — was it a coincidence? Since the Spaceblazer had entered the atmosphere of Ær, he had sensed a Power all around them, familiar and welcoming. Had they been guided by this Power to explore the array before any other place on the planet? The synchronicity was too remarkable to ignore.

A hand on his right shoulder brought him back to the scene. It was Laidé's, his face beaming with gratitude.

"It wasn't me, friend", Ethën whispered to him. "Something else is at work here."

"Those Humans?"

"Perhaps…"

It was clear to him now, they, the expedition, had been clumsy in accessing the power of the array. Those three Humans at the center had called forth with mastership a portion of Åkhas without abandoning physical Space, and controlled it with no apparent effort.

Those in the gathering were now studying the scene inside the sphere. At times, the scene zoomed in to show a close-up of a group of the youngsters; at other times, the close-up was of their craft. Then, after all the youngsters' faces and behavior had been shown closer, and after the outside features of the craft had been fully surveyed, one of the two men at the center began to speak. His voice was soft and solemn, yet it was carried by the acoustics of the place for all to listen clearly. And from the man's thought projection, Ethën understood:

> "Thank you, fellow Star-Born, for coming on such a short notice to *The Mirror of the Soul*. You can now see for yourselves the nature of the urgency. These visitors arrived early this morning to a forest in our district. They are, without doubt, sisters and brothers from the stars. The people in our district first heard the commotion their conveyance created when it landed, and next we sensed the presence of their souls and their kinship with us.
>
> "The three of us here were chosen to observe them, without letting them know of our presence, and also to ascertain they were unharmed since the disturbances our people heard suggested something was amiss with their conveyance.
>
> "As you see, these visitors are young and of an exuberant friendliness. Their thoughts we could understand with ease, and from them we learned they came full of hope. They are voyagers from a people who love the freedom of the stars. In response to a call they came here, which they sense our planet broadcasts. Listen to this: They are of the mind our planet is of the lineage of Aïdin!"

The two companions of the speaker nodded in confirmation when a loud murmur of shock rose among those present. A few leaped to their feet wanting to speak, among them a woman, older in years than most of those present, though still young. She next rose her hand, and the one who had been speaking nodded in deference to her. She then asked the three of them:

> "Are you certain, Conveners, these visitors didn't see you nor detected your presence in any way?"

The man replied:

> "Yes, Soree, we are sure. We remained at the edge of the forest, veiled by a thought, and moved around the periphery of the clearing as 'the Forest Lights' move in their woods. Besides, it became clear to us, as soon as we heard their thoughts, the newcomers believe themselves to be the first Humans ever to set foot on this planet. Thus, they don't expect nor are looking to meet others here."

Once more a loud murmur rose from those listening. Soree the woman, who apparently elicited great respect from all those present, waited to speak until she had everyone's attention. Then, addressing not just the three but all those present, she said with disquiet in her voice:

"These are grave news, Conveners of our people's ways. This planet mustn't be known as of the lineage of Aïdin, because then its destiny, and ours, would be thwarted — that much I know. The Chronicles of the Horizon foretell of the coming of visitors from the stars, although at a time far ahead in the future. We aren't yet ready for these travelers, nor is the planet. Our knowledge of the journey of our people along the spirals of Time still has many gaps, past and future, and we aren't yet ready to understand our destiny. How can we, I ask you, expose ourselves to visitors when, for instance, our planets of origin are still veiled to us? We—"

A man, younger than most, standing not far from Soree, startled Ethën when he interrupted her with a sonorous voice and a furrowing brow:

"On the contrary, it's among the many suns beyond where we will find the answers to the questions assailing our souls. That's the reason I advocate traveling to the stars!"

The power of will and the magnetism emanating from that young man was impossible to miss to Ethën — *Here is a natural leader of peoples*, he thought. Yet he also noticed that, similar to the woman, he didn't have the jewel on his chest but the same multicolor sash she had across the left shoulder.

Not annoyed for his interruption but with the patience of a teacher, Soree replied to the young man:

"You know well, Tiá, the Lords of the Horizon, before they departed from the shores of this planet, advised our ancestors not to reach towards the stars but to remain guardians of Æl~Ur and to grow in wisdom until their return."

Still sounding defiant, Tiá asked:

"But why, Keeper of the Chronicles? Why is that so? Why are we bound to this planet when our souls long to soar among the luminaries that beckon to us from afar during the night?"

Taking a deep breath Soree replied:

"You know well we aren't privy to the designs of the Lords of the Horizon. The Keepers before me could not answer that question either. And as you too have searched, and many have repeatedly sought, that answer isn't in any of the Nomöi of Aïdin. Yet, one thing is clear to all those who follow the path of Keepers of the Chronicles of the Horizon — and that includes you: The Power hidden in our land must remain veiled until the return of the Lords; were it not so, a storm would rise that would darken even the stars on their paths across the heavens!"

The young man shook his head unconvinced, then, in silence, sat back on the grass. Those near him smiled to him in understanding. He returned their gesture with a slight bow and a weak smile. Ethën could see in his demeanor that the man carried a heavy burden of doubt, and that this wasn't the first time he had had that interchange with Soree. When Soree said no more, one of the three who had called the meeting, the woman, spoke to all:

"Star-Born, we must face what life has brought to us — What are we to do about the newcomers? We can't leave them by themselves. Our way is to welcome all. Besides, these visitors may need our assistance. The light of their bodies, in some of them, shows an ebb and flow, and this could mean the onset of an illness. On occasion, I've seen the same fluctuation in the light of some Luman, and soon after they have fallen ill."

A man among those sitting replied:

"By all means we must welcome them — they are family! I too sense their presence, and the kinship of our souls is beyond doubt. It may well be they are heralds of the Lords of the Horizon's return. How could they not be when they are the first to come from the stars since the Lords departed! Æl~Ur wouldn't have allowed them to enter and to land on Mu'a, unless their destiny is to be here."

Voices of agreement rose among many, including Tiá. Ethën noticed Soree had an unreadable face, surveying everyone's reaction to the man's words.

The man of the three, at the center, who had spoken first rose his hand to ask for silence, then he said:

"Because not all of us would be of the same mind in this affair, it was the reason the three of us decided that, of the twelve Nomöi of Aïdin, this Nomös was the right one for having this gathering. Let's then now ask 'The Mirror of the Soul' to show us what our collective soul holds for us from this encounter with those youngsters."

A silent assent went through all those present. Next Ethën sensed they all focused within, in their innermost being, while holding in their minds the thought of embracing the Nauthian youngsters with a welcoming heart. At this, the scene inside the sphere of Åkhas began to shift through a series of new and successive scenes. The shifting, though, was so fast, Ethën didn't have the time to grasp what each scene represented, nor its details. In some of them he identified the young Nauthians, in others the expedition members, and still in others beings and events he couldn't recognize. There were also strange cities and places, and buildings and seafaring craft of unknown make. Land quakes, floods and mighty storms were in others. In several scenes armies clashed, and in one of them bursts of a blinding light defaced the planet. It all ended not long after, and with it the sphere also vanished.

Ethën was at a loss. Nothing had made sense to him.

Those in the gathering remained silent for a time. They all gave him the impression they hadn't anticipated that outcome: it confused and frightened them. The most disturbed of them all was Soree. She was the first to speak with a trembling voice:

> "None of this is foretold in the Chronicles of the Horizon! How can it
> be in our soul? — That can't be our fate!"

Tiá stood up again, and with intensity he said slowly:

> "Now you all understand what I sense in my heart since my earlier
> days. Our souls long for boundlessness — we all feel it — while the
> Chronicles are nothing more than the views of others. They limit us!
> They seek to define us in a set identity while our souls move us to
> keep looking for the answer to who we are.
>
> "I don't doubt we were visited by those we call Lords of the Hori-
> zon — this place and the other Nomöi are a confirmation of their
> time with our people. But neither these Lords nor anyone else can
> claim to be masters of others' souls!
>
> "What we just witnessed, I don't understand either. All I grasp is
> our future appears turbulent. Yet, I can't allow that knowledge to
> burden my soul. All I accept is the present moment and, as it is with
> every other moment along life, I can choose to embrace this present
> one guided by my heart and not by the Chronicles."

Looking at Soree he then added, not in defiance but with an understanding love:

> "I'm going now to welcome the voyagers from the stars. My heart tells
> me they bring what we lack."

Tiá turned around as he finished, not waiting for the reaction to his words, and climbed the slopes of the array with decisive steps. Others, about two-thirds of those present, followed him, including the three who had called the gathering. A few, just a handful, went to talk to Soree. The rest remained by themselves, sitting on the grass, confusion on their faces.

Immediately after, Ethën had the sensation of losing his footing and that a cloud, momentarily, hid the light of that place. When he recovered, the scene of the gathering of Humans had vanished. So had the Waters of Åkhas. Althesal and the other members of the expedition were all close to him. They were standing on the grass of the array where they had been observing the scene. They all regarded each other in wonder, not only because of what they had just witnessed, but because they weren't alone!

The young rebellious man who had been among those in the gathering — *Tiá* — with a heartfelt smile, stood now regarding them. Using Galactic Standard language, in musical words he said to Ethën and the others:

"Sisters and brothers from the stars, you are most welcomed among my people, *the Atelë.*"

Tiá was accompanied by nine of his kind, representing all the distinct types Ethën had observed in those Humans. The three Rangers Mhali had sent to the rim of the plateau were also with them, holding amused smiles on their faces as they looked at their wonderstruck fellow expedition members.

38

The Gardens of the Chronicles

After the initial surprise Tiá gave Althesal, Ethën and the other members of the expedition, he said to all, "You heard our call this morning! Thank you for coming to help my people in this hour of need."

This morning? Help? — At first Althesal thought it was Tiá's faulty use of Galactic Standard. But she sensed a dread and urgency in the young man's heart. And so it was. The initial mirth and joy of the encounter turned into alarm when Tiá forewent the use of verbal language for direct mental communication.

"A threatening Darkness has descended upon our land," his thoughts reached Althesal and the others, "and Naleean and his friends are the only ones daring enough to confront it. They—"

"What! Where is Naleean?" Mhali spoke aloud.

Upon hearing Mhali's commanding voice Tiá recoiled from him, his face contorted in pain and his body unsteady and shaking.

Before Althesal could react, Mhali steadied the young man and said softly to him, "Excuse my use of the voice, Star-Born. I spoke as for rough stone-cutting, while your voice and ears are those of a delicate jewel maker."

Tiá nodded slowly, his eyes locked into Mhali's, and promptly recovered with a grin on his face. "Naleean is safe", he next said. "He and most of his companions are now with the Forest Lights requesting their assistance. The rest of them are with a group of my people."

The young man projected clear mental images as he communicated with them. Yet his mental language was so speedy, Althesal couldn't grasp in their entirety some of those images — 'the Forest Lights' was one of these.

And this is the story Tiá proceeded to tell Althesal, Mhali and the others:

Yesterday some of my people in the western district of our land witnessed four large and ugly conveyances descend from the sky and land at a short distance from the Nomös of Aïdin we call 'the Sphere of Tears'. Soon after, strange and fearsome shadows, accompanied by beings of another race, exited these craft. Like mad creatures they all next darted towards the Sphere and surrounded it from all sides. But as my people expected, their onrush was halted when the Sphere exerted its work upon their minds and hearts. Then, for the afternoon, the entire night, and until early this morning, these strangers remained transfixed under the spell of the Sphere.

Those of the other race were the first to be released from the allure of the Sphere. Yet, they weren't whole, as if the Sphere had failed to do its work upon their souls. They were greatly confused, and in panic retreated back inside their craft. As for the shadows, they too were set free from the spell this morning. And they too awoke with a madness but of a different kind — they rushed to do violence to the massive Sphere itself — at first with their bodies and later with their craft, smiting it repeatedly. For a time the Sphere withstood their attacks, each failed attempt eliciting a cacophony of wails from them. However, after many assaults and when three of their craft smote it together one more time, the Sphere vanished in a flash of blinding light, leaving them more confused.

That was this morning. Last evening, however, when the news of the landing of these off-worlders spread, and when images of their looks were shared, my people in all the districts were overcome with fear. For an unexplainable reason those fiends awoke the memory of a horror we didn't know was buried in our hearts. This prompted most of my people to flee, throughout the night, to the mountains in the north. Only thirty us remained, and that's because, when we received this news, we were in the company of Naleean and the others, who requested of us to stay.

At first Naleean thought the strangers were a reconnaissance team of a people he calls 'The Others' and that these, probably, weren't aware this is a planet of Humans. Thus, unafraid, he led us all to study the newcomers while they were still under the influence of the Sphere of Tears. Yet, once he saw those shadows he told us they weren't of The Others and that something else had to be in the works. So we retreated to observe them under cover and with much greater caution. Then this morning, when the shadows awoke mad, Naleean lost his resolve and ordered everyone to retreat.

"A powerful Darkness is working through those fiends", he told us. *"We need the Rangers! I feel we all are in grave danger, not just us on this planet but everyone among the stars where there is goodness and light. We need to contact the Chancellor of the Union and let her know… Right now! Let's hope the communication beacon will work this time."*

So Naleean hastened this morning to their craft with a few of the other Nauthians, while leaving me and others to keep watch of the off-worlders.

It was when Naleean was away that the shadows destroyed the Sphere of Tears and that they moved their craft to their present location — close to a place we call 'the Gardens of the Chronicles of the Horizon'. What they are after, we fail to guess.

Later, when Naleean returned from his craft, he told us he had been able to send to the Chancellor only a voice message, and that he wasn't sure it had been received. Thus, full of doubts the Rangers would come to our aid, he decided to go to the Forest Lights to ask for their help. Once more he left me, most of the other Nauthians, and a number of my companions observing the movements of the off-worlders from a hilltop nearby the Gardens.

It was there, while on watch, not long ago, when we sensed the landing of your craft and your presence.

"It has to be the Rangers coming to our help!" I told my companions, even though I didn't know who Rangers were. Yet, if Naleean trusts the Rangers, I trust them too.

"And so the ten of us you see here rushed to transport ourselves to these eastern savannas, to the base of this hill we call 'the Mirror of the Soul', where we found your craft but only three Rangers.

"There has to be more of them!" I told my companions. *"I sense them."*

When the Rangers told us that you had activated the array, we were greatly surprised you knew how to do it. At the same time, we were forced to wait, unable to stop the operation of the array until the right moment when you would do it, or we could safely do it for you.

To end his story, Tiá said to Althesal, Mhali and the others, "Naleean is still there, at this moment, in the Forest of the Dancing Lights. Although I doubt the Lights will leave their abode to help us. In all the history of my people They have never wandered beyond their forest's borders."

Then, regarding Althesal, he pleaded, "Let's make haste! I fear the worst from those fiends!"

"The Spark!" Althesal said to Mhali and the others when Tiá said that. "That's what the Dwellers are after. I have no doubt of it now."

"Yet, it appears they don't know of its looks, nor of its location", Daothel said. "Their assault upon the place Tiá calls 'the Sphere of Tears' tells us that much."

"This is to our advantage", Mhali added. "But, then, where is the Spark?"

All eyes turn to Althesal — How could she know? For what she had heard during the gathering of the Atelë's Conveners, none of the Atelë knew of its location either. They spoke of a Power hidden in the planet, but that was it.

Thus, doubting she could answer Mhali's question and taking a deep breath, she nonetheless closed her eyes in an attempt to sense the presence and power emanating from the Spark as she remembered it. To her surprise, right away a wave of energy washed over her body accompanied by a single and powerful sound. It had come from beyond Space and Time, yet it was also near to her heart and contained in its sounding an entire symphony of indescribable beauty. Opening her eyes, she spoke in a whisper, "Directly west of us."

The look of concern on her companions made her notice her body was shaking from the impact. "I'm fine", she added.

"Are you sure?" Ethën came closer to her.

"Yes, I am. I heard…" She couldn't find words to describe what she had just experienced. But that sound had also carried a Call, an urgent Call. Thus, without knowing where the knowledge came from, she added, "Its location is somewhere overshadowed by the twelve structures Tiá's people call *the Nomöi of Aïdin*… Were I to hide it, I'd use their combined power… All I now know is its Call comes from a place west of us."

Mhali quickly turned towards Tiá. "Friend, what is west of us that isn't a Nomös but part of the Nomöi of Aïdin?"

"The Gardens of the Chronicles!" the young man answered. "The Gardens are at the geometric center of the twelve Nomöi. They are the heart of Aïdin."

Mhali looked at Althesal and with clenched jaw said, "That's where the Dwellers are right now!" Without waiting for her to react, and facing the Rangers, he spoke: "Everyone! To the Spaceblazer! Now!" Next, he invited the ten Atelë to come with them on the craft, to show them the location of the Gardens.

While they reached the base of the hill, Althesal asked Tiá about the dangers the three sleeping Children of Ær — *Luman,* the Atelë called them — would be exposed to. Tiá, puzzled by her question, answered, "On the land of Mu‘a, no animal ever harms a Human!"

As soon as they arrived to the Spaceblazer, in silence each took their positions inside, and Althesal could not fail to notice Tiá and his companions gravitated towards her, as youngsters seeking for the protection of an adult.

"Rise the Spaceblazer", Mhali ordered the pilots, "to the second ös-harmonic light-field and situate us where Tiá showed you. Remain on that harmonic level when we arrive."

In less than two seconds, they were there, invisible to those on the lower light-fields. Next, with the exception of the pilots, everyone rushed to look through the panoramic windows.

Althesal's heart sprinted into a gallop at the spectacle. The Gardens were much more extensive than she had pictured — more like a large city park formed by several tiers of well-kept concentric gardens. The Dwellers, dozens of them and mad with rage, encircled the perimeter. An invisible barrier prevented them from entering the place, and they made attempt after attempt smiting it with their bodies. Every time they did it, the phosphorescent red blotches on their spectral forms flashed, and otherworldly wails were heard. By all appearances it was an uncoordinated assault.

In the confusion and chaos they made, slithering through the air to and fro, Mhali had nonetheless identified their leaders, five of them, and had pointed them to Althesal. She felt disgusted and horrified. These didn't have the reptilian shadowy and blurred form of the others. They had a more solid body, each made of an amalgamation of Human body parts with the reptilian form. Although they looked as deranged as the rest with their inability to enter the Gardens, at times one of them made the effort to slow down its madness to herd a group of subalterns to batter the barrier together.

Once Mhali assessed the situation, he told the pilots to land the Spaceblazer inside the Gardens. Yet, when they proceeded to comply, Althesal's suspicions were confirmed — the craft couldn't penetrate the barrier either. Althesal suspected it was a Time field, attuned to the Human essence, after Tiá explained to them that only Humans, while holding an empty mind, could enter the Gardens; that the creatures of the land couldn't wander into it.

Soree, the Keeper of the Chronicles, stood inside the Gardens, near their center. She hid among the twelve sets of light-made spirals that sprung from a circular mirror-like surface. With a terrified face the Keeper stared at the assailants — *She can't be the power behind the barrier,* Althesal knew it. She felt the woman was paralyzed by fear and unable to think. Her attempts to contact her with the mind to let her know that help had arrived had been futile.

"I remember this place", Althesal whispered to Mhali. "It's the place of my dream right before we left Thel. The place where the Asli urged the seven of us to go."

Mhali, studying the situation, didn't look at her when he spoke. "We can do nothing if we remain in the second ös light-field. However, their numbers are more than I had expected, and if we descend to their level, our powers may not be enough to stop them."

"We must try. This is the reason we came here", she replied, even though she also realized the Dwellers appeared to be even more dangerous than what they had imagined.

"I'd feel more confident if Tiá and his people helped us", he said to her, still studying the Dwellers. "The powers of their minds and voice are much greater than those of a Galactic Human. I suspect they have the capacity to immobilize those shadows and send them back to the place they came from."

"Yet, would you order your Rangers to take children with them to a dangerous mission?" she asked — "The Atelë are like children, with an innocence of heart that speaks aloud they have lived in isolation from the drama of the history of our galaxies for all their existence. My heart tells me they represent both the beginning and the end of the journey of Humans in this Universe. For this reason alone, we must protect them and this planet!"

Mhali turned to regard her with his deep green eyes and whispered, "Atelë, they call themselves — curiously, a word in the language of the Åh meaning 'Star-Born'. Their name should be other. They strike me as those beings to whom some of the Legends called *Manaï.*"

Althesal assented with a silent nod. Protecting the Atelë from the Dwellers and from The Others looked to be an easier task than protecting them from contact with Galactic Humans. Her people had lived through a similar experience, and they had lost much in the process.

Mhali next ordered the Spaceblazer to land on the south side of the Gardens, at about 100 paces away from the invisible barrier. He directed the pilots to keep the Spaceblazer in the second ös harmonic light-field level, invisible to the others on the ground, until he decided on their next move.

The Gardens occupied a large circular area of land, close to one-quarter of one ont across [0.7 kilometers]. The four craft of the Dwellers were clustered together, at about 200 paces from their perimeter. The Spaceblazer now rested to the left of these craft, at that same distance from them, giving those inside the Spaceblazer a clear view of them.

Near these craft, Althesal and Mhali counted six Dreki bodies laying on the ground. The bodies' positions suggested they had been running away from their craft, in the direction of a nearby woods, when they fell. They were dressed as elite forces of Overlord Ankepum. The reason for their death wasn't apparent, yet each had multiple burns, similar to those Althesal had seen in the Rangers who explored Ankepum's base on the planet Mal'ek.

Tiá told them they had counted fifteen individuals of that other race when they were at the Sphere of Tears. Thus, the other nine Dreki were probably inside their craft. If they were alive or dead, the Rangers hadn't been able to ascertain. With their higher senses they could usually sense the presence of The Others from a distance, but in this case the walls of the Dwellers' craft prevented them from sensing anything inside them.

"Where is Overlord Ankepum in all this?" Mhali voiced the question in Althesal and in everyone of the expedition members' minds. "He can't just be lending his best forces to those shadows!"

In truth, they had no way to figure out that mystery, and with a deep breath Mhali added, "Let's focus on the problem at hand."

Dealing with the Dreki wasn't a problem for the Rangers or the Wanderers — the Dwellers were. No one knew for certain if they could be stopped. Thaël's plan was to contain them inside a force-field so that they could be transported to the planet Mal'ek to return them to their realm. Once this was accomplished — although no one knew yet how the door to that realm could be opened to send them back — the Rangers were going to destroy the base but not the towers. Following this, the quarantine of that planet would continue for an undefined length of time.

To contain and transport the Dwellers, Lyel's team, following Thaël's designs and Ethën's adaptations, had prepared three portable photo-sonic generators to create an energy enclosure similar to that of the në material forming the hull of the Spaceblazer. They had been tested on Thel, and the në enclosure thus generated was unaffected by any force or energy that Lyel's team had applied to it. Everyone was counting it was also going to contain the Dwellers.

Three Rangers were going to carry and operate the generators — Thaël had astonished Mhali when he had handed them to him: each fitted in the palm of Mhali's hand and weighted as a feather. "It is a technology my people won't share with others, for now," Thaël had said, "but essential for your success. Thus, I want them back."

There was the problem, however, of inciting the Dwellers to cluster together before the energy enclosure could be raised around them — this was the task assigned to the Rangers and the Wanderers; they were going to be the bait! From the analysis of the debriefing of the Rangers sent to Mal'ek, and from the recordings made by their suits' sensors, Mhali and his strategists had concluded that the Dwellers, for a mysterious reason, were particularly attracted to Humans. On this too, everyone was counting.

None of the Thelians in the expedition, nor Laidé, were going to be outside the Spaceblazer during the maneuver to capture the Dwellers. They had other roles to play.

The number of Dwellers was difficult to determine. They hurtled around the invisible barrier at speeds and in such a chaos that the eye couldn't fix on them well. "I count sixty-six", one of the Rangers had ventured to say. "Though I'm sure there are more. They contract and expand their bodies, and at times each seems to split itself in two or three entities."

Althesal had also observed their bodies were smaller than those she had witnessed during her experience in the Null-Time chamber, observation which Tiá confirmed: "They were larger when they landed next to the Sphere of Tears." Althesal suspected something in the Gardens was affecting them.

"Regardless," Mhali said to all, "they are still the most powerful adversaries Rangers have ever confronted. So, be ready!"

Mhali turned one last time towards Althesal, and she said to him but for all to hear, "There is a great Power and Light behind us. We will succeed!"

Next, she heard Mhali command with a force of will that could move a mountain: "Now!"

A Wrinkle in Time

As the pilots lowered the craft to the dense ös light level, following Mhali's command, they also opened the main hatch of the Spaceblazer, facing the Gardens. The twelve Rangers had arranged themselves in a circle around Soen, Mhali and the five Wanderers. Next, in the split of a second they transported the entire group across the opening to a place midway between the Spaceblazer and the invisible barrier protecting the Gardens. The pilots immediately closed the hatch.

Althesal was now in command of the Spaceblazer — her mind, linked with Mhali's mind, was ready for any eventuality. She could, nonetheless, feel the apprehension of those inside. It was good that Mhali had given each a task to perform. The pilots and the manning crew were ready for her orders to move the Spaceblazer, if required. Laidé and Daothel were in charge of watching the four craft, alert to any change coming from that direction. Ethën and Lyel were, too, ready to activate the towing ray that was going to be used to transport the në-made enclosure with the Dwellers inside. Nesdil had her mind open and receptive to any communication coming from those in the group outside.

As for Tiá and his nine companions, Mhali hadn't assigned them any role, but Althesal had thought it wise to engage their help. Their task was to be alert for anything happening in the surrounding land, or for anyone approaching. Naleean was still out there, unaware the expedition had arrived and taken control of the situation. If he approached now, that could be a problem for Mhali's carefully orchestrated plan. There was also the mystery of Ankepum's whereabouts. She had the feeling they were going to meet the

Overlord before everything was over.

Outside the Spaceblazer one the Dwellers noticed the Rangers and Wanderers. The creature halted with some hesitation to look at them with its bizarre and misplaced eyes. Next, others around this one began to slow down in their mad rush, also sensing something. Mhali's strategists had been right — Humans were more attractive to these entities than what they were after. In no time, it all became a chain reaction, with everyone of the Dwellers, including their five leaders, turning and slithering through the air towards the circle of Ranges and Wanderers.

When they came close to the group, there was a long moment during which all the Dwellers halted and became still. Althesal heart thumped as she waited for their following move.

Then, what happened next came so quickly Althesal couldn't identify what was first. She saw the Dwellers slither with lightning speed to close the distance to the Humans… heard Mhali in her mind say with a calm but power-filled voice, "Enclosure!"… sensed the Wanderers and the Rangers project together a wall of violet light around themselves… saw a golden light-field enclose the Dwellers and Humans… and heard a chorus of wails coming from the Dwellers that chilled her bones.

In the silence that followed, everyone inside the craft held their breath — was the në enclosure strong enough to contain them? The Dwellers appeared to be confused after they had hit with great force the wall of violet light surrounding those in the circle.

"It worked!" Althesal heard Ethën shout behind her. "They're trapped!"

Others inside the Spaceblazer echoed Ethën's euphoria.

"Quiet!" she ordered. "This isn't finished."

The next move would be for the Rangers and Wanderers to exit the në enclosure through the top of its toroidal form. Yet, already she could see two of the Wanderers waver in their concentration. Something wasn't right.

Nesdil was the first to sense it, and with consternation on her face turned to tell Althesal: "They prey on the energy of Mind! That's what attracts them to us, and the Rangers and Wanderers have a great store of it!"

A frigid cold had begun to penetrate the Spaceblazer. Outside, the ground vegetation was wilting around the në enclosure, covered with a black frost. Dark ice crystals were also appearing on the wall of violet light separating the Dwellers from the Rangers and Wanderers.

In all their preparations no one had considered the Dwellers could behave otherwise than what it had been witnessed of them before. But inside the në enclosure they all had become still and appeared to be working as one entity. Their wild and erratic movements were gone, and their spectral shadows undulated in synch as if moved by a single will. The frigid cold was their doing as they siphoned off energy from all directions in their attempts to drain Mind energy from those in the circle.

Everyone inside the Spaceblazer felt the cold. Yet, it wasn't just a physical cold. It also chilled their souls!

"We'll have to retreat", Althesal whispered to Laidé and Daothel, who had come close to her, knowing also that Mhali would be listening to her thoughts. "We didn't come prepared for this. We underestimated the power of those entities." She felt wave after wave of a force that was Fear itself coming from them and seeking to instill itself in everyone inside the craft.

"We can't leave those outside by themselves!" Laidé rushed to add. "Since they can't transport themselves through the walls of the Spaceblazer, I don't see any other option for them than to exit the enclosure through its top and transport themselves here through the open hatch."

"Agree", she said. "Let's move the Spaceblazer closer to make it easier."

"Althesal! No!" Mhali's thought-words came to her. "We can manage. Move the Spaceblazer away from here. It too may be at risk."

Then she saw what Mhali was seeing. Six of the shadowy entities were breaking free from the në enclosure by changing their forms into a diaphanous, vaporous substance that exited the enclosure as if passing through a permeable membrane. One of their leaders also made the attempt to exit, but its Human-body parts prevented it from doing so. Then, when the six became free from the enclosure, more of the Dwellers followed their example and began to change their forms. Yet with this, the Dwellers' concentration as a single will broke, and the light and warmth of Sol began to melt the frost covering everything.

"Go!" Mhali communicated to her once more. "Take the Spaceblazer away!"

She was turning towards the pilots to give them the order to move the Spaceblazer to the nearby hilltop when a cry, accompanied by a strong emotion of concern, reached her. She thought the worst had happened, that Dwellers were coming inside the craft! But no, a picture came next to her mind, and she turned back to look outside.

The cry and the picture had come from Tiá, who in a state of great agitation was showing Althesal and all the others what was occurring on the right side of the Gardens.

With everything that was happening, they had forgotten Soree. Not so Tiá. She had left the central area of the Gardens and was now zigzagging in a desperate run through the many plants adorning the periphery. There was no doubt her intention was to exit the Gardens. She carried an object in her hands covered with a purple cloth. It didn't look heavy, but it was cumbersome to carry. It appeared to be rounded and about three handspans across.

"What is she carrying?" Althesal asked Tiá.

"The Flaming Core of the Chronicles."

"Explain", she said to him.

Althesal and Tiá were now surrounded by all those inside, except the pilots. He appeared uncertain and turned around, first to his fellow Atelë, next to the others. Then, as if having made a decision to reveal a secret, he said:

"In my training as the next Keeper I learned that, if for any reason the Chronicles are destroyed, they can be rebuilt; but, only if their Flaming Core remains intact. The Keepers have always known of this, although there has never been the need to use it." Next, turning quickly to watch Soree, he added with concern, "I don't understand. Why is she leaving the safety of the Gardens? Where is she going with it?"

At that moment Soree crossed the perimeter of the Gardens, where the invisible barrier rose. Almost immediately, a fast-moving shock wave accompanied by thunderclap struck the Spaceblazer, and Althesal felt split into two individuals, momentarily. Reaching for Daothel's shoulder to steady herself, she heard him say, "Two loci of Time just collided!"

Everyone else had experienced it too. Those outside, including the Dwellers, had paused in their movements. To her horror, however, that wasn't the only change. Whatever had happened had likewise rendered inactive the në enclosure where most of the Dwellers were still confined. Worst of all, the wall of violet light protecting the Rangers and the Wanderers was gone too!

The Dwellers were quick to recover their wits. The first indication the invisible barrier protecting the Gardens had also vanished was a large number of them herded by their five leaders and slithering through the air towards the light-made spirals at the heart of the Gardens. About a third of the Dwellers, however, didn't follow these and went, instead, towards Mhali and his group. The attack launched by these ones was so vicious that Rangers and Wanderers broke their circle to dodge their shadowy forms. It became everyone for himself and herself, fighting for their lives. Soon, however, under Mhali's direction they managed to reorganize themselves in small groups for a better defense. But the attacking shadows weren't acting randomly — with precision and coordination they were separating and isolating from each other these small groups.

For their part, Mhali, Soen and the others produced through their hands balls of a violet fiery light which they hurled with swift and deft movements at the attacking Dwellers. These caused the Dwellers to recoil with a wail as the violet fire bore a tear in their forms. Yet, this didn't stop their offensive. With renewed force they sought to ram the Rangers and the Wanderers.

As for the other Dwellers inside the Gardens, they had slowed down their initial rush and, under the direction of their leaders, were now systematically inspecting, and then destroying, each of the light-made spirals Tiá called "The Chronicles of the Horizon" — *They must be looking for the Spark! But, is it there?* Althesal couldn't sense its presence.

"Althesal!" Laidé's shout startled her. "Ankepum is here!"

Althesal's heart sank. A worst-case scenario couldn't be happening! During the confusion a fifth craft, similar to the other four, had descended north of the place where Soree had exited the Gardens. It had landed behind a group of trees, which couldn't completely hide it. Now Overlord Ankepum and five of his lieutenants were moving towards the Keeper.

When Soree saw Ankepum's party, she made a quick turn away from them and in the direction of the Spaceblazer. Her desperate race was, however, halted by a discharge of a reddish light Ankepum sent through his right hand. The discharge hit the Keeper in the back, who stumbled, falling to the ground, face forward. As she fell, she lost hold of the object she carried, and the cloth covering it floated away. The object tumbled free towards the ground in a slow motion, but it never reached it. At about four or five handspans from the ground, it kept floating away from her until it halted in midair, ten or twelve paces from where she had fallen.

Laidé and Althesal gasped in unison when they saw the object Tiá had called 'the Flaming Core of the Chronicles' — It was Stïel Key!

Wills in Collision

Planet Ær, Sol System

Mhali and Soen were by themselves. Dwellers had them trapped in a tight space surrounded by a thick wall of a vaporous substance oozing from their forms. It was a cold, dark miasma that burned everything it touched and siphoned their strength. Worse, they were immersed in an otherworldly twilight their senses couldn't penetrate, and the deep loneliness they felt increased moment by moment.

Mhali didn't feel like himself. He felt shaken and hesitant. The other Rangers and Wanderers had to be in the same predicament. He hadn't expected an organized attack of this type. The Dwellers were cunning and had learned quickly to anticipate their movements.

He had at some point given the order to his Rangers and the Wanderers to rise their bodies to a higher dimensional light-field. But the Dwellers had then rushed towards the Spaceblazer. Thus, he had to tell everyone to descend again, to drive the attention of the Dwellers away from the defenseless craft. Now they were in a stalemate, which gave him the impression that was the Dwellers' plan — to neutralize them while the others searched the Gardens.

He hadn't fully grasped the reason for the disappearance of the në enclosure and of their protective wall of light, nor for the strange wrinkle in Time they had experienced. Althesal had communicated to him what was happening with Soree, and that she, Laidé and her other friends had decided to leave the Spaceblazer to help the Keeper. The only thing Mhali could do right now was to hope that Althesal and the other Thelians would improvise something to save the day with Stïel Key. He had never in his entire life felt so powerless and afraid.

"It is them", Soen whispered to him. "Don't let their unwholesome emanations control your mind and heart."

The two had attempted to sound the fundamental chord of their souls to drive away the shadows, as Althesal had taught them during the days of preparation for the expedition. But in their condition they weren't able to raise their awareness. All they could do then was to radiate through their bodies the little light they could harness from their inner being, and hope it was sufficient to hold the Dwellers and the darkness at bay.

⚡

When Althesal saw the Stïel Key, she knew they had to do something to protect it and to help Soree. With a quick decision she informed the others and rushed out of the Spaceblazer followed by Ethën, Laidé, Nesdil, Daothel and Tiá. Lyel and the rest of the manning crew of the Spaceblazer remained behind, in charge of the craft, together with Tiá's nine companions who were scared witless with all what was happening.

Althesal needed to reach Soree before Overlord Ankepum did. The Keeper had managed to rise from the ground and was limping towards the Spaceblazer, carrying the Key. The Overlord had his eyes fixed on the Key, as if he knew of it.

With every step Althesal took, however, a power grew in her. She felt the power not just inside her but all around. Yet it wasn't a power to destroy but a power to be who she was — "This planet has no master, and it's going to remain as such!" she told her companions as they ran. As if in answer to her statement, a strong wind began to blow from the west, parting the dense clouds that had been casting a shadow over the land. The rays of Sol shone now upon them with the intensity of a midday sun, even though it was late afternoon.

Althesal had never met Dreki before her experience with them in the Null-Time chamber, but as they rushed towards Soree, Laidé confirmed her observation. Something had befallen Ankepum and his lieutenants because they ran with difficulty, as if wading knee-deep through water — "This planet must be affecting them", Laidé said to her. Nonetheless, Dreki were agile in the extreme, even when they were seriously injured, and Ankepum caught up with Soree moments before Althesal and the others reached her. His lieutenants still struggled in their run, twenty or so paces behind.

Soree froze in terror at the sight of the bipedal form towering over her — Ankepum was two heads taller than her and with the ferocious look common to Dreki, who artificially exaggerated the saurian and scaly features in their humanoid form to infuse terror in those they confronted. Looking at the Keeper directly in her eyes and with a swift movement, the Overlord yanked Stïel Key from her hands. Soree collapsed on her knees, speechless and unable to react.

Ankepum began turning towards his craft but halted when he saw Althesal and her friends approaching. With a defiant snarl he regarded them. Stïel Key shone a soft iridescent light on his naked torso and arms, highlighting his light-brown, scaly skin. The dark and glassy oval implants on his chest, which Althesal knew were weapons and protective force-field generators, gave off a greenish and sickly refection.

The Overlord's five lieutenants arrived at that moment and surrounded their Lord in a protective formation.

Tiá went directly to help Soree, chanting a soft tune to her which contrasted with the wails of the Dwellers inside the Gardens. But Althesal didn't stop there. Though she slowed her pace , she continued with determination to confront Ankepum.

For a moment, as she approached the group of Dreki, Ankepum locked his eyes with hers, widening his vertical, slit-shaped pupils; then, with a dismissive snarl, the Overlord turned again towards his craft while saying something to his lieutenants in the breathy and croaky language of the Dreki. Immediately two of these rose their left arms and pointed their stretched hands towards Althesal. A reddish light had started to circulate throughout the convoluted wire implant covering the back of their left hands.

"Stop!"

The command came as a thunder, and all the Dreki, including Ankepum, were forced to stop in their tracks, as if the sound of it had immobilized them. The reddish light coming from the two Dreki's hands vanished.

"That object doesn't belong to you!" Althesal continued with her normal voice but infusing each word with the power swelling in her. "You are trespassing on a planet of Humans. Return that object and you can go. Otherwise—"

"Otherwise what?" The Overlord's voice rumbled while turning to face her. Then, with a snarl that could have been a laugh, he added, "You? You will stop me? You are nothing!" He spat before continuing. "I've been looking for this weapon all my life, and you aren't going to stop me now, Human. With this in my possession, the Union is over."

He paused to regard the effect of his words upon her. Althesal didn't feel intimidated. She continued to look at him directly in the eyes — *So, Over-lord Ankepum thinks Stïel Key is a weapon... Perhaps it is, but not in the way he imagines.*

Her friends arrived at that moment. Nesdil and Daothel went to stand at her right while Ethën and Laidé went to her left. She sensed something new in them too, and it wasn't fear. Whatever it was, she felt it circulating among them. One thing was clear in her mind — Stïel Key wasn't going to leave the planet! Thus, with the power rising in her, she spoke again:

"Otherwise, Overlord Ankepum, your life will end here, on this planet."

He was about to reply when the Overlord became aware of something Althesal had already noticed. With each of her words the flaming sparks inside Stïel Key increased in quantity and intensity, and now the Key had a faint glow. The Overlord extended his arms to study it. Yet, instead of the reaction Althesal expected, he let out a loud snarl that echoed in the distance, then said:

"You have just confirmed a tale from the old legends. This weapon is activated by the sound of the Human voice!"

She hid from him the surprise she felt — so he knew what she had suspected of Stïel Key. However, it didn't matter at that point what the Overlord knew.

"No Human will ever cooperate with you!" she replied.

"There you are wrong, Thelian." Then, turning to one of his lieutenants at his left, who appeared to be a Dreki with not-so-well formed features and shorter than the others, Ankepum added, "My friend here, Aldiarlim, is Human, and he will help me use this weapon to end the ascendancy of your scum race."

The man Ankepum had called Aldiarlim regarded her. The peeved twist of his lips lasted a fraction of a second, but her skills at reading other people's hearts told her that, like her, he had been surprised by this latest revelation of his Overlord's plan. Yet, with the skill of someone who must have lived a life hiding his true nature, his face soon assumed the snarl the Dreki grafts on his cheeks and forehead allowed him to make.

The power all around them continued rising. Althesal felt it, and Stïel Key was reacting to it too. The light in its interior now had a rhythmic beat, and the musical quality of it didn't escape her.

Ankepum also noticed the change and inspected the Key once more. Dreki knew nothing of music, nor could hear the complexity of sounds Humans heard. However, the change in the Key appeared to delight instead of intimidate him. Not that she had expected it. After all, he couldn't have carved out the largest dominion in the history of The Others if he was easily intimidated. What puzzled her was that Ankepum was known as a reasonable individual, more so than the other Overlords. She expected his common sense would stop him from taking such an object into his craft without knowing its nature. But he wasn't himself. Something on the planet appeared to be clouding his reasoning.

Once the Overlord finished inspecting Stïel Key, with a hiss he said to the man he called Aldiarlim, "This interchange bores my mind, and this planet tires my body. Enough! End them!"

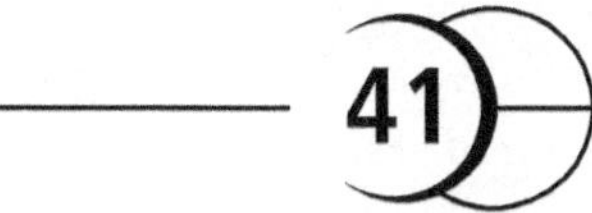

Darkness and Light

Soen was at the end of her strength, exhausted and unable to move. Mhali and she had dropped together to the ground, facing each other and holding their hands in each other's to sustain the little light they managed to radiate from their inner light-fields. The shadowy miasma surrounding them was now no more than a handspan away from their skin. Her mind was muddled and unable to think. All she had left was the light of her heart, flickering and void of hope.

"Sorry…" she heard Mhali whisper. "We shouldn't end like this."

Unable to reply, she bent forward and touched his forehead with hers. Then, she closed her eyes and released Mhali's hands… and her body. As a point of awareness, she floated away from physical existence.

⚡

Lyel's mind was in overdrive searching for a way to help Marshal Mhali and those trapped by the Dwellers. Dean Althesal had left her in charge of the Spaceblazer, but she couldn't remain a passive spectator to what was happening. Her teammates and Tiá's nine companions were as anxious as she was.

"We must do something, quickly, to help the Rangers and the Wanderers", she said to her teammates.

They regarded her with a mix of reactions that went from hesitation to fear.

"I-I've an idea", one of the pilots said to her with a quiver in his voice while some of the other team members talked to each other in low voices.

"Speak!" Lyel said to him louder than what she had intended. She could feel he was afraid to tell her his idea.

All the talk ceased, and the pilot studied each of his Thelian companions before saying under his breath, "A song of restitution!"

Lyel froze, breathless, and for a long moment her mind refused to process what he had said. Every Thelian inside the craft had also stopped breathing. She blinked and shook her head to be sure she had heard from him those words. Then she sighed. He was right. They had nothing among the provisions and supplies they had brought that could be used to immobilize or to draw the Dwellers away from those outside. But they had their voices.

"No!" the team's tactician cried with dismay. "Never in the history of our people the target of a song of restitution has been a living being!"

"Then, the Rangers and the Wanderers are going to die", another team member replied, biting his lip.

The tactician opened her mouth to say something but nothing came.

No one offered another idea. Some had their eyes closed, others stared at their feet. Then, one by one they all looked at Lyel. She could see and feel their distress and the dilemma wrestling in their minds. She felt the same. Songs of restitution were the means their people used to break down into their basic light-wave components all objects, buildings and tools made for their daily living when they didn't need these anymore, or when better ones could be constructed. They were called 'songs of restitution' because they returned to the universal light-field of Space what belonged to Space. This type of song was target specific. It wasn't difficult, however, to come up with the song that would disintegrate the Dwellers' bodies. It was a matter of studying the music their forms made to reverse its harmonies and to introduce certain dissonant beat chords.

She shifted on her feet before speaking:

"I can't force any of you to do this. Besides, it may not work and we may lose our lives in the attempt. Our people know little of life outside our planet. We tend to think others in this vast Universe share our principles — this is our comfort zone. However, when we accepted to participate in this expedition, we also accepted to venture outside our comfort zone. It's clear, life out here operates under different principles. These aren't good or bad compared to ours… They're just… different… as different as another set of harmonies is when intended for another type of music." She halted, realizing that with her speech to them she had made her decision.

The nine Atelë had also listened with great attention to each of her words. They may have not understood her Thelian words, but by the look on their faces it appeared they had captured the meaning of her thoughts — and most of them made a slight inclination of their heads when she ceased speaking, as if approving.

Without saying another word, Lyel opened the main hatch and took a step outside.

"You will need all of us." The team's tactician spoke behind her.

The eight of them quickly formed a semicircle on the broad ramp of the craft. Most of the Dwellers close by were occupied with the six groups in which they had managed to split up the Rangers and the Wanderers, and were now completely still. But a few others were by themselves, hovering close to the ground and telescoping their bizarre multiple eyes towards the west of the land, where Sol was setting.

It took Lyel no more than a few seconds to assess the song of the assailants' bodies. She next did a quick survey of her team, and each and all nodded to her. Then, they began to sing.

None of the Dwellers reacted to their song, not even to their presence, giving Lyel the impression they were deaf.

The Thelians continued singing, improvising while listening to the shadowy forms' music, and the notes that came from their mouths had a fast tempo and followed harmonies that surprised them. Lyel was full of wonder — the Dwellers must have been once creatures of great beauty, because the song of their inner being was one of great harmony. Then, when the eight of them grasped the fullness of the song, the time came to introduce the dissonant chords that would start the restitution.

Lyel sounded the first chord, clear and loud, and with that power of will which only Thelians among Galactic Humans infuse to their voices. The chord reverberated throughout the space between the Spaceblazer and the Gardens, and its dissonance contrasted with the beautiful sounds of Nature on that planet.

The Dwellers who had been by themselves were the first to react — their forms began to twist and wriggle, though they continued staring towards the west.

Next, one by one and at the right moment in the song, each of the other Thelians sounded a chord of restitution, and with this the discomfort of the Dwellers became more apparent. Those Dwellers surrounding the Wanderers and the Rangers had also begun to twist and wriggle. Still, no Dweller had taken notice of the singers, and Lyel's confidence rose — too soon, though. In a sudden reaction, five of the Dwellers staring towards the west, all at the same time turned towards the Spaceblazer and began, slowly, very slowly, slithering through the air in their direction.

Lyel's reaction was to sing louder. Her teammates followed her lead. But that didn't stop the Dwellers, who continued moving towards them as if crawling through the air. For a moment the thought came to her that they were about to die, and her chest tightened. Without stopping her singing, she closed her eyes waiting for the worst.

Voices! — She heard new voices. These had joined their singing and were adding something new to it.

Opening her eyes she realized Tiá's companions had exited the craft and were now behind the eight of them. Soon these nine Atelë revealed mightier voices than those of her team and took the song in a new direction. Yet that wasn't the only surprise. As if they were one people who had sung together all their lives, the Thelians and the Atelë composed, as they sang, a masterpiece song of restitution not heard before.

Yet, the music and its dissonances, to Lyel's surprise, didn't do to the Dwellers what a song of restitution would do to an object. Instead, those Dwellers approaching them halted and let out a series of soft, rasping wails while their forms started to release a thick greenish and brown vapor from their craggy skins. It may have been a trick of the setting sun, but Lyel saw behind those dark emanations glimpses of a golden-white lighted form.

The song was never finished. Unannounced, at that moment bright rays of a bluish-white light, coming from the west, shone upon the singers and upon everyone between the Spaceblazer and the Gardens. In no time, these rays condensed into a dozen beings, ethereal and magnificent. Such was the majesty of their presence, and of the music of their forms, that they silenced not just the singers but the Dwellers as well.

None of the Dwellers appeared to have been permanently harmed by the song of restitution. However, while the song hadn't achieved to free the Rangers and the Wanderers, the arrival of those beings did it. With great haste the group of Dwellers were retreating away from everyone to cluster together, their bodies trembling, their grotesque eyes darting to and fro regarding the newcomers.

Spellbound by those magnificent beings, neither Lyel nor anyone of those standing on the ramp noticed that someone approached them from behind the craft. Thus, she startled when she heard a thud on the ramp.

"Better go inside your craft, Thelians", she next heard a sonorous male voice said in Galactic Standard. Turning in its direction, she recognized the one who had spoken — Naleean, the Nauthian youth.

⚡

For Soen, an eternity could well have lapsed before she felt a hand on her forehead and another on her chest. With difficulty she opened her eyes and saw light all around. The hands were Mhali's, and there weren't shadows surrounding them anymore. He was giving her of his life-energy for her to return to her body, and she had entered it with the swiftness of a soul entering a new body at birth.

It was then when she heard a music coming from all around them and above the wailing of Dwellers in the distance. Mhali greeted her with his beautiful smile and said, "Naleean brought the Forest Lights!"

Her friend helped her to stand up. To their left the other Rangers and Wanderers were helping each other recover — all had survived the ordeal, though all looked exhausted. However, to their right the spectacle was other, and what she saw was going to remain forever etched in her memory.

Space… Infinite Space in all its beauty she beheld in and through the starry forms of the Forest Lights, and her heart leaped with joy in recognition — "Old Ones!" she cried to Mhali. "The Forest Lights are Old Ones… the Åh!"

The Åh described in the ancient legends were of many different groups, having many different functions in the processes that made stars and planets. All were benevolent and cared for all that breathes and grows. Soen now beheld a group of Them made of light patterns resembling a tapestry of stars in the form of a living, radiant, white-blue flame. Two blazing extensions of the flame, resembling the wings of a mighty bird, issued from their backs, and these undulated with a rhythm both musical and life-giving. Twice as tall as any Human they were, and only their heads and faces remained unchanged as their flaming forms danced and scintillated with grace.

"Yes, Soen, the legends have caught up with us", Mhali grinned in reply. "Their presence enlivens everyone and everything. Look at the ground and the vegetation, it's fast recovering from the foul emanations of the Dwellers!" Then, with the delight of a child who has discovered the beings of his childhood tales are real, he added, "Who but the Åh can do this!"

The Forest Lights had already contained all the Dwellers in the vicinity of the Spaceblazer, and these darted back and forth with uncontrolled rage inside a sphere of flaming light enclosing them. But the Åh were undisturbed by their behavior and appeared to be communicating with them in a language of sounds and thoughts new to Soen.

Soen's joyous moment didn't last, however. It was interrupted by a loud hissing, followed by a rumble of thunder that shook the ground. Both had come from the right side of the Gardens, in the direction where Althesal had told them Ankepum had landed. She felt dizzy for a split second and had to lean again on Mhali. It was the same sensation she had experienced when the në enclosure had failed.

"Hurry!" She heard the thought in her mind when the closest of the Åh addressed the two of them. "Go to your friends, Harbingers of the Horizon! This isn't finished. We can only contain these Fallen Ones for a time, and many of them are still loose over there. Go to the others, sing the song of your soul and restore what has been hidden — It is the only hope! Our path is here. Yours is into the Horizon!"

Mhali turned to regard her with a look of understanding. With the thought-words the Åh had shown them an entire vision of possibilities. The two of them bowed to the one who had thus addressed them, and darted towards the right side of the Gardens.

42

A Life-Long Struggle

Aldiarlim reacted with the speed that countless years of training had given him to compensate for his smaller frame among the Dreki. His entire body was now tense. His heart pounded. Like a volcanic eruption, the anger in him was about to explode… the anger he had carried for most of his life. But this time he wasn't going to suppress it. Only Ankepum knew the weapons in his body weren't for subjugating others to one's will, as all other Dreki weapons were. That was their secret. Aldiarlim himself had designed and constructed them to be tools of destruction, killing tools — and Ankepum had asked him, not his bodyguards, to execute his order to end the Thelians!

Before he could act, however, out of nowhere a Mestar, one of the leaders of the Dwellers, had appeared in their midst and had rammed unconscious Ankepum's bodyguards in the attempt to reach their Overlord. In the struggle to protect himself from the foul creature's attack, Ankepum had let go of the ancient weapon he had taken from the Human woman. The weapon now floated in midair between his Overlord and the attacker, each attempting with furious movements to grab it while wrestling to keep the other at bay.

For a timeless moment Aldiarlim observed their struggle. He was witnessing what he had witnessed at the beginning of his life journey, and many times since — blind lust for power! The spectacle filled him with loathing.

It was time to act, though, before anger would overwhelm his reasoning. Ankepum expected him to execute his order. Thus, without hesitation he sent the command from his brain to the power source grafted on the right side of his chest, and with a deft movement of his right hand he aimed and sent the deadly discharge towards the target, made more powerful by the load of anger it carried.

He closed his eyes. All he felt ended at that moment, and an inner peace welled up inside him. The life-long struggle between his mind and his heart was over.

He knew too he had reached the end of his life. He had signed his own death sentence. It was a matter of moments before Ankepum took notice of him. He was now a liability, and his Overlord was going to exact from him the maximum payment. It didn't matter. More than before, at that moment he knew the weapon Ankepum had taken from the woman… that weapon with the destructive power the legends described… shouldn't have been created.

He was ready to die.

Right then, the ground shook under his feet, and a close-range hiss, followed by a thunderclap, deafened him. He felt in two places at the same time. Searing, burning pains all over his face, arms and body came next. Then, there was silence. And stillness. Death had arrived. He waited for it to carry him over… Nothing… A few more moments and still nothing — *Am I still alive?* — That wasn't what he had expected! Then the realization came to him that the hiss and the thunderclap, and that the burns he felt, couldn't have been produced by Ankepum's weapons or by a touch from the Dwellers. He then attempted to open his eyes, but the searing pain on his forehead and eyelids was so excruciating that for a moment he thought his eyelids had fused together. Nonetheless, with a supreme effort he managed to open them.

He was alone! — Ankepum and the foul creature were gone. So were his Dreki friends. More so, there was nothing to indicate they had been there. There wasn't anything left either of the cursed weapon. He took a deep breath, not in relief but in confusion, and felt such a pain that it forced him to inspect his chest and arms — he was stark naked! Lacerations and open gashes, too regular and precise to have been produced by an explosion, had replaced the implants and grafts that had made of his body a Dreki — all what remained was his Human form!

In wonder and with the keen sense of observation and analysis that had propelled him as Ankepum's greatest strategist, he realized nothing in close proximity to the weapon had been destroyed, except that which wasn't Human or didn't belong to that planet. The grasses and vegetation where the struggle for the weapon had taken place were tramped, otherwise they were alive and healthy.

Turning around to assess what had happened to the Dwellers who were inside the Gardens, he felt *It* more than saw *It*. So too, apparently, did those Dwellers who, with their four surviving heinous leaders, circled *It* in silence.

He didn't know what that *It* was. Only that a mighty Power was there, at the center of those Gardens. It called to him, and he felt an irresistible attraction to go to *It*.

Overcoming the pains in his body, he took a step towards *It*, yet voices and hurried movements behind him broke some of the spell. Glancing sideways he saw the Thelian woman and her four companions. Like him, they must have heard the Call because they hastened towards the center of the Gardens. Without thinking, he ran after them.

43

Unbidden Visitor

Planet Ær, Sol System

The wrinkle in Time shook Althesal more than the thunderous noise that had hit them right before it. For an instant she felt living in multiple loci of Time; then, she felt whole again. It all happened so fast that when she saw the man called Aldiarlim alone, for a moment she thought the two of them had been moved to another locus. Yet her surroundings were the same. At that moment she remembered the burst of energy which that man had sent in the direction of Stïel Key. A sinking feeling took prey of her — he had destroyed the Key!

"Nooo!" Laidé's contained sob told her he too had realized they were now doomed. They had no means to close the door to that place where the Darkness dwelt. The Dwellers were now on the loose in the Sol System and would do as they pleased. Already they had started. They were on a rampage in the Gardens and wrecked the light-made spirals which, Tiá had told her, had encoded in them vast sums of knowledge regarding Humans everywhere in Space and Time.

To ward off the despair that sought to overwhelm her, she again focused on her surrounding. Nothing in them explained the disappearance of Ankepum, his bodyguards and the one leader of the Dwellers who had attacked him. With the exception of Aldiarlim, who was now unclothed and with multiple lacerations, the vegetation and their own bodies and clothing were undamaged.

She took a deep breath and closed her eyes. Sol had just set in the west, and the absence of its comforting rays added to the coldness that crept up all around her. She needed to think, fast, to figure out the meaning of those wrinkles in Time, and their next step. Her body, however, cried for attention. Her people weren't used to the noises and to the many unwholesome vibrations they had experienced since arriving to the Gardens. Yet, as soon as she closed her eyes, she heard the Call — the same Call she had heard in the star-map chamber of the Asli's island of her planet. She opened her eyes right away and turned towards the center of the Gardens. A soft and ethereal radiance indicated the location of its source. It beckoned to her.

"The Spark!" Ethën, to her right, cried with a muffled voice while resting a hand on her shoulder. His hand trembled. "I hear its Call", he added.

"Y-Yes!" Nesdil said faintly, her body also shaking. "W-Why didn't we hear it before?" A tone of desperation was on her voice, prompting Althesal to embrace her. "That thunderclap still runs wild throughout my body", she then breathed to Althesal.

"Attune to the planet's soul, and let it drain through your feet."

Althesal released her, and her friend did as she was told. Soon her shakes were gone and color returned to her face.

Daothel and Laidé looked better. Ethën was also fast recovering. Not far from them, Tiá helped Soree back to her feet. The Keeper was grief-stricken and distraught, and Tiá spoke softly to her.

"Hmm…" Ethën mumbled at that moment. "Stïel Key must have kept the Spark hidden." Next, wheeling upon his feet and still somewhat unsteady, he looked around as if searching for clues.

Althesal regarded him. He was right — the Key and the Spark had been connected.

"The Key was…" he continued slowly, speaking his thoughts aloud as they came to him, "more surely… a Time-shifter of sorts… with two phases, each attuned to a different locus of Time… No, perhaps three. That would explain the disappearance of Ankepum and those others; which leads to the question: Are they dead or were they—"

"Not now, Ethën!" Althesal warned him. "We can worry about their fate later. They aren't here, and that's good for us. This isn't the time for your quests."

He pretended not to have heard her and added in rhyme, "Then, to know how the Key came to be the Spark's guardian, two steps it takes."

That caught her attention — two steps? — Something immediately connected in her mind, and in a fraction of a moment she understood. There was still hope!

She reached for his face with both hands and kissed him. "You are a blessing!" Then, she sprinted towards the center of the Gardens, knowing

Ethën and the others were going to follow her. About 300 paces separated them from the Spark.

"You realize the Spark is surrounded by Dwellers… lots of them…" Laidé said to her as they navigated, as fast as they could, around the many plantings and shrubbery forming the outer rings of the Gardens, "and that we have no weapons?"

"We aren't alone, friend. Look to your left and behind."

To their left, Mhali and Soen ran to meet them. They were followed by the Wanderers, the Rangers, and Lyel's team. Behind them, Tiá marched with his nine companions. Naleean and his friends had joined them — all the youngsters carrying in their hands something resembling a coiled lightning.

"This is madness!" Laidé snorted as he tried to keep pace with Althesal. "We all are rushing to meet our deaths!" Turning again his head to look at his fellow Nauthians, he asked, "And what are those lights in their hands?"

"This world must be affecting your wits, Nauthé", Daothel teased him. "Don't you recognize the Fire that made Space?"

Laidé regarded Daothel and replied with awe in his voice, "What kind of planet is this?"

"That's what we are going to figure out", Althesal said sharply to end their interchange. They needed to focus on what they were about to do.

When Soen, Mhali and the rest of the Rangers and Wanderers, and Lyel's team caught up with them, Althesal forced them all to a halt. Not wasting time she explained:

"You all remember the words Stïel of the Nine said to the Nauthé of old when she appeared to them on the world of the Aenrelm. You also remember the ritual she instructed Rïal, their leader, through dreams, to keep alive in their traditions. Bring those two instructions together and that is the complete message the Nine wanted to pass to posterity — the message revealing the key to close the door to a realm where a Darkness dwells."

She regarded her six friends. Understanding was on their faces, also on each of the expedition members.

"Why we didn't think of that before! More so us Thelians!" Ethën let out a heavy sigh. "Not a crystal but the power of the Human Voice acting upon the Spark!"

Knowing this, however, didn't make things easy — Althesal knew it. They still had to approach close to the Spark through the many Dwellers now surrounding It.

"Our best strategy is to approach It from all sides", Mhali said. "That will divide their attention. This is going to be dangerous in the extreme, nonetheless. Those creatures already know enough of us to anticipate our movements."

"This time you won't be alone", Daothel replied to him. "We Thelians can use the power of our non-spatial Self to drive Dwellers away."

"We are here too, Marshal", a young and sonorous voice rose in the back of their gathering — Naleean's. "Besides, by now you should have realized this planet is much more than what is apparent."

The youth and the many others had arrived and flanked the expedition members. Each of the ten Atelë and all the twenty-seven Nauthians carried in their hands a smooth metallic staff, silver in color and crowned with three strands of a flowing electric light, coiled around its upper third. "A gift from the Forest Lights", Naleean added with a smug smile when Althesal and the others regarded them with questioning eyes. "Those fiends are for a surprise—"

"Naleean!"

The angry cry coming from Laidé startled Althesal and silenced everyone. Quickly, they all moved aside when, with brisk strides, Laidé stomped to meet his cousin.

The youth's face turned pale as Laidé confronted him with such a glowering look that Althesal thought Laidé was going to strike him. She had never imagined Laidé could lose his temper!

Mhali took a step towards them, but Althesal rested a hand on his arm to stop him — "Let's wait. This is a family affair."

Everyone watched the two Nauthians. Naleean had lost all his determination and confidence, and waited for the worst with a submissive face. He had dropped the staff to the ground, and the coiled energy had vanished the moment it had left his hand. Laidé's body trembled, his eyes boring into his cousin's. The other youngsters had stepped back a few paces to give them room. They too had a submissive posture. After all, Laidé was their senior and a leader, a Nauthé of their people. He could order them to return to their planet to submit themselves to the ruling of the Council of the Nauthé for having violated galactic protocols and for having created a nightmare for the Union.

Then, when Althesal expected the worst, Laidé grabbed Naleean by the shoulders and brought him closer in a tight embrace. He next said to him, unable to hold his tears and loud enough for her to hear, "Cousin! Don't forget your own now that you have become one of the Nauthé of old!"

The other youngsters hesitated for a moment before leaping to join the two in the embrace.

Mhali assessed the situation at the center of the Gardens from a distance of fifty paces. The Dwellers hadn't taken notice of them. Althesal had told him they needed to be near the Spark. She suspected the sequence of words chanted at the end of the ritual of the Nauthé to activate Stïel Key were the same words to activate the Spark. When she had visited the Island of the Nauthé, the Song Keeper and the Story Keeper had told her the chant had to be sounded at the exact distance of seven paces and from all sides, and that the words made the Key glow with great intensity while the chant lasted — "More surely the seven paces are required to comply with the principles of sound to form interference patterns", Ethën had remarked.

Thus Mhali's plan was to divide all of them into twelve groups around the central area of the Gardens, each led by a Ranger, while he was going to be with Althesal, Daothel, Nesdil, Naleean and two others of the Nauthians. The group opposite to them was going to include Laidé, Ethën and Soen. At first, Mhali had been reluctant to divide them, even though it was the best strategy at the moment. However, when Naleean had explained to him the power of the staffs with the Fire of the Forests Lights, he had felt more confident with his plan. They didn't have to defeat the Dwellers. They just needed to drive them aside so that Althesal, he and their other five friends could approach the Spark.

The early evening twilight descended as they took their positions. By then the Spark's cold white light dominated the place in all directions, from a height about thrice Mhali's height. In spite of its intensity, he could look straight into It. It reminded him of the singularities normally seen inside Pulsar Stars, though much more radiant. Another difference was that something more than light came from It — a power that had nothing to do with Space; a power that reached to his inner being saying, *Be!*

Now that he saw It, Mhali doubted anyone could take possession of the Spark; least of all, remove It from that planet. It wasn't a spatial singularity. It was more like an opening to something beyond the Universe.

The four remaining leaders of the Dwellers had taken position at about ten paces from it, hovering above the ground, motionless and facing the Spark, each in one of the four directions of the winds. A dark mist shrouded them. The other Dwellers, now only about three dozen of them, had split forming two rings outside their leaders. Each of these two groups slithered slowly through the air, in an opposite direction to the other, and in the process making a rustling noise that sounded like an eerie chant. None of them took notice of the Humans.

"I've a bad feeling about this", he whispered to Althesal and those close to him as they entered the central area of the Gardens. "Those creatures are nothing of what we imagined of them. Everything they do tells me they came here with a carefully designed plan. I would give up my rank right now to know what their plan is!"

The central area of the Gardens was a perfect circular space, about eighty paces across. It was covered with countless thumb-size glassy tiles that reflected, in the darkening twilight, the light coming from the Spark. Three spirals of light, barely visible and born at the center of that space, flowed embedded in the tiles. None of the light-made vertical spirals remained.

Mhali was about to send the mental command to his Rangers for all the groups to advance at the same time when Daothel said, "Look at the leaders!"

Through the dark mist surrounding these, Mhali saw their misshapen forms swell and, in addition to their many irregular appendages and Human body parts, something more was now coming from their bodies. Each was extending a tubular organ towards the Spark. A polyphonic hum in a crescendo, in four notes, came from these tubes. At the same time, the two rings of Dwellers around them began to increase their rotating speed and the volume of their chant.

"Mhali, we must move!" Althesal grabbed him by the arm. "They are—"

She didn't finish. The light coming from the Spark vanished, and a gust of pure Evil hit them with gale force. Mhali and the others were thrown backwards, and a Darkness seized them. He heard It bellow in his mind — *Caught you! Now you are mine!*

'Human'

Mhali embraced Althesal to steady her as they were buffeted by that howling gale. Daothel had done the same with Nesdil. When they recovered, instinctively the four of them crouched down holding onto each other. So did Naleean and his two companions. But that was more than a physical wind. It was an otherworldly Force charged with an uncontainable rage that sought to snatch their mind-souls, not to possess but to destroy. Yet, after Its initial attempt, Mhali likewise felt the powerlessness of this Force to achieve its purpose.

When the gale subsided, they stood up. The only light now was that coming from the staffs in the hands of the three Nauthians. Adjusting his eyes to better see in the direction of the Spark, Mhali discovered the leaders of the Dwellers had been replaced by a wall of darkness, darker than anything he had ever beheld. The Spark had vanished behind it, and now he couldn't sense Its presence.

Turning to assess everyone's condition, he saw they were unharmed and now stood gazing towards the impenetrable darkness.

"It's still there", Daothel murmured.

"They didn't want to take the Spark with them", Althesal added with a strained voice. "Their plan all along was to use Its power to set their Master free — the Ancient Darkness!"

Mhali regarded her. A deep frown creased her forehead, yet the light of her eyes shone brighter in that deep twilight.

He next attempted to contact his Rangers, but none answered to his thought communication. A quick visual survey told him, nonetheless, the

four groups he could see appeared to be fine. He felt bewildered by the endless array of surprises the Dwellers gave them. Thus, he confessed to Althesal, making an effort not to reveal in his voice the desperation surging in
him: "If you have an idea on how to proceed, let me know because I have
none!"

⚡

Althesal studied the Darkness with a growing sense of defeat — It rose as
an impenetrable fortress of macabre, writhing and bloating shadows from
which claw-shaped appendages darted here and there in attempts to crush
them into nothingness.

She had failed. The Dwellers had opened the door to the Darkness foretold by Stïel — and, of all places, on planet Ær! She had been mistaken the
entire time. She had thought the Dwellers themselves were the Darkness
Stïel had warned about, and that their base on Mal'ek was the door. But no,
the Dwellers themselves were minions of an indescribable primeval Force.

The Dwellers, she could see, were terrified of their Master and had retreated at a distance from It. They had ceased their slithering and were now
still and silent. Their eyes switched to and fro between the Darkness and the
Humans.

But she and the Dwellers weren't the only ones who had been manipu-
lated. So too had been all those who had answered the Spark's Call, including Ankepum. The Darkness had twisted everyone's perception and
understanding of the situation in the Sol System with the purpose of discovering the location of the Spark… to unveil It… so that the Spark itself
would provide the power to open the door to let It in. It had succeeded.
Now all was lost!

Her entire body shuddered — not just because of her own failure, but
because a frigid cold was spreading throughout the Gardens carrying the
Darkness' hatred for all living beings.

It was her fault!

She should have taken control of the entire affair from the very beginning when she was given the assignment to come up with answers to the
questions posed by the catastrophic events on the planet Yfel. She should
have listened to her heart. But no, she had played the good Thelian, the
good Galactic Human, the good Director of Sciences of the Union, while
all that time her intuition was telling her just to come to this third planet
to meet her fate, nothing more. She didn't know how that would have
played out — certainly much different than the terrifying defeat they now

faced!

Feeling at the edge of desperation, she lifted her eyes towards the night sky. It took her a moment to register it — the Darkness wasn't there! On the contrary, because of It she was met with more stars than those a clear night would reveal. And in that moment of agony, those countless stars twinkled at her. Then it happened. A childhood memory came to her. She remembered the many nights she had spent gazing at the starry heavens and feeling the wonder and joy of belonging to something much greater than the Universe itself. And in that instant, the memory of that wonder and feeling broke the spell imprisoning her.

Enough of regrets! — she told herself when she realized the source of that brooding wasn't her. Using guilt as a tool, someone wanted to immobilize her will — most surely that Darkness!

Instinctively she took a step back, away from the Darkness, and noticed that Mhali, Nesdil and Daothel regarded her with questioning faces. Searching for the right words to say to them, she met their gaze. She wanted to assure them they were going to succeed — even if she didn't know how. Yet, while looking at them she realized a change had happened in them. Even Mhali, who moments before had confessed his impotency as a Marshal of the Rangers to deal with the situation, now had a bearing that accepted no defeat. What was more, their eyes shone with a new light that told her: 'Yes, she was going to do it — take them back into the Light.'

One by one they next spoke to her with the confidence of those who had rehearsed that moment, or perhaps had already lived through it in another existence.

With a calm voice Nesdil was the first to speak to her: *"Friend, the song coming from the Silence pregnant with Life is infinitely more powerful than the bluster coming from the silence where there is only emptiness."*

Next, Daothel added with a slight bow of his head: *"Remember, Darkness abhors Light and ceases to be in Its presence!"*

"Brute force is of Space", Mhali followed. *"The Darkness expects that. Yet, the Essence of Humans, It fears the most!"*

Althesal was at a loss. What were they saying? She understood their words — power came with every one of them — but she couldn't see how that helped. They needed to be near the Spark to sing the ancient words the Nauthé had preserved in their ritual, and which Laidé had them memorize a short while before.

Shouts elsewhere, however, interrupted her pondering. She wheeled around to see the reason — the Dwellers had swollen in numbers with more coming through the Darkness' door! They too had regained their confidence and were slithering fast towards them. This time it was different, though. She felt it — they wanted all Humans dead!

While she dodged the attack of the first of the creatures that plunged into her group, through the corner of her eye she saw Mhali erect a light-field around himself. She knew the momentum the Dweller had in its speed would give her time to sound the chord of her soul to protect herself before it could turn around to come back after her. But a second attack came from another direction, and she had to launch herself to the ground, face forward, to avoid being rammed. She flipped over quickly, with the speed and agility of a Thelian body enhanced by a Ranger suit, and effortlessly rose back to her feet.

She then saw Naleean assist his two companions to their feet, and that Daothel and Nesdil were already inside the light-field Mhali had erected. The three of them beckoned to her. Yet before she took a step in their direction, something hit her with great force from behind. She was hurled through the air and crashed against the hard, tiled floor. Momentarily she became disoriented before realizing she needed to get back to her feet, that on the ground she was an easier prey.

Before she could rise, however, strong hands grabbed her — Mhali and Naleean were helping her to stand up, and in the youth's hand the light of the staff shone with the power of a star. Most of the Dwellers now kept their distance, wailing in rage and afraid of the staff's fiery light. A few made attempts to reach their group, but Naleean pointed the staff towards them, and a burst of fiery light spread out from it. The assailants then turned away. At that moment Naleean's two companions joined him to form a shield to protect her and all in their group. It was clear, a stalemate had developed because the Dwellers had retreated back, closer to the wall of Darkness.

She took a deep breath — How long would that respite last before those fiends, or the Darkness would come with a new trick?

Then she saw it! On the ground, close to her, lay a body, unrecognizable because of the dark frost and burns that covered it all over. With a jerk and holding her breath, she spun around looking for Daothel and for Nesdil. To her relief, they stood behind her, safe and sound, though holding grave faces. Mhali then spoke:

"Aldiarlim… The man called Aldiarlim sacrificed himself to save your life. He pushed you out of the way when one of those fiends came to ram you. He's dead."

She regarded Mhali as Time seemed to slow down. Then her legs felt weak, and she collapsed to her knees next to the body of the man who had known nothing of her but had given his life for hers.

"Why? Why?" she cried to him, with tears flooding her eyes. "It is I who should have saved you all." Touching his lacerated chest with her right hand, she felt his heart — it was silent, and she couldn't sense his soul either. "The life that is in me I would give for you to be alive! No one… no one should cut short his life journey because of me!" Then, with no thought of it she began to sing to him, softly, an ancient Thelian song that spoke of the longing of Humans to return to their Source. And again, with no thought of it, while she sang, she let the light of her soul flow through her hand towards Aldiarlim's now empty form.

Nesdil and Daothel came to kneel across from her, and the two joined in the song. It was muted, although of such a majesty it silenced the wails of the Dwellers. So absorbed was she in her desire to guide Aldiarlim soul's departure towards the higher realms that it took her a moment to notice Daothel and Nesdil no longer were singing and that Daothel had cried out, "He breathes again!"

Indeed Aldiarlim stirred, and the flutter of his heart she could now sense!

Mhali hurried to kneel beside her, and using his Ranger training, gave an additional quota of life energy to Aldiarlim. Soon the man opened his eyes long enough for her to thank him with a smile before he lost consciousness again. Then it hit her what had just happened: she had brought a man from the dead!

"How is this possible?" she cried looking at her hands. "I'm a simple mortal!"

Mhali lifted his head to face her. His eyes held such an intensity that she had no choice but to look at him. Then, with a thunder-like voice, he spoke to her:

"Not so, Human! Even your sorrow is a command to the deepest forces of this Universe!"

A lightning-like energy swept through her body when she heard Mhali address her as *'Human'.* From the crown of her head to the base of her spine and into the ground the bolt traveled — and up again to rest in the center of her chest. And from there a power filled her entire being. For the first time in her life she understood the real nature of being *'Human'* — *the Essence, the Beginning and the End of all existence!*

She wasn't the only one, though. Her friends likewise understood. They now regarded her with a face that also spoke to her of that timeless and non-spatial Essence which makes Humans 'Human'.

The sorrow, the doubts, the confusion she had felt before, all had vanished as shadows cease to exist with the arrival of light. She felt renewed… She felt more… She was awake — It was time to be *Human!*

Rising to her feet, she turned in the direction of the center of the Gardens and was met by Naleean, face to face. The youth nodded to her with obeisance as if knowing already what she was going to do next. She placed her right hand on his cheek and smiled to him — he beamed at her. The youth indeed knew what needed to be done. His innermost being and hers, and that of all Humans, were, after all, of the same Stream and Source.

Mhali, Nesdil and Daothel also rose, and the Marshal, resting a hand on Naleean shoulder, said to him, "Nauthé, protect Aldiarlim until we return."

The youth gave him a silent assent.

Althesal next reached with her mind to Ethën, Soen and Laidé, and heard their answer. Then, filled with the power of THAT which is beyond this Universe, she directed her steps to meet her destiny — the destiny of all Humans.

A silence had descended on the Gardens. Even the writhing shadows forming the Darkness wall were now still. The Dwellers, too, knew something was about to happen and retreated in haste as she, flanked by Mhali, Daothel and Nesdil, crossed the distance with unhurried steps. Soen, Laidé and Ethën soon joined them.

With every step she took, she felt more of it — She hadn't come to answer the Call… She had come to sound a new Call!

And when she arrived, with the bearing of those who are lords and masters of their journey along Space and Time, she entered the Darkness.

45

Tidings from the Nightside

Planet Esdänl, Alcyone System

Councilor Thaël dashed to the Chancellor's office. Aides and other members of the staff in the halls were startled to see him racing. "You better come to my office", Chancellor Vuensé had said to him through the omnicom. "We have news of the expedition!"

Ten standard galactic days had passed since the Spaceblazer had left Thel. The only news during that time had come half a day after — that one more of the Dwellers' craft had entered planet Ær. It had come from outside the system and had cunningly avoided detection until the last minute by using the same cloaking field the other four craft had used. Since then, nothing else had happened, and no communication had come from those on the surface.

The Rangers on the transport outside the moon's orbit had seen the Spaceblazer arrive to Ær's upper atmosphere. After that, they had lost sight of it in the unexplained variabilities of the ös-sphere of that planet.

All those days of silence and waiting had Thaël on edge, and he burst into the Chancellor's office without waiting to be announced.

The Vice-Marshal of the Islnom-1 halted in mid sentence when he entered. Two other Ranger officers, the Strategy Commander of the Corps and the Science Director, were with him and bowed their heads to Thaël.

The Chancellor sat on her chair, looking tired. She pursed her lips to acknowledge him and said to the Vice-Marshal, "Please, do start again."

"As I was saying, our craft *Mni* is one of the seven transports we have now in the Sol System. Since the Spaceblazer left planet Thel, the Mni has orders to remain on a stationary orbit with respect to the large continental land of planet Ær. It has maintained a continuous survey of the surface and is recording everything its sensors can detect. As you know, it isn't much besides general conditions and indistinct land visuals. Today, however, at approximately noon time here, the Mni's sensors recorded a single flicker of data that would have passed as a glitch in the sensors but for the Ranger in charge of the monitors at the time. He noticed the data had been recorded by every sensor, simultaneously, and concluded that a malfunction affecting all of them at the same time was highly improbable. After informing his captain, they ran a preliminary analysis of this recording and discovered it contained much more data than a normal recording during the same length of time. Immediately the captain sent it to us.

"Our people here passed this data through a series of filters and soon found it wasn't one recording but three, at short intervals the one from the other. Each appears to be a snapshot of visual, sound and other telemetry, but the only component we are able to isolate is the visuals. The other measurements in the recordings are lost in the background of the planet's ös-field, atmosphere, sonosphere, ionosphere and electro-magnetic fields. In the three cases, the snapshots are of the same geographical location on the planet — a small area of land in the central northern region of the large continent.

"The question of why the Mni was able to detect something at that specific point in time is difficult to answer", the Vice-Marshal continued. "Using what we know of that planet, it appears that for a moment three separate events at that location created, each, a pause in the planet's anomalies for the Mni to detect it — that's the best explanation we have."

The Vice-Marshal next gestured to the Science Director to continue. She stood up, spoke a word to activate the first recorded visual, and began to analyze it for Thaël and the Chancellor:

"As you can see, this first recording, similar to the other two, gives us a view of an area of approximately one-half square ont [1.9 square kilometers], at an early time in the evening. The visual isn't good, but when we zoom-in to the center, we can see what appears to be the Spaceblazer next to a large land feature probably built by an intelligence because it is perfectly circular, is covered with a different vegetation from that of the surrounding land, and has a central reflective area, which is also circular. In the vicinity of this land feature we can also observe four other craft, next to each other. By their shape and size, our people think these are the four craft that first entered the planet. There are also these dark—"

Thaël looked at the dark blotches the Science Directed pointed at and couldn't contain himself. "The Dwellers!"

"Yes, Councilor, that's one possibility. However, there isn't anything in the image that can help us identify their real nature."

Thaël had been standing all this time and felt the need to sit. He knew it in his heart — the expedition had engaged the Dwellers! His anxiety and frustration rose to a new level. He felt like a general who knew his troops had engaged the enemy but was completely blind to the happenings on the battlefield.

The Science Director continued next with her analysis of the second burst of data:

"The first difference on this second recording is the twilight of that early evening. It has deepened some, indicating that about twenty minutes have elapsed since the first recording. Another difference is that the dark blotches have split in two groups — one is now inside the reflective area at the center of the strange formation, and the other has remained near the Spaceblazer. This second group is now surrounded by a strong bluish light-field of unknown origin."

"There is one more thing in this second recording", the Director added. "You can see, on the north side of the land feature, inside this patch of greenery, which appears to be a group of trees, another craft has landed that wasn't there in the first recording. It is similar in shape to the other four craft. We can only conclude it is the fifth craft that entered the planet half a day after the Spaceblazer arrived. Why those on that craft arrived later and chose to land away from the others, apparently under cover, we can only guess."

"Ankepum!" The Chancellor said with a frown while looking at Thaël.

Thaël agreed, and this could only mean one thing — Ankepum and the Dwellers had different purposes! That conclusion could be confirmed. They needed to send Rangers to track the base or bases the Overlord had used on his trip to the Sol System. That was an easy thing to do. In their endless bragging, Ankepum's people wouldn't keep that a secret.

The Science Director, being a Human from the Seïnn System of the Cealaïs Galaxy, had a strong natural empathy with all those around, and her next words sounded to Thaël like a mother addressing her young children:

"I want you, Chancellor and Councilor Thaël, to understand that my Rangers don't know how to interpret the third recording I am about to show you. It is the shortest of the three and has the least amount of data. Therefore, it's better not to draw conclusions from it until we find other means to know more."

Her words had the opposite effect on Thaël than what she had intended. He braced for the worst.

The image on the third recording appeared in mid air, in front of the chair where Thaël sat. After a long moment studying it, the Chancellor came to sit next to him, and in silence the two of them continued looking at it. None of the Rangers said a word.

Thaël couldn't make sense of it. What was it? What had the Mni's sensors recorded?

The Spaceblazer, the five craft, the dark blotches that were the Dwellers, and the strange circular land formation had all been replaced by a landscape that appeared to be completely natural. To add to the puzzle, and if the Rangers were right in their calculations, not more than thirty standard galactic minutes had elapsed between the second and the third recording. However, the place was now illuminated as if it was midday, while the surrounding area of land showed that it was still night!

"An explosion…" Thaël whispered. "Only an explosion could have erased them in such a short time and leave that afterglow." He sighed. He felt defeated. His worst fear had come to pass. He had sent Althesal and the others to their deaths! He rubbed his forehead with the tip of his fingers, hard, to arrest the tears about to spill from his eyes.

"An explosion of what?" The Chancellor turned to regard him. She looked as miserable as he felt. "What in this Universe erases people, craft and structures, and leaves behind Nature as if nothing had touched it?"

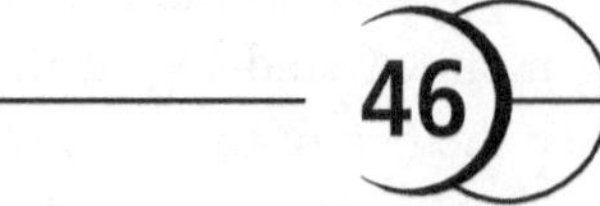

46

The Song of Aïdin

The Darkness wasn't just an absence of light, it was also a nothingness — the utter negation of existence. It had embraced Althesal and her friends as they had stepped inside It. A tendril extending from It grazed Althesal's cheek but jerked away as in pain. She shivered at the thought It left in her mind — *"You are my creation! Fight me not!"* — In response, the light from her body wavered… just once… a fraction of a moment. She knew the Darkness' tricks and wasn't going to be deceived again.

The only light there was hers. She couldn't see her friends. They were close to her, though. She felt them and the strong link with their minds and hearts. She could sense they too were the target of the Darkness' deceiving tactics, but all remained steadfast.

Raw rage and a deep stillness also pressed in on them, and not even the song of her body she could hear. Her feet touched no ground, and her body no longer sensed the coldness that had invaded the Gardens when the Darkness had first appeared. Involuntarily, she took a deep breath and became aware that, yes! she was breathing air! It all had to be a deception. They were still in the Gardens.

Time to end this! — she told herself.

Then, as she held the intention to gather the power of her soul essence, she discovered it was remote and unreachable. Once again her resolve wavered. The power surging in her before entering the Darkness, she no longer felt it either. Yet Mhali's words were with her — *"Human, even your sorrow is a command to the deepest forces of this Universe!"* Thus, soul power or not, she still had her voice, an extension of her innermost being.

"Begone!" she called out with might. "Return to whence you came!"

Spasms traveled through the Darkness, and with a jerky motion It retreated a few paces from her. She then saw her friends standing close to her, now adding their bodies' light to hers. But the nothingness still pressed in on them seeking to extinguish their existence.

They too must have noticed the power of their soul essence wasn't reachable because Ethën cried out, "We can't do this by ourselves!" A pained stare framed his face.

"Don't falter now!" she replied and took a step towards him. "All this is a deception. The Spark is twenty or so paces in front of us. Let's move!"

Following her, it took them only a few strides to exit the dark miasma that was the wall. Then, they saw It! — It had changed! It had grown! It had become more!

In wonder they halted.

The Spark continued to be a dimensionless point, but its intrinsic luminosity and its radiance had increased more than ten-fold. So too the singularity or window around it was now much larger — a Human could easily walk through it. More mysterious was that through that window they could see a 'Beyond' that beckoned to them. Yet, their path was barred. A chasm all around, bottomless and sickening, obstructed their way.

The Spark wasn't free either. Tendrils of the Darkness, entering through the south pole of the singularity around It, formed a throbbing funnel that syphoned Its power. A stench of rotten flesh came from that funnel, and as it rotated Althesal caught a glimpse of body parts. *The remains of the leaders of the Dwellers!* — she knew right away.

Doubts then assailed her. She had understood from the words Stïel spoke to the Nauthé that only Humans could summon and control the power of the Spark. How, then, had the leaders of the Dwellers been able to call forth Its power to open the door to the Darkness? Was her reasoning wrong? Could anyone, Human or not, summon the power of the Spark?

She had just finished formulating that last question, when all the threads of the mystery connected in her mind. For a moment she froze in shock at the realization, and her heart began to pound — her reasoning had been correct all along! Stïel Key was truly of the utmost simplicity! As she had concluded before, the Key wasn't the crystal. The crystal had been a conveyor for the first part of the message, as the ritual had been the conveyor of the second part. The message was a simple reminder: 'To close the door use the most *Human* in Humans — the means of expression of one's Essence: the power of the Voice!'

The Darkness couldn't summon the Spark — It hadn't — nor could the Dwellers themselves — they hadn't. The Darkness had used the leaders of the Dwellers. These must have been Humans at some point, and their mind-souls must have remained trapped in those forms. That explained the presence of Human body parts in them. The Spark did respond to all Humans, even to Humans twisted to such a fate. That too explained the polyphonic notes sounded by the leaders to summon the power of the Spark and thus open with it the Darkness' door.

But there was more. Now she knew that the chant of the Nauthé to activate the crystal wasn't the actual words to call forth the power of the Spark. That realization was confirmed by something the Master Chronicler had told her about the sacred utterance used to name the legendary planets of the Manaï.

"Time to sound the Call!" she told her six friends, who one by one nodded to confirm they had followed her reasoning through the link of their minds.

Next, with the simplicity of those who know *to be* Power itself, they focused their attention on their mind-soul essence, and using the harmonies of the Voice which only a Human can sing, they sang together a single song-word:

"Aïdin!!!"

Time stood still as the song-word went forth… for a moment or for an eternity… it could well have been both. Then, of its own, as a mighty wave its volume rose in the silence, and the seven of them braced for the explosion of light and power that was coming. It didn't happen. Instead, the Spark took their song-word and began to weave with it a full song of great majesty and beauty, filling the oppressing nothingness with its harmonies — *the Song of Aïdin!* A song not heard since ages past.

At once, the many tendrils of the Darkness draining the power of the Spark melted away, releasing a cloud of sparkling white-blue light which slowly rose towards the heights accompanied by Human cries of relief. A wordless shriek followed, carrying a primeval rage. It came from the Darkness as It rushed to retreat through the chasm, chased away by the harmonies of the Song of Aïdin.

Then the Song changed its rhythm, and a mighty torrent of light erupted from the Spark in the direction of the Seven. It swirled thrice around them, leaving them untouched, yet in the process becoming a maelstrom of light and harmonies. At the sight of it, the Dwellers who were inside the Gardens reacted with a cacophony of wails and sought to flee. Yet, they had barely started to retreat when the maelstrom engulfed them, hurling them into the bowels of the chasm.

At that point, once more, the Song of Aïdin rose its tempo and volume, and with it the maelstrom expanded beyond the Gardens in all directions, seizing with its windless gale of harmonies the Dwellers held by the Forest Lights, together with their five foul craft. Again, with a cacophony of rage and fear these shadows resisted in vain as they were cast into the bottomless depths.

For a moment the Song paused. So did the maelstrom. Not for long. With a great crescendo it resumed, this time the Spark calling to Itself its own light and harmonies. Thus, as swiftly as it had first formed, the maelstrom collapsed upon the Spark, and in its wake closing the chasm to the realm of that primeval Darkness.

The door was no more.

Yet, when the Song of Aïdin ended, Althesal and her six friends no longer were in the Gardens of the Chronicles of the Horizon on planet Ær — the Song had transported them to the Beyond!

47

Trailblazing

Althesal was momentarily confounded when the Song of Aïdin ended. She blinked — *Where are we?* — An expanse made of a clear light extended before her. It resembled an immense basin. High above, spirals of light, made of twinkling points, formed shifting patterns of beautiful designs against an indigo background. An ethereal and remote music also reached her ears. It came from a single point throbbing with life at the center of that space. *The Spark of Aïdin!* — she knew it; she too felt its power.

Although the place evoked a familiarity in her, she had no recollection of having visited it before — in dreams, visions or otherwise.

Her six friends, next to her, also studied the place. Their minds were closer to hers than their bodies, as if they were one mind. They were as puzzled as she was. Since there was nothing in that space but them, in the silence of their minds they decided to go towards that single, faraway point of energy. To their astonishment, as soon as they had agreed to it, they were there!

So too were ten other Humans! — Five women and five men.

By now, after all they had encountered, she was used to experiencing levels and aspects of Space and Time still unknown to most. Nonetheless, the sight of them was breathtaking. They were the perfection of Human, not just in form but in presence and soul. But there was more — though she didn't remember how or when, she knew them all! They were kin, and with a wordless greeting they welcomed them.

Only of the woman right in front of her did she recall her name — *Iolthel.* While the other nine were clad in garments of light, she was dressed as a Thelian and looked the same as she had in the recording Ciän the Wise had shown her. The only difference was that, similar to her companions, a soft light came from her that extended in all directions and blended with the light of the Spark.

Iolthel's smile widened as she took steps to embrace each and to kiss them on their foreheads, as Thelians do among their own. The others too approached to greet them by placing their right hand on each one's chest and giving each a wholehearted welcoming.

When it was the turn for one of the other women to greet Althesal, she took hold of Althesal's hands and locked her eyes with hers. A brief, silent and wordless communion reached Althesal's mind, and in that communion a picture formed where she saw the world of the Aenrelm and the group of the Nauthé of old led by Rïal.

"*Stïel!*" Althesal cried out. She and her friends were in the presence of 'the Nine'!

"It wasn't difficult, was it?" Stïel said while embracing her. "The message, I mean. We knew it was a gamble, yet we also knew you would decipher it. By the laws of this Universe we couldn't intervene directly. The flows of Time with the various possible outcomes laid clear to us, but we had to respect your free will and let you find the way."

In reply Althesal pulled Laidé close to her, resting an arm across his waist. He was regarding Stïel with a dazzled expression. "His people did most of the job", she said to Stïel, "with their great love for that which is past and future, and for all beings and paths."

Stïel regarded Laidé for a long moment with the loveliest of faces. "Once I too was a Nauthé," she said to him, "long, long before Rïal. It was then that, like all of us here, after much inner struggle and realization I found the way to the fulness of 'Human' — I had to rid myself of my misperceptions on the nature of Humans, Space and Time, of the ideas of the One Source of All I had erroneously constructed, and of my self-imposed illusory limitations."

Laidé couldn't control himself and burst into tears while giving her a tight embrace. "I knew you were a Nauthé the moment I laid my eyes on you — I must tell of you to our people!"

Once the greetings were finished, Iolthel addressed the seven of them, both in their minds and with words in Galactic Standard. Like a celestial music her words sounded to Althesal as these created almost invisible, sparkling waves in the light of that place.

"Though joyful, an unexpected encounter is this, dear ones", Iolthel began. "You surprised us with your boldness to confront the Darkness in its own midst. Even the Darkness was taken by surprise! Yet, for a moment we were uncertain you would succeed. But no, you gathered upon yourselves the power of the Human Stream and made of that which was most difficult an easy task. And now you remember some of what the fullness of Human is — unconquerable!

"With your boldness, however," she continued, "you have also placed yourselves — and us here — at a crossroads. You shouldn't be here! Not yet. We don't understand how you did it. Regardless, a decision you now must make: either to remain here, or to return to your path as physical beings."

"Do we have that second choice?" Mhali interrupted her with a tone of uncertainty in his voice and narrowing his eyes. "I, too, wasn't expecting for us to end here." Then, with stilted words he added, "By the Light! I don't even understand where 'here' is!"

"Yes, you do have that choice, dear", Iolthel replied, regarding him with tenderness. "We all 'here' can return and tread again the path of Humans. It isn't easy, though, when your sensitivity to both, the joys and the suffering of others develops in fullness, and when you see the patterns formed by the threads of Time and know of the challenges ahead for those who travel them… Yes, you can return."

Mhali turned to Althesal. "Let's go back! Our journey there isn't finished."

"I'm torn between those two choices", Daothel spoke at that moment with an uncharacteristic solemnity. "I am torn because my heart tells me that 'here' is also a journey, although a different one, along the vast avenues of Consciousness that give origin to Space and Time. Yet, my heart also tells me that disregarding the ways of Space and Time when I haven't yet mastered them will make of me incomplete. It will as well rob others of the opportunity to bless me with their uniqueness, and myself of the uniqueness I can offer them."

Althesal couldn't contain a smile. The youth, in his innocence and wisdom, had just described the essence and the implications of their choices.

She wasn't the only one who felt surprised by his words. The astonishment on the faces of Iolthel and the Nine was something almost out of place there.

Then, one of the nine, a man, took a step forward. "You may not recall it — *Ríordáin* is my name", he said. Next, addressing Daothel while shaking his head in wonder, he said in Standard Galactic, "It took each of us here, wise one, much, much longer to arrive to the understanding that took you but a moment. You are right — those are the two paths of which one you now must choose. Know, though, one doesn't exclude the other. Regardless of the one you choose, at one point you may feel the need to also travel the other until you know in your heart that you have become master of Space and Time, and of That which sources them. What happens after? Those who so have become don't tell." He ended with a smile.

"Are there others like you?" Ethën asked, gaping at Ríordáin.

"Oh, yes!" Ríordáin replied with his winsome voice. "Many, many, and not just Humans — including those you call *Manaï*. This Universe, the others and the Beyond teem with life — intelligent, advancing, conscious life. It just happens that the journey of the ten of us crosses the journey of the seven of you and forms a pattern which extends into the Beyond. Thus, this isn't the first time nor the last one we meet."

Something had been nagging in the back of Althesal's mind since they had arrived there. Now she realized what it was: her memories of her existence as a physical being, including the events at the Gardens, were receding, becoming blurred and less relevant to the choice confronting the seven of them — not because she was purposefully ignoring her physical existence but because, she suspected, that realm had the effect of placing all things in a broader perspective. She didn't want to lose those memories, however. In her heart she felt the fate of the Atelë and of planet Ær was also at stake in the choice they were about to make. Mhali was right. They hadn't finished. The seven of them had started a chain of events for that planet for which they were responsible.

"What's going to happen to the Spark of Aïdin now that the door to the Darkness is closed?" she asked. "Is it still visible to those on planet Ær?"

Iolthel looked at the Nine, who in turn regarded each other. They all seemed uncertain, and Althesal sensed a silent interchange, not of the mind but at a higher level, taking place among them. When they finished, another of the Nine — a man — spoke:

"I have been known before by the name *Ösel*. I will first answer your second question: Yes, the Spark is still visible to those in the land of the Atelë — Its nature is multi-dimensional both in Space and in Time. Know too the Spark of Aïdin isn't unique. Other similar projections of the Beyond, not too many, are found in Space and in Time. Some resemble the Spark, others take other forms. Yet all work as passageways for streams of Consciousness to travel across and in between Space, Time and the Beyond, and as outposts of the Essence of the Beyond."

Ösel paused for a moment to study the seven of them — even though young in appearance, he reminded Althesal of an old and tried teacher who wanted his students to understand well his lessons. Then, he resumed, "Regarding the first question, telling you the fate of the Spark is the reason the ten of us are also at a crossroads with your coming 'here'. Until one becomes a Time Seer, one isn't supposed to know anything of one's journey along Space and Time. This blindness is the incentive for one to alter Space and Time, and for leaving one's beneficial imprint on them, which is what this Universe intends for self-conscious beings to do — to make of Space and Time more. For this reason, anything we disclose to you of your journey will have effects none can predict. However, since you are 'here', we realize you need clarity — just enough of it — for the decision. And here is what we can tell you: *The journey of the Spark of Aïdin across Space and Time, the journey of the seven of you, and the journey of the ten of us here, is one and the same from its beginning to its end! And those in the Beyond who know of this journey marvel at the daring and wondrous tale that is unfolding.*"

"I suspected as much of the first part of what you said", Althesal replied with a grin after a moment. "Thank you for your light." Turning to her friends, she then said, "Since we discovered the existence of the third planet of Sol, I've felt in my heart that my destiny is tied to its destiny. It was by ignoring the promptings of my heart that matters became twisted and complicated. Not this time — I'm going back."

"So I feel", Soen said to her. "Since my first visit to that planet, I have felt in my heart that connection. I know not the reason. Forging new paths — trailblazing — has been the joy of my heart, and I'm not going to miss this opportunity!"

Next, one by one each of the others stated their decision to return.

Once again the ten communed with each other. This time it was clear to Althesal they were pleased.

No other word was then said, and at the right of Althesal a wide opening appeared. Through it she saw Naleean with Tiá surrounded by their friends, they were still in the Gardens. The other members of the expedition were also with them, and two Rangers attended to the wounds of Aldiarlim.

Looking at Iolthel and the Nine one last time, even though she had decided to return to Space and Time, Althesal had tears in her eyes. "Will we see each other again while we follow the mortal path?" she wanted to ask them, but she already knew their answer — "Perhaps!"

Iolthel, though, came to her and, placing a hand on her cheek, spoke to her mind: *"The path of a new type of Time Seer you have entered, and loneliness is not of it! Be strong. You are to forge a path of great promise with those of the*

Source Path — they and the Atelë are now one, and you too shall become one with them."

Althesal nodded to Iolthel, brushed her tears, and gave her a quick embrace. Next she turned towards the opening, to return with her friends to that new world, Ær, to continue their journey — as Soen had said it, trailblazing!

48

The Lost and Found Prince

Planet Ær, Sol System

Althesal regarded Aldiarlim with solicitude. The life of his body ebbed away, and nothing she or the healers had done was going to change his fate. Once he had been a Human, from a planet in the Cealaïs Galaxy. Now his appearance was something else… something which defied her comprehension of the Human psyche. But his soul was still Human — that much she knew — and he had requested from her to listen to his story so that she could understand and, perhaps, forgive him and his turbulent path.

Tarlal was the name Overlord Ankepum had initially given him when he had joined his clan 630 standard galactic years before. His Human name had been *Aldiarlim,* and that is how he had pleaded with Althesal to remember him.

From the start Aldiarlim had become Ankepum's most trusted advisor and confidant because of his intelligence, great military wit, and knowledge of races and worlds. Born as a prince, in his youth Aldiarlim became dissatisfied with his duties and with the idea of monarchies, rulers and all those who placed themselves above everyone else — *"By whose right are you a king and I a prince when Humans are all equal?"* he had asked his father countless times. Thus, in his early adulthood he had renounced that life and had left everything behind to become a drifter, moving from planet to planet in search for something he couldn't define.

When his traveling took him to the Laïs Galaxy, he applied to the Ranger Corps Academy to become one of them. He had started his training distinguishing himself from his fellow cadets, but a taint of rebelliousness soon became apparent to his superiors. They thus decided he was unfit to continue since he couldn't accept authority. He had left the Corps with a bitter heart and had vowed to dedicate his life to oppose the Union. That was when he had decided to join The Others. Fate took him to Ankepum, who, although then an upstart Overlord, recognized his worth and adopted him into his clan.

To find more acceptance among the members of the clan, Aldiarlim had undergone grafts and genetic changes in his body to look more as one of the Dreki race. The results had exceeded his expectations. The changes had given him a more ferocious and dangerous look than the humanoid Dreki had with their distant resemblance to dragons.

But after the transformation he experienced in his heart, right before destroying Stïel Key, Aldiarlim no longer pretended he was a Dreki. Thus, when he regained consciousness and found himself under the care of healers, he had surrendered to Althesal for his final judgment.

For days Althesal had met with him, sparing an hour or so to listen to his story. He laid on an air-bed mixed with a mist of remedies the Atelë healers had made to diminish his discomfort and pain, and to improve his breathing. The only story left for him to tell Althesal was Ankepum's involvement with the Elite of the planet Mal'ek.

Today she sat next to his bed ready to listen to him one last time.

Before Aldiarlim could begin, however, voices sounded outside the room. Althesal rose from her chair and went to open the door. Naleean, Nadé and three other of the Nauthian youngsters talked to the Ranger whom Marshal Mhali had assigned to protect her in case some of the planet's natives decided to explore once more the provisional settlement they had established nearby the Gardens.

When Naleean saw her, he whispered, "Issën Althesal, the healers tell us Aldiarlim's condition is deteriorating fast. We know his heart longs for company, and we promised him we will guide his passing in the tradition of our people. Could we come in and listen to the last of his story?"

A faint voice sounded behind Althesal: "Please… let them in."

Althesal nodded to the Ranger, and the youngsters entered. They had taken to visit Aldiarlim since his surrender to her twenty days before. It was them who had penetrated the barriers he had erected around his heart for most of his life, and Althesal knew the healing of his soul had begun all because of the youngsters.

The Nauthians greeted Aldiarlim as if he were an old friend, and Althesal marveled once more at the disinvestment they had experienced on Ær from the conventionalities and grievances of the Union, and from the prejudices many Galactic Humans embraced. For them Aldiarlim wasn't a traitor who had loathed Humans most of his life. No, he was someone who had come to the end of his path and, after seeing the fruits of his labors, wept in his heart at the suffering he had caused to so many, and to himself. They didn't judge his actions, only knew he shouldn't have to walk alone the last steps of his path.

The youngsters sat on the floor in silence while Althesal returned to the only chair in the room. Without anyone asking, Aldiarlim began the last chapter of his story with the raspy voice left in him:

Ankepum was unlike any Other and not so easy to understand. Yes, he was ambitious and thirsted for power and for controlling as many star systems as possible. But since his youth, he had advocated to his people for a different approach to end the stalemate with the Union. When I came to know him, at times I thought he wanted to make a final peace with Humans. But most other times I knew all he wanted was to close the technology gap that gave the Union its supremacy. The fact is, as all Others, he harbored a visceral fear of Humans disguised as a hatred.

While growing up he had taken to study the old legends, and his fascination with them never ceased. Because of this, when he carved for himself a dominion in this galaxy and became an Overlord, he started to collect ancient artifacts, old records, and antique maps. This was something his people and the other Overlords never understood since those things are rubbish to them. I knew better... He looked for something.

Hundreds of years passed, and his quest produced no results. He refused, nonetheless, to give up and continued searching while becoming the most powerful of the Overlords.

Thirty-two standard galactic years ago we stormed a planet in the outer regions of the Laïs Galaxy and annexed it and its inhabitants to his dominion. In that too Ankepum was different from the other Overlords. He always gave the choice to the inhabitants of the worlds he conquered to either remain under his rule or go somewhere else; and when a people remained under him, he never destroyed their culture. He just made of it one more tool for the exercise of his power. It was on that planet where he found records describing what he sought.

Ankepum had always wondered at the way the ancient War of the Kskiln had ended — we spoke of it countless times. He had read of the weapon used to destroy the Kskiln, and he wanted it… That's what he looked for… and on that planet he found an old story telling the whereabouts of that weapon. The story was an account of a conversation, sometime after the War, between the inhabitants of that planet, who themselves had suffered much during that War, and a group of the Åh. According to the story, this group of the Old Ones had themselves participated in the ending of the War.

The interesting point is that the story told that the weapon had also destroyed those who had used it against the Kskiln, and that it had been left abandoned in Space in the same region where the last battle had occurred. The account was, as expected, vague and adorned with mythological weavings. However, it spoke of detailed changes and anomalies the weapon produced in interstellar and interplanetary spaces, and on those worlds that were near it.

To me the story was all fragments from the old legends strung together. I doubted its value. But Ankepum took it seriously and began a search for the anomalies in Space and the changes in sentient beings described in the story.

Years came and went during which he offered rewards for any information. Many leads he so obtained, but all came to nothing. All this time no one bothered to understand Ankepum's obsession with this search, thinking he just wanted more archeological artifacts for his collection. I knew otherwise.

Three years ago his search took a new turn.

In one of those rare meetings the Overlords of The Others convene from time to time, Overlord Kapshug told of entire crews losing their minds, and of craft mysteriously disappearing in the interplanetary spaces of a star system which the independent traders called 'Sol'. Kapshug also mentioned that some traders had found two planets in that system where their inhabitants were afflicted by the madness of slaving and killing their own kind.

Ankepum kept silent while Kapshug spoke, and only a quick glance at me revealed how happy he felt at that moment — he had found the place he looked for!

But his initial euphoria turned into anger when we visited the Sol System and discovered the inhabitants of those two planets were Humans. That's the last thing Ankepum wanted — for the entire system to be off-limits to The Others. Some of his lieutenants suggested we could sneak in, but Ankepum was apprehensive of the possibility Wanderers could be living on, or visiting those planets. The irony of the situation was that Ankepum himself was a great advocate of the Armistice and had helped write many of its terms.

He wasn't going to give up at that point, however. If he couldn't enter the system as an Overlord of The Others, he was going to do it as nobody of consequence. Thus, he acquired a nondescript merchant transport, with its crew and goods, to enter the system and explore it in disguise. I and his four personal bodyguards accompanied him during that trip. We wanted to observe the two Humanities and to search for any anomaly in the interplanetary spaces.

Of course those two Humanities surprised us as much as they probably did you when you learned of them. At the same time Ankepum was delighted because they confirmed the changes told by the old story of the weapon. But where was the weapon? Our craft sensors had by then failed to detect any technology or anomaly adrift in interplanetary space. Was it on one of those planets?

Then, as we were about to study the ös-sphere of the fourth planet, we received the information Ankepum had requested from one of his deputies back home:

"The Order of the Wanderers and the Armistice Inspectorate have no knowledge of Humans in the Sol System, nor does the Union have any contact with the system", the deputy told us.

This news emboldened Ankepum, who ordered his pilot to bring to us his personal craft and several of his fleet commanders to enter the system to search for anything out of the ordinary. Once on board his personal craft, which had a much better sensor technology, we continued our exploration of the fourth planet, Yfel. Soon after, however, we ruled out the weapon was there. All we found there was a fallen Humanity tearing itself to pieces in a perpetual conflict. We regarded them with disgust and left them alone to their meaningless fate.

Afterwards we were going to visit the other Humanity, on the fifth planet, which you already know as the planet Mal'ek. Yet, by a twist of luck, at that point the leader of a scout unit informed Ankepum that they had detected an unknown craft, with a bizarre shape and strange wart-like protuberances, following an erratic course from the fifth planet towards this one... the one you now call Ær.

We then followed that craft while concealing our presence. Something in its behavior and shape was too strange to leave it alone.

When that craft arrived to this third planet, it encircled it from pole to pole, twice. Next, it entered the upper atmosphere and did some maneuvers inside it incomprehensible to us — as if the pilot had difficulty controlling the craft. Then, the craft returned to Mal'ek, also following an erratic and spasmodic course.

Ankepum, cautious as he always was, immediately ordered two survey craft to do a preliminary inspection of the surface of this third planet since the sensors on his craft couldn't read much. "This is the place", he told me at that moment with a rare display of emotion. "I feel it in my blood!" However, much to our surprise, right before entering the atmosphere of this planet, the two survey craft vanished in front of our eyes, leaving no trace!

After that setback, undaunted, Ankepum sent a small, unmanned spy probe, thinking that this planet had a sophisticated defense system. It also vanished.

For hours we attempted to figure out the defense system protecting this planet. To our instruments, nothing was out of the ordinary. More puzzling was that they couldn't penetrate the lower atmosphere to read details on its surface. Ankepum wanted to continue our efforts to get to the bottom of the mystery, but all of a sudden many in the crew became agitated with fear... some even lost all control and had to be restrained. That was atypical for Dreki and new to us. Thus, Ankepum, remembering Overlord Kapshug's account of entire crews losing their minds, ordered the pilot to leave orbit.

He knew at that point, without any doubt, the weapon that had ended the ancient War was here, on this third planet. He, of course, became obsessed with possessing it. He also suspected the key to get his hands on it was on the fifth planet... and that the strange craft we had seen had the capacity to bypass the defenses of this planet since it had entered and exited its atmosphere without challenge.

Ankepum was a master of timing and, before rushing to act, decided to observe the situation on Mal'ek. At first we were puzzled that an undeveloped civilization, such as that planet had, could have an interplanetary craft of the speed and maneuverability we had witnessed.

For two days we surveyed Mal'ek and discovered that its civilization was characterized by a sophisticated slaving system imposed by Humans upon other Humans through a control of their economy.

The Dreki in our crew enjoyed the sight of it because it debunked the moral superiority Humans claim to have. I must say, though, I felt both shocked and sorrowful. I was shocked because I had seen slavery before but only in a few primitive, non-Human sentient races... and sorrowful, because no sentient or sub-sentient being should ever be submitted to slavery of any kind!

It was at the end of the second day studying that planet when we found the landing port where the craft was kept — there were two of them. What we didn't expect was that these craft belonged to a race of shadowy beings working with the Humans on that planet. More surprising was that those shadows came through an opening from a twilight realm into our light-field dimensions and that the Humans of the planet feared them in the extreme. 'Stwg' was the name Ankepum gave to those creatures, which means "Evernight Dwellers" in the language of the Dreki.

Who is then in control? Ankepum and I asked ourselves. *The Humans or the Stwg?*

The more we observed the situation, however, the more we became convinced we weren't seeing the entire picture, that something else had to explain that uneven alliance. Ankepum saw in this his opportunity. Thus, in a bold move we introduced ourselves to the native Humans manning the port. The Dwellers seldom remained for long in our side of Space, and so we chose a time when they had returned to their own realm.

Once the initial reactions of the Humans to our presence calmed down and the communication barriers were bridged, Ankepum requested to be taken to the rulers of the planet. We had to wait an entire day at the port before we received a reply. During this time various Humans came and asked questions to us. They also requested to inspect our craft. Ankepum didn't feel intimidated by them and complied with their requests. Then, the reply came — we were to travel to their main city to meet with the rulers.

We had thought we had seen all that was strange on that planet. How wrong we were! To start, the rulers of that planet were a reclusive group who controlled the affairs of the civilization from inside a large fortress. The exercise of their power was through an administrative and policing force called 'the Controllers'.

Ankepum, his personal guards, and myself were the only ones allowed to enter the fortress. We were received by a lone young man who had the look of being in a trance — *"I am the Spieler"* — he introduced himself in their language and through a weak mental impress that we understood, and said no more. He then led us downwards through many passages and stairways until we arrived at a large chamber beneath the fortress. As we descended towards it, the feeling of danger grew in me, but Ankepum had made up his mind and ignored me when I told him so.

A gloomy twilight surrounded us when we entered that chamber. It was difficult to see how far it extended because unlit spaces were all around. The Spieler then directed us to the only place in the chamber that was thoroughly illuminated, and told us to wait there.

I am not a person given to fears, yet at that moment I felt very afraid. I noticed too I wasn't the only one of our party in this: Ankepum's bodyguards were bunched up close to me.

Not long after, we saw a group of shadows advancing towards us. At first I thought the light had shifted and the shadows of an unlit space had extended in our direction. But no, the shadows were five monstrosities of beings, difficult to describe, which slithered towards us along the air right above the floor.

Aldiarlim paused to drink some water. Then, he regarded Althesal and Naleean. "You two saw those monstrosities too, but some of those here didn't... Thus, I want to describe those leaders to them. Althesal made a silent nod, and he continued:

The leaders of the Elite were a mix of Evernight Dweller and of Human. They looked as if someone had cut into pieces Human bodies and the bodies of some of the Dwellers we had seen at the port, and then assembled them again, mixed and without knowing what they were doing — each creature had more than two Human arms and legs, and three of them had two Human heads, but all attached to the wrong places... and still alive!

I altered my body many years ago to find acceptance with the Dreki. However, in the past few days, here, with all of you, I have come to realize I never ceased being Human — I just closed my heart and masqueraded myself as a Dreki. This isn't what I saw and sensed in those monstrosities. Of Human they had only a few appendages left in their bodies; and if they still had a mind-soul, it was deeply buried.

Those shadow monsters were something one doesn't encounter

even in the worst nightmares. Fear, hostility, rage, pain and sadness issued from them! Not that they were afraid of us, or hostile or angry towards us... No... These feelings came from them as light comes from a star. Even Ankepum recoiled when they came close to us. Each was different in shape, and the foul smell of burning and decomposing flesh surrounded them. In silence they studied us for a time with their bottomless eyes, evidently not having seen a Dreki before. But more time they spent studying me and touching my body with their malformed limbs — they knew I was an altered Human, and it pleased them. I remained still and with my eyes closed while they did this. It was all I could do not to panic!

When they were satisfied of the inspection, they spoke to us, not directly but through the Spieler. As an introduction this man told us that his masters — *the Mestar,* he called them — could receive thought communication from us but could not speak directly to our minds. They thus wanted to know our story and the reason for our visit.

Ankepum was the one to answer, and he told them of himself and of his dominion, also of his desire to enter into a relationship with them — of course, leaving aside his interest in the weapon. He ended by offering them to have an exchange of technology to build spacefaring craft and other things. I knew Ankepum was scheming to give them as little as possible in exchange for information about their craft and their interest in the third planet.

Afterwards they asked many questions, including the capacity of our fleet and, especially, on the manner each craft was piloted. They too wanted to know about the Dreki race and their capacity to fight and to withstand fear. They ended by interrogating me. They were interested in how I had been altered, and if I had difficulties exposing my body to the daylight — I think they believed I had been assembled from parts of Human and Dreki because they never understood the concept of genetics and grafts.

Ankepum and I were, of course, reading their intentions, their strengths and their vulnerabilities through their questions. They had a great sharpness of mind and a keen understanding of the forces of Space, which was, probably, their greatest strength. At the same time, they couldn't hide the fact they wanted to use us in their plans. We also understood they could kill anyone instantaneously, with their bodies, without the use of any weapon. Yet, likewise, we discovered they were prisoners in the chamber, could leave it only at night, and that the radiations of Sol weakened them. We suspected they were slowly dying, based on the stench of decomposition coming from them.

When they were satisfied with our answers, Ankepum asked of them to tell us their story.

For the first time we saw them hesitate, and I knew then no one had ever asked them that question. Next, they ordered the Spieler to tell it to us. Immediately a change took place in this man who, with a more lucid air and as if awakening from a dream, told us:

"The Mestar remember little of what happened to them, so I can only tell you the events I experienced and witnessed.

"We were a group of sixteen engineers and technicians, working under the Consortium that built and operated the energy-supply system of our planet, when, six years ago, a problem occurred at one of the energy stations in the place known as the Eltish River Valley. The few inhabitants of the valley didn't know what was happening and informed the government that there was something wrong with the towers. In turn, the government informed our bosses. Thus, with our bosses and our equipment we traveled to the valley, wondering what could be happening since never before had towers malfunctioned.

"Once there, we immediately realized the problem wasn't with the towers. It was with the direction of the energy they siphoned from the planet. Their condensed beams had converged to form a strange phenomenon in the center of the valley, at the ground level. It was a hole in the air, a doorway to another place because we could see through it to a space filled with a twilight. Our bosses then decided to explore it. For this they chose eight of our group, forcing them to enter it with threats of dismissal since none of us wanted to do it. I and seven others were left on this side, each with one end of a rope attached to a body harness, which each of our friends donned.

"We all were scared, and none of us wanted to be there... I still remember the faces of the eight before they entered the ominous twilight...

"To our astonishment, our friends vanished from view as soon as they crossed the threshold. Soon after, the ropes became taut, and we sensed our friends pulling for more rope. Then, when the lengths of the ropes inside that gap were about fifty paces, these suddenly went slack. We waited for a long while hoping our friends would return, until our bosses directed us to pull the ropes back. Another surprise came next: the eight ropes still had the harnesses attached to them, fastened and undamaged, but of our friends, there was no sign!

"I hadn't seen our bosses afraid until that moment. They immediately ordered everyone to leave that place and contacted the government to send security forces to cordon off the area.

"I, however, couldn't abandon my friends and decided to remain in the valley to assist in some way. The few people still living there were, as might be expected, afraid… We all were… Nonetheless, I took lodging with the family closest to where the opening appeared. From then on I entered the cordoned area using my credentials as an engineer of the Consortium and kept watch on the mysterious opening. During that time the opening appeared at random — some times for a few minutes, other times for a whole day. I didn't know what was going to happen next, but I kept my hopes high that my friends would return at any moment.

"Then, one evening, seven days after my friends had disappeared, they came back as you see them now. I knew they were them because I recognized the faces in the heads attached to those bodies."

Lowering his voice, the Spieler added:

"Their Human side is receding with every passing day. Now the Mestar are more of them than of us!"

That was all the Spieler said of that sad story. After he finished, his look changed again to the one as in a trance. Then, he led us out of the fortress and told us to wait at the spaceport until the Mestar decided on Ankepum's offer.

On that same day, in the evening, under the cover of darkness the Mestar and the Spieler appeared at the port, alone, to visit Ankepum's craft. They were pleased with it, and asked several times to the crew if they were afraid of them. Naturally we all were! but Ankepum replied for the crew otherwise.

Next, the Mestar told Ankepum they accepted his offer with a different set of terms. They wanted us to pilot their craft to help them neutralize something on this third planet whose emanations were slowly killing their kind on the other side of the door — they called the thing a *Wo'ar,* which the Spieler translated as 'a parasitic spatial anomaly'. They told us the Mal'ekian pilots were having a challenge steering the two craft already built.

Ankepum couldn't believe his good luck. He suspected the thing they called the Wo'ar was the weapon — well, he was going to take it away and solve their problem!

I warned him, however, not to trust those creatures, that they weren't telling us everything. Ankepum assumed as much, but again he ignored my warnings. Thus, in the following days, as instructed by the Spieler, he called several of our craft to land on the port, to expand its capacity and for some of his crews to learn to pilot the Mestar's craft.

I was right in my misgivings. The first surprise came when we asked about the power-drive of their craft. There was none! It was the Dwellers themselves! — three of them per craft... not the Mestar but three unaltered Dwellers. Somehow those beings have the power to displace themselves, and physical matter, through free Space without the need for any conveyance. But they have limitations on our side of Space. One is that the light radiations of stars damage them, and for this reason they can only stay for a few days at a time. Thus, their craft weren't craft at all but protective shells for their bodies. That's the reason the craft had attached on their outer hulls the rock-like structures... the ones that made them look as if the craft had warts. These were hauled from their own realm to insulate them from the light of Sol and the other stars.

Their other limitation is they need someone from our side of Space to guide them to any destination because, on this side of the door, they can't see well or sense where they are going — they are able to perceive and sense only within a radius of no more than forty paces. That's the reason they needed our pilots.

Ankepum readily accepted this arrangement. Yet, it wasn't to work out as easy as he had expected, and two standard galactic years were spent in making possible a way to communicate between our pilots and the Dwellers. I still don't know how exactly the communication worked. It required direct physical contact, with one Dweller touching a Dreki on the head with one of its appendages. In this way they could see through the Dreki's eyes. The challenge was that, with their touch, a flood of dark feelings rushed to the pilot, causing an overwhelming fear. Ankepum asked for volunteers and offered a great compensation. Yet, most of the volunteers quit after the first try. Those who remained did so but not for long — it was clear that over time the contact damaged their minds and made of them empty shells. Thus, Ankepum had to continually replace his pilots. The Dwellers were also affected by the contact; they convulsed and wailed at times, and appeared to be drained of energy after a while. The fact is they had to go away, to their realm, after every trip, and we never knew if it was the same group that came back.

I didn't like any of that and tried to distance myself at every opportunity. I found it difficult, however, since Ankepum didn't trust any of his deputies but me in managing the agreement with the Mestar.

During those two years Ankepum had regular meetings with the Mestar. I attended all of them at their request and Ankepum's. It was apparent they felt, somehow, fond of me. I felt the opposite. My revulsion at them increased with every visit, and I began to feel for the first time in a long while that I wanted to be fully Human again. I felt my existence slipping away, and that the only thing real was my Human essence.

During those meetings the Mestar thirsted to know more about Galactic Humans and all the other races, their civilizations, and their power and technologies. Ankepum was too forthcoming with them, and I thought his obsession with the weapon was affecting his judgment. Thus, in this way the Mestar discovered the superiority of the Union, both technologically and culturally, as well as Ankepum's desire to bridge this gap.

I wasn't happy with the way the situation was unfolding and told Ankepum so. He agreed with me they were manipulating us to an end we hadn't yet discovered. But Ankepum continued with the arrangement because this was the only way to get his hands on the weapon. We had made attempts, multiple times, to penetrate this third planet's defenses with no success.

Eventually, after two years of failures, the interaction between our volunteers and the Dwellers improved when someone suggested to us to drug the volunteers with the extract of a plant used for treating madness. Thus, the first test flights to this third planet started in earnest. At this point Ankepum requested from the Mestar something in exchange. Well, they had already thought about that and provided him with the blueprints — drawn by the Spieler under their instruction — to build a prototype mobile power to translocate an entire fleet through the higher galactic ös light-fields. They also offered to Ankepum to use the base and resources from Mal'ek to build it, away from the prying eyes of the Union — of that craft, you already know.

Once the issue of the pilots was solved, two more of their craft came through the door. Then, the real plan of the Mestar began to unfold. They told us the four craft were going to be used to spread matter from their own realm in the ös-sphere of this third planet — the same reddish substance sustaining them here, on this side of the door, and the same one attached to their craft. With this, the Mestar wanted to weaken the emanations of the Wo'ar before they could neutralize it.

Ankepum and I had been thinking all this time, of course, that the defense system of this planet and the Wo'ar had to be the same thing: the weapon he coveted!

However, when the Mestar revealed to us these details of their plan, alarms sounded within me. I kept going in my mind over all the things they had told us, seeking to discover why their plan didn't feel right. Then, a realization dawned on me... which I don't know why we hadn't seen it before. I realized that *the only thing that wasn't affected by the emanations of the Wo'ar was matter from the other side of the door.* Next, a question occurred to me — *Why are the Dwellers affected in their own realm, as the Mestar claim, if the Wo'ar is on our side of the door? If their kind is always surrounded by matter that shields the emanations of the Wo'ar, why are they dying there from its emanations?*

"The Mestar are lying to us!" I shouted, startling Ankepum. "Their kind isn't dying! The Wo'ar isn't killing them. They don't want to neutralize it. They don't need to. They want the weapon for themselves!"

Ankepum regarded me speechless for a long moment after I told him my reasoning. Then his face changed into a dark, angry snarl. "I'll destroy them," he hissed, "even if I have to vaporize this entire planet!"

From then on, a race started between the Mestar's plan to alter the ös-sphere of this third planet and Ankepum's plot to steal one of their craft, to retrofit it with a drive, to reach the weapon first.

To our advantage the spreading was a laborious and slow work. The reddish substance had to be brought from the Dwellers' realm, and only they could handle it and disperse it from their craft. The entire enterprise was odd to witness, and for a reason that wasn't apparent to me, this substance dissipated without leaving any residue once it exited the craft. Again to our advantage there were many idle days, during which both our pilots and the Dwellers had to rest.

The Mestar never suspected we knew of their true intention, nor of Ankepum's plot. On the contrary, they wanted to keep Ankepum happy. Thus, at various times they gave him blueprints for new weapons and for improvements to the craft of his fleet, which Ankepum used to rebuild his Elite Forces.

But stealing one of their craft wasn't as easy as we had thought since, when the craft weren't in use, they were taken back through the door to the Dwellers' realm — "To recharge their power", the Spieler told me when I asked the reason. Yet I was dubious of his answer. "And where is their realm?" I continued prodding him — "Far away, beyond the rim of known Space", he added and walked away from me.

One day our fear of failure rose to a new height when the Mestar informed us the work was going to be completed in a short number of days.

I wonder now if a higher Power was involved in the way events unfolded after that moment, because what happened next couldn't have produced a better outcome.

It all began when Ankepum was so desperate that he was ready to steal one of their craft using an attack force. It wasn't going to be so. He and I were summoned by the Mestar once more. In that meeting they told us another measure was needed to neutralize the Wo'ar since the alterations of the ös-sphere hadn't produced the expected result. Thus, they needed to alter the orbital harmonics of the Sol System to weaken the ös-sphere of the third planet. To do this, one of the small planets of the outer orbits was going to be moved to a new orbit, and that for this, a new craft of theirs, different in its geometry, was going to be required to do the job. For this, three more pilots were required.

We were, of course, perplexed by this new development. I told Ankepum that the Mestar probably had had from the beginning a much more elaborated plan than what we had imagined. To me it looked as if they were preparing to use the weapon for something, and the stage was going to be the Sol System.

Aldiarlim pause to drink more water and, before continuing, said to us, "Our challenge with the Mestar was they were revealing to us only bits of information at a time, and they were very clever, so we needed to guard our words and actions to avoid revealing our true intentions."

"We have to stop them! Now!" I begged to Ankepum after that meeting. "Once the weapon is in their hands, they aren't going to need us anymore and will destroy us first." Ankepum ignored me, and I thought his repeated contact with the Mestar and with the Dwellers was affecting his mind. His thinking was becoming slow and muddy.

A few days after the moment to move the small planet came. Ankepum wasn't in the Sol System at the time because urgent matters somewhere else in his dominion required his attention. He then left me in charge of supervising our involvement in it, and from a distance on my craft I witnessed and recorded the unusual operation.

The relocation started as planned, with the Dwellers in the craft generating, or perhaps passing through their bodies, a force aimed to capture and move the small planet — it was an eerie sight to see how easily they did it! However, as I observed their progress it became evident to me that Sol wasn't going to permit its re-insertion in the normal plane of the orbital harmonics. I had no means to communicate with our people inside that craft, so I waited to see what the Dwellers on it were going to decide about that. Then, unexpectedly, the entire maneuver stopped, and I concluded they were satisfied with the planet's new, although skewed orbit.

As I was readying my craft to return with them to the base on Mal'ek, I noticed their craft was adrift. Puzzled, I approached it and waited. Eventually it became clear to me that something had happened to our people inside it. After considering options and a long wait, I decided to call one of our transport in the system to retrieve the Dwellers' craft. We loaded it inside one of the cargo bays and carried it back to the nearest star system in Ankepum's Dominion — Aric is its name [Barnard's Star].

On our way there I contacted Ankepum and told him of the situation. He rushed to meet us. Once at our base we unloaded the craft under a heavy guard. Next, we opened its main hatch. No one came out. Ankepum then sent inside ten Dreki heavily armed. They soon came back outside with the news: "Our people are dead, and there aren't any Dwellers inside!"

To this day I don't know the events that occurred inside that craft. All we found of the Dwellers was a colorless dust scattered all over. Ankepum was, however, more practical and immediately ordered the craft to be retrofitted with engines, sensors and piloting systems. The hull of this craft was, like the others, covered with the foul substance from the Dwellers' realm. We expected it was going to allow us to enter this third planet.

Meanwhile, to cover up our plan, Ankepum and I rushed to Mal'ek to inform the Mestar of the result of the small planet operation. We ended telling them that, by all appearances, the pilots had lost control of the craft and it had collided with one of the many large asteroids found in that region of Sol.

I don't know if the Mestar believed us, but they brushed off the issue as if it was nothing. They were more concerned with the exact location where the small planet had ended up. When I told them the exact coordinates of its new orbit, they were satisfied. Next, they told us that in seven days the work in the ös-sphere of this, the third planet, was going to be completed.

"What is going to happen after that?" Ankepum asked them.

"We will wait until the interplanetary harmonics are aligned in the proper way", they replied through the Spieler. "Then, we, and some of our own, will travel to that planet on the four craft, to fully neutralize the Wo'ar by destroying it."

To finish his story, Aldiarlim lay back and, closing his eyes, told Althesal and the Nauthian youngsters:

"From that moment on it became a mad rush to finish retrofitting the craft that we had taken from the Dwellers, for us to travel first to Ær and locate Ankepum's weapon. But, again, a higher Power was also at work because the Mestar weren't able to act as they had planned.

"In the end… you know… we all came here, to these Gardens, at the same time… including you, Issën Althesal…" After a pause, he added, "Good it happened in this way. I don't know what that singularity is, but in my heart I know it isn't for The Others or for the Dwellers."

Aldiarlim took a deep breath, he looked exhausted after such a long tale. Nadé then rose and helped him to lie down more comfortable.

"You deserve to rest", Althesal said to him softly. "And I mean, more than body rest. Your story tells me you were always loyal to the highest ideals. You just didn't know, until recently, that the ideals you pursued were in your own heart and not outside you. The fact is, you always have been noble of heart. You always have been the true prince you believed you had left behind!"

⚡

Aldiarlim went through transition nine days after he finished the account of the story of his life. All the members of the expedition, all the Nauthian youngsters, and a large number of the Atelë attended the last rite of his passage.

His body was placed on a polished stone slab, in a clearing of a forest nearby, a slab which the youngsters somehow had procured. Then, all the Nauthians present, including Laidé, sung in the old language of the Nauthé a canticle whose words none other could understand but whose melodies moved Althesal and many others to tears. Althesal knew in her heart, however, the canticle spoke of the longing in all Humans to be free from Space and Time. When the canticle was finished, Naleean and Nadé walked to the slab and placed two small spheres close to Aldiarlim's body — one by the head, the other by the feet. Next, they retreated and, at a word sounded by the two, an effulgence came from the spheres. Bathed on that effulgence, Aldiarlim's body transformed into an iridescent light that soon ascended towards the sky. Nothing was left of him, not even dust — solely the memory of his courageous transformation on that new world.

As Althesal beheld the transition of his body to the higher realms of light, his last words to her resounded in her heart and mind:

"I pray to the Source of All, Althesal of Thel, that when I return into a physical form, it will be with the wonderful people you are. There is something about this planet that makes me feel at home. That singularity isn't a weapon... I know it — It doesn't affect the minds of people... I know it — It doesn't destroy craft approaching it — No! It simply asks of all and everyone who approaches this planet to surrender the old and be new and more!"

$$\left(49\right)$$

The Turning of the Ages

Seven days after the Ranger transport Mni made the recordings of the events on planet Ær, new tidings came from other quarters to Thaël, the Chancellor and Ulhloom.

The first news came from the commander of the Rangers in charge of enforcing the quarantine around the planet Mal'ek. She first informed them that no activity had been detected at the base of Ankepum and the Dwellers since the quarantine had begun. Then, she reported that a political change had started on that planet. The Elite had disappeared, and no one knew what had happened to them. The first indication of this was that the man called 'the Spieler' had taken over the leadership of the planet. His first action had been to invite all his people to re-establish the cooperatives and the former government of community councils.

The second news came from various sources telling that Ankepum, his bodyguards and his closest advisor, Aldiarlim, had disappeared. The rumor among his people, and through the Underworld, was that they had departed for a secret mission to a distant world. But Councilor Ulhloom suspected, and so did the Rangers, Ankepum had disappeared on planet Ær together with the expedition. Their conjecture was validated soon after by the events that followed.

In a surprising move, Ankepum's new craft with the power to translocate a fleet through the higher ös light-fields appeared inside the atmosphere of Mal'ek. It arrived with three fast-acting combat units bearing no insignia. These craft then razed to the ground the entire base there, together with the tower collectors. Next, as quickly as they had arrived, the four craft had left the planet. At the same time that the base was laid waste, the other six Overlords of The Others in the Laïs Galaxy, in an unusual joint communiqué, warned their own not to venture near the Sol System, for any reason. Immediately after they began to partition between themselves Ankepum's dominion and to hunt down his closest associates and Elite Forces.

For the Chancellor, Ulhloom and Thaël these events meant only one thing: Ankepum was gone for good! That wasn't a good news, however, since, unlike Ankepum, the other Overlords had no attraction to enter into a direct dialogue with the Union when circumstances required. Besides, they had now become more powerful — replicating that craft was going to take them some time, but they were going to do it.

With these news from Mal'ek and from The Others, the Chancellor had no reason to continue with the quarantine of that planet. Its fate was now in its inhabitants' hands.

All this time, and for days after, the three of them studied and discussed the recordings made by the Mni, until every detail became familiar to them. The Rangers brought outside experts to do the same, and many attempts were made to extract more data. In the end, no one knew what had truly happened on Ær. A main obstacle to obtain more information was that the Time anomaly around that planet deepened and became more variable in the days and months that followed.

To Thaël there was only one course of action: to build another Spaceblazer and send another group there.

All his people on Thel wanted to help with this undertaking, and many volunteered to be part of that second expedition — so did others from a multitude of worlds. However, Lyel and her team had been the sole experts in the në material and, in the rush to build and finish the Spaceblazer, they had left only a few notes on the processes they had followed. Thus, it was going to take some time before a new craft could be fabricated. It was, at least, a consolation to Thaël to see that all the Guilds had set aside their differences and were working together to make this other expedition possible.

Ciän the Wise told Thaël that the Synod had means to see far and beyond, as witnesses only, and that they too failed to see or sense any of the expedition members. "I can't even sense Daothel, which I should", the Wise One told him one day, not hiding his sadness. Then another day he said to Thaël, "Time and its mysteries are the only reason left in my mind to explain their disappearance. Do what your heart tells you to do, but also give Time its own time. No one can control it."

The affairs in the Sol System and the fate of the expedition affected likewise the Union, at large, in a way which took the High Council by surprise — a spontaneous wave swept over a large number of worlds to renew the bonds of membership and friendship, and greater cooperation was offered in areas which had been, until then, politically contentious. Not since the founding of the Union had peoples felt such a desire to look at the factors that brought them together. Curiously enough, at the same time, so too The Others experienced a closeness rare among their diverse peoples.

These changes reminded Thaël of his last conversation with Althesal. During it she had said to him, "I hear, as do many far and beyond, the Call from that planet. It brings renewal."

As the routine of daily activities in the Union returned, and events in the Sol System quieted, many thought the expedition lost forever. Not so for Thaël, the Chancellor and Ulhloom who kept their hopes alive. If one thing they had learned from the entire affair was that no one had yet arrived to a full and complete understanding of the workings of the Universe.

Thus, with the support of the entire High Council, the Chancellor petitioned to the Armistice Inspectorate for the inclusion of the Sol System in the Union. The petition didn't meet the normal requirements. Yet the Order of the Wanderers didn't oppose the motion, and the Sol System, with each of its planets, became a legal member of the Union under the umbrella of the Pleiades~Eir League of Planets. As a second motion the Chancellor proposed to the High Council for the delegation of planet Thel to the Union to also represent the interests of the inhabitants of the Sol System until they would develop enough to participate in the Union by themselves. This second motion was likewise unanimously accepted.

Immediately after, the Chancellor ordered the Rangers to establish a permanent, unmanned monitoring station of planet Ær outside the orbit of its moon, and to deploy with it a permanent communication beacon. Regular manned surveys of the system were also included in the normal tasks of the Ranger Corps. Planet Ær and Sol would never be alone again!

50

A New World ~ A New Horizon

The sparkling blue fire burned bright and warm through the beautiful lattice-work of the sculpture functioning as an outdoor fireplace, and with a song only the Atelë could have created. The evening was chill, and Althesal moved her chair closer to it. Her six friends sat also in silence, brooding over their fate. She had called them to meet, alone. A decision needed to be made.

It had been forty-five days since they had confronted the Darkness, and Althesal already observed that, like her, her six friends had accepted Ær as their new home. It wasn't so with most of the other members of the expedition in spite that the Atelë, aware of their loss, were doing all they could to make them feel welcomed and comfortable. These others longed to return to the freedom of the stars. Althesal knew that if their situation continued unchanged, despondency would take root in their hearts. Thus, it was imperative for the seven of them to provide a path for hope — that was the reason she had called the meeting.

She still wasn't used to the splendor of the night sky on planet Ær. Gazing at the myriad of stars she wondered once again at the unusualness of the world where they were now stranded. Something on the planet seemed to multiply the number of stars one could behold — "We may be witnessing not just the present, but past and future loci of the starry heavens", Ethën had remarked.

Turning to face him, she asked, "What news do we have of the Spaceblazer?"

He sighed before replying, "Not much. All its systems are in perfect order, yet the riser-drive still refuses to work. The only explanation we have at this time — though it could be other — is that the drift of the light-fields of Sol impinge upon this planet's light-fields at an angular vector which isn't the normal one elsewhere in Space, rendering the drive useless. Until we confirm this and discover the precise four-dimensional vector, we aren't going anywhere."

For the expedition the days hadn't been idle. On the contrary, none of them had had much time for themselves. The peoples of the various cities of the Atelë wanted to meet "the Harbingers of the Lords of the Horizon" — as they were now called. At first, groups of Atelë had come to visit them, one after the other, to the homes of Tiá, his family, and his friends, where they were lodged. But, when the number of visiting groups hadn't abated, Tiá had suggested for the expedition members to better travel to other cities in small groups. Althesal and Mhali had agreed to this to avoid the feeling of being on display. Besides, traveling would give them the opportunity to know more about the land and the lives of the Atelë. However, only after ten days of traveling the two of them wanted the trips to stop. They needed to regain control of their lives. Althesal could already see the tiredness in Lyel and the others from her planet. The five Wanderers were too under strain. That was one characteristic the Atelë didn't share with Galactic Humans. Unlike these, the Atelë didn't show much need for times of solitude and quietness. They were gregarious and happy in the company of each other at all times.

"Communications also remain silent", Mhali said next. "The good news on this area is that we now have a long line of volunteers from the Atelë to help us monitor communications both on the Spaceblazer and on the Nauthian transport at all times. I also have my Rangers figuring out the periodicity of rotation of the folds of the planet's ös-fields to see if we can discover the right moment to send messages. It won't be easy either. There is a variability in the rotation whose source may be Sol."

"It appears the planet doesn't want us to leave." Soen looked them one by one. "This confirms one thing Soree tells me: that the Lords of the Horizon introduced a modification in the song of the planet before they departed, to protect it. But she doesn't know more of this matter. Thus, if we could, somehow, assist the Atelë in recreating the Chronicles, we may obtain more information on the nature of this modification."

"I had the same idea of studying the song of the planet", Daothel said. "Nadé and two of the other youngsters theorize that the Nexus of Aïdin has something to do with it, and they have already begun, with some of the

Atelë, to study the twelve nomöi of the Nexus. The youngsters invited me yesterday to help them with this project. Some of the Atelë think the nomöi contain, encoded in song, light and geometry, vast sums of knowledge. Others could join us in this research, including Soree and you, Soen."

The suggestion stirred the others to speak, which was what Althesal wanted.

Mhali was the first. "We can't continue as guests of Tiá and his people. We need our own place… each of us… and a place that both the Children of Ær and the Atelë will respect as *our home* and *our space*. This means we will need to build a new city for us. Some of my Rangers and Wanderer Eleaph have already thought of this idea. This is, of course, a huge enterprise and we will need the assistance of others. Nonetheless, it will give us the sense of belonging to this planet and provide a foothold for our journey into the future."

Althesal beamed to him. "Great idea! The sooner we start the better."

"I'd like to coordinate a study of the history of the Atelë", Laidé said after a moment. "They don't remember their coming to this planet and their previous history, nor their early history here — not even those who were of the Source Path on Thel remember. However, we Nauthians have learned to read and to uncover the past from the most unexpected of sources. I think it's worth a try. As Althesal says, the Atelë truly symbolize the beginning and the end of the Human journey, and we have much to learn from them."

Of the Seven, Nesdil and Daothel were the ones who felt at home on that planet more than the others. Thus, it didn't surprise Althesal what Nesdil said next:

"I've noticed that the song the Children of Ær sing with their daily living marks the beats of the music which Nature plays on this planet. We shouldn't then ignore that our coming to this world has introduced new voices and harmonies to this music — as did the arrival of the Atelë millennia ago. It is imperative, therefore, that we discover, as soon as possible, the chords and sounds we should sing with our lives here to avoid a dissonance. And by this I mean, we need to figure out the way to relate in harmony, not just to the Atelë, but to the Children of Ær, to Nature, and to the planet itself."

It could have been the reflections of the flames upon the bodies of her friends when, for a moment, Althesal saw them change to a sparkling bluish form. She blinked and they returned to normal. It wasn't the first time in recent days that she had experienced what appeared to be flashes of a deeper reality. Daothel was also noticing them. This wasn't the moment, however, to address the subject; although it was on her list of things to study.

She was about to speak when Ethën spoke again: "We shouldn't ignore either in our plans the recent land tremors and changes in the weather, which Tiá says are new. Something happened to the planet when the Dwellers seeded the atmosphere with matter from their realm, and also with the unveiling of the Spark. We have no idea of the consequences of these two events upon the planet, its ös-sphere and its bio-sphere. Thus, my team — I mean, Lyel, her group and myself — is going to use the sensors of the Spaceblazer still working to start monitoring these changes. Naleean's transport also has some functioning systems, which we may use too. Later, as we understand more this planet, we will design better ways to do it."

Land tremors and erratic weather were also new and unexpected to the expedition members. Worlds where Galactic Humans and Amethen dwelt were stable and with harmonious flows in their natural processes. There were seasons and variations, yet all fine tuned to their planets' normal balance. It appeared that Ær was a rebel in this way too.

"Ethën, don't forget that your research could also help us rebuild our lives here", Mhali said.

"We have already thought of that," he replied, "and ideas are circulating among us to adapt certain technologies from Thel to this planet."

At that moment the song of the fire shifted to an allegro tempo, surprising and silencing all of them.

"Light! There is so much we need to learn from the Atelë." Ethën said after a moment, contemplating the fire. "Everything they build makes of us look like beginners!"

"Well," Althesal replied with a smile, "at least we know the fire of this planet appears to approve of our plans!"

They all flashed a grin at her before she continued:

"My heart tells me, dear friends, we aren't here to rebuild our former lives. No, we are treading a new and uncharted path. No one from our expedition had expected to be stranded on this world, nor was any of us prepared in our hearts and minds for this eventuality. Yet, that's how this entire affair has been from its start — a surprise at every turn — and our journey has only begun. Thus, it's good and necessary that, as we agree, we start organizing our lives here for the long run. Your ideas and suggestions can and will give meaning to our presence here — and we will come up with more as our lives start to move again. As I see them, our priorities here should be: to protect the purity of the culture and psychology of the Atelë and of the

Children of Ær, to understand more about this planet of wonders, and to study the Spark of Aïdin to figure out its nature and its effects upon living beings and the planet."

Everyone nodded back at her with a gleam of confidence, and Althesal realized the seven of them had, at that moment, become a guiding force for Humankind on planet Ær.

⚡ ⚡ ⚡

The End of *Book One* of The Legacy Saga

About the Author

Both, *L. Z. Dáin* and the works made available under this name were born from the present need to cast a light on the journey we human beings are traveling on this Earth. Our sciences and religions, our studies on history, our philosophies and our art, and our educational systems, regardless of their advances, do little to illuminate the path through Time and Space that we started traveling in a distant past and that will take us to a distant future. We human beings have arrived at a moment in our history when we are ready to face that journey and add the weight of our will power, of our creative capacities and of our love to make it joyful, easier, more productive, and closer to the intended goal — instead of all the pain, suffering, and trial and error we have endured until now.

Most of the works penned by *L. Z. Dáin*, though not all, are in the form of storytelling in the genre of Science Fiction — more specifically, in the sub-genre of *Visionary Science Fiction*. There is a reason for this choice:

> Storytelling bridges in us the sub-conscious with the supra-conscious, and in so doing it 'speaks' to the innermost self in each of us, eliciting realization and understanding at the conscious level.

Visionary Science Fiction was chosen because in Science Fiction, even though this genre pushes the present-day boundaries of our understanding and of our sciences towards greater horizons, most times the imagined future of scientific and technological advances, and of social and environmental changes, is nothing more than a transplant into that imagined future of our present psychological and social situation on Earth, and of the challenges we face today. Visionary Science Fiction seeks to avoid that. In storytelling of this nature, not just the scientific and technological advances are pushed to greater and positive horizons, but the natural world and human beings themselves — their psychology, their understanding of themselves, and their development and lives — are also envisioned in greater heights than those achieved so far.

The central principle in Visionary Science Fiction is:

> The Universe in its entirety, and we all with it, is advancing or evolving along a path of an ever-growing perfection, and the future cannot be less than the present but better, brighter and more.

⚡

The name *L. Z. Dáin* is a pen name chosen to express the guiding principle in the works of storytelling that constitute the story universe so created — *Tales of the Horizon Story Universe* — and in other works of visionary philosophy.

The letters *L* and *Z* were chosen from the expression "Limitless HoriZon" so that the two would sound harmoniously with each other.

The word *dáin* is a grammatical form of the word *dán,* which is an Old Gaelic term with various meanings that have evolved through time. It is usually translated as *bard*.

Thus, the loose expression that inspired the name *L. Z. Dáin* is: STORYTELLER OF GREATER HORIZONS!

⚡ ⚡ ⚡

About the word *Aïdin:*

Central to the stories in the *Tales of the Horizon Story Universe* is the idea that the 'voice' is the most remarkable power to create we human beings have and that the capacity to sing is the greatest expression of that power. It was then early in the writings, in spring of the year 2012, that the word *"aïdin"* came to the inspiration of L. Z. Dáin to describe the idea of "song-made" creations, specifically of a song-made planet. The term 'aïdin' later served to inspire other words and terms used in the stories, and no present-day language from Earth was used as a source. Thus, any similarity with words from modern languages is a coincidence.

⚡ ⚡ ⚡

Discover something new at:

TALES OF THE HORIZON™
Visionary Science Fiction Books & Stories

www.talesofthehorizon.com